Lessons in Forgetting

Anita Nair is the bestselling and critically acclaimed author of the novels *The Better Man*, *Ladies Coupé*, *Mistress*, *Idris: Keeper of the Light* and *Alphabet Soup for Lovers*. She has also authored a crime series featuring Inspector Gowda.

Anita Nair's other books include a collection of poems titled *Malabar Mind*, a collection of essays titled *Goodnight & God Bless* and six books for children. Anita Nair has also written two plays and the screenplay for the movie adaptation of *Lessons in Forgetting*, which was part of the Indian Panorama at IFFI 2012 and won the National Film Award in 2013. Among other awards, she was also given the Central Sahitya Akademi award. Her books have been translated into over thirty languages around the world.

She is also the founder of the creative writing and mentorship programme Anita's Attic.

Praise for *Lessons in Forgetting*

'*Lessons in Forgetting* is like an experience in fine dining – it tantalizes your palate and makes you want to chew slowly upon its offerings, and it makes you want to linger at the table just a little while longer … Here, indeed, is a novel well worth remembering.' – *India Today*

'[An] intimate exploration of duty, betrayal and the frail beauty of second chances …' – *The Times of India*

'[A] memorable read … Nair writes with exacting precision about the disintegration of marriages among the middle-class … With carefully orchestrated shifts in points of view, Nair describes how every woman has had to make painful choices to assert and retain their sense of self.' – *The New Indian Express*

'This is Nair's fourth book and there is no doubt about one thing: she gets better with each one … it's all there in the book: cyclones and catastrophes, man-made and wrought by nature; love, dependency and betrayal, female foeticide, Page Three parties. It's a story told at an unhurried pace by an accomplished writer.' – *The Hindu Literary Review*

'Anita Nair weaves her story with the consummate skill of a born storyteller with hard-to-forget nuggets. Never once does the interest of the reader falter. She completely reinvents storytelling … a story of real people in a real but far from perfect country … it is also a story of forgiveness, redemption and second chances. It is a story that inspires, moves, motivates and forces you to think, all this even as it holds you spellbound.' – *Business World*

'Satirical, topical, reflective of new-age desi definitions … Nair picks her way through emotional upheavals and social asides while toning down sentimentality to just the right pitch …' – *The Week*

'*Lessons in Forgetting* provides an ultimately satisfying read.' – *Outlook*

'The distinguishing features of Anita Nair's fiction, exhibited right from her debut novel *The Better Man*, are her command over the craft of storytelling and her ability to navigate between the more nuanced demands of literary fiction, of character and plot and the broad brush strokes, the drama, the excesses, the grand stands and the Manichean play of pulp. The impact of Nair's writing depends upon how well she balances between the two, and in *Lessons in Forgetting* she hones her art to perfection.' – *Sunday Herald*

'An intense look at marriage, parenthood, destiny and relationships, the book also packs in themes such as the cyclical nature of events in our lives and redeeming our mistakes – all this along with strong portraits of finely etched and far-from-perfect but identifiable characters.' – *DNA*

'Over her novels, Anita Nair's finely delineated characters have got etched into our memories, especially the women. Meera and JAK, both caught up by unexpected disaster, add to that canon.' – *The Financial Express*

'The realistic portrayal of Nair's characters is inducement enough for the reader to keep turning the pages … a perfect fit for those in-between times when Salman Rushdie seems too much and Sophie Kinsella too little.' – *Mint*

Lessons in Forgetting

ANITA NAIR

HarperCollins *Publishers* India

First published in hardback in India by
HarperCollins *Publishers* in 2010

4th Floor, Tower A, Building No. 10, Phase II,
DLF Cyber City, Gurugram, Haryana -122002
www.harpercollins.co.in

First published in paperback in 2012, 2018

6 8 10 9 7 5

P-ISBN: 978-93-5029-453-6
E-ISBN: 978-93-5029-237-2

Typeset in 11/14 Minion
by Jojy Philip New Delhi 110015

Printed and bound at
MicroPrints India, New Delhi

To the memory of Paul Marsh

O, what land is the Land of Dreams?
What are its mountains, and what are its streams?

—William Blake

Why is this happening to her? All this grace, such joy, all of life heeding her bidding, this perfect September day…

Once again Meera raises her face to the sky and smiles. Liquid sunshine melds with distilled fragrances. Top notes that tease and waltz. Apples. Jasmine. Walnuts. Roses. Musk. Wine. A solitary chrysanthemum. The plop of corks. The steady arc of the stream. Cool glass against her cheek.

In the Greek myths that Meera loves, there is a goddess who could be her. Hera, wife of Zeus, god among gods, and queen of the universe.

It is a vivacious Meera who stands in the pathway of the breeze and allows it to play games with her. It ruffles the chiffon of her skirt and raises a strand of hair and teases it across her cheek into her mouth.

Somewhere in her a little girl skips. One two, buckle my shoe, three four, shut the door, five six, pick the cheese sticks, seven eight, eat them straight, nine ten, let's do it again!

Meera feels as if she can't stop smiling. It is the most perfect September day anyone could wish for.

Why, everyone else here seems to think so as well. The poolside is rapidly filling up. All these beautiful people, Meera thinks, emerging from their beautiful homes in their beautiful clothes to congregate around the softly lapping waters of the hotel pool under a blue blue sky.

She takes another sip of the white wine. It tastes sour in her mouth. Only for a moment. Then it races through her, the cold sourness plopping every single knot. Plop. Plop. Plop. With the dissolution of each knot, Meera finds another reason to smile.

The hosts of the brunch, wine makers launching a new wine, will be delighted at the turnout. What more could they want? The beautiful people with their heads pertly held, fingers wrapped around glass stems, striking poses as photographers foxtrot from group to group, clicking, capturing beautiful moments.

They will never allow themselves to feel absurd, these beautiful people, not like me, Meera sighs. That is their hallmark. A deep rooted belief in their own 'I am inviolable no matter what'. Giri must be pleased that we are here with the beautiful people of Bangalore. He will be even more pleased if one of our pictures makes it to Page Three.

Meera watches a tall svelte woman talking to a podgy man in a ponytail. Meera aches to be that woman, Aphrodite deigning to play knuckle bone with a goat. She knows who he is. Pan by the poolside, chasing his own echo. It would be nice to be pursued if only by a goat-legged Pan. But where nymphs roam, what place for the frowzy, middle-aged Hera?

Nursed too well by the seasons, each seeking to feed her their libations, each wanting to fill her with their goodness, she, Meera Hera, earth goddess, corporate wife, will have to be content to loll amidst the aqua cushions of the poolside. Inconspicuous, quietly corpulent, and on the pale side of neglected.

The nymph tugs Pan's ear, throws her head back and laughs. Meera sees the curve of her throat and unconsciously, she touches the underside of her own chin. When did this fold of flesh creep up on her?

Sunlight glints on the gold hoops in the woman's ears. She is wearing a halter-necked blouse and capris. Meera looks at the expanse of lacquered skin and toned muscle and raises her eyes to the skies. 'All I ask of you is upper arms like those!'

If she doesn't do something about hers, she will have bats' wings very soon. Meera stifles a sigh and takes another sip. Plop. The weight lifts. Another knot of worry unravels. Tomorrow she will call Fitness One and make an appointment. Until then, plop, plop, plop.

A crow caws, its head tilted, its beady black eyes surveying the poolside world. Meera smiles at the crow. What does it see? Elephants knee deep in slush and still brooking no interference. Leopards on the prowl, and hungry hyenas waiting. A bloat of hippopotami and gazelles at a waterhole? Stately giraffes, a zeal of zebras and dumpy warthogs. A shoal of fish gliding. Yellow cabbage butterflies to whom flowers and animal urine exhale the same attraction. And all along, a carpet of vultures scrutinize, ready to pounce. The animal planet. Meera giggles.

A camera stares at her. Meera looks away, schooling her giggle into a demure smile. It wouldn't do to be seen with her mouth slanting into a snigger, giving away her dissembling thoughts.

Meera nibbles on a tartlet. I would have gone easy on the dill, she thinks. She longs for some more of the calamari rings. That they got right. Most restaurants turn calamari into rubber rings. But these are delicious. Just a hint of garlic and glistening with olive oil.

Meera sees the steward with the calamari at the farther side of the patio. She rises from the cane sofa. 'Nikhil, I'll be back in a little while,' she says. 'Will you be all right?' she adds, a little uncertain.

She hadn't wanted him here. 'He'll be bored, Giri. He is thirteen, for heaven's sake. What will he do at a wine launch?'

But Giri had insisted. 'It's not a cocktail party. It's a Sunday brunch. I am sure there will be other kids there. Probably a few from his class even. Besides, it's time he got out and saw how real people live.'

Zeus spoke as he worked his way through the Sunday newspapers. Zeus, whose bidding even the heavenly bodies obeyed, would tolerate no interference. He made the laws. She, Meera Hera, listened. Or he would hurl that vicious thunderbolt of sullenness. Silence and quiet, but determined pacing through the rooms, which frightened her more than any fanged words could.

'A poolside brunch and real people? You must be joking,' she had wanted to protest but she was afraid to shatter the fragile peace between them.

It seemed to her that they had done nothing but argue these past months. Hushed, so no one else in the house knew that they were warring. Hissed accusations, deflected by cold mute anger. Spilling over emotion erased with composure. So she said nothing and coerced and finally bribed Nikhil into going with them.

She touches his elbow now when he doesn't respond.

'What?' he asks, drawing his iPod earphones out.

'I need to circulate a bit. Would you like to eat something? Shall I fix you a tray? Some tartlets, a quiche slice, calamari rings?'

'Ugh! Do they have pizza?'

Meera shakes her head. 'No, I don't think so.'

'Then I don't want anything.' He puts his earphones back and opens his book again.

Meera frowns. Either he eats all the wrong things or he starves. What is she to do with him? Hera had a son too. Python. What did she do with him?

She takes another sip. Plop.

The smell of sizzling meat wafts through the air. She looks around. There are only so many gods and goddesses and they are all here. People she recognizes from the society pages in the newspapers. People she knows. And some strangers. Even a maharaja, with an entourage of bodyguards and attendants. The sun catches the gems on the rings he wears as he reaches for one salted cashew nut after another from a bowl an attendant holds out to him. Eventually they would all meet and play out the upper epidermis of emotion. That is the nature of such parties. You network with a drink in one hand and a smile on your face, clasping hands, air kissing, and all the while stewards tag you: mothers with trays of canapés to tempt the errant, wandering child.

Where is her Zeus by the way? She hasn't seen Giri since they got here. Meera thinks again of Hera. How strange that the trajectories of their lives have followed almost the same path. Like Hera, she too has gathered a bedraggled cuckoo into her bosom. It has eaten and drunk its fill, nestled in her warmth and love, and now it wants her home. What is she to do? Be Hera who wised up to what Zeus in the disguise of that cuckoo wanted of her? Or allow herself to be manipulated like a guileless crow mother with a cuckoo child in its nest? Her head throbs suddenly. She can't be drunk already!

Where is Giri? She thinks she sees the flash of a turquoise blue shirt. She hears his laugh emerge from a group of men. Meera smiles. The wind is Hera's own. But it is only when Zeus smiles that Hera can puff the sails and winnow the fields. Or what use is the wind to Hera? Wives are the same everywhere. When Giri smiles, so does she. A wife in love. Meera Hera.

She starts towards him, then pauses. She tugs the ruby teardrop clusters in her ear, runs her fingers through her hair and stands undecidedly. Should she go up to him or mingle with the others?

Giri doesn't like it when she stays attached to his side. 'We might as well stay at home then,' he said once. 'What's the point of going out if you don't socialize, meet a few new people? Circulate, Meera, circulate. Chat. Introduce yourself if no one else will. Give them a sample of that famous Meera charm!'

Meera didn't speak then either. She didn't know if that last throwaway line tossed at her was a compliment or a barb.

Increasingly, with Giri, she never knows.

Meera walks towards the barbecue. She would fix a plate for Nikhil. She knows exactly what he won't be able to resist.

'Hey Meera,' a voice breathes in her ear. Meera turns abruptly. It is Akram Khan. A fashion photographer she knows rather well and likes immensely. She helped style a shoot for him once, a long time ago. She smiles and kisses three centimetres of air on either side of his face. And waits for him to do the same. Gods and goddesses seldom deviate from the rituals. 'How are you?' she asks.

'Great! What about you? How's the book doing?'

A diminutive woman with the snout of a shrew drifts towards them. 'I hear the book is essential reading for every corporate wife these days,' the rodent says in greeting.

'Hello, Lata,' Meera says, wishing she could cut her dead instead. Queen Lat. Mouse cunt. Meera bristles. The rodent was so patronizing in her review. She called Meera the Madhur Jaffrey of the boardroom. And here she is, continuing to patronize her.

Meera smiles as she does when fazed. A vague tremulous smile that gives nothing away but a benign sweetness. And Akram, reading Lata's veiled insult as an accolade, beams, 'That's great news, Meera.'

Please don't go, she pleads in her head as he shows signs of drifting off to another group.

What am I going to say to her when what I really want to do is bash her head and her little mouse snout in with my cast iron skillet. She takes another sip of the wine. Plop.

It doesn't really matter. Mice will be mice. And a single Ms Mouse? Sneaky, furtive, and almost laughable in its attempt to damage. The woman is just doing her job. And it seems to Meera, wife of Giri, queen of her world, mother of two, author of cookbooks, mentor of corporate wives and friend to the rich and celebrated, that she who has everything can afford to be forgiving. All the rodent has is an occasional book review. So Meera can afford to be generous. She gleams at the woman. 'I meant to call you and thank you for the review. You were so...' Meera gropes for a word, '... insightful in the way you approached the subject. Not everyone understands how demanding it is to be a corporate wife!'

'Hello, my dear,' a voice purrs in her ear. Meera swings around, a smile lighting up her eyes. It is Charlie Fernandez. He holds her firmly by her shoulders and kisses her resolutely on both cheeks. Meera doesn't bother to hide her pleasure.

'So how's my favourite cookbook writer?' Charlie says, loud enough for everyone around to hear. 'I tried that Thai prawn recipe. It was just brilliant! Which idiot found fault with it?'

Meera sees the flicker of uncertainty in the rodent's eyes. The small rodent's small eyes. If she had whiskers, they would have twitched. Queen Lat, not so queenly any more. Everyone thinks of Charlie as the high priest of culture. His taste can't be faulted. And the Thai prawn curry had come in for much criticism in the rodent's review. Something to do with the coconut milk and how tiring it is to actually make it yourself, etc. Especially for women battling with sloppy home help.

Hasn't the woman heard of coconut milk in tetrapaks? You snip the end with scissors and pour. Or there is coconut milk powder that you stir into water with a spoon and if a spoon is unavailable, the tip of a finger will do. Can't even the most harassed of cooks manage that? Meera fumed reading the review. Now seeing the rodent's discomfort, Meera tries very hard to hide her glee. A glee that morphs into a confident voice as she cocks a finger at a steward.

'Would you give this to the boy sitting there?' she says, thrusting a plate of barbecue into the steward's hands and gesturing to Nikhil. 'And oh, do give him a glass of Coke.'

'More wine, ma'am?' Another steward stands at her elbow.

'I shouldn't. This is my second glass and it isn't even noon yet,' Meera dithers.

'Go on, you are a big girl,' Charlie urges. And then: 'Oh, look what's come in through the door,' he murmurs.

Meera sees a well-known society hostess and dancer sweep in.

'What a number! There was a time when she was doing so many openings, cutting so many satin ribbons tied across doorways, that Deepak called her Edward Scissorhands in one of his columns. She doesn't talk to him any more.'

Meera giggles.

Suddenly Meera realizes she is having a splendid time. These are all her friends. And this is the life she so wanted. Meera knows for certain that there is nowhere else she would rather be.

The afternoon wears on. Meera forgets to count the number of glasses. She sits by the pool letting the water lick at her feet. She has an anklet on. Her daughter has the other one. Her grown-up daughter leading a very grown-up life in another city…

What will he say if I tell him that I have a nineteen-year-old daughter? A tall girl with skin like porcelain and grey-green eyes, studying at the Indian Institute of Technology. She looks at the handsome aspiring actor who sits by her side with his feet in the water. He has his trousers rolled up far enough for her to see the hair that covers his legs. Mia macho. Mia maxima macho…

Zeus, are you looking my way? Meera throws a glance over her shoulder. Do you see him, this Adonis, with a doric column for a throat and a damp well at the base? Where locusts feed, so can I, Giri, so can I.

Meera smiles honey at the actor even as he speaks the most inane rubbish; he wants, among other things, a chessboard patterned floor and to write a book about his childhood spent in a small town. Why is it, Meera asks herself suppressing a yawn, that everyone wants to write a book about their suburban childhood? Long bicycle rides, skinning mango trees, cricket matches and other wholesome things – why not one about trawling the alleys of a city, strangling cats and smashing car windows?

But every now and then Meera sees him dart a glance at her ankles and feels his eyes on her lips. When he reaches across and touches the tip of her nose, she wonders if she should say something. She knows what Giri will accuse him of when they get home. 'He just wants to fuck you. Guys like him have only one thing on their minds. I know. I know how men think!'

Meera thrusts the thought away and puts on her everything-you-say-is-the-most-interesting-thing-I've-ever-heard-in-my-life face and focuses on the actor.

'You are so …' the actor begins.

'Charming? Sexy?' Meera giggles.

'I was going to say easy to talk to. That I feel a great connection with you. But yes, you are charming and sexy too!' he whispers huskily.

Someone must have told him that his voice has a sexy timbre when lowered. What an ass! I ought to shut up and not encourage him. I am drunk, Meera thinks, and searches the poolside for Giri. Where is he? She wants to go home and lie down.

Just then Nikhil comes to her side. 'Mom, I can't find Dad!'

'He'll be here somewhere.'

'No, he's not. I checked the men's room. And the parking lot too. His car's not there either.'

Meera rises abruptly. She thrusts the plate and glass into the actor's hands and looks around. 'He should be here somewhere,' she says again, wandering back towards the seating area.

'Are you looking for Giri?' Charlie asks from near the bar.

'Yes, have you seen him, Charlie?' She tries to hide the worry in her voice. She sees Queen Lat's eyes glitter. The speculation.

'He stepped out as I was coming in. That was about two hours ago, Meera.'

That is when Meera feels her perfect September day with its blue sky acquire an underbelly of grey.

A wail gathers in her. But she clamps it down and improvises, 'How silly of me. The flight must be early…'

The words trail away. Meera sees the knowing look on the faces around her.

My Giri is not Zeus. He does not frolic with nymphets or even goddesses. He is prone to fits of rage; he is ambitious. But he is eminently trustworthy.

Meera hears again the censorious voice in her head: That's exactly what Hera must have thought each time Zeus disappeared from her horizon!

The horizon is darkening. A steely cast settles on the blue skies of the afternoon. There is none of the oppressive heat that announces the arrival of the rains in June. Instead, thunder rumbles from deep within the massing greyness. From the corner of his eye, Jak sees the woman shiver and pull the ends of her stole closer together. He frowns. It isn't all that cold in the little tinbox that is his car. He glances at his watch. It is half past three. 'Hmm... the monsoon will soon be here,' he says, filling the silence in the car.

The woman and the boy are quiet. Their stillness fills him with unease. If the goddamn car had a radio, he would switch it on. Anything to dispel the pall of mourning. Their colourless faces match the leaves of the trees they pass, an ashen sheen that seems to have taken on the reflection of the grim skies.

He waits for one of them to speak. When they don't, he continues.

'I love the rains. I think I missed it more than anything else while I was away. That pure loamy earth scent after the first rain. It's funny how we miss these little things more than the really important ones. Did I mention to you that I used to live in the US until I relocated to Bangalore... Oh, do you call it Bengaluru?'

Meera shakes her head. 'Hardly anyone does, except announcers at airports and railway stations. And politicians perhaps. It will always be Bangalore for me.'

'Like Chennai will always be Madras for me.'

A scream rents the car. He brakes abruptly.

'It's your phone! It's your phone!' a tinny voice screams.

The boy pulls the phone out of one of his numerous pockets and shuts it off. 'I'm sorry,' he mumbles. Then he grins, unable to hide his glee at the shock his ring tone has caused.

Jak tries to grin back, but his heart is thudding. Idiot boy, he thinks.

The woman looks as if she is going to burst into tears. 'Nikhil,' she hisses. 'Didn't I tell you to change that ring tone?'

'I'm sorry,' the boy says. 'I meant to. I forgot.'

'It's all right,' he says. 'But I must confess that for a moment it scared the shi…' He stops abruptly, conscious of what he was about to say, and clears his throat. 'I was petrified.'

He looks at the woman and boy.

He had gone to the brunch on a whim. He knew hardly anyone there. But Sheela, who was a director of the PR firm that was organizing the brunch, was an old friend and she had been very persuasive. 'I need you. I need some new faces in the pictures. It's almost a joke… whether it's a wine launch or a book event, the same people are everywhere. Credibility is becoming an issue, so you, Kitcha, can be the credibility man. The new kid on the block. I love that combination of grey at the temples and the designer stubble. And all those bracelets, the diamond stud and the cigar. Epitome of cool! Professor JAK, visiting from the US, etc.! Also, how else will you meet people in the city? Come on, just for an hour or so.'

He shook his head in amusement. Epitome of cool indeed! She'd say anything to drag him to her wine event. He didn't bother too much about his appearance, settling for comfort in clothes rather than elegance. He was a tall man, six feet two in his socks, and his broad shoulders made him look fitter than he was. Standing in front of the bathroom mirror, he would often pinch with a sigh the roll of flesh around his middle. He was a man going to fat, he told himself as he angled the mirror this way and that, quite aware in a detached way that he would do nothing about it.

He didn't mind growing old and didn't particularly seek ways to hide the toll of age. No dyeing the grey in his hair or styling it in such a way as to disguise the receding hairline. He didn't gym or diet. Sometimes when he was truly restless, he went for a run or a swim. That was it. So when women found him attractive, he wondered why. In his mind, he was still the lanky awkward boy he once was, unable to figure out what to do with his arms and legs. In time, he had learnt to accept the female attention with an easy regard. He didn't go looking for it but he didn't disdain it either when it came his way.

Sheela had known him when he was Kitcha. She still called him Kitcha and not Jak as everyone else did. It did something to him to hear himself being called by his boyhood name. She must sense how starved I am for companionship, he thought. No, the word was diversion. His life had fallen into a rut and he was not given to staying in one place for too long. Yet, here he was, bound to Bangalore for the last seven months and there was no telling when he would ever be able to shake the dust off his feet.

He had smiled again at Sheela's description and leaned forward to light her cigarette.

And he went. He drank a few glasses of wine. Stayed on the fringes of groups and out of arguments and was wondering if he could leave without offending Sheela, when she asked him if he could offer a lift back to the woman and the boy – 'If it isn't a bother, that is? They live in the same part of town as you do. The husband had to leave suddenly and they are stranded.'

So here they were, in his car. The woman was supposed to be a cookbook writer. A gracious woman, but quiet. He wondered what had happened for the husband to leave so abruptly. Did they quarrel? He hadn't noticed any unpleasantness. Or, maybe it had happened before he reached there.

In the rear-view mirror he glimpses the boy: bewilderment and hope jostling in a child's face, waiting for things to right themselves. In the presence of the thirteen-year-old with his nose pressed to the glass, he knows a stilling of time.

I was that boy, he thinks.

Bright thirteen-year-old Kitcha, unsullied by adult troubles, who thought every mango worth a shy, every shell a conch with the sea's song trapped in it, and every blank page waiting to be turned into a picture of his making.

Kitcha, who couldn't fathom the hunted look in his father's eyes and puzzled at what could frighten an adult. Kitcha had a history teacher waiting to pounce on him, but whose relentless scrutiny did Appa fear?

Kitcha had watched his regal mother, two inches taller than Appa, and with the wide shoulders that she bequeathed to him, crouch into a whimpering huddle the day his father made known his decision to join an ashram. To renounce the world. Their world.

His father no longer cowered and all his twitches had ironed themselves out. Appa was no longer his appa, and all he would say was, 'The time has come!'

His mother raised herself on an elbow. 'Whose time are you talking of? Yours or mine? Do you understand what you are condemning me to? Has it occurred to you even once? Tell me, what did I do wrong? Tell me, what was my fault?'

Appa shook his head dismissively. 'It is not what you think. You are not to blame. If someone is to be blamed, it is me for being such a coward. I should have told you. My parents knew I never wished for any of this. A wife, a child, the murkiness of grihastha ashrama ....

'It was my duty to provide them with an heir, they said. For the family line to continue. Don't forget who we are, they said. Who are we? I wanted to demand. The Hoysalas or the Cholas, for all this talk of an heir? But I couldn't hurt them. So I was obliged to shelve my desire.

'So you happened. And then Kitcha. Their heir. But I discovered that you had me wrapped in your coils.'

For a moment Kitcha thought he saw hatred in his father's eyes. How could his father look at his mother like that? Then he heard his father say, 'I told myself I would wait until Kitcha's brahmoupadesham. Once his upanayanam was conducted, I thought I could leave. I was such a fool! '

Kitcha rolled between his thumb and forefinger the sacred thread. Was this already yellowing slender thread, testimony to his brahminical destiny, the cause of all this trouble? If he hadn't had his upanayanam, would Appa have had to stay on?

'But then I couldn't go. I wished to see him, be with him, hear his chatter and his laughter. I still couldn't sever the ties. But now the time has come. None of this.' Appa flung his arm out in a gesture that encompassed everything – Kitcha, who sat with a sketch pad and box of Camlin watercolour tubes and two brushes in a glass of water, his weeping mother, the long bare hall with a swing, the veena propped in the corner, the old clock on the wall, and the sofa-cum-bed that Kitcha opened out in the night and slept on. 'None of this means anything any more. I see all of it as bandhanam. Bonds. Shackles. I am suffocating!'

Appa had turned to him. He had raised his hand as if to gather him into an embrace, then dropped it abruptly. Kitcha thought, was he a bandhanam too? How could Appa have turned himself into this cold stranger?

Kitcha's mother Sarada Ammal, the perfect wife who observed every auspicious date and ritual, who braided jasmine for the evening puja and played the veena, who on Janmasthami laid a trail of footprints through the house and lit a hundred and one lamps on Karthika Vilakku, lay on her side muttering, 'For fourteen years, I never ever disagreed with you. Your will was mine. And now, you call me a chain tying you down. How can you? What am I to do now? What do I do now?'

When Appa spoke next, he addressed only Kitcha. It was as if he had already erased the presence of Sarada from his life. 'One day, Kitcha, you too will know it. A moment of truth and then everything else will cease to be of any significance. Everything else will only seem a deterrent then. An irritant standing between you and your goal.'

Kitcha wondered if Appa was possessed. He was using words he didn't understand. What Appa said made no sense. Yet, there was a ring of certainty in his voice.

And Kitcha felt torn. Admiration for a father who already seemed to have turned into a demigod and anguish for his mother whom he had never seen so desolate or broken.

Kitcha ran then. He threw aside his paints and brushes, crumpled the painting into a messy wet splodge of paper and ran to the slatternly Marina with its side shows of the two-headed woman and the monster child, the horse, the camel rides, the vendors and other strays like him. To the swell and plish plash of waves against the shore.

He stared at the sea, counting the waves. He saw the sea wash away the debris and the words he wrote on the sand. Fuck you Appa, he wrote. Fuck you. Arsehole. Jerk. Motherfucker. Bastard. He wrote all the words he had found in the Harold Robbins novels he borrowed from the lending library. A calm settled on him.

He leaned into the cold gritty brush of the wave and learned in its touch an infinite sense of hope. The wave. It came. It went. It came. It went. It came. It went. Nothing changed that. Perhaps his world too would right itself again. When he reached home, his horizon would be the one he had always known: Appa with the shortwave radio pressed to his ear, as if by osmosis he could make the world of BBC and VOA his own. And Amma? She would be picking bits of husk and grit from the rice for lunch. She would look up from the plate and frown. Even before he had crossed the threshold, she would rage and rant at him for having run away. And Appa would rush to his defence. 'Let the boy be, Sarada. He won't do it again, Will you, Kitcha?'

Nothing had changed when he reached home in the evening, grimy, wind tossed, hungry and tired. He discovered a mother who lay stone faced and a father gone.

'What do I do now?' his mother asked the silent rooms of their home. 'They tell me I ought to feel blessed to have been married to a man who has taken up sanyas. I am cursed, Kitcha, that's what I am. Neither a wife nor a widow. Who am I, Kitcha? You tell me. He says – it's not you. That's what I can't bear. If he left me for another woman, I would woo him back. I would bring him back to us. But this! How do I fight this, Kitcha?'

Kitcha didn't know what to say. He was embarrassed by

this needy woman who lay on her side tracing circles on the cement floor with her index finger. Some of what she said he understood and the rest was a mystery, like his father's decision to go away. Besides, how did one console a mother? I don't know, I don't know, he whispered. I am as lost as you are, he thought.

It is Kitcha the boy who sneaks a look at the woman's face. He wants to speak words of consolation to her and the boy. 'Maybe he has just gone for a drive. I've done it myself. Several times. When I have worked the demons out, I go home. I don't think you should worry. Really!'

But it is Jak who speaks. Urbane, suave Jak with his vestibule brand of chit-chat. 'Sheela said you are a fantastic chef. And that you have authored cookbooks. You should give me a few recipes. Something that's really easy to make,' he says.

Perhaps it's best to not get involved. Meera, he remembers. That is her name. He thinks suddenly of the Meera bhajans his mother took to singing in those first fallow years after Appa left. His mother found in Meera a soul sister. Another woman languishing in a manic unreciprocated love. Another woman wedded to an image.

Jak shivers. He doesn't want to dwell on the past. In fact, he doesn't want to have to dwell on anything.

Besides, he wants to forget about the scream. It had disturbed him more than he realized. Even as he pulls away from the lilac house, it echoes in his head, reminding him of the screams that sometimes emerge from Smriti.

Which one of the fates had hovered as he named his child thus? For that is all there is to her now. What is remembered...

His fingers clench the steering wheel as though he means to hurt it, and he feels the tightness in his chest again.

STAGE I

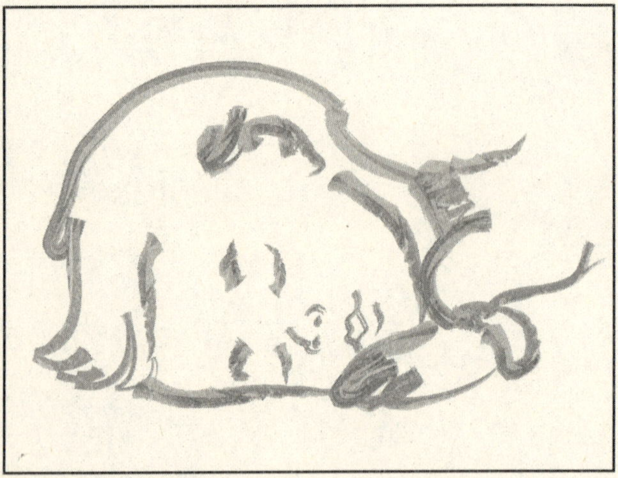

Cyclogenesis of Despair

A child, awake or asleep, has no sense of evil. No presentiment of what may happen in the time to follow. A child's brow rests smooth, unlined, untroubled, until knowledge descends upon it.

In the painting *Infant Moses Brought Before Pharaoh's Daughter* by William Hogarth, let us for once turn our eyes away from all the supporting cast – the maids and the Pharaoh's daughter; let us not dwell on the dark shadows or the building clouds. Instead, let us seek the child Moses who is a child as children should be, without the burden of a past or the knowledge of a future. It is that perfect moment when we believe all of us and all around us are in harmony. Only children know it, and the clouds and the seas.

But even the clouds and the seas are not untouched. For with no real warning, with neither portent nor omen, it is quite possible for a quiet wave to begin within what is considered a closed system. A stream is activated. When the wave turns counterclockwise, it does so by turning on its head all that is known and understood, causing a deeply intense and unstable atmosphere.

When despair strikes, it is the same. There is a mad scramble to make sense of what is happening. The mind whirls, turning every event over, seeking an explanation, a reason... The only certainty about a cyclone or despair is the uncertainty it triggers. And as with despair, the cyclogenesis of a tropical storm is seldom announced. What is certain is the resultant turbulence.

Professor J. A. Krishnamurthy
The Metaphysics of Cyclones

The scream pierces the house. The lilac house. A long drawn out scream of terror.

Meera wakes with a start. Her hand goes to her mouth. Has she been screaming? She waits for the lights to be switched on, doors to be opened. But there is only silence and darkness and hair that stands on end.

Meera gets out of bed, pushes her feet into flip-flops and creeps into the corridor.

A grove of shadows, where Meera who fears nothing can chase that shout of panic, shackle its goat legs and slit its throat. In all these years, Meera has forbidden panic entry into her lilac house.

When Daddy died leaving very little behind, when a silver oak came cascading down on the kitchen, when Giri was laid off work, when Nayantara left home at seventeen, when Lily's ankle broke, when the septic tank overflowed and the mushy sweet pong of faeces began permeating their every breath, when Lily's maid and Meera's anchor decided that henceforth every new moon night the goddess of Melmarvathur, Parasakhthi, would seek her out as an oracle, high priestess and repository, when nine-year-old Nikhil's class teacher called Meera to say that he had smuggled in a bra to school as part of a dare and Meera didn't know whether to laugh or cry or worry if the bra was an ancient one with frayed lace or an extravagantly sexy red confection of nipple net and under-wire hoist, when silverfish chewed their way through all the notes she had been making in the hope that one day she would do her dissertation 'on the role of water tanks in American fiction rooted in suburbia', when she discovered a lump in her breast and in Giri's briefcase a secret sheaf of bills – lunches, drinks for two, a bottle of perfume – each time the furies and fates disturbed the quiet fabric of siesta that was her life, Meera strangled panic even before it made known its presence. Who dares panic in her home now?

She pauses outside the door of a bedroom. Her mother's. She can hear even breathing punctuated by a gentle snore. She smiles, a curl of grimness. Mummy, who actually claims that most nights she doesn't sleep a wink, and that's what causes the dark circles around her eyes. The next time she uses her sleepless nights as an excuse to get out of something she doesn't want to do, Meera will tell her. It just might wipe the smugness off her face for a second.

Next, she pauses outside her grandmother's door. Two sets of snores heave within. The old woman on the bed. The maid on the floor.

As she walks towards Nikhil's room, she hears the muttering. He is talking in his sleep. Meera opens the door and creeps in. The thin quilt he covers himself with is tangled around his legs.

She caresses his brow. 'Hush, hush, baby!'

Nikhil's eyes snap open. 'Daddy! Is Daddy home?'

'Go to sleep, darling. He'll be home in the morning, you'll see!'

'I dreamt Daddy's car was perched at the edge of a cliff. He was trying to get out before it went over. He was shouting for me to help him.' Nikhil shakes at the horror of it. 'I tried to run to him. But my legs wouldn't move. I really tried, Mummy, I did…'

'Ssh...' Meera murmurs, cradling his head against her.

Sheela, the woman from the PR company, had arranged for someone to drop Nikhil and her home. A man who was at the party and lived in her neighbourhood, Sheela said. He was perfectly safe, even if he was a stranger. She and he had been friends from their college days.

Meera was relieved to hear that he was a stranger. She preferred that to going with someone she knew. A stranger would ask few questions and wouldn't speculate about Giri's going away.

She had watched Nikhil's eyes scan the road. He searched faces, parked cars, number-plates. When the scream resonated through the car, the blood drained from her face. What on earth? Then she saw Nikhil's grin and felt as if she wanted to burst into tears. How could he?

And Giri, she wanted to scream. What is this game you are playing? Where have you gone?

As if from a distance, she thought she heard the man say something. And she heard herself replying on auto pilot, 'Oh, what you need is a recipe for a quick cold soup! A gazpacho, perhaps.'

What had he asked?

The car pulled up outside their gate. Nikhil and she stood watching it drive away. A little blue car.

'Did you see the inside of his car? What a mess! He has groundnut shells in a paper bag along with a million books and files. Do you think he treats the back seat as his office?' Nikhil chattered.

She listened without registering what he said. All she could think of was Giri and his disappearing act. What was it all about? So when he suddenly asked, 'Did Daddy text you?' she said automatically, 'No.' Then, because she was afraid of what she might see in his eyes, she said carefully, 'Nikhil, don't tell anyone yet that Daddy went away without telling us. You know how they are…' she finished, not knowing what to say next.

'But where do you think he went, Mummy?' Nikhil asked, more curious than afraid.

Meera shook her head. 'I don't know. Maybe he had an urgent business meeting to go to.'

'Why couldn't he have just told you that?' Nikhil said, accepting her explanation and kicking the gate open in one swift boyish act of innocence.

Meera watched him walk in. She followed, wondering what excuses she could make for Giri's absence. Unless, of course, he was already home. She hurried in, the thought lending speed to her step. Maybe that was it. Something, the heat or the alcohol, had triggered a migraine and he had rushed home before it became unbearable and he couldn't drive. He knew, if he told her, she would have insisted on their leaving together and he wanted her to have a good time.

He must be in their room with the curtains drawn tight to block the light and with the fan whirring at top speed. He would be lying there reeking of Tiger Balm, his arm over his forehead, as if only by this careful arranging of his limbs would he be able to leash the pain. If she were to even exhale, he would growl, 'Can't you keep it low? I have a headache!'

The bathroom would bear the stench of vomit. That, too, was routine. The throwing up. Mostly, he cleaned up himself. He was a meticulous man. But if he was really unwell, then that too would be waiting for her.

For once Meera longed for the growl and the irritation, the bits of food and bile splattering the toilet bowl. For the stench and for her own insides to heave involuntarily. Poor baby, Meera thought, rushing to minister comfort to the migraine stricken Giri.

Meera walked into the house to hear Nikhil say, 'Dad's gone to the golf course.'

Her mother said, 'Your father doesn't play golf!'

'Actually, he doesn't play anything.' Her grandmother laughed.

Nikhil pushed his hands into his pockets. 'Did I say he was playing golf? He's gone with a friend.'

'What friend?' her mother asked.

'He has no friends,' her grandmother added.

She wondered if she should go to the police. The very thought was daunting. She had never been to a police station before. What did one do? What did one say? Then there was the matter of bribes. She could hardly slip notes into the policeman's waiting hand under the table or into his pocket while muttering, 'A little tea money!'

From the movies, she knew that twenty-four hours had to go past before a missing person complaint could be made. She was panicking for no reason. He would be back soon. She would wait twenty-four hours before she worried, she told herself as she removed her earrings, sitting in front of the dressing table.

In the mirror, she could see the bed with its coverlet stretched tightly across and the plumped up pillows resting against the bolsters. A pristine bed, strangely forlorn.

At seven her mother settled in front of the TV with a notebook and pen. 'Please Nikhil, no chit-chat!' she told the silent Nikhil who was plugged into his iPod maze of 1756 songs.

'Why don't you just ask me to shut up?' her grandmother said.

'Please Mama, it's my favourite programme. I have a library meeting next week. I need to know what to recommend!'

'Rubbish! Do you think that man reads any of those books? All he does is read the back of the book! How can you be taken in by him? And I think he wears foundation cream. Can't you see that line by his jaw?' Lily mumbled querulously.

'What do you know of books? All you do is watch movies or talk shows all day. I don't know how you can watch such mindless nonsense.'

'Better than those travel and living programmes you watch. Where do you think you are going? Or, for that matter, when was the last time you cooked anything? Ha!'

The bickering continued. Meera rubbed her forehead. Her head throbbed. She wished she could turn and snap, 'Shut up! Shut up! Can't you see that I am worried? I don't need this as well.'

But she couldn't. No matter what, Meera never lost her temper. She never flared or snapped. She was just not like that.

Hoping to restore peace and some calm in her head, she intervened with a 'Lily dear, can I fix you a drink?'

Lily dear gleamed. 'I thought you would never ask. And pour her one too. She'll say no if you ask and then steal sips from my glass when no one's looking.' Lily gestured to her daughter with her chin.

Meera sighed.

Lily pounced on the sigh. She scrutinized Meera carefully. The drawn face and the shadows beneath her eyes. Lily frowned. What was wrong, she wondered. Then she put it out of her mind. One of the benefits of growing old was this: being able to push aside any troubling thoughts that entered one's mind with, it will resolve itself or somebody else will do it! No need to get your knickers into a twist.

Nevertheless, Lily reached across and touched Meera's elbow. 'What about you? You look like you need one!'

Meera shook her head. 'I had plenty to drink at the party. Too much, in fact!'

She caught Nikhil's eyes on her face. What was he thinking?

Meera thought of the image they must make. Three women of three generations and a young boy, cast in a room of fading splendour. The pools of light, the shadows, the long convoluted histories of how they came to be where they were.

In the 1930s, when Raghavan Menon began working in Calcutta, he fell in love with a way of life. Calcutta reminded him of his Calicut in many ways but there was more. Art flourished in every home and in one of those soirees he had taken to attending, he met Charu, a Bengali woman. When he married her, he became a born-again Bengali. Charu died some years later and Raghavan Menon decided to send his daughter Leela to Santiniketan. 'I want culture to course through her veins. I'd prefer culture to blood, in fact!' he told his brothers who advocated that he send Leela to study in Calicut instead.

The brothers shook their heads in sorrow. If the girl had come to Calicut, he would have returned home perhaps and made a life there. Now, he was lost. Soon thereafter, they sent him a cheque as his share of the family estate.

Then a well-known Bengali director spotted Leela, and Lily was born. Hindi cinema already had a Leela and so it was decided that the name she was called at home would be her screen name. Lily the actress did only offbeat cinema and just as the movie-going world was getting interested in her, she married Sandor, a Hungarian painter. They came to live in Bangalore in this house that Raghavan Menon found them.

Saro was born. Saro was sent to expensive schools. Saro fell in love with her best friend's brother and married him. Sandor died, and a year later Saro was widowed when she was thirty-nine. It was to this house she came then, seeking refuge for herself and her nineteen-year-old daughter Meera.

A window rattled, shaking Meera out of her reverie. She ran a hand through her hair and leaned back in her chair, pretending to be absorbed by the breaking news on TV.

Lily and Saro had settled their differences and were sipping their drinks. The bickering was customary. Like Saro's book buying. One book of fiction preferably by someone who had just won an important prize, or was being hailed by the literary establishment that month as the voice of the century. And another of non-fiction, usually a biography or a historical account, preferably by an Englishman. Saro only bought books that had sold at least 100,000 copies or would post a major prize. And the books programme steered her towards these titles. It was completely beyond her to consider a book merely because the title excited her, a book no one had ever heard of. She couldn't take the chance. Her reputation was at stake after all. Saro liked to be thought of as a woman of taste, whether it was in clothes, jewellery or books.

In contrast, Lily picked her reading by the book jacket. 'Give me a book with a man and a woman searching each other's eyes. Or one with a knife and a red blob. Or some such thing. I assure you it will be truly unputdownable. Though she won't agree, of course! She is such a snob.' She cocked an eyebrow at Saro, her daughter, Meera's mother.

They quarrelled through the day. If it wasn't books, then it was a plant or a piece of furniture or a memory they both remembered differently, or a recipe that each swore was the authentic version. If they didn't, one of them was ailing or troubled. So Meera gauged the well-being of the old ladies by the vitriol they hurled at each other. That night, they were well enough. They didn't seem perturbed by Giri's absence.

Nikhil worried her, though. He was quiet. Too quiet. 'Are you all right, baby?' she asked.

He peered at her. 'Don't call me baby!'

Then he asked suddenly, 'Did you try his mobile?'

Meera nodded. 'Unreachable.'

'What will you tell them if he doesn't come home by midnight?' Nikhil whispered. They looked at the old ladies watching a programme that they both enjoyed. A talk show with a hostess who was sophisticated enough to satisfy her mother. And an ex-movie star, which made her glamorous in her grandmother's eyes.

'No whispering in public,' her mother said.

'Naughty secret, is it?' her grandmother added, speculation lighting up her face.

Meera sucked on a melting ice cube. She hoped it would freeze the scream that threatened to erupt from her mouth any moment now.

Her phone beeped. Nikhil looked up. Meera grabbed the

phone. New Message. It would be Giri texting, explaining, apologizing, saying he would be home soon.

It was an advertisement for ring tones. Meera dropped the phone and reached for another ice cube.

'Can we order a pepperoni pizza?' Nikhil said.

'No,' Meera snapped. 'You had pizza three days ago!'

'It's not good for you to eat so much pizza,' Lily chuckled. 'All this junk food will show itself twenty years from now. You will be a very fat man.'

'And a poor one,' Saro added. 'Pizza doesn't grow on trees. It's expensive. Do you realize your mother could buy groceries for all of us for a week for that much money?'

Nikhil slammed the book down. 'We never have money for anything. What I can't understand is how we can afford to live in a house like this. Look at it!'

'Nikhil…' Meera growled. She looked beyond him and saw the stillness that had swept into the other women. She sensed it inch into her too. The house. The lilac house. Somehow it always came to that. The house.

Meera asked herself, if it wasn't for the house, would Giri have lingered that first day?

Had the house lost its power to enchant and keep?

Meera kisses the brow of her sleeping child. In the morning, if Nikhil remembers, he will be embarrassed by how he clung to her. He might even deny it outright. 'You must have dreamt it,' he will say defiantly.

But for now he is her little boy again. A little boy who doesn't know what to make of a father who disappeared mysteriously one Sunday afternoon, on a perfect September day.

I

It had been a perfect September dawn when he saw her first. He said he had been enchanted. He said he didn't know if he wanted to collapse with laughter or lean against the gatepost and watch her forever. Giri said that was when he fell in love.

'Imagine this,' he said, leaning forward to coil a strand of her hair around his finger, 'a girl in an ivory dress. The sun teasing glints of amber in her hair. A barefoot girl chasing a flock of geese through the grass!'

'A gaggle. Not flock,' she murmured.

'Flock! Gaggle! How does it matter? All I knew was, that's where I want to be. With that girl and her pet geese in their lilac house.' He sighed and leaned back in the chair.

His eyes swept over the house and the garden, the blossom laden trellises and borders, the trees and the carp pool with its little stone frog. She saw his eyes pause on her face with the same rapt pleasure. And she knew she couldn't tell him that the white dress was a faded nightie. Or that she had heard the geese in the front lawn and leapt out of bed and run out to chase them away before they trampled all over the newly planted aubergine plants. Or that the geese were merely biding their time as they were fed and fattened to be sold to Hamid Bhai in time for Christmas. (For every goose was worth its weight in gold or would at least help pay for changing the termite infested rafters of the back kitchen.) And that she didn't waste tears or sentiment over the geese as they were taken away to have their long necks wrung and their down plucked. That she feasted on the goose, with as much relish as anyone else. He would have been horrified. He called her his pet goose. Goose girl of the lilac house.

She smiled. She liked being his pet goose.

'All I could think of was, how am I going to get my foot into this door? I was the prince inching around the enchanted house, seeking to find a way in.'

'You just had to say hello and I would have hello-ed you back!' She grinned.

He frowned. 'You don't understand. A hello would have been way too ordinary. I had to discover you, my goose girl of the lilac house.

'So when the model coordinator suggested that we use this house for the photo shoot of Coconut Kisses, I didn't think twice. I said yes.'

She saw it in her mind then. The inward jerk of the elbow, the clenched fist, the explosion of a yes as it conveyed from deep within the desire to discover her. His goose girl of the lilac house. And she gleamed in reflection of that yearning.

The model coordinator couldn't stop beaming. She had never had it so easy. The location and props in one place, with a stylist thrown in for free. Meera had brought out the crocheted doilies and organza napkins with their delicate scalloped edges, the silver napkin rings and the silver tea service, the tiered porcelain cake stand and the Royal Doulton teacups. She had arranged the Coconut Kisses and even found a way to position the biscuit packet in such a way that it blended in, and then set the table. Meera heard the pleasure in the art director's voice. 'Gracious living! It's exactly what we had planned for!'

Meera smiled. She wondered how much she could pad her bill for the props. Gracious living doesn't come cheap, she wanted to say. Then she met his eyes and she saw herself there. And she didn't say anything. She would talk to the model coordinator on the side and she wasn't going to budge from the figure she had in mind.

But he had found reasons to not leave her alone. Again and again he lingered at her side, chatting between the shots. Could it be that a miracle had occurred? Could it be that he was drawn to her? When he came by the next day with a small basket of flowers for her, she laid out gracious living once again, just for him. It was her only weapon. Other girls showed the tops of their breasts or batted their eyelids. Meera had just this to offer and she wasn't going to shy away from it. And the old ladies, they played their parts.

They sat there, mother, daughter and granddaughter, each one of them wooing him, and he didn't even realize it. Lily with her lace fan, fluttering it ever so often with an elegant little movement of the wrist. Saro in her pearls and crisp cotton sari and 'Shall I be mother?'

Only Meera was as she always was. Uncertain, tremulous and hiding behind a façade of remote charm. She prayed her hands wouldn't shake when she offered him the cake. She so wanted it to be right. For Meera had utterly and hopelessly fallen in love.

She crossed her ankles, laid her hands in her lap and said little.

She could see he was charmed. Giri offered adulation as if it was a ginger biscuit on a plate. 'I love the colour of your house,' he said.

Lily widened her eyes and began, 'The painting contractor ...'

But Saro cut in with, 'It is very pretty, isn't it? We have such trouble matching it each time we repaint.'

Meera swallowed convulsively. Lily, she realized, had intended to bring forth the story of the painting contractor who had offered them the paint for half the actual cost. He had made a mistake elsewhere and was trying to salvage some of the cost. And they didn't have to pay as much as they would have had to if they had chosen the colour themselves.

Meera rose. 'I need to check on something on the stove,' she said. Her heart wouldn't stop hammering. Would Giri be bored with them? She couldn't bear to see it when it happened.

Lily was silent for a few minutes. Then she set about playing grand dame of the house. 'Meera, wait. Where are you running away to? She's such a shy thing and so conscientious.'

Virtues any prospective husband would want.

'You must tell him about the time David Lean was almost here, when he was shooting *A Passage to India*!' Lily began.

Meera paused. 'Lily, it's your story… Go on, you tell Giri!'

And Giri said, 'Yes Lily, may I call you Lily, do tell me.'

And then Saro matched celluloid reels with stories of Meera's daddy's tea estates. Not once did they break the rhythm as anecdote followed anecdote.

Lily's brief career as a movie actress in Hindi cinema. The scion of a minor royalty family who fell madly in love with her. The cluster of rubies he set in a ring and had delivered at the doorstep. 'On a cushion held by a turbaned man who looked like a maharaja himself,' Lily giggled.

The meeting with Sandor, the portrait painter from Hungary. Their whirlwind courtship and elopement.

'Saro was a good girl,' Lily said archly. 'None of her mama's madness. When her best friend's brother proposed marriage, she accepted. Meera's daddy was a very handsome man. And the bungalow they lived in at Coonoor, what a splendid house it was!'

'There were four house boys apart from a butler and two cooks,' Saro added. 'The parties we threw…!'

'Meera picked it all up then. How to lay the table and do the flowers, plan a menu and seat the guests. Meera will make an exemplary wife!' Lily leaned forward in a stage whisper to Giri.

From where she stood by the garden door, Meera saw her mother talk in low tones to Giri. She could see that he was enchanted as the old ladies wove their spell around him. For a while Meera continued to worry. Any moment now, it would happen. He would see them for what they were. But Giri didn't. Giri sipped the tea and ate his cake. And Meera slipped into the chair alongside his.

When Saro rose, he jumped to his feet. She smiled her imperious I-am-the-queen-of-this-fiefdom smile and gave him her hand to kiss or hold, but not shake as the rest of the world might be inclined to do. 'Come again, young man. Meera is such a shy creature, it will do her good to meet more young people like you.'

Like you. Meera's heart trilled in joy. Mummy liked him. She actually liked him. And Lily, incorrigible rascal Lily, peered at him with a coy smile and said, 'And so handsome. Meera, don't let him go!'

He blushed then and looked at her. What now? Meera wondered.

'Such lovely ladies,' he murmured.

For now they were the keepers of the gracious lilac

house. And protectress of Meera, his goose girl waiting to be discovered.

So when he leaned across and said, 'Would you like to go for a drive? We could stop for an ice cream at the Corner House!' Meera widened her eyes in pleasure, tried not to look at the remains of the tea tray, the sandwiches, patties and biscuits, cakes and crumbs. The thought of an ice cream sat heavy. But she wasn't going to let him slip away from her.

She wanted him. Poor Meera. She never asked what he wanted. Her, the lilac house, or together what they represented.

She let her lips flower. 'I would love to,' she said.

Love to place herself and all she had in his hands, Giri read.

Giri rose six inches high. What man wouldn't? He thought of the riches laid out before him. A bride with social graces and a beautiful old home. A grandmother who referred to Sir Richard Attenborough and Satyajit Ray in the same breath. A mother who breathed finesse. She even had a fork to extract meat ever so daintily from a crab claw.

Giri had never known such people before. He thought of his father in his yellowing banian and dhoti in Palakkad. He thought of the old decrepit house and relatives as stringy and penurious as his father. He had been fortunate in his brains and a Maths teacher, Sivaraman Iyer, who had shepherded him away from home. First the Regional Engineering College, where his eyes widened at a world he never knew existed. Then the IIM in Ahmedabad. Campus recruitment ensured that he found a foothold in the corporate world.

Giri had made careful plans about where he would be by the time he was thirty, forty, forty-five… thereafter would be the playing fields of his life. To accomplish this, he needed to round off the edges that still clung to him from the small-town, lower middle class boy he was. Meera would make this possible, he knew with certainty. Meera, who exuded upperclass-dom like the L'air du temps she wore. Discreet, elegant, and old money.

Giri, on his jaunts abroad, spent many hours in the duty-free area, filing away in his mind accessories to gracious living as epitomized by designer merchandise in international airports. Mont Blanc pens and Burberry coats, Louis Vuitton bags and the crystal world of fragrances. It was here that he almost gave up. The eye could remember patterns and shapes but the nose almost defeated him. The nose was easily tricked. In the end, he got around that too. Each time, he chose a couple of perfumes that he liked the most and persuaded shop assistants to spray them for him on white slivers of cardboard. He would sniff at them diligently, keeping at it until the top note was committed to memory. Giri knew he had to acquire that veneer of polish Meera seemed to be born with.

Giri exhaled. With Meera, he would be able to move on. Finally, he would be free of the yellowing past and the stench of making do. Meera. His. Like the lilac house. L'air du temps.

Meera was to know an occasional qualm. Was Giri in love with her for all the wrong reasons? She thought of the young women who were part of his professional world. Tall young women who wore their suitability like their hair. Shining, groomed and never out of place. Why does he prefer me to them? she asked herself. They are smart, competent, and have careers. Whereas all I have is a postgraduate degree in English and stewardship of this house.

'Don't be silly,' he murmured against her cheek. 'I don't want a journalist, a teacher, a brand manager – it's you I want as my wife. Let me assure you, it takes a really smart woman to be a corporate wife.'

Meera rested her cheek against his. She would be that. A corporate wife. The woman behind his success. It was what she wanted. To be there for him. They would build their lives together.

A few days before the wedding, Saro asked her, 'What now, Meera? Will you move out or will you live here? What does Giri want? Do you know? Have you two even discussed it?'

Giri wanted them there. 'In the lilac house,' he said. 'Why would we want to live elsewhere? It is your home. Our home. Besides, after this, how can I ask you to live in a poky flat?'

Meera felt another qualm. 'Giri, you mustn't get the wrong idea. I…we… don't have much. This house…' she began.

'Ssh. I know what you are going to say. This house is all there is. It is enough, goose girl! Just you in this house is all I ask for.'

Meera wrapped her arms around his neck. She knew what she would do with her doubts and suspicions. Pat them into balls like the tamarind they dried every year in the sun and put away with rock salt in a terracotta jar. Out of sight. Out of mind.

Meera stands at the window and looks out into the darkness. There is a streetlight by the gate. A blue beacon that would show up anyone who stood at the gate.

She is hopeful as she waits. Any minute now, the headlamps of a car will pale the blue light. Any minute now, a rattling, noisy autorickshaw will pull up.

Meera continues to stand there. Suddenly, the streetlamp near the gate splutters and crackles. She watches it for a long while, timing the intervals between each splutter and crackle. Maybe Giri went for a drive to clear his head. His car had a breakdown; she knows how hopelessly incompetent he is when it comes to cars. He doesn't even know how to change a flat tyre. Maybe his phone ran out of charge or there was no signal. The outskirts of Bangalore have many such pockets. This is the only explanation, Meera tells herself repeatedly. What else could it be? She grasps as desperate women do at any straw to prevent her thoughts from going down one particular, obvious alley. A narrow, dark, fetid lane called the other woman.

Had Hera sat thus? Meera asks herself suddenly.

Hera, who had a wedding night that lasted three hundred years. Hera had known how to core the golden apple, scooping a hollow in each half. Into it she had poured all of herself: her fragrance and breath, spit and mucus, milk and wellness, sweat and soul. She had cut a quarter off the half and run it along her limbs, gathering into its juice all the sweetness of her youth and hope, and fed it to Zeus with her lips. His tongue snaked out of his mouth, and fed from hers. They feasted off each other and Hera thought, what other woman will offer him this? What goddess, nymph, mortal creature can match the extent of all I have given unto him?

So Meera had thought when Neruda and then Pushkin first sat on Giri's bedside table where once Deepak Chopra and Thomas Friedman had. When Giri took to twilight walks out of her sight with his mobile hidden in his breast pocket as if it contained a rare pearl. She pretended not to see the changes in his wardrobe or hear his mobile as it beeped a spell first thing in the morning and last thing at night. The pink translucence of a youth rediscovered seldom lasts, she told herself.

I am not Hera, she tells herself. I will not panic. I will not spew venom or make known my rage. I will not lower my dignity or shame myself. I can live with these shadows as long as it is me he comes home to.

Besides, Giri is not Zeus. He isn't a compulsive philanderer, merely a middle-aged man who has had his head turned. Meera tells herself, don't panic, who else can offer him this cornucopia of elegance? Which other woman can lay his table as I do, or make a home for him as I do? The felicity of our lives may be shadowed, but will never be tainted or violated. Giri will not risk losing any of this.

And yet, where is Giri?

Meera squares her shoulders and decides to fill up the time until Giri comes home. There are books to dust in the living room. Hundreds of books Giri has accumulated with his Books & Periodicals expense account.

One by one, Meera wipes them clean. But Giri is yet to come home.

Meera switches on the computer. On a whim, she opens Giri's email account. He has forgotten to sign himself out and Meera enters his private world, heart hammering. But there is nothing for her to discover. All of it is empty. His Inbox, Outbox, Sent box… It is as if he has erased himself out of his own life. And then, in the drafts folder she finds an unfinished email.

When the developers called again last morning, my hand shook as I wrote down their offer. It was serious money. I would never again have to eat shit with that kind of money in the bank. With that kind of security, I could finally do what I want to do. Start something on my own. M mocked me when I tried telling her. 'Oh Giri, first figure out what it is you want to do and then we can talk of selling the house.'

You are being stubborn. No one will ever make such an offer, and for this old house? I said again.

Sometimes I think I could strangle her. She refuses to listen to reason. I tried explaining it to her: Listen to me, Meera, if we did this, our lives would change.

She stared at me with a strange expression. 'Why would you want our life changed? It's perfect. I am happy. Aren't you happy? I thought you were happy.'

I wanted to reach across and slap her face. Her face that she has slathered with half a tin of fucking Nivea cream. That's her greatest fucking concern. Wrinkles.

Does she for one moment understand what I have to put myself through, day after day? Does she know what I have to do to keep my place on the corporate ladder? The endless dents to my self-esteem? The fear of being made redundant or, worse, passed over for a promotion? What does she know of any of this?

'We have growing children. Can't you see that? You have to stay on in your job. You can't risk everything we have. We owe it to them to provide them the best. Besides, you are too old to play hippy, Giri. Organic farming is all very well. But do you know a spade from a hoe?' she said as if talking to a petulant six-year-old.

Don't patronize me, I said.

But what I really want to do is shake her till her teeth rattle and tell her, Fuck you and your fucking old house!

But I can't stop seeing the figures the property developer quoted. There's nothing to be done but try again. She just needs to be persuaded. I will wait till I catch M in a more affable mood. There's nothing else to do. After all, it's Madam's lilac house.

Meera stares appalled at the unfinished mail. Who was he writing to? And who is this Giri? Where is such rancour and bitterness coming from?

Meera never dreamt big dreams. She had no desire for designer clothes, diamonds or expensive holidays. In those hard years after her father's death, she learnt to worship at the altar of enough. That was all she ever hoped for. Enough to keep the roof over their heads and food in their bellies. Enough to retain dignity and not have to ask reluctant removed relatives for a temporary handout. Enough to live as they did.

Then Meera had her moment of epiphany: Giri. He was the god of her enough. She hugged her relief to herself. The enough she had always wanted was hers.

Only twice did she know pangs of anxiety that ruffled her sense of peace. Then Meera, the otherwise reticent Meera, bellowed out her pain in the labour room. The nurses had tried to shush her but she had screamed and shrieked to hasten the process whereby she could revert to her state of enough.

When the babies were laid in her arms, the fulfilment she knew drowned her in its completeness. How could anything else compare to this, she thought as her eyes sought Giri's.

Meera reads the mail again. She has been so blind. Giri had wanted more than enough.

And suddenly she is overwhelmed. Meera, goose girl, corporate wife, had forgotten that suspicion, like tamarind, never loses its sourness. It knows how to wait. And when to emerge as a humming swarm with a sting.

II

Suspicions swarm and hover, ready to sting. Is this the place? How could it be? Perhaps the taxi driver got it wrong…

Grey painted doors line the corridor. A regulation grey that makes the dirty cream coloured walls seem like watered down chicken curry. The mosaic floor is chipped and grimy. He follows the boy down the corridor, feeling his heart sink with every step. Why did she choose to come here?

'There is only one other deluxe room. But that is reserved for the doctor,' the boy says. 'He comes and goes but the room is always kept ready for him. Now this is a very good room too.'

The boy unlocks the door and pushes it open. A swash of warm fetid air rushes out. The boy switches the light on, and the fan. Jak looks around him.

At one end is a bed with a batik patterned sheet stretched across it and a pillow on top of which is a folded sheet. There is a mirror on the wall with a wooden ledge beneath it. By the main door is another door. The bathroom, he thinks, postponing the inevitable shudder at what he would find. A tiny cake of Medimix soap and a sachet of shampoo. A threadbare towel, a grimy bucket and mug. And a toilet he would need to exorcize all his acquired American standards of hygiene to squat upon.

'Tea, coffee, mineral water? Sir! Sir!' The boy's voice splices his thoughts. His eyes are expectant as he stands by the door.

Jak pulls out a fifty-rupee note from his wallet, knowing very well that he is over tipping. The boy beams. He will be useful, Jak knows.

He places his bag on a low wooden table. On the farther side of the room is another door. A grey door flanked on either side by windows. Grey window frames. Overhead, the fan whirrs, stirring air in the still room. He asks himself again, but this dump, why did she choose to come here? What on earth was she thinking of?

Then the boy walks towards the closed door and with the aplomb of an amateur magician pulling a rabbit out of a black top hat, he flings it open.

The tang of the sea. The boom and splash of the breakers. The salt of the spray. The skies. All of it gathers and rushes into the room. Jak walks out into the balcony. He feels his legs tremble. He sees the sea as she must have. And he feels that familiar crouching ache rise and stretch its muscles. She had come here chasing a memory. His memory of this little seaside town, Minjikapuram.

He begins to understand now. He had described to her his first time in Minjikapuram, dredging out the only phrase he remembered from his Perry Mason days: 'Out there what you get is a lungful of storm!'

He had painted a picture for her. The surprise of it, the grandeur. The overwhelming of the self by the sea and wind. She had wanted all that he had known. And so this.

The taxi driver had looked at the piece of paper he had written the address on. 'I'll take you to a better hotel. With cable TV and fridge in the room.'

He shook his head. 'No, I want to go here,' he said, stabbing the paper with his forefinger.

The taxi driver shrugged. Each to his own, but don't blame me if you hate it, the set of his shoulders bristled.

The hotel at Madurai had arranged the taxi for him. 'The driver is from those parts. He should be able to find the place you want to go to,' the reception clerk said.

Jak had nodded. 'Good,' he said. 'That will save me some time.'

'But sir,' the man's eyes had brimmed with curiosity, 'what is there in Minjikapuram? Why are you going there? Are you visiting relatives?'

Jak shrugged. 'Research! Just research work. I am a cyclone expert. And there are some interesting developments on this coastline that I want to study.'

'Ah, I see!' the man said, printing out Jak's bill. 'After the tsunami, some scientists came here. They were on a research trip and were going further south, they said. But you know what I think…' He paused expectantly.

Jak stood there silently, knowing he would hear it anyway. 'You can study nature as much as you want, but you can't ever predict it. Actually, there is nothing in life you can predict.'

Jak remembered this as the car turned onto the market road. Had he ever thought he would come back here again? It was almost thirty-one years ago that he had come to Minjikapuram. After the hustle and bustle of Madras, it had appeared quiet and provincial. He searched the road for some familiar landmark. All he could remember was the bus stand with a façade of shops in front. And the temple on the hill.

'Do people still come to the temple here?' he asked.

'Not as much. Everyone's rushing to Tirupati or Sabarimala these days. But the people around here still pray to Minjikaiyan and Minjikammal for the welfare of their children. My wife comes once a year and she insists on dragging me along. When it is for one's children, I suppose you don't want to take chances. Our children are our wealth, after all.'

The driver's matter-of-fact pronouncement was something he had heard several times before. But now it had the edge of a gutting knife. It tore into him, eviscerating in one sudden turn.

Jak scanned the shop fronts that flanked either side of the road. The familiarity of it all. Aluminium vessels in one. Sacks of grain in another. A barber shop and an old newspaper and bottle shop. Rolls of fabric at an entrance and saris draped from hooks on the ceiling. The glint of gold from a secluded interior. The fragrance of coriander and coffee that filled the air. The row of flower vendors with huge garlands of marigold and jasmine. A pushcart vendor frying pakodas in a giant frying pan. Beneath a tree sat another vendor with an array of brightly coloured plastic articles spread on a tarpaulin sheet and further ahead, a fortune-teller with his parakeet in a cage. Nothing much seemed to have transpired in the last three decades. It was still a town that happened to be there, going nowhere.

Which was why Jak had been puzzled at first. Why had she even wanted to visit Minjikapuram?

The taxi continued down the market road, past a church. The shops began to thin out and Jak could smell the ocean.

'How far is the sea from here?' he asked the taxi driver.

'Behind the lodge,' the man said. 'But it is not a sea you can swim in. The coast is dangerous.'

'I know,' Jak said. 'I have been here before.'

'Then I don't have to tell you to be careful,' the man said.

'No.' He spoke quietly. If only someone had warned Smriti to be careful.

When the taxi pulled up outside an ugly bleached building, he asked, 'Are you sure this is the place?' The driver stared at him blankly, then shrugged. 'This is the lodge. Not at all suited for people like you. You want me to take you elsewhere? I know of a really good place…'

Jak held up his hand to pause the flow of words. He paid the driver and pushed open the metal gate. Somewhere in this dingy seaside lodge he would find the first clue, he thought.

The reception clerk made him wait as he filled a register. There was a wall-mounted date sheet. 30 September. A line of red plastic chairs stood alongside a wall. A few men sat there, idly flicking through different sections of the newspaper. One man was talking on a mobile phone.

He felt their eyes on him. The smoke from their cigarettes stung his throat. Were you here when it happened, he wanted to ask them. It was in the last week of February. On the twenty-eighth. Do you remember? Wasn't there something you could have done? Anything?

You sir, he wanted to ask an elderly man in a cream coloured half-sleeved shirt and dhoti who was reading a newspaper, you look like a father, a grandfather; an educated man. Shouldn't you have said something? Asked her why she was here. Damn it, isn't that what we do, poke our nose into everything, probe and question all we see? She wouldn't have liked it. She may have asked you to mind your own business. She may have walked away muttering, 'Indians!' But if you had asked her… Maybe.

As he walked away, he heard the elderly man ask the clerk, 'Who is that? Not the type we see here.'

He heard the clerk mutter a response.

'Who is that man?' Jak asked the hotel boy, feeling the elderly man's scrutiny brand his back.

'He owns the hotel. Dr Srinivasan sir. He owns everything here in Minjikapuram. Shops. The hospital. The theatre. Everything. He is a very important man.'

Jak nodded, feigning interest. He felt his thoughts crowd in on him again.

Jak shifts in the chair and puts down the book he is trying to read. He has read the same line twenty times over and it is still only a series of meaningless syllables. He lights a cigar but it tastes bitter and dry in his mouth. He decides to go for a walk. The reception clerk pretends not to see him as Jak walks past. Jak wonders at the hostility of the man's averted glance. It makes no sense at all. They don't even know each other.

He ambles slowly along the road. It is dark by the time he reaches the Minjikapuram main road. He looks at his watch. It is a quarter past six. He stands on the side of the road rubbing the bridge of his nose. What is he doing here?

The cinema theatre is where it used to be, ahead of the bus stand. Jak buys a ticket and enters the darkened hall. He has a seat in the balcony, right at the back. But the theatre is almost empty, so he chooses for himself a seat in the front row. He leans back, propping his feet on the parapet wall in front. He can't remember the last time he was in a cinema theatre.

Appa had liked going to the movies. They would go for the night shows – Appa, Amma and he. It was the one weakness his otherwise austere father allowed himself. Amma wouldn't say it, but movie nights made her especially happy. She would dress in her silks and braid jasmine into her hair. Her laugh would echo through the house and she would cook something special for dinner. As Jak sat there watching the story unfold, of caring husbands and patient wives rewarded, of villains being beaten to a pulp and of a life blessed with fairness, he wondered if in the movies Amma had found hope, while Appa had sought something else – respite from his everyday. Escape from the life he was condemned to. Or perhaps what he saw in them was the banality that strengthened his resolve to abandon this life.

Late in the night, Jak approaches the bed. Did she sleep on it? Was she alone? Or was there someone else with her? Did they share this room that trapped the sea within its dingy blue walls? Did they make love here? Please god, he prays, let her have known what it is to be made love to gently, carefully and with tenderness. The horror of what happened will never be mitigated. But it makes it one fraction more bearable to know that someone loved her. And that she knew how to give, not just be ruthlessly plundered and violated.

He slams his fist against the wall.

He didn't mean to do this, go back to where it happened. Recreate each moment, examine and deduce. What is the point? Knowing the how and why isn't going to reverse Smriti's condition.

But what is Smriti remembering? He knows he has to find out the genesis of that scream, the source of that terror.

III

An undefined terror threatens to pull him deeper and deeper into the maze.

He wakes up shivering, cold. Icy fingers clutch his toes.

Smriti used to do that. Hold her hand under the cold water tap, come into his room, lift the bedclothes and grab his feet. When he woke with a start, she would crouch behind the footboard, trying hard not to giggle and give herself away. If he looks now, will she be there?

The sea breeze has an edge. He stares at the sky. The clouds are the colour of brushed steel. He can smell rain.

It has been a long time since he was in the field. But he has always had it. A stirring within him that warns even as the winds gather and collide. Kitcha, the reader of omens, the collector of warnings, the storm warning buoy, his professor called him, only half in jest. That was how accurate Kitcha used to be in his predictions. Then he became JAK. The guru of simulated cyclones. Shorn of his powers, deserted by that intuitive knowing, he didn't know that across the world, his child was being mauled and ravaged. Instead, he was in a Florida beachside home, fucking a colleague's wife against a wall.

'You've wanted this for so long, haven't you, you bitch?' he growled in her ear. And she murmured her willingness, biting down on his shoulder. Bitch. Cunt. Whore. He knew with that unfailing instinct of his that this one was definitely not a blueberry muffin, sweet darling, or *mon petit chou* sort of a girl. That inside the quiet academic wife lurked a slut only he could excite with his magical incantations of filth: Bitch. Cunt. Whore.

Did someone say that to Smriti? The thought wrenches itself out of his mind. He stumbles out of bed. From his bag, he takes out a blue denim shirt and a photograph. He swaddles the photo frame like he once swaddled her in a shirt, and takes it to bed with him.

You never wanted a child. It frightened you, the thought of being a father. We bring to our adult lives what we learnt from the adults we knew as children. How could you be a proper father? It terrified you that you would be unable to keep the commitment a child would demand of you. That you would fail the child somehow. Just as your father did. Who knew, when the time came, how you would be? Would an innate selfishness emerge? And then there was the responsibility. What did you know of how to bring up a child?

But Nina pooh-poohed your fears. 'You are not the first man to be a father; I am scared too. But this is what I want,' she said, pressing your palm to her still flat abdomen. 'In here is a life. Our life. Our child! Imagine, Kitcha!'

When Smriti was born, you spent all of that first night gazing down at the sleeping child. Your child. You had never known anything like it before: this liquification, this snagging of your heart when her tiny fist clutched at a finger of yours. Mine. My daughter. My life.

When she woke in the night, you would wrap her in an old blue denim shirt soft with many washings. She seemed to prefer it to the gaily patterned baby things Nina and you had bought at the baby shop. And you would take her into the living room. For a while you would walk her slowly, humming under your breath, and then you would sit in the rocking chair by the window and rock her to sleep. Slowly, ever so slowly, the softness of her baby cheek nuzzling the side of your neck, her baby breath of milk and sweetness fanning the skin, the warmth of her body seeping into you. In those dark solitary hours of osmosis you knew yourself to be one with the universe and your child. If her eyelid fluttered, you felt it in the beat of your heart. If her breath paused for even a quark, you felt your heart stop: My child. My daughter. My life.

His eyes feel hot and heavy. His throat aches. The dampness beneath his cheek spreads. In the grey dawn, he lies, a man felled by a thought: why did it have to happen to her?

He draws the sheet to his chin and turns on his side, cradling the bundle.

A sound startles him. He has never heard it before. He hears it again as it escapes his throat. A whimper, a low call of helplessness, a querulous note of fear. And then, because he can't bear to be strong any more, he cries. Quietly at first, muffling his pain and anguish. Only, he can't hold it within any more. The hurt wrenches itself out of him. Jak weeps.

In the morning, he wakes up with a thought: someone would remember. He would ask around. Someone would know. He leaps out of bed and rifles through his bag again. In the documents pouch is the printout. He had folded it into four and thrust it there. Now he draws it out and smoothens it on the table.

She had sent it to him two days before she arrived here. A smiling girl, and behind her, three boys. 'Papa Jak, these are my friends. Asha is not in the picture. The five of us are heading out on the "save the girl child" programme. I am sooo excited!' she had written.

Jak looks at the faces. Where are these children now? The three boys and Asha. Why didn't they come to see her even once? Guilt, perhaps. He could understand that. That they hadn't been there for her.

Yet, something niggles. A feeling of disquiet at such complete silence. There have been a few calls and even a couple of visitors. But none from those in the photograph. The invisible Asha hasn't been in touch either.

What happened here in Minjikapuram?

Lives changed. Smriti's, and his. That much he knows for certain.

The knots will need to be undone. The knots of silence that seem to surround the days before the accident. But how and where will he find that first slack in the string?

IV

Jak unties the string carefully. He opens the newspaper wrapping and within, on a banana leaf, lies the masala dosa he ordered for breakfast. A blob of red chilli chutney smears an edge of the dosa. A composite wave of memory and aromas rides up his nostrils. The hiss of the batter on the griddle, the dollop of ghee melting and turning the batter to a brown crispness, the onion and chilli from the chutney, the fragrance of food wrapped in banana leaf. Jak feels his mouth water.

Despite everything, despite the world falling around our ears, our bodies will never let us forget that we are alive and needy. That our hunger has to be appeased, our thirst quenched, our desires slaked; our lives spent. There is no escaping that, Jak thinks, as his hand reaches greedily to tear a piece of the dosa.

The boy peers anxiously at Jak's face. 'Is it all right? I had the sambhar and chutney packed separately!' he says, pointing to two plastic sachets brimming with a green and brown fluid each.

Jak nods. 'It's fine. What about you? I asked you to get yourself something too. I hope you did.'

Swami smiles. 'Shall I pour the coffee?' he asks, unscrewing the lid of the flask.

'How long have you been working here?' Jak asks.

'Some months now. Why?'

'Nothing,' Jak says, feigning indifference. 'Someone I know came here earlier in the year. I was wondering if you remember her. She was your age. Nineteen. She came from Bangalore.'

Swami shakes his head. 'There was some problem with that girl. A police case. They sent the clerk and the hotel boy who were here then to Tuticorin. But why? Why do you want to know?'

Jak looks at the floor, schooling his features to not give anything away. 'Just curious. I read about the accident.'

Swami begins cleaning up. 'I could ask Chinnathayi. She works as the sweeper here. She'll know, I am sure. She knows everything and everyone.'

Jak thinks of the elderly woman he has seen sweep the corridor and knows a flaring of something akin to excitement. A feeling that has evaded him for a long time now.

'Chinnathayi hasn't come in this morning,' Swami comes back to tell him.

What do I do now? Jak asks aloud of himself. But Swami

has an answer. 'Sir, why don't you go to the government hospital? All police cases are taken there.'

The doctor at the district hospital glances at him as he walks into his room. He has the attendant call Jak in despite the long line of patients. 'Yes, yes, what can I do for you?' he beams, eyeing Jak with the rapacious hunger of a vulture waiting for road kill.

When Jak explains who he is, the doctor's eyes drop. The smile vanishes. 'Please wait outside. I have a long line of patients, as you can see. Actually, why don't you come another day? I am very busy now,' he says, ringing the bell to alert the attendant.

But Jak refuses to leave. He sits there, peering through a crack in the door each time a patient leaves, hoping to catch the doctor's eye.

'Naked. I remember now. It happened some five-six months ago, right? First week of March, if I am not wrong. How can I forget? How can anyone forget? We were all shocked by the state they brought her in. You know how it is usually… we have to cut the clothing off an accident case but in her case, someone had just flung a cloth over her. It was quite obvious that she didn't have a stitch of clothing on her when she had the accident. It makes you wonder what she was up to.' The government doctor turns the pages of the file in front of him, each flick of paper suggesting the contempt he feels for a young woman who is so careless of her modesty and her NRI father who brought her up so.

You stare at the man's bent head and want to punch his face. That's my child you are talking about. If it was your daughter, would you be as callous? Would you sit there exhibiting your disapproval and emanating this 'she deserved all that happened to her' attitude?

And it wasn't an accident. You know that just as I do. They paid you off to turn it into an accident. Is that what paid for the expensive watch you wear, the mobile in your pocket, the car parked outside? You bastard!

You clench your fist, restraining your impulse to haul the man up by his shirt and slam him against the wall.

'Please, sir,' Jak grinds the sir out with as much servitude as he can muster, hoping to evoke a slightly less guarded response. 'We, her mother and I, still can't understand how it happened.'

The doctor looks up and beyond him. 'Is her mother here?'

'No.' Jak wipes his forehead with the back of his palm. 'No, she is not here.'

'You see, that's the problem with you people. You NRIs. You don't understand that grown-up girls need to be with their mothers. You think this is America. You send your daughter back filled with all the permissive ideas you teach them in the West and then when something goes wrong, you blame India for it. She was here with a man, I hear. By herself.'

'She wasn't here with a man. She was part of a group. They were volunteers in an NGO programme,' Jak tries to interject.

The man shrugs. 'A man, a group… Would any Indian girl be so bold? They may have been classmates, but she was alone and who knows what transpired? Didn't you or her mother teach her what to do and what not to do? If you ask me, I would lay the blame at your feet. Her parents.'

Jak rises from the chair. He will not sit here, listening to this pathetic, corrupt creature lecture him on parental responsibility. What does he know about them? Or her? To him, she is just the naked accident case.

'How is she now?' the doctor asks suddenly.

Jak pauses. He stares at him. He sees the tapping fingers, the beads of sweat on his forehead; he sees the evasiveness in his eyes, the compromise he has made with his conscience. He sees a man who has doctored the case sheet.

'You do know the condition she was in when she left here. What do you think could have changed?' Jak says, feeling his shoulders slump.

'But hope is all we have. Don't you see that? You have to believe that somewhere in her, there is a part that is still alive. It tells her that things will change. It will bring her back to us. We have to cling to that thought, Kitcha,' Kala Chithi said in that low, measured voice of hers, which he knew so well and loved. All through his life, hers alone had been the voice of reason.

They were sitting in Smriti's room the day before Jak left for Minjikapuram. 'Look at this,' he had burst out, demanding she see what he did. The room was filled with all the little odds and ends Smriti had collected in her lifetime. Postcards and pebbles. Feathers and paper clippings. Photographs and books. All day they played her the kind of music she used to listen to. On a wall were shelves of her books. And on all the remaining surfaces, the dolls. Plastic, shell, bone, terracotta, metal, rubber, poly-fibre-filled velvet shod dolls… All of Smriti's dolls that had lain in storage in Nina's attic for the last four years. Nina had complained when Smriti packed them away, 'I wish she would let me give them to the Children's Hospital. Why does she want to keep them?'

Box after box of dolls from day one to age fourteen and two months, when Jak and Nina separated.

When Jak sent for them. Nina's voice had cracked on the telephone: 'What perverse idea is this, Kitcha? What are you planning to do with the dolls? You are not making this any easier for any one of us… to handle this… to deal with this tragedy.'

'Tragedy! You sound like one of those plastic women in a TV newsroom,' Jak had snarled. 'She is our daughter. You do not get past her or deal with her. Smriti is our child!'

Nina's voice was quiet when she spoke next. 'What about Shruti? Think of what this is going to do to Shruti. Do you remember you have another child? Think of her, Kitcha, for heaven's sake! You haven't even asked about her.'

But Jak had wanted to surround Smriti with all that she loved in her once picture perfect world. In every doll was a wealth of memories. Who knew what would bring her back? The boot black of an eye, a blonde curl, a gingham pinafore, a white rubber shoe…

'It's like the tombs of the kings. Everything she loved, all that was precious to her – except that she isn't dead. Do you know what we are doing? We are burying her alive.

'Look at these dolls.' His fingers trailed along a row of cabbage patch dolls. 'Her babies, she had a name for each one of them when she was just six years old. "I am going to have a houseful of babies," she'd say and we would laugh at the notion of our Smriti becoming a mother. Can you imagine our Smriti a mother, Nina and I would smile at each other.

'It kills me, Kala Chithi, to think that my Smriti's life is over. That she will never have anything of what she wanted... Nina thinks I have forgotten Shruti. That she doesn't exist for me. But I am scared to even think of her. How can I love again? How can I lay myself open to this again?'

He stared at the floor and as a glassiness entered his eye, he heard himself say, 'It would have been better if she had died.'

He waited for Kala Chithi to gasp. To tell him that he was a heartless creature, an unnatural father. What parent would say such a thing?

When she didn't, he raised his eyes and saw in hers only a deep sorrow. Did she, he wondered, feel the same? That despite all the reassurance she felt she owed him, there really was no hope of Smriti ever recovering.

In the shadows of the room, Kala Chithi seemed more gaunt than ever, the stubble on her head a million grey dots. 'You look tired,' he said.

'I am tired,' she said. 'I am tired of worrying about you. Will this never end?'

'What are you talking about?' He frowned.

'Look at her, Kitcha. If her life is on hold, it's because of an accident. But you, Kitcha? You too have put your life on hold. You behave as if to recover and move on would be an act of betrayal. Nina is dealing with this better than you are. What are you doing to yourself?'

He ran his fingers through his hair. 'I am all right. I just need to sort out a few things, then I will be fine.'

Kala Chithi touched his elbow. 'Why are you doing this, Kitcha?'

'Doing what?' He affected ignorance.

'I know you too well. Don't hide it from me, Kitcha. I

know you have been going to Smriti's college, probing and questioning.'

He shrugged. 'I have to know. I can't believe it was a freak accident!'

'Would that make it easier to bear?'

'What I can't get past is a detail…' Kitcha spoke haltingly.

'What detail?'

'That there was evidence of sexual activity before the accident. With more than one man… That my daughter, my Smriti was… The accident happened on the beach. Do you think she would…' His voice broke, unable to continue the thought – fuck on the beach like a bitch on heat with more than one man.

He straightened. 'I cannot accept what they say. If someone did this to her, they should be punished.' Jak spoke slowly. 'I am her father. I have to make it right for her.'

The old woman sat next to Jak, her Kitcha. 'This is not a book or a film, Kitcha. There will be no happily ever after when you have finished playing avenging father seeking retribution!'

'I know.' He sank his head into his arms. 'I know… the consequences. But I need to find out what happened to her. I am a scientist, Kala Chithi. It is my natural instinct to seek, to try and fathom, to make sense.'

Jak waited for Kala Chithi to speak. To refute his claim of scientific need with an exclamation of 'That's rubbish'. When he raised his head, he saw on her face a twisted mendacious smile of disapproval.

As he watched, the smile slipped. 'How will you know when to stop?'

He rose from where he was sitting. The need to get out

tussled with his need to retreat into some back room where he could bury himself amidst books and long columns of data and graphs.

'I don't know. But it is the way of all scientific investigation to end in a conclusion. Perhaps then I will stop.'

'And Kitcha, what do you do with the conclusion you arrive at?'

Jak shook his head. 'I am a scientist, but I am a father too. It depends on what I discover. I can't promise you anything now, Kala Chithi.'

He walked out of the room, deep in thought. He even forgot his customary tickle under Smriti's chin. A wiggle of fingers and 'You better wake up, little girl, in the next two minutes, or Papa Jak will be very angry!'

Jak sits in the balcony of his room and stares at the horizon. It is the hour that always causes in him an ache. The boy Kitcha had vested his hopes in the evening sky, but it only fills the adult Kitcha with fatigue. Yet another futile day gone.

Chinnathayi seemed to have disappeared, Swami said. 'She is not at home either. I went there looking for her but the house was locked.'

'What about the doctor? Was he here then?' Jak asked Swami suddenly. 'The doctor who stays here at the lodge?'

Swami shook his head. 'He doesn't pay. He comes to Srinivasan sir's hospital with the scan machine every now and then. So there will be nothing in the register. I can ask Dorai sir at the reception.'

But neither Dorai nor anyone else at the lodge had anything to say. 'In fact, Dorai sir asked me to mind my own business. He asked if I was working for you or for the lodge. And did I want to keep my job or not?' Swami said, standing by the door and avoiding Jak's eyes.

And Jak knew he had come to the end of yet another road.

It was like trying to climb a translucent glass wall. On the other side was the truth, and on this side a hazy shaping of conjecture.

He waited all afternoon at the police station. A new humility had crept into him. These were busy people. He was the one who needed them to make time for him. He waited, every second an iron-shod peanut his tongue teased in his mouth, that he ached to sink his teeth into and crack.

'Come back later,' the policeman admonished. 'I need to look for the files. I need at least a week's time. We are busy this week. It is Gandhi Jayanthi tomorrow, or have you forgotten? The MP is coming for the celebrations!'

Jak stares at the sky, rubbing the bridge of his nose. What is he to do now? He knows the police file will merely corroborate the doctor's statement. Accident victim. Name. Age. Sex.

What of the others? The three boys and Asha. Jak draws the printout from his pocket and looks at it again.

Strange that the doctor at the government district hospital should say Smriti was with a man. No one seems to mention the other two boys or the girl. So where were they when the accident happened? Or, did Smriti lie to him? But why would she? He is not that sort of a father, to lay down the law or impose rules. They have always been able to discuss everything. Why then would she lie to him?

Jak stands up abruptly. The plastic chair jerks back, catches in a dip in the chipped mosaic floor, and topples backwards. He reaches to set it upright, then kicks it away. His daughter lies on her back, will perhaps never sit up again. What is he getting so uptight for, about a fucking chair?

From where he stands on the balcony, Jak can see the strip of sand behind the lodge. The sand bank. Did it happen here? Or was it further up the coast? Or, perhaps down in some secluded cove?

Would this self-inflicted torture never end?

Jak stuffs his still wet towel into a plastic bag and locks the door behind him. The coast is treacherous. Only fools and idiot tourists would swim out into the sea, he knows. But he cannot contain the restless beast that paces within him.

He strips his clothes off and in his boxer shorts runs into the sea. The waves break against him but he pushes through the swell. This isn't the gentle ocean he swims in most days of the year. This isn't the placid sea he has vacationed by. The violent rough seas here hoist him and throw him back towards the shore. But Jak won't turn back. He won't heed the sea's warning. I know you as well as I know myself. Do you think you scare me? What's the point? The worst that can happen has already happened. What do you think you can do to me now, he screams at the waves. And then, as he knew it would, the shelf of sand beneath his feet falls away. A bottomless abyss. He is on his own now.

Alone.

V

He didn't mind being alone any more, he was used to it. Sometimes he feared he would never be able to live with another person again. His space had become important to him. In fact, some days it was almost with relief that he walked into the silence of his apartment. That afternoon, he had been glad that there was no one waiting as he turned the key in the lock.

He had whistled under his breath as he opened his apartment door and sauntered in. It was one of those irritating things: a tune without words. He'd forgotten the words but the tune had stuck in his head that first time after Lisa called, and stayed there ever since.

A week before, he had hosted a party in his home for a few of his soon to be ex-colleagues and their wives. He was leaving on an open-ended sabbatical to research the book he was going to write. If he didn't do it now, he never would, he laughed. From the corner of his eye, he saw Lisa devour him with her large blue eyes.

That was when it began. The wooing of Lisa Sherman.

He had enjoyed flirting with her. He did it rather well and effortlessly. All he had to do was stick to a pattern. Cyclones had taught him as much. That there is nothing random about life, ocean currents, clouds, or affairs with married women, even if they are the wives of colleagues. He had singled her out as the one he knew to be most vulnerable and hence most eminently fuckable.

She wore a single string of amber beads around her neck and her need on her face – twin creases of discontent at the corners of her mouth and hunger in her eyes. Her fingers teased and played with the amber beads while her eyes swooped on him from across the room. '*Come back Liza, come back girl, wipe the tear from me eye*,' Belafonte sang on the stereo, his Bose speakers speaking only to her.

And then he brought out his Leonard Cohen. The only poet who sang within him. Cohen, who had a line for every man, woman and moment. For Lisa and her sisters. For every woman who bore her loneliness like a sin.

She called him the next day. That too was part of the pattern. Good wives calling to say thank you. Two days later, the next call was to tell him about a documentary on Bangalore on CNN. Wasn't his daughter there? She thought he'd like to see it.

He had felt that familiar curl of excitement spiral in him; it was like spotting the eye of a cyclone through a cirrus canopy in a satellite picture. Once he'd seen it, he knew what was coming.

It was late afternoon and already the room was sunk in a shadow of dying light. Jak threw his keys on the table by the door. The clatter of the keys against the metal tray filled the hallway. Jak paused. The emptiness of the apartment, its silence, filled him. In two weeks he would be in Hawaii. At forty-eight, it was daunting to start life all over again, like when he was twenty-two and had moved to the States. If he could relive those years, would he have done things differently?

The tune wouldn't stop in his head and Jak felt it escape his mouth again. He went to the fridge and took out a carton of fruit yoghurt. And from a bag, a handful of carrot sticks.

The fridge was almost empty. He would pick up a few things tomorrow. Then it would be time to close up and leave.

Jak leaned back in the sofa and flicked the TV remote on. The sounds of a ball game filled the room. He pressed the mute button and opened the carton of yoghurt.

Lisa's armpit. A cloud of strawberry with an undertow of a cheesy pong. Lisa, who hadn't been washed and deodorized and prepared for him. He had caught her unawares that first time with armpit stubble and lank hair, her jeans pulled over panties soft with many washings and the beginning of a fray in the elastic. Slatternly, ripe Lisa, hidden behind the façade of a proper wife. Feral Lisa with sharp pointed teeth and an insatiable hunger. 'Not here, not here,' the amber beads clak-clakked against the door as she moaned. 'Not in this house! Not in his house.'

You had wanted a fuck, a series of fucks perhaps. But you didn't want to break up Lisa's marriage. Yet, when she suggested that the two of you meet at a beach house a friend of hers owned, you agreed. What was the harm? She knew what she was doing. Between two consenting adults, etc. She had planned it all to the last detail. The babysitter for the kids and an alibi for herself. A hamper with little things to nibble at, wine, and even a corkscrew. Sexy lingerie, freshly washed hair and painted nails. As she sucked you on that hastily made bed, you wondered how long she had been thinking about this.

And then, as you latched the windows shut and locked the door, she clung to you. 'When? When can I see you again, darling?'

And you felt that curl of postcoital content crumble. 'Darling!' You saw how her fingers wrapped themselves around your wrist and ash coated your tongue. Didn't she know you were leaving?

Images flickered in front of him on the TV screen. What had he gone and done? He could hear Nina say, 'You never think. You never do. You just give in to that wild reckless impulse. Did you for one moment think of the others involved?'

Then the phone rang, echoing through the apartment, its ring soft but persistent. Lisa, he thought. That too was the pattern. They always called after that first bout of dammed hunger was released. No woman would call a fuck just a fuck. It had to be tarted up and sanctified with words of love. He sighed and picked up the phone. 'Jak here,' he said.

It was Kala Chithi. 'Kitcha.' Her voice was wary as it reached his ears. 'I received a call from the police station in Minjikapuram.'

And he felt the floor slide away.

VI

Each time he thinks he has found a sand bar to rest on, it slides away.

The waves continue to slam into him. Jak fights the water, the heave and push necessitating every ounce of his strength. If he allows himself to slacken even a little bit, he will not be able to breathe. The water stings his eyes. His arms ache, his legs tire, but he cannot turn back. He needs to flee the guilt that haunts him. He was the one who created the magical land of Minjikapuram. In his telling of all that happened to him there, he planted a seed in Smriti's head. He thinks of that first time now.

She was seven. Leaning against him with a rag doll clutched in one hand and her thumb in her mouth.

'There is a temple on a hill by the sea. But it is not like any other temple. This one has two deities. Minjikaiyan and Minjikammal. They were born when Shiva's seed was split on that hill.'

'What seed? Is Shiva a fruit?'

Jak laughed. 'No, silly. The lord Shiva with the third eye. If he opens it, you and I, Mama and baby Shruti, and your Melissa and Sita, Tinkerbell and Kokila,' he gestured to the dolls she had brought into the living room, 'will be barbecued meat.'

'Oh, how do you know? Have you met him?' Smriti asked, her eyes brimming with admiration for her Papa Jak.

'I almost did. It is believed that if you swim in the sea by the temple at Minjikapuram and then climb the one thousand three hundred and thirty-three steps and make a wish, it will come true. So I leapt into the water. All I meant was to go for a little swim and make my wish. But the sea had other plans for me.'

'And then, Papa?' Smriti touched him on the shoulder.

Jak looked at his daughter's face and tried to laugh off the horror of the moment when he knew there was no escaping the current.

Besides, how could he admit that he had been terrified? To confess to fear would make him and his reassurances suspect: *You are a big girl now, you don't need a night light. Papa is in the next room, what do you have to fear? It's just a bad dream, baby. Too much pizza. No monster will get you. Papa is here.*

The waters off the coast were violent, the currents unpredictable and almost demonic in intent. 'What are you playing at, you silly fool?' the man had hurled at him as he pulled him onto his catamaran. 'This is the ocean, not some stupid pond for you to paddle around in. You have to understand the ocean, read the skies before you venture in.'

Fifteen-year-old Kitcha had lain with his head hanging over the side of the boat. His chest had hurt and he had felt the rasp of salt in his throat, the bloat of water in his belly. Dead. He could have been dead and his body would have washed ashore on the coast three days later.

He caught her searching his face. Her little fingers were wrapped around his wrist.

'Papa, did your wish come true?'

Jak smiled. He had been so afraid that he had forgotten to make his wish. 'I never feared the sea again.'

'You are not afraid of the sea! Really?' Her eyes sought his. They had been teaching her to swim then. 'All that water around you, over you, you were very afraid at first, right Papa?'

Nina came in from her study then. 'Kitcha, you know you shouldn't fill her head with your stories. As it is, she is a reluctant swimmer. And now you are going to scare her even further!' As if to erase the sting of her words, Nina ruffled his hair as she went past.

She hadn't yet got to the point when all he did, all he said, even the way he breathed, was an affront to her.

'Of course I was scared at first. But then I learnt something. I learnt to respect the sea and I was never afraid again. You must always treat water with respect,' he said. 'No silliness.

No taking stupid risks. You see, that's why Minjikapuram has a very important place in my life. I learnt a lesson there. You don't run away from things that terrify you. The water scared me but not for long. If you understand it, it will never be able to dominate or scare you.' Jak was trying to be at his paternal best. A father imparting life lessons and guiding his child through the complexities of living.

He saw the intensity of Smriti's gaze. She was a child who took everything he said to be the holy truth. She would never allow him any fallibility or weakness. And so, feeling a sudden qualm of disquiet at how seriously she took him, he reached across and pulled her pigtail. 'Do you know when I was really scared?' He lowered his voice to a whisper. 'When I asked your mother to marry me. I was shaking. Now that was scary!'

Nina smiled at him from across the room. 'Liar,' she mouthed. 'Liar, liar, liar…'

Jak pretended to cringe. 'Do you know who she was?' He turned to Smriti.

'She was the Madras Girl. The only Madras Girl in all of Syracuse. And I was this really wide-eyed boy from a little alley in Mylapore. A little brahmin boy who couldn't even figure out which jeans to buy. But the Madras Girl knew everything.

'And that wasn't all. When I asked her to marry me, she gave me the Madras Eye. Do you know what that is?' Jak narrowed his eyes till they were slits. 'She looked at me through her sunglasses with her Madras Eye and said, "I don't know Kitcha, I don't know."'

'Kitcha, stop filling the child's head with misinformation. I don't know why you do it. Smriti, listen to me. Madras Eye is conjunctivitis. I don't know what Papa means by saying I gave him the Madras Eye…' Nina stirred her coffee and licked the spoon.

'But she knew, Papa, she knew she wanted to marry you. That's why you married each other and I am here and baby Shruti,' Smriti cried, aching to be part of that moment when Kitcha and Nina, Papa and Mama had found each other.

Kitcha, Nina, Smriti and Shruti. When did it all change?

A wave breaks over his head.

The middle phase. It is this period that you need to watch for, Jak thinks.

He has seen it happen. How, sometimes, even a well developed wave, a young cyclone full of promise, will not grow into the mature one they had predicted it would.

Jak wonders why he didn't see it coming. As his life became more and more contained in classrooms and labs, he failed to sense the change. And Nina and he grew apart… until one day the marriage was over.

The embarrassment, the shame, the disappointment… You resorted to the God of the Gaps theory to explain the dying out of promise to your children. You felt the eyes of your older child trail you and Nina. You saw her gather her younger sister into the fold of her embrace. She didn't trust either Nina or you as parents any more. You tried logic; all the theories you knew, all the reasoning you could muster to make sense of the situation. That was all you had, to help her make sense of the constant bickering, the fault finding, the relentless criticism, the snapping and snarling that grew into cold quarrels that wounded and crippled. The palpable resentment when Nina and you were merely in the same room together.

Smriti became a child caught between two fronts. She wouldn't buy into the sometimes-people-grow-apart-it-is-inexplicable explanation. Was that what caused her to flee their warring world? And from a distance, she tried to instigate Shruti's relocation. 'We will be happy here,' Smriti wrote. 'This is our home. Here family means everything!'

Were Nina and you the perpetrators of what happened to her? Was that ass of a doctor right after all?

All your life, all you ever wanted to do was protect your children. From demons and heartbreak, big and small. From hurts and wounds inflicted by a careless, callous world. Even when all you could do was watch from the sidelines: when Smriti was not chosen for the school play, when Shruti's friends didn't turn up for her birthday party, when Smriti's boyfriend dumped her.

You shared with them all that life had taught you about life itself so they could avoid the mistakes you made. And yet, when they chose to make their own mistakes, you had no option but to be there for them.

How can you cease to be a parent even if your child is determined to shrug off the mantle of being a child?

When do you let go? Where do you stop? How does one draw the line?

Jak treads water and looks around. He can see the temple in the distance. How could you have not looked after my child? When she came here, it meant you became responsible for her. How could you have let this happen? Jak rages at the brother and sister duo and then abruptly ceases. What is he doing? Trying to shift responsibility to deities of stone in a derelict temple on a hill?

If he is swept into the sea, there will be no one for him to throw accusations at but himself.

And Smriti, what would happen to her then? Nina would have her put in a home somewhere. Nina is no longer the woman he knew. What was once a chitinous shell, easily cracked, has turned into stone.

Nina sat there by Smriti just before she returned to her life in America. An inert Smriti, for once. She often sat at her bedside, looking at her daughter's face, studying it for some sign of change. 'You, Kitcha,' she snarled suddenly, 'I hold you responsible for this. You and only you. I don't want you to come anywhere near Shruti. I will get a court order if I need to. I won't lose another daughter to you, to India.'

'Nina.' He reached out to take her hand in his. But she flung his hand away.

'You wouldn't listen to me ever, the two of you. You ganged up against me. I was the stick in the mud. I was the gargoyle spitting advice, I was the one you had to defy and even spite. Fine! Now you look after her. You take the responsibility.'

Jak turns towards the shore.

Out there on land is Smriti. The responsibility of her life. The burden of the past. Her petrified future.

VII

Meera's petrified future. It begins thus:

The raucousness of a rowdy flock of mynahs in the avocado tree by the bedroom window.

Just for a moment she knows respite as she stirs from sleep. A sleep she had lured in the early hours with a Restyl tablet. She had lain on her side reading the chemical composition of the little angel who would lull her nerve ends to repose.

She keeps her eyes shut and holds her breath. What if Giri crawled into bed while she was asleep? A movement at her side. A breath. A hand that snakes its way to drape around her hip. A clearing of throat. The presence of Giri.

She lies there with her eyes pressed tightly shut.

Meera lets her fingers crawl and encounters the unslept side of the bed. She knows then it is the morning after Giri's disappearance. In the span of sixty seconds, her mind leaps, vaults, hops, skips, tumbles, cartwheels, gyrates and contorts into a million possibilities of anguish in waiting.

Explanations. Nayantara. The police station. Mummy, Lily and Nikhil. The neighbours. Colleagues. Friends. The driver, the maid, the people in the park. Telephone calls. Credit cards. The bank manager. Hospitals. Telephone books. The morgue where bodies wait to be identified… Stop it, stop it, Meera tells herself. She catches sight of herself in the mirror and thinks, do I know that woman? Sitting with her arms wrapped around her knees, rocking ever so gently, as if to soothe herself. Do I know that woman with bereavement written in her eyes, face and limbs? A woman who doesn't know what to do next except alternate between grief and abasement.

There was a time when Zeus decided to punish Hera for her wilfulness. He hung her from the sky, shackled by golden bracelets at the wrist and an anvil at the ankle.

In the oceans below, Hera saw herself reflected. She quailed at the image of what she had been turned into. Worse was the knowledge that she would be seen thus: a woman petrified.

How could something like this have happened to her? Hera didn't know what hurt more, the pain or the humiliation. A cry escaped her.

And so Meera Hera cries as she opens her eyes to a dank September morning.

'Where's Giri?' Saro asks at breakfast, forking a papaya cube.

'I don't know,' Meera says. Her mother needs a whole papaya every morning, one half of which she cuts into cubes and eats. The rest she smears on her face. Meera gapes at her now, as if seeing her for the first time. This orange-faced silly woman, my peacock of a mother, is this the woman I am to turn to for comfort and succour?

'Isn't he having any breakfast?'

'I don't know.'

'What do you mean, I don't know? Is it too much to expect a civil answer?'

'Now now, Saro,' Lily interrupts. 'No need for you to get so upset! Meera means she doesn't know if Giri is in the house or in the garden.' Lily smears butter on her toast. 'He'll be here soon!'

The scraping of the knife on the crisp surface of the bread. Scrape. Scrape. Scrape. Meera feels it grate inside her skull.

'No, I don't know. That's what I mean. I don't know where he is. I don't know where he spent the night or who he is with. I don't know if he will be here for breakfast or back in this house ever again. I don't know if he is alive or dead or lying in some hospital in a coma… I don't know a fucking thing!' Meera snaps. Her eyes fill and she brushes the tears away. 'Satisfied? Does that satisfy your curiosity, Ma?'

Saro's eyes are round with shock. Lily's crafty old eyes narrow. Meera drops her head and rests her forehead on the table's edge. She wants to crawl into a deep dark hole and stay there. Away from their prying eyes, their questions, and the sight of Nikhil, a mute Nikhil pretending that he has heard nothing, trying to hide behind a tightly clenched face his perturbation at a suddenly foulmouthed, raging mother and a mysteriously missing father. His fingers alone give him away as they shred a piece of toast into crumbs.

'But he must have said something,' Saro begins.

'Did you try calling him?' Lily asks.

Meera rubs her forehead on the edge of the table. Each time the children or Giri fumed at the old ladies for making a fine art of stating the obvious, Meera had frowned at them.

'Then tell them to lay off. I don't need them telling me what I can see for myself,' Nayantara would snap back.

Now Meera wishes she could do as Nayantara does. Toss her head and flounce off in a rage. 'What do you think?' she asks between gritted teeth.

Precisely eighteen hours after Giri disappeared, Meera's mobile lights up with a message from him: Check your email.

She stares at the screen in shock. Check your email.

She calls him. But there is no response. Either Giri is ignoring her or he is not being allowed to access the phone. Meera's hand goes to her mouth. Has he been kidnapped?

The papers are full of such stories. Of men robbed at knife point on their way home. Of missing 'techies' and murdered businessmen. Was Giri… Meera races to the computer.

Meera.

Her heart pauses.

In its very baldness is a statement of intent. Meera speed reads the letter, unable to believe what she is reading. Then she reads it again, slowly, so that each syllable brands itself on her mind.

Meera, I know you must be worried by my disappearance. Furious even. I am sorry if I have caused you some anxiety over this. Please believe me, I didn't plan to do it this way. I wanted us to sit down and discuss it. If I told you how I was feeling, I knew you would understand. That our life together weighed on me.

But I didn't think it would come to this. That I would find the courage to just up and leave. I woke up this morning in Chennai asking myself, what am I doing away from you and the children? Then I felt a sense of relief. I don't know how to explain it.

I tried, I want you to know that I tried, but I can't go on like this any more. We have just one life to lead and I can't waste it.

I need to be more clear in my head about what I want to do. I will be in touch. Bear with me, Meera. Bear with me until then.

Bear with me until then. Meera reads the line over and over again. Until when, Giri, until when?

Meera looks at her hands. Shouldn't they be shaking? Shouldn't her mouth wobble and her eyes well up? But for a moment she feels nothing. Then a pulse in her forehead begins throbbing and in the pit of her abdomen, she knows a heaviness. A heaviness that envelops her in a chill. What is she to understand of this?

Has he left her? Or is he coming back? Is this an interim phase, a temporary madness, or is he never coming back? What does he mean by 'our life together weighed on me'?

Outside the windows, the sky heaves. The blue skies of September have turned. Dense grey clouds pile up, swamping the light and air. The room closes in on her, a giant beast squeezing the confines of space with its gargantuan paws. Thunder growls. Meera sits staring at the computer screen unseeingly. She knows she ought to get up and switch off the computer, pull out the plugs of all the electrical appliances. The electrician had warned her about the faulty wiring. 'Madam, we need to redo the wiring entirely. It can't take the load. Until then I suggest that you pull out the plugs during the rains. Or there could be a short somewhere.'

It begins as a hiss. Then sheets of rain. Meera looks out of the window. Nikhil will be soaking wet by the time he reaches home. Again she feels unable to rouse herself.

Meera gropes within herself, searching for some clue that will tell her how to react. Grief. Betrayal. Anger. Fear. Loss. Resentment. Hatred. What is she to feel?

She sits there, not knowing what to do. It would come to her soon, the knowledge of how to decipher the significance of this moment. It would reveal itself and take precedence over the hammering in her forehead that demanded with every throb: But what are you going to do? What are you going to do now?

VIII

What are you going to do? Meera asks herself, putting the phone back on the hook gently.

He was here for the day, Giri said. And he wanted to meet. 'Not there,' he said. She noticed that he balked at using the word home. Our home. The home he had fled. 'Not with those old bats listening to every word and interfering.'

Meera flinched. Her mother and grandmother were not easy to live with. But she couldn't bear for Giri to reprimand or ridicule them. The first time he jeered at them, Meera had recoiled as if kicked in the chest by his harshness, his irritability with them. She turned on him furiously. If he found fault with them, it was like finding fault with her.

'How can you, Giri? How can you be so nasty? It isn't done,' she said when he emerged out of the spell they had initially woven around him. Disenchantment made him acerbic. Odious even.

Giri looked at her as if he couldn't trust his ears. Meera, his goose girl, telling him that he was wrong. Meera met his stare even though she knew he was hurt. Perhaps she should have flung her arms around him, declaring total allegiance, and whispered in his ear, 'I know, they are rather hard to live with. They try my patience too!'

But how could she make such an admission of disloyalty? If she was so easily a traitor to her mother and grandmother, one day she would betray him too. Didn't he see that? But Giri didn't. Instead, he chose to remain aloof. When Meera went to him, wanting to share a moment of distress triggered by them – a careless word spoken, a thoughtless deed, wounds inflicted carelessly and with little malice, nevertheless painful – when Meera turned to Giri for handholding and comfort, he removed himself from her confusion and hurt. 'I don't want to get involved. They are your family. You won't like it if I say something. Just leave me out of this squabbling. Though civil war would be more appropriate a phrase.'

Only, now, Giri doesn't feel the need to be civil any more. He can say what he pleases. And if she doesn't like it, she can stuff it, his tone implies.

And yet, Meera can't help a fugitive thought from taking residence in her mind. He is here, isn't he?

Meera waited until the next morning before she mentioned the email. 'Darling,' she told Nikhil. 'Daddy is in Chennai.'

Nikhil looked away. 'When is he coming home?' he asked.

'I don't know. He didn't say.' Meera looked at her tightly clenched fingers. 'Time to go to school. We can talk about this later,' she said, injecting a breeziness into her voice. If she didn't show how perturbed she was, maybe he wouldn't be too worried.

Saro and Lily read the email together. They looked at each other without speaking. Then Lily began, 'I don't understand why he sounds so trapped…'

'Is it us, Meera? Are we the reason?' Saro asked tentatively.

'I don't know, Ma, I really don't understand what's got into Giri.' Meera found she couldn't put on a brave face any more.

'Call him. Tell him we'll leave,' Lily said. 'He can have the house and you to himself.'

'We'll tell him that!' Saro added.

Meera shook her head. 'I don't think it's that. Really. I think he just grew tired of us… this life!'

Lily snorted. 'He isn't a four-year-old. He is the father of two children. He has responsibilities.'

Saro put her arm around Meera. 'I don't think you should worry too much. It's just a phase. Most men go through it. Even your daddy did. A few days away, and he'll back here. You are a good wife, Meera, and he'll never be able to replace you. Trust me, darling!'

Meera wished she could.

Meera next called Nayantara. How did one tell an adult child about her father's flight? As a childish bid to escape the monotony of everyday? But Nayantara snarled into the phone, 'If this is about Daddy, I already know. He called me late in the night after he reached Chennai. What have you done to him, Mummy? How could you? You were never supportive. That's why he had to run. You were stifling him. I can see it now….'

Meera clutched the phone to her ear. Her daughter's voice shrilled through it.

'He drove from the hotel straight to Chennai that afternoon,' Nayantara said. 'He couldn't bear it any more. He was crying, Mummy. Do you know what it is to hear a man cry? To hear Daddy say again and again – I am sorry, baby, but I had to leave. I didn't know what else to do… It broke my heart. You did this to him! I can forgive you anything but this. You stole his dignity. You did this to him!'

Meera thought, how is it that my life has never risen above a series of clichés: Big house, poor inmates; boy comes on work to house, falls in love with house and girl; they have two children – boy and girl; man rises in career, wife trails him, happy to be his helpmate; the crisis of middle-age; man abandons wife; family divides – boy with mother, daughter declaring her allegiance to the father…

'Shut up, Nayantara,' she hissed. 'You don't know anything about Daddy and me. He has always spoilt you and that's what you are – a silly spoilt brat sitting on judgement on her mother merely because she's been the one to lay down the law.'

She heard Nayantara draw in her breath. The enraged silence. And then the click of the phone.

One more cliché. Daughter hangs up on mother, unable to face the truth. Nayantara doesn't mean it. She is frightened, confused, and needs someone to blame, Meera told herself again and again when her daughter's accusations came back to haunt her.

Meera crosses her legs. Giri is late. She glances at her wrist. She would have liked to go to the bathroom, put on some lip gloss, and check her sari. But what if he comes then? She doesn't want him thinking that she failed to turn up.

Her eyes travel across the room once again, halting at the large floral arrangement of birds of paradise, ginger lilies and ferns on an antique round table. The plump cushions on the cane sofas, the glistening leaves of the indoor plants in gigantic brass planters and the sparkling floors. It is exactly the kind of setting Giri fancies himself in. She smiles, unable to help the bitterness that corrodes the stretching of her lips.

She goes to stand by the plate-glass window. Outside, it is an idyllic world. A butterfly hovers over a cluster of frangipani flowers. The breeze rustles the leaves. In the pool, koi carp frolic.

The perfect world as glimpsed from an air-conditioned room. Nothing to hint at the scorching sunshine or the grime outside. Neither sweat nor dust. Pretty much what my life used to be like until now, Meera sighs, and then catches herself in time.

She has taken to watching TV documentaries at night, these last few weeks. Stories of tribal women in Afghanistan dying in childbirth; the starving children of Darfur; the wounded, the maimed. The more suffering that is unveiled before her, the less isolated she feels. In her head echoes the refrain of a woman speaking about her seventeen-year-old daughter's death: The god who gives is also the god who takes.

Then the children found her one night. Nayantara, still unwilling to absolve her mother of blame and yet longing to comfort her. 'Mummy, why do you watch such depressing programmes?'

And Nikhil, poor Nikhil, who has appointed himself her chief cheerleader: 'I have a DVD of *Heroes*. Shall we watch that? It's all about people who discover that they have special talents – supernatural powers.'

Meera sighed. 'I wish I had supernatural powers. I don't. I am just an ordinary…'

'Please,' the children cried in unison, coming to sit by her side. 'Please don't start. We know what you are going to say.'

Nikhil slipped his hand into hers. 'Why do you sigh so much, Mummy?'

'It's depressing, that long intake of breath, the loud exhalation, I tell you, it's depressing.' Nayantara took her other elbow.

Meera looked away and said, 'Do you know what Keats wrote – There's a sigh for yes, and a sigh for no/ And a sigh for I can't bear it/O what can be done, shall we stay or run?'

Meera caught the children staring at each other with an

almost comical look of horror on their faces. Mummy had taken to reciting poetry. What next?

So Meera resolved to never sigh. Or, at least, not as often as she seemed to these days.

She sees him come through the lobby doors. And it seems that he has seen her, for he walks straight towards her. Meera looks at the floor, trying to still her heart, trying to control her features from collapsing into a scream of reproach, trying to still her tongue from incoherence – accusations, reproach, pleas… In how many ways do I confront thee?

She raises her eyes to his. What can she expect? Remorse, perhaps. Petulance, too. She knows Giri hates to admit he is wrong. Even when his misdemeanours stare him in the face, he seldom apologizes. And when he does, it is with poor grace. Awkward, bitten down words giving away nothing but that which is absolutely necessary. Meera has learnt to accept these as his best effort. What will he say now?

She knows what she must do. She must make it easy for him. Meet him halfway. That is what marriage is all about, she will show him. A tree that will not be uprooted even if it has taken a rather bad battering. Whatever happened is best buried, she will say. I won't ask you anything, unless you choose to tell me. I will not ever bring it up and no one else will either. We'll just go on as if you were on a business trip these six weeks. It is enough, Giri, that you are here and we are together. Nothing else is important, she will murmur, and slip her hand into his. See, I am not that cold unfeeling woman you accuse me of being, the warmth of her hand in his will tell him. See, see, see how important you are to me…

He stands there. And in that stance, arms tight against his sides, his feet at ease, his face clenched and his eyes obtuse, Meera reads a disavowal. Even before he speaks a word, she knows. She has lost him.

'Meera,' Giri says.

She stands up. The words dry up in her mouth. What is she to say? Hello? Goodbye? She feels wrung out. She wants to go home and lie down. Pull the quilt over her head and burrow herself in a warm, dark place where nothing will change and all is safe and restful.

'Come,' he says and leads the way to the coffee shop.

Something, is it a sob or a fishbone of anguish, shifts in her throat.

Doesn't he remember? When the Oberoi opened, they would come to the coffee shop late in the night. The kids, Giri and she. They would drive into town for ice cream at Lake View. Apricots and cream in winter. Strawberries and cream in summer. And then for coffee to the Oberoi. For cappuccinos in wide shallow cups with cinnamon dust speckling the froth. Enough, Meera had thought then, spooning the foam into her mouth, was this. What more could she want but Giri and the children and these quiet moments of content?

They sit across each other. 'What shall I say?' he begins.

She waits. What will he say?

'That afternoon, I hadn't planned it, I swear. I hadn't meant to disappear like that. Or frighten you. I had wanted to sit down with you somewhere quiet and talk to you. Tell you how I was feeling. You would understand, I knew. You were the one person I could say anything to. You know that, don't you?'

Meera moves the cutlery around, as if to get it right. She doesn't give a toss really. But if she doesn't give her hands something to do, occupy part of her mind, she will grab him by his collar and scream, 'What the fuck are you leading up to? What am I supposed to have understood? Just say it and let me go.'

'So there I was. Standing with a group. They were all young, the men and women. But it was the men who made me want to sit down and howl. Their confidence, their zest for life… Meera, I watched them. I smoked one cigarette after the other. I thought, if I could get that buzz, all would be well. I wouldn't feel so completely left behind. But I couldn't bear the taste of wine. I asked for scotch then. That didn't work either. I couldn't drink. I took one sip and left the glass on a table.'

Meera shudders at the word scotch. Whisky, single malt or blended malts, she aches to correct him. Then she shuts herself up. How can she be such a pedant? Insisting on the right word when her husband is trying to explain why he did what he did. Somewhere in me, she thinks, I feel this is all a joke. He will finish with his explanations and we will go home together.

'And I watched the young men so full of ambition and dreams and I thought, what have I done with my life? I felt as if I was being strangled, slowly but surely. I had to move on,' Giri murmurs.

He waits for Meera to speak. To interject, to question, to merely react. But Meera, done with the cutlery, is rearranging the stack of sweeteners in their silver dish. Later she will ask herself, if she had spoken then, would the ebb of conversation have receded in another direction?

Was it her silence that goaded Giri to finish on the note of 'there-is-no-room-for-negotiation-here'?

'So I left. I didn't understand or even realize why I was doing what I was doing. I didn't think you would understand how I felt either.'

'What?' Meera asks. 'I thought you said I was the one person who would understand. And now it seems I don't understand you. Is that what you are bringing this down to? This middle-age caper of yours… Is that what this is about?'

Giri shakes his head. 'You just don't get it, do you? How I feel, what I am going through. How do I make you understand?'

That is when something snaps in Meera and she rises, her teeth baring into fangs and her eyes daring him to speak further. 'What about us? The kids, I… What are we to do while you find yourself?'

'Sit down, Meera. Sit down. Everyone's looking at us!' Giri hisses.

Meera looks around her wildly. Then she drops into the chair. What is the use anyway?

She hears him speak. Nuts and bolts of how they would separate and what would need to be done. Their lives, their children, their joint account and what they had shared once. How simple it is to unravel a skein if one wants to.

Long ago, Giri told her, 'Patience, Meera, patience. That is all you need to work any knot open. Keep teasing it and you'll find a knot with a bit of slack and once you do, you are home.'

Giri, Houdini of matrimony. Where did he find that slack bit?

'Then there is the house. I asked you, begged and pleaded

with you to sell the house. With the money, I would never have had to work for someone else. I could have pursued my dream, my chance at happiness... but you wouldn't listen. You kept brushing the thought away. You indulged me with a "not now, we'll do it later", as if I were a child hankering for the moon. I have to move on, Meera. I don't know what it is I want to do. I know it is too much to expect you to understand what I am going through. Or for you to look at this objectively. But I want you to know that I didn't intend to hurt you or the children.

'You may have to seriously consider selling the house now. I won't be able to contribute much till I have sorted things out. The kids' education and their essentials – that is my responsibility.' He pauses and looks away. Then, in a firm voice, as if to beat down any protests she may have, he says, 'I have other responsibilities, too, now.'

Meera searches his face. Is that what it's all about?

All those times when he was working weekends, the late evening meetings... how did I not see it? Mummy is wrong. I am not a good wife. Or, wouldn't I have sensed it? The presence of another woman in your life. How did I go so wrong? Who is she? Where did you meet? How long has it been going on? But I won't ask you who she is. I won't give you the chance to unburden your guilt. I will not sit here and listen to you say, 'Meera, you are the only one I can say this to... you are the only one I could ever say anything to.'

From somewhere in the back of her mind a thought rises: if you love your life, you are lovable. If you hate your life, you become hate worthy. Did she read it somewhere? Or is it one of those Lily–Saro aphorisms that after a while became a part of her system, swimming to the surface with unfailing accuracy of time and circumstance? Making her mouth fill with ashes as once again she realized the truth of all that she had dismissed as their narrow-minded nonsense.

Meera sits there one last time with Giri, spooning the cinnamon speckled foam into her mouth and tasting nothing.

She watches him leave and thinks: what now?

IX

What now?

They have already kept her waiting for ten minutes or, as Meera calculates it, for Rs 52.65. This is the fourth time. The last three times they kept her waiting only to tell her that Randhir Sahi was in a meeting or elsewhere. 'What about his mobile? Has the number changed? I can't reach him on that either. Can't you give me the new number?' Meera tried to keep the plea out of her voice.

But they refused. 'Please try again, ma'am.' 'Please call back later.' 'We'll tell him you called.' And Meera waited for him to call her. He didn't.

Meera gnaws at her lip. The meter is ticking. The theme song of *Titanic* plays on in her ear. A hysterical giggle flutters in her throat. What could be more appropriate? A sinking ship and her…'Hello,' she says into the phone. 'Hello, hello, hello…'

As she stepped out of the house, Nikhil asked, 'Why aren't you calling from home?'

'It is cheaper,' she said. 'I can keep an eye on the meter. Here I'd just prattle on.'

'You don't prattle. They do!' he retorted. 'They are the ones who talk too long on the phone.'

'Hush! It doesn't matter. They are trying, Nikhil. It is not easy for them,' Meera said, trying to not let her lip wobble. These days even the slightest hint of kindness unsettled her. She could handle rage and anger, frustration and even rudeness. But kindness… it unnerved her.

The old ladies tried. Meera watched Lily and Saro meticulously move one button into the box after each call. Meera had said they must. 'Each button represents one free call. We will be billed after a hundred free calls. And you'll have to ask me when you need to make a long distance call. I have locked that facility. We need to economize now. Really. I've also changed all our cell phone connections to prepaid plans.'

They looked at each other, Lily and Saro. This was a Meera they didn't recognize. A Meera with home economies. A button a call. The pink papers and news magazines cancelled. No more half loads in the washing machine. Lights and fans switched off when not needed. Reheated leftovers. And a measuring spoon that didn't brim any more. But they said nothing. The stern cast of her face alarmed them more than Meera realized. At night, in the privacy of their bedrooms, they heard the echoes of the clamour in Meera's heart: What are we to do now?

It was Lily who said, 'I don't need a cell phone, Meera. Anyone who wants to reach me can call here. It is too much of a nuisance really! All kinds of strangers calling at strange hours, wanting to sell you things you don't need.'

And Saro, who couldn't even bear the thought of sharing a bottle of marmalade with anyone else said, 'She and I can share mine. Why waste money on two connections?'

'It's fine for now. I'll tell you when we may need to give up one of the connections,' Meera said quietly.

'Yes, Meera,' his voice booms over the line. Her publisher and lifeline.

'Hello, Randhir,' Meera says in as steady a voice as she can muster. 'I tried calling you several times but couldn't reach you.'

'I heard,' the voice at the end of the line says. Meera waits for him to make excuses, even apologize, perhaps. In the past, he never failed to call back. And at book events, he was always there, ebullient and full of gruff humour and telling anyone he could grab hold of, 'My bestselling cookbook writer. Except, how can you call her a cookbook writer? She's more than that. She's the corporate wife's Spencer Johnson, an inspiration for every woman whose husband is part of the corporate world!'

Meera would smile, partly in embarrassment at his exaggerated claims for her and partly out of affection for him. He had been a rock all along.

She didn't actually set out to write a cookbook. In fact, if Meera had nurtured literary ambitions, she would have chosen loftier, weightier themes from her Greek myths. Or traced the life and writings of a poet, perhaps. Or crafted a series of literary essays on books and writers.

Then one Saturday evening, three years ago, she found herself at a loose end. Saro and Lily were away visiting friends. The kids had gone out for a movie and Giri was in Singapore on work. Once upon a time Meera used to go with him on his foreign trips. But after that time when they were in Brussels and Nikhil fell ill, Meera was increasingly reluctant to leave the children alone. Now they holidayed abroad once a year, with the children. Meera preferred that to sitting around in hotel rooms all day or strolling aimlessly through the streets of some foreign city, waiting for Giri to be available after a day of meetings and presentations.

She sat at the dining table, cutting up vitamin pill strips into neat little squares of aluminium foil. She kept them in a round glass candy jar so that each of them would see it and remember to swallow one just after breakfast. She thought of the dinner party they had been to a week before. A young colleague of Giri's had hosted it. They had arrived at the apartment two streets away, exactly at 7.15 p.m. as they had been asked to, only to find a flustered host and a distraught hostess.

'The maid didn't turn up and the baby kept crying through the day…' Tina, the young wife had murmured, trying to hide the fact that she had been weeping all evening. 'And there was a power cut last night and the food I had kept ready in the fridge has spoilt. Neeraj is angry with me for calling in food but what else could I do? And then the dog ate up the kebabs I had placed on a platter for heating up and serving. And he says it's all my fault. That I should be more organized.'

Meera saw the red-rimmed nose and the puffy eyes, heard the wobbly voice and felt her heart go out to her.

'Don't worry,' Meera, the legendary hostess, smiled. 'We'll put a smile on Neeraj's face. Now, what do you have in your kitchen?'

Later, as she sat watching Tina charm Giri and the other men with stories of her former workplace, Meera smiled to herself. At least she wasn't as clueless as Meera had been. Meera, at her first dinner party, had tried to introduce literary trivia into the dinner table conversation, thinking it would amuse and entertain and perhaps even start a discussion. 'Did you know that Sylvia Plath actually used a thesaurus?' she had said.

Giri's boss had spooned pulao into his plate and murmured, 'Sensible woman! What's poetry anyway but the same thought in different words? One might structure it better with a thesaurus. Now Meera, did you make all of this? Excellent food and a superb menu! I especially love the flavour of pineapple you have brought into your pulao. Giri, you are a very fortunate man. She is an asset!'

Meera had felt her smile falter, her topics for discussion sink in the middle, and she dwindled into silence. Over the years she had learnt to rein in her impulses and seek those worlds where it was enough to float rather than probe or analyse. The price of gold was good, as was a new restaurant they had eaten at, or a movie she had watched; international celebrities and a description of a visit to a quaint place full of atmosphere and antiquity were perfect, especially when one had overseas guests. And when all failed, Meera brought in Daddy's tea estate years and Lily's cinema days. Meera's parties would never be a riot. Instead, they were elegantly structured, perfectly orchestrated symphonies with never a wrong note. Meera, conducting with a twirl of her wrist, had just one mission – that the boss went back happy and Giri's colleagues went home envying him the life he had.

The magazines referred to people like her in rather dismissive terms. The soufflé sort. The Teflon type. It hurt, especially because deep in her it rankled that she who in her student years had worshipped at the feet of Germaine Greer and Marilyn French, Andrea Dworkin, Gertrude Stein, Dorothy Parker and Simone de Beauvoir – the devis of womanhood who taught her how to shape her femininity and female thinking – had become this. All it took was one long look at

Giri, and the devis and their theories had evaporated. And now she was the kind of woman who mouthed gibberish.

'Thanks, Meera,' Tina had whispered in her ear as the party progressed without a hitch. 'You should really write a book for wives like me. For corporate wives like me so they don't make a hash of their husband's career and their marriage!'

Tina was more than a little drunk by then but Meera, sitting at her dining table with a fistful of vitamins, found herself taking one of Nikhil's exercise books and scrawling on the first page:

THE CORPORATE WIFE'S GUIDE TO ENTERTAINING

1. Thou shalt be dressed, perfumed and ready by the time the guests arrive.
2. Thou shalt not drink too much alcohol.
3. Thou shalt not forget to show appreciation for the perfumed candle brought by the boss's wife. (The very same candle you gave them a year ago during Diwali.)
4. Thou shalt not dawdle over serving, or race through the meal.
5. Thou shalt not monopolize the conversation.
6. Thou shalt not discuss thy office politics, or thy ailments, maids, drivers, servants and in-laws.
7. Thou shalt not air thy views on company policies even if thou hast a management degree from IIM or Wharton.
8. Thou shalt not flirt with thy spouse's boss. Even if he looks like Richard Gere, Alec Baldwin or Saif Ali Khan.
9. Thou shalt not find fault with thy spouse even if thou would like to crack his knuckles with a nutcracker.
10. Thou shalt remember to smile at thy spouse ever so often. Bosses know a happy man is a happy employee.

Over the next few months, Meera no longer had empty evenings. In those hours, she worked on her book and with the same detached secrecy with which she had written it, she took a printout and sent it to one of the best known publishers in India – Watermill Press.

One of the news magazines that specialized in literary gossip reported how Randhir Sahi was so enchanted by what he read that he called Meera the night he finished reading the manuscript and signed her on. In six months' time Meera became the bestselling author of a book that corporate men gifted to girlfriends, fiancées, wives and in some cases, their mothers as well.

'If you don't get through to me, all you have to do is email me, Meera. I may not always be able to come to the phone,' he says. 'And now, what can I do for you?'

'Well, it's about the new book,' Meera begins. 'I was waiting to hear from you on the proposal I sent… the one on desserts.'

He sighs. And Meera feels her expectation curl at the edge.

'I am not so sure that we will be able to publish it,' he says. 'I sent you an email. Didn't you get it? It just doesn't sit well on our list!'

Meera had read the email in puzzlement. What had the editor meant by saying it wouldn't fit into their publishing programme for the year? A mistake, surely? She had run her fingers through her hair and thought, I will have to talk to him myself. The editor perhaps didn't realize who she was or what Randhir thought of her. His star, he called her.

'Randhir, I was taken aback by the email. I thought you hadn't seen it…'

'I see every email that is sent out, Meera.' His voice wears an edge now. '*The Corporate Wife's Guide to Entertaining* was a hit, I agree. But *The CEO Lunch* hasn't taken off as I expected it to. And Giri, after saying at the book launch that he had found a tie-in to buy back 1000 copies, hasn't reverted. I had to make some enquiries and I hear that you are separated. That changes the whole angle, you know. And 'Just Desserts – Desserts for When the Boss Comes to Dinner' is too niche and too much of a risk!'

Meera listens. I will not beg. I will not plead, she thinks. But she hears herself say, 'What am I to do now?'

'I really don't know. Think of something else. A cookbook that no one else has. Like you did with *The Corporate Wife's Guide to Entertaining*. Send me the book proposal first, though.'

A container truck thunders past the narrow road. A medley of horns blare. 'Where are you calling from, Meera?' the voice asks, suddenly curious.

Meera hangs up quietly. Later she would send him a polite email explaining she had been cut off, and couldn't connect again. She needs him more than he needs her and she is prepared to grovel. But for now, she takes a deep breath and stares at the phone as if it were Randhir. 'Bastard! The fucking bastard!' Meera mouths softly in the confines of the telephone box. Abuse trips off her lips easily these days.

Why hadn't she signed the two-book contract he had proposed after *The Corporate Wife's Guide to Entertaining*? Why hadn't she done what authors everywhere were doing? What use now this mad bid to hold her freedom to herself? Giri had urged her as well: 'You could have asked for a bigger advance!'

'It's not the money, Giri,' she had tried to explain.

'It's always the money,' he cut her off. 'It's a commercial book you are writing. He is going to make money from it. You should too! But when do you ever listen to me?'

Now Meera walks back to her home quietly. She has spent Rs 110 on a call that has amounted to nothing. At least she has been spared the humiliation of her mother and grandmother hovering, eavesdropping and then huddling together to speculate about what would happen next.

X

There is no knowing what will happen next in our lives, Meera thinks, walking past the gates of the lilac house. Did Lily and Saro ever know such uncertainty, she wonders. Perhaps they did, which is why they are the way they are. Wary of everyone and everything, jealously guarding what is theirs. In time, will I, too, become like them? Watching out for myself rather than for anyone else? Meera dislikes the woman she is turning into.

The cane chairs sit forlorn and vacant in the patio. A breeze ruffles the tops of the palms in planters. Meera stands by the pillars and looks at the house. Her lilac house wreathed with creepers, its garden abloom. Bees drone, squirrels chatter, birds call. An oasis of peace flanked by tall apartment blocks on either side and a shopping complex across the road. Meera sighs and asks the house, 'How could you do this to me?'

If a few months ago someone had said that this house, her beloved lilac house, would fracture her marriage and throw her life askew, she would have laughed herself silly. And then reached across and tapped their nose playfully. 'What did you eat last? A magic mushroom omelette? I've never heard anything more bizarre! Is this the house in *Amityville Horror* or what?'

Meera walks into the house. Where is everyone? She can hear the television. She goes to the kitchen and pours herself a glass of water. She takes the glass and sits in the patio.

She has been clutching at straws. Cookbooks are fine for corporate wives with husbands who pay bills and settle the dues. Abandoned corporate wives need more. Meera draws out a diary from her bag. All her household accounts are in it. It seems to her that this is all she does these days. Tabulate the figures again and again as if by doing so she can arrive at a sum that will assure her all is well: Giri may have left but they will survive. One way or the other.

Meera finds Nikhil in his room. He is lying across the bed with his head resting on one arm.

'So what happened?' Nikhil asks.

Meera shrugs. 'Nothing really. He wants me to come up with a book idea like *The Corporate Wife's Guide to Entertaining*! This one doesn't work, he says.'

'Is it because of Daddy?'

'No, darling. Daddy has nothing to do with this.' Or us any more, Meera thinks but bites down the words. Nikhil still believes that his daddy will come back.

She sits by his side and ruffles his hair. Her eyes sweep the span of his room. A child's room, though he hates it when she refers to him as one. She thinks of how he clamoured for a book every week. And now he doesn't any more. Instead, he reads again the books he has. She thinks of how he reads the newspaper, making an effort to seem responsible. He sits in

Giri's chair and holds aloft the pages as his father once did, seeking to fill his place.

Nikhil looks at her. 'What will we do, Mummy?' he asks and Meera thinks her heart will break at what she sees in his eyes: Nikhil knows his father isn't coming home any more. 'Will you have to sell my iPod?' he asks.

'Not yet,' she says quietly, hating herself for not being able to say, 'Of course not!' This way it won't be such a shock if we have to, she reasons.

One more nail in your coffin, you SOB, she tells Giri in her head. I can forgive you for what you are doing to me. For the anxiety you are causing my mother and grandmother. But not this. Not for robbing my son, our son, of his childhood. Nothing you ever do, even if you come back, will remove that shadow in his eyes. Somewhere in your new happy home in your new happy life, I hope it occurs to you that you have a child who has resolutely willed his tongue to never again utter 'I want', or 'I need'.

'What will you do?' he asks again.

'I don't know yet, darling. But we'll manage. I know we can.'

Meera's eyes swoop on the books. 'But I'll tell you what we are going to do, right now.'

She goes into her bedroom and drags out a trolley dolley. From the shelves in the bedroom and the living room, she pulls out books. All the advertising and marketing books Giri bought with the rapacious greed of a child who can't have enough. He merely needed to possess them; some of the books are still in their plastic jackets, uncut, unread.

'What are you doing?' Nikhil asks from the doorway.

Meera smiles. 'Come with me.'

They take an autorickshaw to an old bookstore Meera has run in and out of when book buying was a necessity rather than a luxury.

She watches the bookshop owner price the books. A small price to pay for stealing a childhood, Giri, she thinks.

'Buy yourself two books for Rs 200 each,' Meera tells Nikhil, stuffing the money into her purse.

'What about Nayantara?' Nikhil asks carefully. He knows Meera isn't pleased with her.

Meera wants to reach across and hug Nikhil. Her son who so wants to right the world, their world, where Mummy and Daddy live together and siblings don't have to choose between parents. 'When she's home for the weekend, she'll have her book allowance too!' Meera smiles.

Through the aisles of books they wander, seeking paperbacks whose marked price doesn't exceed their budget and will buy them solace for a while.

Through the mustiness of age, from the patina of dust that clings to the air, a soft voice rises. A child singing – '*We Shall Overcome*'.

Meera turns and sees a pixie faced little boy sitting on the floor with a picture book. He is singing as he turns the pages.

Meera's eyes seek and meet Nikhil's. They smile. Complicity and hope.

Meera feels a warm rush of love for the child, that unknown child.

We shall overcome, she thinks.

In the newspaper that morning, Meera had paused at an advertisement for editors in a software company. She has a postgraduate degree in English language and literature. Would she be considered too old? What if the working hours are long? What would they – Lily, Saro and the children – say? It doesn't matter, Meera thinks. I can put up with anything if it will exorcize this constant fear of penury. If it will just let me cope until we figure things out. If it will buy me time…

STAGE II

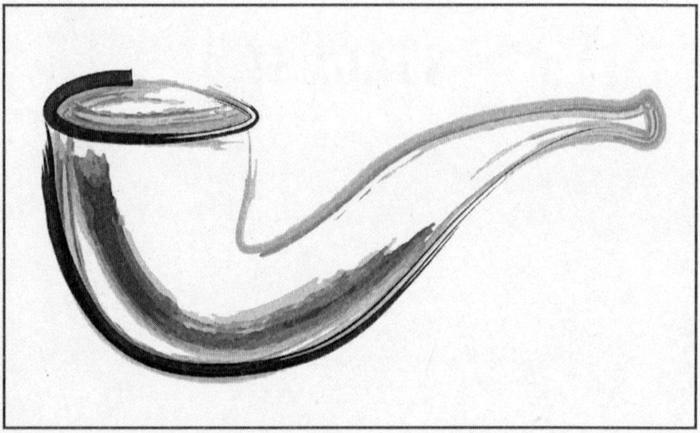

The Cirrus Canopy of Denial.

Let us compare mythologies. In the mythology of all civilizations, heaven represents an acme. The divine realm where all human destiny is decided before it is etched on the forehead of the life that springs in the womb. The clouds then are what separate the mortal from the immortal, the known from the unknown. As long as we do not see, we do not know.

We expect joy as our birthright, but despair? Though logic assures that where there is joy, there will be despair, we are never prepared for it. Not truly. And when it happens, for a while there is yet another phase before the acceptance of the inevitable.

Like the cover of clouds, it is the scrap that the all-powerful being allows us: the power of denial. When it comes to self-deception the human mind is capable of the infinite. At the Los Angeles County Museum of Art is a singular painting that is an ironic expression of this human trait. *Ceci n'cest pas une pipe.* This Is Not a Pipe is one in the series 'Treachery of Images' by Rene Magritte. Look at it. It is the image of a pipe. A larger than life pipe.

But Magritte maintained: 'And yet, could you stuff my pipe? No, it's just a representation, is it not? So if I had written on my picture "This is a pipe", I'd have been lying!' (Harry Torczyner, *Magritte: Ideas and Images*, p. 71)

So it is in the world of cyclones. As if to deny its very presence, the intense and unstable convectional clouds produce an outflow. An exhalation of a lofty white, fleecy cirrus formation that hides the eye of the cyclone. The cirrus canopy above the storm area puts everything on hold. That which is not seen does not exist. Meanwhile, the eye grows in strength and ferocity.

Professor J. A. Krishnamurthy
The Metaphysics of Cyclones

t . i . m . e
e . m .i . t
m. i. t. e

Meera moves the cursor back and forth over the jumbled letters. i . m . e . t. In one glance, she can see three ways of putting it right. But they only want one. Which one is it to be? Meera frowns.

t . i . m . e, Meera decides.

'I am done,' she tells the girl who looks like an older version of Nayantara.

'What do I do now?' she asks the girl.

The girl stares at her blankly, removes her earphones and says, 'We'll let you know in a couple of days or so.'

Meera smiles at the girl. She had shown her where to sit. She helped her locate the tests on the desktop, found her the earphones and said, 'There are two parts to the test. One where you have to watch the movie clipping and type in the dialogue. There are four clippings. You can watch it as many times as you want but you can't take more than half an hour for all four. Then there is the language test. You have half an hour for that too.

'Try and guess if you don't know the right answer,' she added as an afterthought.

Meera sat in the cubicle with the computer. Around her men and women who were young enough to be her children walked around taking long deep swigs from their cans of Red

Bull or bottles of Gatorade or Coke. There was a pizza box stuffed into a waste-paper basket brimming with cartons and cans... What am I doing here? Meera asked herself. What will I tell the children? Perhaps I could just point to a subtitle when we watch a movie and say, 'That's my new job. Subtitling movies. What a great profession, huh? Watching movies all day...' Meera pondered as she watched the movie clip.

At first, none of it made any sense. Then the words began to fall into place and Meera let her fingers fly on the keys.

I can do this. I can do this well. I have to do this. Our survival hinges on this. Meera's fingers flew.

Meera looks at the girl in front of her. Her blouse ends a few inches above the waistband of her cargo pants. The lobes of her ears are festooned with tiny silver ornaments. 'Bye,' Meera says. But the girl has already put her earphones back on.

The steel walls of the lift reflect distorted images. And that is how Meera sees herself.

Meera, with her hair pulled back and dressed in her daughter's clothes. Meera, who at forty-four hopes she will pass for an aging thirty-five. Meera, desperate Meera, desperately seeking employment in a world that has little use for corporate wives of even an exemplary kind.

Meera pulls away her hairband, yet another of Nayantara's castaways, and lets her hair swing free. Her head hurts. Meera, the masquerader. The abandoned wife pretending to be protectress.

Hera had never dwelt on it too much. For Zeus had always been there to rush forth to her rescue. And so in the battle between the giants and the Olympians, when Porphyrion placed his enormous hands round her neck and began strangling her, Hera's last thought wasn't: I am dying. Instead, it was the harried but secure wife's anger that made her wriggle: 'Where is Zeus when I need him?'

Hera couldn't even consider the possibility that Zeus wouldn't rush to rescue her.

Giri has always been there. All these years Meera had Giri to lean on. Only now, Giri is gone.

All these years Meera never knew what it was to be stripped of dignity. She feels as if she is laying herself bare for the entire world to see and speculate about. Her hands splay across her chest and pubis. She feels naked and vulnerable.

She cowers as the lift door opens.

I

Through the open doors of the lift, Vinnie sees a woman huddled against its steel side. A woman with her head bent and her shoulders shaking. Is she giggling into her phone?

An eyebrow arches by itself. What do these women chatter about all day?

Then the woman raises her head to look at her and Vinnie thinks she has never seen anyone look as depleted by anguish. Or as naked.

Vinnie has a split second to choose. To ignore the woman in tears or get involved. She doesn't know why, but she finds herself touching the woman on her shoulder and saying, 'Come. Let's get a coffee. Whatever it is, you will feel better then.'

The woman stares at her through her tears. Then she goes with her.

'I am sorry, I am sorry,' she keeps whispering, trying to dry her eyes.

Across the road is a Café Coffee Day. Vinnie doesn't like going to these places much. They are teenage haunts. For children on whom tall drinks of fattening chocolate and milk don't show. 'A lot can happen over a cup of coffee,' Arun had grinned at her. They had met there one evening and Vinnie saw how his eyes flicked over the girls, pausing at the smooth, unlined midriffs only a twenty-year-old can possess. And how the young girls feasted on him. 'They must wonder at us,' she said.

'Let them,' he drawled. 'What is it to us?'

Nothing to you, perhaps, but I feel like a fool. A middle-aged fool, Vinnie had ached to snap.

It hasn't been an easy morning for Vinnie either. Arun wants a loan.

Vinnie has been unable to stop the voices in her head and heart. The voices have alternated between raucous heckling and blandishments, trying to out voice each other.

'Give it to him,' one of the voices said.

'If you give in now, you are doomed,' another said.

Give it to him, the voice in Vinnie's heart whispered. Give it to him and he'll give unto you all that you desire, it simpered.

Lady, there's a name for people like you who need to buy desire, the other voice in Vinnie's head curled its mouth.

Vinnie patted the coil of hair that sat atop her head. A crown that allowed her to disseminate businesswoman efficiency with the raising of an eyebrow and a curl of the lip. It was the cornice atop a façade of control. Don't mess with me, it warned the world of employees, shop girls and all minions who contributed to making the earth a better place for Vinnie.

'I don't like it when you do this to your hair,' Arun had said a few days into their relationship and pulled down the careful coiffure. 'I hate it,' he said, running his fingers through her hair. 'As for this,' he continued, dropping the chopstick she used to hold her hair in place into her hands, 'it belongs in a Chinese restaurant!'

Vinnie smiled and popped it into her bag. Other women wore brooches and rings; Vinnie had her chopsticks. A whole tray of them to match her clothes and hold her knot in place. In jade, bone, horn, porcelain, wood, and even a couple of plastic ones. Needles to pierce the heart of all her surreptitious wayward longings and keep them coiled and in place.

'Wanton, wanton,' Arun murmured as he played with her, her nerve ends, her restraint.

'Now this is you,' he said, coiling a strand around a finger. And Vinnie couldn't speak a word. For the mere sight of him, her lover, opened a ravenous greed in her. His long musician's fingers sang on her skin, his mouth feeding tickling licking sucking cupping, how could a pair of lips and tongue know so much, the smoothness, oh the smoothness of his skin, the ridges of muscle on his back, the mat of hair on his chest grazing her breasts, the back of her thighs, her nipples, her pubis, his to do as he pleased. And she could give as good as she got, reaching for his cock, the arc of his balls, hers, hers, hers, to do with as she pleased, her back arching in the pleasure that began at the curl of her toes, riding up through sinew and muscle into the cells of her brain – a thought: I could go on and on. As the thought turned back to her toes, enough, enough, enough, she thought as she collapsed in a heap of satiation, spent fluids and a deep deep sense of regret that it had to be like this. Frantic afternoon groping and fucking, noises escaping his mouth and hers but no words of love or forever. All of it a slaking of lust and loneliness. It was what he and every fortune cookie knew but her husband didn't: a woman needs to be loved, not understood.

Vinnie clutched her purse tight. In that older man, mature voice of his when he asked for the money – 'Only a loan, you understand, I'll return it as soon as my transfer comes through' – she saw the deep clavicle that crested his mouth. And she thought of how he had picked from the floor her blouse which she had tossed away carelessly in her hurry to be in his arms and how he had ironed it carefully. Smoothening each wrinkle and crease with a housewifely hand so that when she put it on, she was Vinnie again. The hard, indestructible Vinnie only he could crumble with a tiny nip on her earlobe. She knew he enjoyed this power he had over her. And a tenderness welled up in her.

Did she love him? She didn't know. But she needed him and was petrified of losing him.

And yet, to give him the money would be changing the trajectory of 'this thing, whatever it is' as he called their relationship.

Would it bind him to her? Or, would it just make her his money-dispensing machine each time he fell short? An edge of a wheedle in that deep baritone voice, a hint of helplessness in those eyes. Would he think that was all it took to send Vinnie rushing to the nearest ATM?

Vinnie didn't know. She couldn't decide what was right, what was wrong.

She pushes her wandering thoughts away as she leads the woman towards another café a little further away. One of the coffee shop attendants saunters to their table. 'Two filter coffees, please,' Vinnie says.

'We don't have south Indian coffee.'

'I don't believe this.' Vinnie's mouth curls. 'Here we are in Bangalore, south India and you have, what is that?' she peers. 'Colombian, Brazilian, Kenyan... and no good old south Indian filter coffee. Bring us two espressos and two glasses of ice water.'

The woman is dabbing at her cheeks with a tissue. 'I am sorry to have imposed,' she says, a watery smile creasing her face.

'Don't. I am Vinnie. I am sure whatever is troubling you can be resolved.'

'I am Meera,' the woman offers shyly. 'Thanks, Vinnie. Thanks for…' She pauses, unsure of how to describe the situation she has been found in.

II

'So this is my situation. Perhaps I should consider becoming a whore! What else am I trained for?' Meera finishes, feeling her lips tremble, her hands shake. It has been a relief to talk to someone, this perfect stranger, of how her life changed; of not knowing; of the questions and answers that hovered over her, every waking moment and in her sleep.

The trembling will not stop. Vinnie notices how Meera's hands shake but she pretends not to see and takes her up on what she has just said.

'A whore!' Vinnie throws her head back and laughs. 'I can just see it. What do you think you will be doing? Offering your clients tea and biscuits and a lesson or two in etiquette? Meera, Meera, what is wrong with you?'

Then Vinnie stops abruptly. Meera, she sees, isn't smiling. She doesn't even look sheepish at having touted such a preposterous idea. Instead, she is nibbling her lip as if that is the only way she can prevent her face from crumpling into a wail.

'Meera.' Vinnie touches her arm. 'What are you thinking of? I don't even know what to say.'

Meera squares her shoulders and says, 'What else can I do? This job I have applied for – I don't even know if I will get it. And if I do, it doesn't pay very much.'

Meera opens her handbag, an expensive Coach, Vinnie sees, and takes out a pocket book. She flips a page and pushes it towards Vinnie.

'Look at this. This is how much money I need every month. Expenses. I have economized as much as I can. My family, my grandmother and mother and my children, why even the maid, all of them are so careful, it breaks my heart to see them like this. But even this tightening of purse strings, it isn't enough, Vinnie. If I don't find a job soon, we will be in serious trouble.'

Vinnie sees the columns of figures in Meera's neat hand. Each item carefully written, every i dotted, each t crossed. How desperate does a woman have to be to consider selling her body?

'But didn't you have any sense of what was coming? Some deep rooted discomfort at what was happening between the two of you?' Vinnie asks.

Meera watches Vinnie as she tears open a packet of sugar and empties the contents in the saucer, her hand carefully trailing the circumference of the cup. Then Vinnie stirs her sugarless coffee.

'Why do you do that?'

'Do what?' Vinnie frowns. She looks at the empty sugar sachet.

'Oh, this.' She smiles sheepishly. 'It's silly but some part of me, the sugar craving me, is quite appeased by this. And I don't have to worry about the empty white calories coming to live on my hips!'

Vinnie takes a sip and asks again, 'Did you really have no idea that everything wasn't well between the two of you?'

Meera stares at the middle distance. 'We squabbled. Which couple doesn't? But I didn't think there would be another woman or it would lead to him leaving...no, walking out on us.'

Meera sits up abruptly, stricken by a memory.

The night before Giri left, he drank steadily. He seldom drank more than his one shot of whisky but that night, he had already had two drinks. He came into the bedroom clinking the ice in his drink. Meera looked up from where she was sorting her clothes for the next day's brunch and smiled at him.

He walked to the dressing table where her few articles of make-up and her bottle of perfume resided. He picked up the perfume and sniffed at it. 'You ought to try a new one. A Dolce Gabbana or an Armani. It's time you had a new fragrance!'

Meera looked up, surprised. 'I thought you said this one was me. I thought you liked it. Which is why I never buy anything else.'

He took a sip of his drink. 'The problem with you, Meera, is that you want everything to stay as it is. You have to allow room for change. For me to change. I used to like this fragrance once. Not any more. I find it boring. Old fashioned, with no zest at all!'

Meera didn't speak. Instead, she held up a skirt and asked, 'What about this?'

'Hmm…' Giri said, feeling the chiffon between his fingers. 'A little too sedate, I would say. Don't you have anything more vibrant?'

Meera's face fell. 'I am forty-four years old, Giri. I can't dress like I am twenty. Mutton dressed as lamb, etc.'

Giri shrugged. You asked and I replied, the shrug said. Meera bit her lip as she hung up the skirt. What did he want from her? She couldn't seem to please him any more.

'I have a daughter who's nearly twenty years old,' Meera began abruptly. 'It looks so silly for me to dress like she does…'

'Please. Let it be.' Giri held up his hand. 'You must dress or do whatever you want, exactly the way you want to. Anyway, it isn't as if you do only what I want you to.'

Meera went towards Giri and touched his elbow. 'Tell you what, I'll lighten it up with some jewellery. Chandelier earrings, the bead anklet, what do you think?'

Giri waved his hand in a careless gesture. Now what? Meera wondered. Is he going to sulk about this?

'Have you thought about what I said this morning?' he asked from the depths of the armchair he had retired into.

'About what, sweetie?' Meera asked absently, staring into the innards of her closet. Should she attempt a quick sorting through of her undies?

'Don't use that fucking tone when you talk to me. I am not a three-year-old child.'

Meera turned in surprise as the vicious bolt of rage hurled itself at her.

'Giri,' she began.

'I asked you this morning to consider the offer from the real estate people. Have you thought about it?' He leaned forward, his hand clenched around the glass.

'What is there to think about?' Meera said quietly. 'I can't. We can't sell the house.'

'Think about it,' Giri said slowly, coming to stand by her side. 'Apart from the money, the developers would give us two flats. One for us and the other for Lily and Saro. In the same block. They don't have to think you are abandoning them. And you can pop over as and when you or they want, so they don't get lonely.

'It would be perfect, Meera, think of it. Money won't be such a priority any more. All you need to do is say yes.'

Meera sat on the bed. She felt that old fatigue suffuse her. What was she to tell Giri?

'No, Giri.' She shook her head. 'I can't. Even if I were to agree, they won't. They never would… And it's their house after all.'

'What about me?' Giri stiffened. He took a deep swallow of the whisky. 'What about me?' His rancour no longer hid behind a façade of civility. 'Don't I have a fucking say? For the last twenty-two years I have sunk so much into the house. Look at it, Meera. Who is paying for its upkeep?'

Something snapped in Meera then. Was it the strain of keeping a lie alive this long? Or, was it having a husband turn into a nit-picking ogre? 'That's true. But come to think of it, you didn't pay any rent either.'

Meera saw his face and felt all churned up again. 'Giri,' she tried to make amends. 'I didn't mean it like that. They won't agree. They won't. I know how they think. They don't like change.'

His face was averted. She placed her hand on his arm. 'What is wrong with us? I can't believe that we are arguing about this house, money, really!'

Giri slithered his elbow out of her grasp and walked away. He picked up his glass and his voice when it emerged from the swallow of whisky and ice was cold. And his words chilling: 'That's what couples argue about. But we are not one, are we? You are the landlady and I am the tenant. There is no us. It is always you. Your house. Your family. Your friends. Has it occurred to you how I feel?'

'But you wanted us to live here in this house with Mummy and Lily. You wanted to meet all my friends,' Meera began. 'You said you wanted to make my life yours…'

'You don't get it, do you? You never did,' he interrupted, moving further away into the shadows.

What is it that I don't get? Meera clenched her fist. Why is it that each time I question him, he throws this in my face? As if not comprehending him is a fatal flaw. As if from that point in my brain where all comprehension begins, from my cerebellum to my vagina, there is a long catheter that drains away my capability to absorb and understand. As if, only by his filling the gap can anything decent, noble, or right be imbibed by me.

'What is it that I don't get, Giri?' she asked, not bothering to hide the bitterness in her voice.

The tirade then. A long laundry list of linen that she had soiled; of hopes thwarted and disappointments endured. Of not finding in her the support he had expected; for turning him against his family, his past. 'You don't want a husband, Meera, you want a fucking puppet.'

Meera felt a foolish grin split her face. What was he saying?

'I knew you wouldn't want to move, to change your life here, so I put my career on the back-burner. I had so many offers but I told myself, no, I wouldn't disrupt your life.' In his voice she heard a deep regret now.

At the door he turned. 'You know what your problem is, Meera? You want to make life fit those lists you are making all the time. You don't see it, do you? That your lists are all about the past or the future. Pending chores. Things to do. What about the present, Meera? What about now? That's what I am worried about. That's where I want to live.'

Meera continued to sit there, on the bed. She felt herself grow cold. Giri had never spoken to her like that. He sounded almost as if he hated her. As if she had trapped him in an unbearable situation. She stuffed her fingers into her mouth to stop a sob escaping her.

In bed that night she pretended that none of those bitter words had been spoken, and snuggled up to him. She was tired. It had been a long and weary day but she wanted to make up to Giri. Smoothen any wrinkles that had crept between them. Restore the limbo their life was all about. If he wanted to make love, she was willing and ready. If somewhere deep within, a little voice taunted her that she was bartering her body for peace, she knew how to silence it effectively. For the greater common good, what was a little desecration of self-respect?

But he lay there, still and unresponsive. Worse, she felt him pulling away. He lay with his eyes closed and an arm draped over his forehead, pretending to be asleep.

Meera rolled on to her back, bewildered. Frightened, too. She had never known him to be so withdrawn. What now? What have I gone and done, Meera asked herself a thousand times as she hovered between wide-eyed consciousness and fatigue that shut her eyes in fitful sleep.

But in the morning Giri smiled at her. Meera clutched at that carelessly tossed smile with the tenacious pluck of the drowning woman groping for anything, even a smile as hollow as straw. I'll make it up to him. I'll try and unspeak those words. I'll try and be his goose girl again, she told herself as she fastened teardrop clusters in her ears and slipped on her daughter's anklet. Then, on an impulse, she daubed herself with Nayantara's perfume.

'He didn't leave much. He wanted us to sell the house. I refused. So he's punishing me. This walking out on us, it's childish vengefulness.' Meera's voice shakes.

'But why don't you sell the house?'

'I can't, Vinnie. I wish I could. That's the whole trouble. The house isn't mine or my mother's or grandmother's to sell. We are just allowed to live in it. It's the strangest bloody thing. My great-grandfather took the house on a ninety-nine-year lease. That was fifty-four years ago. Forty-five years from now, it will revert back to the original owners. I don't know what he was thinking of. Maybe he meant to provide for his daughter and granddaughter; the following generations would have to look out for themselves, etc. I have no idea why such a deal was struck and my grandmother has no logical explanation either.'

'Does Giri know?'

Meera shakes her head. 'He doesn't.' She looks up from the table at Vinnie. 'It wasn't that I chose wilfully to hide it from him. At first when I brought it up, he didn't want to know. He kept shushing me. Then later, I was much too scared. I knew that we came together as a package, the house and I. If he couldn't have the house, I thought he wouldn't want me either. And the lease, I thought, would expire only when we were very old or dead, and it wouldn't matter then.'

'What about the rent?' Vinnie remembers seeing the huge old house and grounds. 'Can you afford that?'

'Two hundred rupees. Six years from now, it will be five hundred!'

'What?' Vinnie laughs aloud in disbelief.

'Exactly. The landlord was my great-grandfather's best friend. His family tried to take the house back, raise the rent, etc. but the old men had drawn up a watertight contract. We may starve to death but it will be in gracious surroundings!'

III

The surroundings fill him with a great sense of loss. Jak rests his arms on the steel table and watches the boy in front of him. For someone his age, he drinks a lot. He drinks too much, Jak thinks. This boy is all messed up. Heavens, how has he managed to put away so much rum without falling on his face?

In the end Minjikapuram wore Jak out. Like that time before, when he was fifteen. It could give him nothing of what he sought. Instead, it did exactly what it had once before. It pushed him into doing what inertia or perhaps even apathy might have prevented him from doing.

The silence of Minjikapuram so infuriated him, he decided he must find out what had really happened, one way or the other. It could mean starting afresh from another point but Jak knew all about that as well. When available scientific data offered only inconclusive answers, one looked elsewhere. In the stories of men who had seen it happen, in remembered portents and stipples of hearsay. On the field Jak knew of fishermen reading storm signals though radars maintained a resolute silence, of the spotting of a cyclone from the crest of a wave and the cry of a seagull. So Jak went home and began all over again.

The boy's hand shakes as he pours rum into a glass and tops it with water from a steel jug. Behind him shadows dance as men come and go. There is no laughter and hardly any conversation in that room lit with a lone naked bulb hanging from the centre of the ceiling.

'How did you know I would be here?' the boy asks.

Jak shrugs. 'I have my ways.'

For a moment you think of the days spent in the college corridors and the canteen, seeking a face from the printout you carried. Faces imprinted in your mind so that you would recognize them anywhere.

They threw strange looks your way. Who was this man who haunted the college campus, searching every face? Then you asked to meet the principal.

'I can't allow it. I can't give you personal information about the students here,' the man said categorically. 'Why do you need to know about them anyway?'

Smriti wasn't a student of this college. The boys were Asha's friends, she had said. What could you say?

'They were my daughter's friends,' you said.

'Were?'

'She is not well,' you said quietly.

'If it is a police matter, they will do the questioning. I can't let you loiter here in the college campus. Please leave…' He looked at the card you had given him. 'Professor Krishnamurthy, oh, I see… at the University of Florida.' A note of respect crept into his voice. Apology even.

As he saw you to the door, he said again, 'I hope you understand my position. I am helpless. Really!'

Outside and across the road was a petty shop. Cigarettes, soft drinks, biscuits, bananas, magazines, betel leaves, chewing tobacco, everything a college boy might need to alleviate the hours spent cooped within the classroom.

You started a conversation with the man there. He knew one boy, he said. Used to be my regular, he beamed, though I haven't seen him in a while.

'Where do you think I can find him?' you asked.

The man shrugged. 'I don't know where he lives.'

You looked away. What were you to do now?

You had thought it would be easier to trace the boys rather than Asha. A girls' college run by nuns would require many explanations. And you didn't even know what you were seeking.

'Come back tomorrow. I will ask some of my regulars and let you know.'

Next day the man said, Shivu, that was the boy's name, had

gone back to Salem. 'That's where he is from. He moved to a college there. I think it is called the A.V.M. Chettiar College.'

This time you knew what to do. You wouldn't waste time inside the college. Instead, you would head for the petty shop outside.

'You could try the Rose Cottage,' the man there said. 'Some of these boys go there, dirty as it is!'

'Rose Cottage?' Your heart sank. A whore house?

'Hawaldar's place. He doesn't have a liquor licence but he sells booze in a back room. These college boys go there for a shot… army quota. It's hard stuff but cheap!'

You waited outside for four days before Shivu walked in. You crossed the road and followed him in. In your haste, you bumped into him.

He turned in surprise at your bulk looming behind him. 'Who the fuck?' he snarled.

You murmured, 'I am Smriti's father.'

The boy's eyes were those of a rabbit's caught in a light. Petrified.

The owner, who is also the bartender, steward and chef, slams a plate of scrambled eggs on their table. Oil glistens on the egg and chopped onion and chillies. 'The hardboiled eggs are over. So I made you this. Anything else?' the man asks.

The boy shrugs. Jak looks at the thickset man with his hair razed to a stubble. He has heard the other men call out to him as Hawaldar. An ex-army type or a man posing as an ex-army man. He continues to stand there.

'What?' Jak asks.

'You have to order something. This isn't a club for you to sit around and chat,' the man says.

'Fine. Bring me a vodka tonic,' Jak says. He doesn't want a drink. But if he has to, he prefers vodka.

'I don't have vodka, gin or all those fancy spirits. Just rum, brandy or whisky. It's all military quota.' The man's abrasiveness rattles Jak.

'Get me one of each.'

'Large or small?'

'Large, and three bottles of soda, and a plate of peanuts. That satisfy you?'

The boy looks up now. 'I am sorry for this,' he says quietly.

Jak doesn't speak. He is furious. Then he asks, 'Why?'

'I can see that this is hardly the place you would hang out in. And the rudeness of Hawaldar… oh, for everything.' The boy's voice rings with remorse.

Jak puts his hand on the boy's arm. 'Should you be here at all? Look at what's around you!'

Their eyes survey the rundown seediness of the room. The decrepit men with shaking hands and the palpable need to toss a drink down their throats. The silence they fill with alcohol in steel tumblers. The demons that perch on their shoulders and urge with slobbering mouths: one more, one more…

'This is a place for alcoholics. For men who are far gone. So why are you here?' Jak's voice is soft but insistent. 'What are you running away from?'

The boy's eyes widen, then he drops his gaze. 'What do you mean?'

'Why haven't you been to see Smriti even once?' Jak asks.

'It is difficult for me to come to Bangalore.'

'That's not the truth.'

The boy continues to look into his glass. He doesn't speak. Then he raises the glass to his mouth and drinks deeply.

Jak flinches.

'I can't,' the boy says. 'I can't. Do you hear me? I can't. I can't. I can't. That satisfy you?' The boy's tone mimics his.

'No,' Jak says. 'I need to know why. You were her friend, weren't you? You, the other two boys, and Asha.'

The boy's eyes are quizzical. 'Asha? Who is Asha?'

Jak looks at his palms, on which the lines whirl in an almost centrifugal pattern.

So Asha is yet another lie in the stream of lies Smriti fed them, Nina and him. Why did she feel the need to create this imaginary girl? Asha, whose mother was a doctor and father an architect. Their dog Snoopy and their lovely old home in Jayanagar, which Smriti had been to several times. Asha, who topped the class and never missed a step. Was she the girl Smriti ached to be? Or was she the veneer of respectability Smriti sought to hide her recklessness behind?

But why? He wouldn't have prevented her from going on a trip with the boys anyway. He never laid down the law; never played the heavy father. He never said, no dating, no doing this, no doing that… 'It's your life. If you screw it up, you'll have no one to blame but yourself. I know how it can feel. That restlessness. The need to push the limits. But take it slow.'

He voiced only what Amma had said when for a while he, Kitcha, had run amok.

'The world is yours to grasp,' Amma said to him, taking his hand in hers and smoothening his tightly clenched fist. There are many ways of knowing life. All in good time. Why must my Kitcha be in such a hurry?'

Kitcha didn't want to dwell too long on it. These days he didn't want his mind to pause at any point. If it did, he knew he would burst into tears. It was better this way. Ever since Appa left, a ball of fury seemed to reside in his chest – his biology teacher called it the thoracic cavity. Home to his anger, it hissed and fumed, burnt and seethed.

It made him aim stones with his catapult at the blackboards in empty classrooms. It had him defile library books and smash windowpanes. There was a strange satisfaction at this wanton destruction. Like there was triumph when he aimed for shins rather than the football. Or, when he bowled to injure rather than contain the batsman's stroke play. A ball of fury with goblin ears that said playing hooky was what any schoolboy could do, go on, do more.

It made him light a cigarette in the playground. It made him smuggle pornographic magazines into the class. It whispered in his ear, 'Be a man! Now! Now!'

It emerged as a sulphurous stream from his mouth: profanity made him feel better. The shock and disgust it triggered made him want to laugh. A wild manic paroxysm of laughs. Koodhi. Amma Koodhi. Appa Koodhi. Loose Koodhi. The words danced on his tongue with glee and Kitcha spoke them loudly, clearly, on the playground, in the streets. He soon came to be known as the nasty boy with a gutter mouth.

Inevitably, he was caught. 'Missing classes to go for a movie is one thing, but your son is a bad influence,' the principal said. He had found his son smoking and the boy had no qualms about pointing his stubby index finger at Kitcha. 'He said I should try it. Be a man, Kitcha said.'

'I am suspending him for a week. This is his last chance. Then it will be dismissal.' The principal bristled.

Amma said nothing. Kitcha waited. They took the bus home, their shoulders and thighs touching, but Amma wouldn't speak a word. Kitcha darted glances at her face. Would she be angry or would she weep?

At home, she went into her room to change her clothes. He waited in the hall. The chains creaked as he swung himself, waiting for retribution.

Amma went into the kitchen and brought out a plate of tiffin and a tumbler of coffee for him. As if it was yet another ordinary school day.

Amma watched him eat. She sat by his side, still wrapped in a catacombic silence. What was she thinking? What was she planning?

When he was done, she took the plate and tumbler from his hands. Then she said, 'I think I know what's making you do this. What can I say, Kitcha? I am sorry that your father and I did this to you. I am sorry, Kitcha!'

He hadn't expected this. For Amma to take the blame for his rowdiness. Kitcha cried then. Large wet sobs that tore themselves from the ball of hate in his thoracic cavity and emerged as gigantic, heaving tears.

They wept together. Then Amma wiped her tears and his. She took his hand in hers and kissed his brow. 'I know you are not a bad boy. It's your age, Kitcha. It's your age. Shall I suggest something? When you get really angry, why don't you draw something? You hardly touch your paints any more.'

The boy isn't drinking in such a hurry now. The level in his glass dips slowly. Jak feels the questions tumble in his head but he doesn't know where to start.

The Hawaldar appears at their elbow. 'Half an hour. That's it! I am closing. If you have any last orders…'

Jak shakes his head.

'I've had enough,' the boy says.

'Don't come back tomorrow if you are going to sit around and gossip. I don't like people staying too long here. Do you hear me?' Hawaldar puts a piece of paper on the table. 'Settle up and leave. Quickly!'

'Can we meet tomorrow?' Jak asks.

The boy shakes his head. 'For what?'

'Just an hour. I won't bother you after that,' Jak pleads. 'But not here. Come to the hotel I am staying at. No one will hurry us there.'

The boy gulps his drink down and Jak counts out the notes.

The boy stands up. He wipes his hands on his jeans. 'Don't you want to know my name?'

'It's Shivu. I know,' Jak says.

'What time tomorrow?'

'Eleven thirty suit you? The bar opens by then.'

'Hey, hey,' the boy protests. 'I am not a drunk. I don't know why you said that.'

'I didn't mean it that way,' Jak placates. It's just that he thinks liquor will loosen Shivu's tongue.

You were there when it happened. Is that what it is, Shivu? You can't face the truth. That you could perhaps have stopped it somehow.

IV

There can be no stopping. Once the unravelling of the past begins, it will be beyond him. Jak knows this. He will not at some point be able to put his hands up and say, 'Stop. I have heard enough. I know enough!'

Does he have the stomach for this?

'We knew that these girls were sluts.' The boy wipes his mouth and then, aghast at his words, he reaches out to pluck Jak's sleeve. 'I am not saying that about her. She, Smriti, was different. She wasn't like the rest of those girls. The NRFs, we called them. The Non Resident Fucks.' Again the boy catches his breath. He sinks his head into his hands. 'What am I saying? I am sorry. I don't mean it like that. I don't know what I am saying!'

Jak looks away from the boy. Do I make this easy for him? Do I tell him, yes, yes, I know it is all those other girls you were referring to. It's not my daughter you meant. You wouldn't. A nice decent boy like you wouldn't make such allegations about nice decent girls. Especially my daughter.

But he doesn't offer a line to the floundering boy. Instead, he taps him on his shoulder and says, 'Go on. I am listening.'

The boy raises his head from his hands. Remorse is replaced by the inevitable need to unburden. To shed the weight of his soul that has driven him to obscure bars.

Shivu reaches for a glass. Booze steadies him. It calms him. It wraps him in a haze of forgiveness. You are not to be blamed. You did not know what you were doing.

'There is a kind of hangout place near the college. They play good music and it has a hubbly bubbly. Most of us go there after college. The girls come too. The day scholars, and sometimes the hostelites. But it was the foreign girls who came there as regularly as the boys did. They had money to spend. And I suppose it was like one of the places they would go to in their own countries. A place where you could hook up with someone. Everyone knew that. It was like a tradition.'

He searches Jak's face.

Jak meets his gaze steadily. He reads the purport of the boy's expression: What is this man thinking as I lay bare his daughter's life?

Jak wills himself to not show any emotion. Shall I tell him that we did the same? That university students all over the world have always felt the need to congregate and stimulate their already burgeoning hormones with coffee, beer, coke, whatever? That I know how plans are hatched, dares sprung and the camaraderie of one's peers makes one feel ready to take on the world.

Jak allows the boy a tight smile. 'I understand. So is that where you met Smriti?'

The boy shakes his head. 'That's where I first saw her. She came there with a group from their college. She walked in and we couldn't take our eyes off her.' The boy gestures.

Jak's eyes drop. The boy's meaning is quite obvious. Smriti's body piercing would make anyone flinch.

'Is this about Nina and me splitting up?' he asked, unable to believe the mutilation he saw. Was this creature with studs in just about every conceivable place his baby girl?

'Why does it have to have anything to do with you?' She tossed her head, her dreadlocks swinging back. He grimaced at the sight she made. She looked like one of those demented creatures you found wandering in temple hallways, claiming to be possessed by the goddess. With matted hair, glazed black-rimmed eyes and a set expression that would accept no truth but theirs.

Was that a stud in her tongue? He could see one in her navel too. Where else? Where else, Eashwara? In moments of stress, Jak found himself reverting to Kitcha, the Mylapore boy who called on his patron deity for rescue and succour.

'Oh, stop it, Papa Jak. Don't act so wet. This is my Goth look. It's what I want for now. Don't be like those Indian parents we know. C'mon, Papa Jak, do I ask you why you do what you do?' She perched on his knee just as if she was eight and not seventeen.

Jak knew what Nina or any of his relatives would say to that. Nina's mouth would narrow into a line of displeasure. 'For heaven's sake, Kitcha, she is not a child any more!'

The male relatives would turn their eyes away while the female relatives hissed, 'Shiva, Shiva, what's wrong with you? Don't you have any sense? As for the girl, has she no decorum, no modesty?'

But Jak had turned his back on Kitcha, the boy he was, and had become a product of the new world he inhabited. He could let his grown-up daughter sit on his knee, close his eyes to the thought of nipple rings and clit studs and pat her head affectionately and ask, 'Isn't it a nuisance? All these studs and rings? Don't they get in the way? Catch on your clothes, your hair?'

She jumped off his lap. 'You get used to it. Papa Jak, guess what? You should get your ear pierced too!'

Jak touched his ear lobe. 'My ear was pierced when I was a baby. But I guess it closed up. I might just do it again,' he said with a laugh.

'Cool!' Smriti grinned. Her Papa Jak would never fail her. And Jak felt as if he had triumphed again. He had tried telling Nina this. No point in getting the children's back up. You have to meet them halfway.

'We hadn't seen anyone like her. The studs in her eyebrows, the nose ring. The under lip stud and then the one in her tongue, her navel. It was like any place she could, she had it pierced,' Shivu speaks easily now. 'But we met for the first time at the Stree Shakti forum.'

Shivu and his theatre company had been invited to conduct a workshop by the forum. Rupa, the forum coordinator, had asked if they would pitch in. 'The least you can do after what you have put us through,' Rupa said, grinning.

Shivu knew what was coming. 'Which means we won't get paid, I presume.'

'You presume right.' Rupa shoved a sheaf of printouts into his hand.

'You mean there is actually a script!' Shivu widened his eyes dramatically. 'Not just polemic. So what is it this time? A Burnt Woman is not a Beautiful Woman?'

Rupa swatted his arm playfully. 'Don't mock us. Female abuse begins early, Shivu. This is serious. Female foeticide. We want to take this play to little towns. Stree Shakti is having representatives from its various nodal cells come here and if you train them to put up the play, they'll take it further. It's like what we did to spread awareness about the evils of dowry. There are fewer cases of bride burning now. And we need to take this up seriously.'

Smriti was roped in by some girls from her college to volunteer, and Shivu had wondered if it was a fad like the piercing. But she was a dedicated worker whose unbridled curiosity was matched by her tirelessness. In the following days, Shivu watched the girl with the strange look take on the work of ten people. When Rupa tried to tell her she was doing too much, Smriti wouldn't accept it. 'This is the least I can do,' she said vehemently. 'All those girl babies! Murdered even before they had a chance! It kills me to even think of it!'

Shivu felt his curiosity transform into admiration. And then something else. One day after rehearsal, he suggested coffee.

'Smriti agreed easily enough and we went to the coffee shop where I saw her first. I was curious about her. What was she doing here? In India? In Bangalore,' Shivu narrated, his voice striated with the sweetness of a time long ago when all their lives had brimmed with promise and hope.

Jak and Nina had been appalled when she turned down Brown and Columbia and announced her decision to move to India for her undergraduate degree. Nina, who was at Berkeley then, had been unable to hold back her anger. 'You are going to regret this! Kids from all over India, from even small towns want to come here, dream of studying here, and you want to go there! If you want to be a sociologist, then it is the US you should be in. India! You want to study in India! I don't believe this! Tell her, Kitcha, make her see sense.'

At first they had been united in their efforts to keep her there. What is all this nonsense about social welfare? We thought you wanted to do women's studies.

Smriti listened to them patiently. 'You are an academic,' she told Nina. 'You do not understand what women's studies ought to culminate in. I do. It has to translate into real life solutions. Do you know what is happening to women in India? You sit in your pretty little house with your labelled kitchen jars and a room full of books and think it is emancipation. Empowerment has to come from within.'

Mother and daughter argued for days while Jak watched

and listened. And, as always, he weakened. He fingered the diamond in his ear lobe – his mother's nose ring – and relented. 'Let her give it a shot! If she doesn't like it, she can always come back. Or she can always come to the States for her higher studies. Maybe it is time she got to know India. Discovered it for herself. She's going through a phase. Of wanting to save the world. Didn't we all? C'mon, Nina, it's not all that bad. Both you and I studied there, remember?'

Smriti, seeing signs of Jak succumbing and Nina flagging, had grabbed the ice cream scoop and crooned into it the lines she knew would elicit a smile from Jak. His very own Leonard Cohen advocating: '*Should the rumour of a shabby ending reach you, it was half my fault, it was half the atmosphere.*'

Nina shrugged. Your funeral, the movement of her shoulders implied. Your responsibility. Remember, you, Kitcha, are responsible, shabby ending or otherwise.

Should he have tried harder to make her stay back? Persuaded, cajoled, bribed, done what he could have to keep her with them. At least they would have all been in the same country, on the same continent. Instead of which, he had succumbed to Smriti's superior will. She was still a young girl, wild, impetuous and wilful, but he had failed to see that. Rather, he had closed his eyes to it. What kind of a father was he? The thought haunted him. That he had been irresponsible. But he couldn't see her unhappy. That was what it had always been about. Jak couldn't bear to see Smriti's eyes shadow.

'So that was how the two of you met.' Jak speaks quietly. 'And the others? The two other boys and Asha?'

'You keep saying Asha. There was no Asha. There was Nishi, Priya, Shabnam and Anu.'

'I must have got the name wrong,' Jak mumbles. 'Tell me about the other two boys. You knew them?'

The boy nods. The lightness that briefly settled on him flees again. 'Matt and Rishi. Mathew was from Kochi but he had chosen to come to Bangalore to do biotechnology like me. Mathew was my best friend. Rishi was a senior. He was from Coonoor. He had actually passed out by the time we met but he was very active in the theatre group we all belonged to. It was kind of inevitable that we became friends. We had so much in common, and in some ways we were also the outsiders. So we hung out together.'

Was. Liked. Hung out. Jak notices the use of the past and that Shivu's hands are trembling.

He pushes the glass towards Shivu. 'Drink,' he orders. 'Toss it down. What happened then? Tell me.'

But Shivu's hands will not stop trembling.

'At first, I thought she was attracted to me. I liked her. I liked her very much,' Shivu says. Suddenly he looks up. 'How can I tell you all this? You are her father. How can I talk to you about what we thought, said, did… It's awkward. Shit man, it's embarrassing.'

Jak doesn't speak for a while. 'Don't think of me as her father. Think of me as your friend,' he offers.

'You are not my friend,' the boy states baldly.

'Then think of me as someone you just met. A stranger in the bar. And that's the truth. You and I have no relationship. No tie. You can tell me anything, you know.' Jak listens to his own voice, amazed. How did he manage to bring that wheedling note into it?

The boy stares bleakly into his glass. 'All of us hoped to have a girlfriend. But Smriti was the girl one dreamt of. She was cute, smart, and she had none of the hang-ups that our girls did.'

Jak flinches. Our girls. My poor baby, did you even realize how your open ways would be misinterpreted? Jak isn't able to hold himself back. 'Meaning?'

'Meaning she thought nothing of holding your hand in public. Or greeting you with a hug. Or wrapping her hands around your middle when she rode pillion on the bike.'

'But don't girls here do all that?' Jak asks in an incredulous voice.

'Yeah, they do. But they don't strip down to a bikini when they go swimming, or sleep over at your place, etc. I am not saying Smriti was easy. She was cool. She was really cool. But she was uninhibited and if we got too physical with her, all she would do was push our hands away and say in that accented Tamil of hers, "Konnudu vein!"'

A nerve flutters at the corner of Jak's mouth. He often mock-threatened his girls: 'Konnudu vein if you play with the matches. Konnudu vein if you stay up late watching TV. Will murder you, little beasties!'

'You were saying you thought she liked you,' Jak says abruptly. Did he really want to hear this boy list in how many ways Smriti allowed the boys to treat her like they would a slut?

'Yeah! We met in the café a few times and soon I thought Smriti and I were a couple. I wanted to show her off. But mostly it was Mathew and Rishi I wanted to impress. So I introduced Smriti to them.'

And the inevitable happened, Jak presumes. He feels sorry for the boy. 'One of the others stole her away,' he says. 'Is that how it happened?'

The boy shakes his head. 'Yes and no!' A note of resignation has entered his telling.

Two weeks later Shivu felt a fist slam into his belly when Rupa called him with news of a sighting. Had they broken up, Smriti and he, she wanted to know. Mathew and Smriti looked very cosy together. 'What are you guys up to with that girl? Playing passing the parcel?'

Shivu wanted to go to Mathew's room and haul him out. Smash his face in and kick him in his belly. That was how angry he was. But he let it rest. What was he thinking of, he asked himself, appalled at the beast that he was turning into. Mathew was his friend and Smriti was his girl. How could he doubt them? Rupa was a jealous bitch out to make trouble. There was perhaps an innocent explanation.

Then came news of more sightings. A casual remark. A tossed aside. It occurred to Shivu that the world had nothing to do but keep an eye on Mathew and Smriti.

Shivu didn't know if it was jealousy that rankled. Or his pride that was hurt – the thought of people seeing them together left a sour taste in his mouth. They are going to think I am a wimp if I let it go on, Shivu told himself the day he decided to confront them. He was afraid, though. He feared his nebulous hold over Smriti and he knew he would lose her if he brought up the gossip.

Mathew was different. Mathew was from here. He ought to know better, Shivu told himself as he pushed open Mathew's door. They used to share a room once. Not any more. Shivu felt his eyes search the room and his glance pounced on a scarf he recognized as hers.

'Isn't this Smriti's?' he demanded.

Mathew shrugged. Shivu didn't know what to say. The shrug was a gauntlet. All's fair in love and war.

In desperation, Shivu turned on Smriti.

Smriti was furious. 'You are not my boyfriend. You are my friend. Why do you have to be like all the Indian boys I meet? Can't we just be friends? You, Mathew, Rishi and I. I've been out with Rishi too. So what?'

Shivu poked a straw into his glass. The ice cubes at the bottom rattled. He felt like a fool. He had probably read too much into what Smriti and he shared. On the heels of that came a sense of disquiet. Mathew was not going to like the idea of Rishi and Smriti going out together.

'You better tell Mathew that you've been out with Rishi,' Shivu told her. 'Mathew is very possessive. He doesn't like sharing what is his.'

'I am not his or anyone else's,' she said, dismissing him and his sense of unease.

'Mathew was a jealous sort, was he?' Jak probes.

'Mathew was one of the most generous people I knew. But he was possessive about the people he loved. At first when Rishi and I became friends, he couldn't bear the thought that I had another close friend. He saw Rishi as an intruder. Eventually, when he saw that nothing had changed between us, he eased up. But I knew he would be furious when he found out about Smriti and Rishi.'

Jak rests his head on his arm. Could Smriti really have been as clueless as she seemed to be? Didn't she realize she was toying with these boys? Or did she enjoy the power it gave her? Children of divorced parents are supposed to be needy.

Did she need the security of knowing these three young men were smitten by her?

Jak stands up and stretches. Where is this story leading?

As long as Smriti's last days are veiled in mystery, Jak is going to put his own life on hold. It isn't that he wants to. But his mind will not obey. His mail box had spewed fifty-six messages that morning. He let his eyes slide over them without a flicker of interest. Some had to do with the book he was researching. One was from the journal he was supposed to submit a paper to. Two invitations to a weather conference, two more to lecture in Waikiki and Brisbane. All of them necessitated his attention and action.

In the end Jak decides on one thing. He will hire someone to deal with all of this, till such time as he manages to shrug his apathy off. He will write to Sheela. She will be able to find him a research assistant.

Outside, the afternoon has settled into dusk. How long must I court this boy? Am I Scheherazade or am I the Caliph? Was there any real difference between them anyway? They were both putting off the inevitable.

So that neither of them would have to decide what to do next.

V

What comes next in Meera's life is a mail from Sheela. Meera is surprised. The PR woman and she barely know each other. Randhir dealt with her directly when he hired her for all the promotional work for Meera's books. Meera had to just sit through the interviews and photo shoots of her home while Sheela bustled in the background, making countless calls and mapping appointments on her Blackberry. All Meera had to do was reinforce the image of the corporate wife with a single tiger lily in a tall vase and plumped up silk cushions, and offer tea from a tray. Sheela was pleased at how well it all went and so Meera became part of her list.

There haven't been as many invitations to PR events of late. Perhaps Sheela has heard of her fall from grace. But here she is, inviting her to a flower arrangement book launch and – 'by the way, would you know of someone who could be a research assistant? A friend of mine, a college professor here on a sabbatical from the US, needs one. He's quite desperate and will pay well and it will be flexi hours. This is his email id.'

Meera ignores the invitation and dashes a mail off right away with her telephone number. The subtitling editor's job has been offered to her. She is to start next week. But what if this is a better option, she tells herself. What if it is something that she would feel less undignified about doing?

On the phone his voice is deep and gravelly. An elderly voice thickened with age and much smoking, she presumes.

'Hello, may I speak with Meera Giridhar?' it asks, a polite, carefully modulated voice.

Meera says, 'Yes, this is Meera.'

'Hello, Meera, how are you? This is Professor Krishnamurthy speaking. I received your mail this morning and thought that I would like to chat a bit.' The voice pauses. 'Get to know if you would be interested in working for me.

'I like your qualifications and the fact that you live in this part of Bangalore helps. We can work the hours around to suit us both without worrying too much about commuting time. But we need to meet so we know we are compatible. Very essential for people who have to work closely,' he adds.

And so a date and time is fixed.

Later that evening Meera discusses it over dinner.

'Do you really have to do this?' Lily asks, spooning her soup noisily.

'Mama, please,' Saro interrupts. 'Meera knows what she is doing.'

Meera throws her mother a grateful look. This is a mother she no longer recognizes. The imperiousness has been replaced by protectiveness. When the children or Lily are difficult, it is Saro who rushes to rescue Meera.

'But it's a secretary's job! How could you?' Lily demands.

'What's wrong with that?' Saro retorts. 'Besides, she is going to work for an academic. Professor Krishnamurthy. Meera says he has traces of an American accent. Meera, you must have him over for a drink sometime. Let him meet your family and see for himself that you are from a privileged background and it is just special circumstances…'

'Mummy, stop.' It is Meera's turn to halt the conversation. 'I don't have the job yet. Besides, he sounds like a very elderly man lost in his books. Not the kind who would care who or what I am as long as I function effectively.'

'How old do you think he is?' Lily asks suddenly.

Meera shakes her head. 'I don't know. Maybe your age. Maybe Mummy's age. I really can't tell.'

'Maybe he is your age,' Nikhil says suddenly.

Meera frowns. 'Highly unlikely, but we'll see!'

'What will you have to do?' Nikhil rolls his egg into his chapatti.

'I am not sure yet. Research whatever he wants me to. Type letters, etc., I presume.' Meera watches Nikhil eat with a frown. 'Won't you have some of the salad?'

Nikhil picks up a lone stick of carrot as if it were a dead cockroach.

'What will you wear, Meera?' Lily looks up.

'A sari,' Meera says. Her mother nods in approval.

'A smart cotton sari, and you can have my pearls. Look elegant always, that's half the battle won!'

Nikhil drinks up his milk, mumbling, 'Why don't you wear cargo pants and boots if it's a battle?' He grins at their horrified expressions and says, 'Why can't you dress like you always do?'

The three women turn on him in unison: 'You don't understand these things!'

Then she sees him. Striding towards her with a long-legged gait. Meera feels her heart sink. She knows the man. He is the one who dropped her and Nikhil home that afternoon. And now he would recognize her, too, and would want to know about her runaway husband. Meera swallows.

He comes to stand before her and in his eyes is a flare of recognition. 'Meera?' he asks. 'Meera, right?'

'Hello.' She smiles. Meera looks past him towards the door. She can't remember his name or anything about him. Right now, she wishes he would just leave.

'What a surprise. How are you, Meera?' He continues to stand there after they have finished exchanging pleasantries.

'So…' he says. 'Are you meeting someone too? I am here to interview a lady for a position as my research assistant. Tell you what, Meera. If you have a moment to spare, why don't you join us? I would like an opinion. I haven't done anything like this before, in India.'

And Meera suddenly realizes that he is the elderly gent, the Professor Krishnamurthy she is waiting for.

'Professor Krishnamurthy, I think I am the one you are here to interview,' she says quietly.

He straightens abruptly. 'Oh! Meera Giridhar. Very silly of me not to have recognized your name. So, shall I sit down?' he says, pulling out a chair.

'This is a surprise but I am glad it's you, Meera. Really glad. But what about your cookbook writing? That can't be easy. I know it's very hard work. And to take this up… Will you have the time?'

Meera stretches her lips in a parody of a smile. 'I am actually between books.'

'Great!' he murmurs, leaning back.

I must say this for him. The man is circumspect, Meera tells herself. He hasn't asked me about Giri yet. Most people would have.

VI

Most people would wonder at this man who sits before her. Lily and Saro wouldn't approve; the children would. And Giri? He would dismiss him as a no-good poseur. But Giri isn't here. So she will watch and wait.

Meera studies him carefully as he talks into the phone. She rather likes what she sees. He is not Giri with his carefully brushed hair, Mont Blanc pen in his breast pocket and gleaming brogues; the Rolex Oyster and pin stripes for workdays and studied casuals for weekends. Giri was always living up to an image of himself and he wanted her to do the same. It is a relief that he is nothing like Giri, this big man with his firm stubbled jaw and twinkling eyes behind narrow spectacle frames in a bright shade of blue. She sees the bracelets on his forearm, the gold amulet strung around his neck on a leather thong and the diamond ear stud.

She can't see him in a suit, hemmed behind a table laden with corporate-alia. Nor can she see him in a classroom. What does he do, this Professor Krishnamurthy?

She teases the image of him this way and that. A smile escapes her.

She feels his eyes on her as she pretends to toy with the mutton cutlet he insisted on ordering, saying, 'Sheela recommended it highly and I want to try it now that we are here.'

Meera smiles and says, 'She is right. It is rather delicious.'

She is hungry and has to control herself from eating it all up in one gulp. And then a little thought on mice feet scuttles through her mind. What does he see when he scrutinizes her?

What do I see when I look at myself? Meera peers at the face in the glass pane. She has always seen herself with other people's eyes. Lily's serious granddaughter. Saro's fussy daughter. Giri's elegant wife. Nikhil and Nayantara's dependable mother.

What does he see? A silly cookbook writer. A pathetic, abandoned wife. A desperate, no skills employee.

She looks around Koshy's. She sees a woman she recognizes and smiles at her. The woman throws a languid wave at her. She must be wondering about Professor Krishnamurthy, Meera tells herself, matching indolence with a careless toss of her wrist as acknowledgement of the wave. 'Hi. Hi. Now get the fuck out of my face!' Meera grimaces.

He snaps shut the phone and says softly, 'It doesn't matter if you haven't done this kind of thing before. You will learn as you go along. All I ask is that you keep an open mind and make a sincere effort. The rest will follow naturally. I really would be very happy if you could take it up.'

Meera's eyes widen. No small talk. No checking up on qualifications or credentials. Is he always as impetuous as this? Her eyes widen some more when he mentions the terms.

The wolves will stop baying at her door. For three months at least. That is the trial period he mentions.

Meera wonders at the state of the car. How can anyone have such a messy car? He drives well and expertly. Giri is a good driver, too, but he prefers to sit in the back and have the driver deal with the traffic, the bad roads, the beggar children and eunuchs at the intersection, while he reads the *Economic Times*. He doesn't want to be bothered. Professor Krishnamurthy, it occurs to her, can't be bothered either. But in a different way. Perhaps I ought to first clean his car for him, she tells herself and then catches the thought in time. What am I thinking? I am his research assistant, not his wife.

'I thought I'd show you where my house is before I drive you home. It's not too far from yours. Just a couple of streets away,' he says, turning into Wheeler Road at Thom's Café junction.

The breeze blows Meera's hair into her face. 'Have you always lived in Bangalore?' she asks, filling yet another silence between them.

'Grew up in Madras. Then the US. I've been in Bangalore

for about eight months now. I am still finding my way around.'

'So how come you chose Bangalore? Are you in the IT industry? This is ridiculous, I know Professor, but I haven't even asked you what I am to help research.'

He smiles. 'I know. We both seem to be novices at this. And no, I have nothing to do with the IT world. I am a weather expert; a cyclone specialist, to be specific. I am working on a book on cyclones. There is a lot of data to wade through, a lot of information to source and collate, and I need help. Which is where you come in.

'As for Bangalore, my wife made me buy this house some years ago. And my daughter chose to go to college here. So when I needed to be in India, it seemed perfect!'

Wife. There is a woman in the house. Meera is nervous. A little. He seems eminently respectable but there is no telling. A wife makes everything so much easier.

'Ex-wife, I should say. We have been divorced for a while now.'

Meera's heart sinks. Oh no! What is she getting into?

'But it is a full household! You will see! I have had to carve out a work space for myself…' His voice trails away and Meera wonders at the composite of bitterness and sorrow that underlines his voice.

It is a nondescript house on Graham Road. Rectangular and low, it echoes the aspirations of a time when people weary of worrying about rafters and tiles switched to concrete roofs. A flat roof where you could lay things out to dry and even string a clothesline if necessary. There is a circular driveway from the gate and the porch stands at its apex. To the left of the house, away from the building, is the garage, abutting the corner. A late sixties' style, low bungalow shorn of the steep gables and monkey tops of her own house. Less pretty, but so much easier to keep clean. Meera thinks with a shudder of her monthly foray with a long-handled cobweb duster.

'Nina wanted an old bungalow. One of those real Bangalore houses. But I thought it would be too much trouble. I am glad that we chose this house. It's not pretty but it's functional,' he says, stopping the car in the porch.

Meera says nothing. Does he read minds? She looks at him sidelong.

She runs a quick eye over the garden. A giant old avocado tree stands to a side, casting dense green shadow and spangles of light onto the side of the house. Bougainvillea trail over the porch roof, the gnarled old stem climbing the porch pillars. At the farther corner is a patch of wilderness. Heliconia droop flowers amidst a pool of ferns. A stunted frangipani stands in the middle of what was once a lawn. The crazy paving is broken in parts but here and there where the sun thrusts its way in, geraniums flourish. Pink, red and white blossoms standing tall and healthy.

Someone is making an effort, or wanting to. A row of terracotta pots wait beneath the avocado tree, and a small cluster of plants in plastic bags.

'I hope to do some work on the garden when I can.' He shrugs.

Again. He is doing it again, Meera thinks. Is he one of those people with a sixth sense or whatever?

Meera gathers her sari pallu around her.

The house is quiet. Meera hesitates at the door. She watches him slide his key in. Didn't he say there were other people in the house? What is she thinking of? Walking into the house of a strange man.

He opens the door and steps in. 'Kala Chithi,' he calls softly.

Meera exhales. There are other people here. Why didn't he ring the bell then?

An elderly lady in a grey sari emerges from an inner room. Meera tries not to stare at the woman's head, the grey stubble that is the grey of her sari.

'This is my aunt,' he says softly. 'This is Meera,' he says, turning to the elderly lady. 'She's going to work for me.' He speaks in Tamil.

The elderly lady folds her hands in a namaste. Meera does the same. Then she says in her best Tamil, 'I live just two streets away. On Bailey Road, next to D'Costa Square.'

He raises an eyebrow at her. 'Tamil, too! So no secrets in this house, I see!'

Meera smiles. 'I grew up in Ooty,' she offers in explanation.

'Sit down, I'll bring some coffee,' the elderly lady says.

'Is it just the two of you who live here?' Meera asks. The room is tidy but spartan, the newspaper neatly arranged on a glass coffee table, cushions stacked on the cane sofas. The TV in its corner. Coasters on side tables.

He looks away. 'No, my daughter is here too. That's why I chose to live in Bangalore. Because of my daughter.' He pauses and begins again, 'I met your son. Is he your only child?'

Meera smiles. 'No, I have a daughter. Nayantara. She is nineteen and is at IIT Chennai.'

'Must be a brilliant girl! You must be proud of her.'

Meera feels a queer sadness wash over her. I must be proud of my daughter, you say. I am. Nayantara. The star of my eye.

But I have also been wounded by her. That is the thing about daughters, you see. Their mothers have to bear the brunt of it all.

Tell me, how old is your daughter? Like mine, did she choose you rather than her mother when it came to aligning herself? Where is this girl child of yours who has appointed herself your confidante, ally and daddy's best friend?

'Smriti. She is nineteen, too.' He rises abruptly. 'Come, we might as well get this over with,' he says, breaking into her thoughts.

And so Meera sees Smriti.

Meera stands at the door trying to assimilate all that lies before her in the room. From the window, a filtered green light of sun trapped through leaves. In the dark corners, an underwater green cast by the constantly moving image of the sea. On the wall opposite the bed, a projector beams a continuous roll of waves. Speakers echo their rise and flop; the sound of water again and again.

A few shelves hold books. The rest of the room is crammed with dolls of every material, organic and man-made; precious and ordinary.

But it is the girl on the bed who causes Meera to grip her bag even more tightly. Her eyes crinkle. Is that a girl? She hasn't seen anything like this creature. Not even in her disaster documentaries. A wave of revulsion washes over her.

It lies poleaxed. Legs separate and hands flung wide apart. Swathed in a blouse and pyjamas of fine cotton, its hair razed to a stubble. Thin as paper and almost as pale, the skin stretched across the bones, causing the cheeks to hollow inwards. The eyes wide open, cast of glass. The mouth askew. A face stricken in a permanent leer. Something about the hardness of the stare and the grim mouth gives it an evil cunning.

I am watching you.

Meera knows fear. What monstrous creature is this?

'Meera, this is my daughter, Smriti. Nineteen, that's how old she is. And condemned for life to be this monster who causes you to flinch each time you look at her,' Jak says.

Meera is ashamed. She raises her eyes and meets his gaze.

'Nina and I couldn't at first forget home. We lived in the States. Our bodies did, that is. But our minds sought the India we had left behind. That was what brought us together. Bound us. And so, when she was born, we decided to name her Smriti. What was remembered. Now that is all there is to her.'

He is slowly unclenching its fists. 'In a little while, her fingers will curl inwards again. We do this every hour so that she doesn't lose the mobility of her fingers.'

One by one he straightens each finger, smoothening the stiffness out, rubbing gently. He squeezes hand lotion from a tube and rubs it in. Meera swallows, the leap of saliva in her throat absurdly loud.

She doesn't speak. She doesn't know how to respond. With comfort or curiosity.

Meera walks home. 'It's just a few minutes away,' she says, closing the door behind her. As she turns the corner, she can't stop the question in her head. How does he bear it? How can he see her like this and be sane?

'What happened?' she had asked. 'How did she...?' Her words trailed off.

He put down the hand lotion and wiped his fingers. 'I don't know. There are so many versions. The doctor's version. The police version. All I know is, she went on a trip with some friends of hers. And there was a freak accident, so they say.'

Meera let her fingers slide towards the creature's. As she slowly straightened the curling fingers, it felt strangely as it used to when she slid her fingers into Nayantara's when she was a baby. They were warm, fragile, and bereft of a will of their own.

'Nayantara,' Meera says urgently into the phone.

'Hi Mom,' a tinny voice trills in her ear. 'How did the interview go?'

'It was fine. I got the job,' Meera says. 'His name is Professor Krishnamurthy.'

Meera rambles. Anything to keep Nayantara on the other end. Anything for a few moments of reprieve. Of knowing that as long as her child is talking to her, she is safe.

'Mom, I have to go,' Nayantara breaks in.

'Yes, yes. Nayantara, baby, you will be careful, won't you?'

'Careful of what?' She laughs.

'Oh, just careful!' Meera tries to interject a note of lightness into her voice.

'Sure.'

Meera holds the phone to her mouth and beseeches into its silence: Be careful, my child. Please be careful.

VII

Be careful. You need to handle this one differently, Jak tells himself.

He wishes Meera were here. She would know how to make this seem natural. Careful, he cautions himself as he lets his eyes wander around the room. Be very careful here. This one will not be as forthcoming as Shivu.

Jak's eyes linger on the altar on the eastern wall. On the wooden crucifix and the candles. Would he be able to prevail upon the boy's religion to make him speak the truth? Bile coats his mouth. Who is this creature he is turning into? Is nothing above or below him in this pursuit to recreate Smriti's last conscious hours?

Sometimes Jak cannot recognize himself. The lost boy he sees in Kala Chithi's eyes. The wayward academic reflected in Meera's puzzled glance. The stillness of the helpless father in Smriti's pupils. We are what we are seen as. Or, are we?

When you walked into Koshy's, you spotted Meera immediately, in a deep cream sari with intricate black designs on it and around her neck a single strand of pearls. An isle of perfect calm in the sea of people and tables. You knew a sense of inevitability. You stood there looking at her. It was a Hopperesque moment she captured. The Chop Suey one. Hopper's painting of the woman in a restaurant.

What was she doing here, you asked yourself curiously as you gathered in the mettle of the rest of the world seated there.

They had barely spoken during that first car ride but you caught yourself thinking of her every now and then that first week. What had happened, you wondered. Had the husband come home? Had they settled their differences? You couldn't understand it yourself, this preoccupation, except perhaps that you could see in her tightly reined grief and helplessness a reflection of your own anguish. Something about her manner, the intense imploring cast of her features as she sat in your car that first time, resolutely not searching the roads, filled you with admiration. You approved of women who didn't give way to the weight of their disappointments. Women who held themselves together.

But in the din of Koshy's, she seemed lost. You didn't know why you asked her to help you interview the person you were meeting, except that you wanted to prolong the moment. When she said she was the one, something leapt in you. A blue flame of hope. The husband was still absent, you deduced. Not that husbands were ever a consideration once you set your heart on a woman.

Later, in your home, you watched her face when you took her to see Smriti. You waited for revulsion and instead saw sadness.

She had watched you straighten Smriti's fingers.

'There is a day nurse and a night nurse. And there are stand-bys if one can't come in. There is Kala Chithi who talks to her, sings to her, sits with her, and there is me… We do what we can, Meera. We have to. How can I give up on her and let Nina take her and tuck her away in some hospice there? It would be like burying her alive, don't you see?' But you didn't say any of this aloud. You didn't want to embarrass or frighten her with a flagrant display of emotion.

Then she took Smriti's hand in hers. It reassured you. She had a daughter. She would understand how you felt.

In two weeks' time Meera became a part of your everyday. Without her to organize your day, you felt rudderless. You had wondered if you should ask her to accompany you to Cochin. But you weren't sure that she would go with you. Perhaps one day when the two of you knew each other better, when she trusted you…

A middle-aged man walks into the room. Grey splattered hair and a paunch that causes his T-shirt to stretch. His mundu, crisp and cream, flicks with every step. Jak's heart sinks. The man must be only as old as I am but his aura of respectability will not allow me to even bring up the subject. He will first be outraged and then deny it flatly. 'You must be mistaken. My son Mathew! He is a very studious boy. And a member of the church choir. I think you have the wrong boy.'

Careful, careful, Jak tells himself and prepares to lie.

Mathew's father smiles at him. He goes to an ornately carved roll top desk and extricates a box of cards. He offers a card to Jak.

'Joseph John. Pleased to meet you.'

Jak fumbles in his pocket for his card sleeve. He dredges a card out and proffers it to the man with a terse, 'I am Professor Krishnamurthy. I am the Head of Department of Biotechnology at the University of Florida.' Jak lathers his words with his most pronounced American accent, determined to make an impression and buy the man's complicity. If Mathew were majoring in medicine, Jak tells himself, he would have introduced himself as the Dean of Paediatrics at Florida Med School. It was Mathew who had hoisted the 'all is fair in love and war' flag.

'Your son is a bright young boy. I have been corresponding with him on email. As I was here, I decided to surprise him.'

The man beams. 'That is wonderful. Mathew has gone to church. He should be back soon. Please do sit down. Would you like coffee or tea?'

Jak settles into the chair and waits. For a man whose very soul is restlessness, the extent of his newfound patience amazes him. Such vast reserves of calm, where has it lain hidden all this while?

So with his newfound patience Jak absently thumbs a magazine, drinks a cup of coffee, eats his way through a plate of banana chips and waits.

Shivu has revealed what he can. It is Mathew's turn to take the story forward. But will he?

'Has he always been a very religious boy?' Jak asks.

Mathew's father frowns. The famous Joseph John frown that the rest of the family knows so well. Don't be an ass, it says. 'We are a very god-fearing family. A Christian family. All of us go to church. My uncle is a bishop, in fact!'

Jak sits squashed and subdued. After a moment, he smiles and wheedles further, 'I am so pleased to hear Mathew is such a spiritual boy. The new generation could do with boys like him. You are a fortunate man.'

Joseph John preens. Which father wouldn't, Jak thinks sadly. We want it all for our children. Health and happiness, the best of grades and the largesse of at least one of the muses. We want our children to be admired even more than loved. We want to see in our children the fulfilment of our dreams, the expansion of our lives.

VIII

'Our lives are not ours. God decides the dictum of our lives. "Many false prophets shall rise, and shall deceive many." The Bible says this. For a while, I was deceived. That was the beginning of my sorrows. Because iniquity shall abound. All of this too is in the Bible, Shivu. But I have seen the sign of the Son of Man in heaven, I have heard his angels trumpet.'

Jak reads once again the letter Mathew had sent Shivu. He folds it and puts it back into his pocket where it lies alongside the printout that he carries with him everywhere. Three boys and a girl. The sides of a square and the trapped past within.

He looks at Mathew's face. Brother Benny Hill, you have seen the sign and heard the angels, but will you speak the truth now?

Mathew starts when he walks into his home and discovers Jak ensconced in an armchair, nibbling on banana chips and discoursing on the merits of the American education system.

'Look who's here.' Joseph John beams. 'You didn't think Professor Jak would come here, did you? Come, come, join us.' Joseph John thinks of his family in Fort Worth and Long Island. And of a possible move there if Mathew made America his home.

'It's just like being here; you get everything you need, except it's a lot cleaner and more efficient,' a visiting cousin had said, showing off photographs of his house, roses, dog and car. 'Here, take a look! You should think very seriously about sending Mathew there for higher studies.' And so the seed of imminent migration was sown.

Mathew looks wildly around. Jak sees the widened eyes and flaring nostrils, then Mathew's features slowly twist into a grimace of a smile. Fear fights with acceptance of the inevitable. The grimace contorts into resignation. The Que Sera Sera look. Mathew probably knows the song from his father, Jak tells himself wryly. Joseph John seems to be the kind of man who would have an impressive collection of Jim Reeves, Kenny Rogers and music from the fifties.

'How was church?' Jak asks. He sounds foolish to his own ears. But seeing the flare of panic in Mathew's eyes, he sees how the innocuous question is striated with sinister serpentine turns: it doesn't escape me, my boy, why you need to go to church!

Mathew is quiet.

'Was the choir practice better today?' Joseph John tries to aid his suddenly tongue-tied child. What is wrong with him? Here is this man, all the way from America, seeking his son out to possibly passage his way into his hallowed institution and the boy is behaving like the village idiot. Alternating between moronic grins and silly grimaces and not speaking a word.

'Well, I'll leave you to it! No doubt you have much to say to each other.' Joseph John rises and as he leaves, gestures for Mathew to follow him.

'I'll be back in a moment.' Mathew's voice finally emerges, low and tremulous.

In the corridor, Joseph John frowns at Mathew. 'What's wrong with you? Instead of making an impression on him, you are behaving like a frightened bridegroom! Go on, talk to him. When he goes back, I want him to consider you as a serious candidate for his course.'

'Chachan, you don't know who he is,' Mathew begins.

His father holds up his hand. 'I know. I know that your future lies in his hands. So go and be as he expects you to be!'

Mathew huddles in a chair. Jak waits for him to speak.

'Let us go for a walk,' Jak says to the hunched boy, feeling a wave of pity for him. 'I think you would prefer that. What do you say?'

They sit in silence by the sea wall. Gulls circle a crop of rock in the distance. The skies are slowly changing colour and Jak feels calm beach itself in him. The sea always does that for him. It is true, he thinks, that tattered cliché about time being a healer. My daughter lies there in her tomb of silence. And I can sit here and gaze at the horizon with what seems to be pleasure. Should I feel guilty? Or should I think that this is wisdom, this acceptance of circumstances. Jak cuts the end of his cigar and puts it into his mouth. He lights it, turning it slowly. In his most reasonable voice he inquires, 'Why didn't you come to see Smriti even once?'

The boy stares into the distance. He doesn't reply.

His new-won calm dissipates. 'Answer me.' Jak grips the boy's arm.

'How could I?' The boy shakes Jak's hand off angrily. 'How could I? Would you have been able to? I can't even ask her for her forgiveness. Do you know what I am going through? Do you know what it is to be tormented by guilt every moment? Knowing I am responsible…'

Jak is surprised. He didn't think Mathew would admit to any responsibility. Not so easily and quickly.

'Shivu must have told you,' Mathew begins.

Jak nods. 'Some of it,' he says, lighting his cigar again. The sea air gathers the sweetness of the cigar smoke with a casual ease. 'Shivu told me that you and Smriti were… that you were in love with her.'

'I was a fool,' the boy says bitterly. 'I was a small-town boy who was overwhelmed by her. By her American ways.'

Mathew thought he couldn't remember a time when he didn't feel like this. All churned up by love, anger, tenderness, resentment, jealousy, clowns cartwheeling and tumbling in the sawdust that was his heart. He found himself writing her name on pieces of paper. Smriti. Smriti. Smriti. Smriti. Smriti. Pages and pages of it as if by committing it to paper, she would be his forever. She lived in his inner eyelid; each time he shut his eyes, she was there, her head thrown back in laughter, the curve of her throat, all his, all his. She perched on every breeze, the fragrance she wore rode up his nostrils so that it came to him again and again. His ears quickened; her footsteps were hers alone. His skin warmed in memory of her skin against his… Smriti. Smriti. Smriti. Smriti. Mathew leaned back against his bike and glanced at his watch again. She was late. She had no concept of time and if he pointed out to her that she was late, she would crinkle her nose and demand, 'How does it matter?'

He would wait another five minutes and leave. She could call him when she got here and if he was free, he would come by. He started playing a game on his mobile. His fingers itched to text: Where are you? But he was already too much of a soppy fool around her.

When Shivu had introduced her to him, he felt a bolt of lightning shoot through him. It really had been that thing: love at first sight. All he could think was, Shivu is my best friend but I can't let it stop me. I love her. I love her like Shivu would never even know how to. I am the one who deserves her. Not Shivu, even if he's my best friend.

He had to employ all his cunning to find out where he could meet her alone. A space to wedge himself in and snare her. Steal her from Shivu, his conscience reminded him, but Mathew wasn't listening. All is fair in love and war, he told himself.

He glanced at his watch. Two more minutes. He wished Shivu was here. He missed Shivu. But there had been an ugly scene at the hostel a week ago. Shivu had found out that Mathew had taken Smriti to Wayanad. 'It's not on,' Shivu had said, white lipped. 'I know Smriti wanted to see wild elephants and I know your dad could arrange it because of his connections but Mathew, she's my girlfriend. You can't go off with her like that. If it wasn't you, I'd think you were hitting on her.'

When Mathew didn't defend himself, Shivu stared at him in shock. 'You are, aren't you? You are trying to take her away from me. But Mathew, you are my friend.'

Mathew turned his head away and said, 'All is fair in love and war. Smriti isn't in love with you. Why else would she go out with me?'

Shivu turned on his heel and walked out. He hadn't seen him since.

Mathew kick-started his bike. He would go to the coffee shop. In its bright interiors and with the music playing, he wouldn't feel so torn and twisted.

As he walked into the coffee shop, he saw Smriti. She was sitting with someone. Shivu, he thought. That fucker, he's trying to snatch her back from me. The *pilayadi mon*!

Mathew strode towards them angrily, his fingers already

clenching into fists and then he stopped abruptly. Smriti, he saw, was sitting shoulder to shoulder, thigh to thigh with Rishi. And that bastard was using the oldest trick in the world to hold a girl's hand. He was pretending to read her palm.

As for Smriti, she sat there resting her chin on her other palm, her eyes half closed, rapt in attention – or was it something else? How could she? Didn't it bother her that someone would see her like this with Rishi? Mathew could see her frown and demand in her most acid tone: 'Like what with Rishi? He was just holding my palm, I wasn't giving him a blow job! What's wrong with you, Mathew?'

Mathew heard another voice in his head. Joseph John's, when he had Mathew admitted to the Deccan College for Biotechnology. 'I am paying a lot of money just for the admission. I hope you understand that! And the course isn't cheap either. I want you to work hard and get very high grades. Do you hear me?'

Mathew had nodded, eager to flee his father's censure and ambitions for him.

'One other thing,' Joseph John said, leaning forward. Mathew looked up from his plate. His mother, he noticed, kept her eyes on her plate, afraid to meet his gaze. 'You are going away from home and neither your mother nor I will be there to watch over you. The devil takes many forms. You have to watch out for yourself. The devil will charm you and entice you. The devil will make you its own with the face of an angel. Do you understand what I am saying?'

Mathew nodded again. Decode to 'Don't get involved with girls!'

But perhaps Chachan had been right after all. Mathew felt bile fill his mouth. The devil smiled and had the face of an angel. The devil played with you, shredding your soul, your mind. The devil called itself Smriti.

Mathew bellowed.

'Who was it who dragged me away? I can't remember. It must have been Shivu. When the red cloud in my head lifted, I found him there.'

Jak can't speak. Something akin to revulsion fills him. Who is this girl these boys knew? It couldn't be Smriti. Not his Smriti, who knows neither guile nor deception.

'Did you speak to Smriti?' Jak asks.

'She said I was silly to think that she was seeing Rishi. For that matter, she wasn't seeing anyone – neither Shivu, Rishi, nor me.'

'And then?'

'I didn't believe her. I didn't want to. How could she not love me? I loved her that much, you see. Shivu insisted that she was just friends with all of us. That he had made the same mistake, reading too much into their relationship. "That's how these girls are, don't take it too seriously!"

'But I couldn't let it go. I pretended to let it all settle down. We were all friends once again. Shivu, Smriti and I. But I don't think any of us trusted the others. Only Smriti, poor Smriti, trusted us. She was so happy to have all of us back together again.

'"My family," she said. "You are my family. Do you understand?"'

Jak closes his eyes. It tears into him, the stab of guilt and sorrow.

'Your appa wasn't happy,' Amma had said one evening. It was a few months after Appa left.

Kitcha stared at his mother. Why was she suddenly talking about Appa? Then he saw her eyes linger on the calendar and he realized it was his father's birthday.

His mother had been in a strange mood all day. Humming under her breath as she bustled about her chores in the morning. In the evening, he had come home from school to discover that she had cooked a feast of 'tindi'. Who was she expecting for tea that evening, he had wondered, surveying the chakkara pongal and bonda, aval uppuma and kuzhipaniyaram.

She had looked up each time an autorickshaw turned into their alley, her eyes on the door, waiting for the appointed knock. Kitcha felt a wave of pity engulf him.

In what desperation had she cast portents for the day? It would be the day he would come home. Her husband would walk in and discover how he lived there even if he didn't any more. So she hummed his favourite kirtanams, dressed in his favourite colour of M.S. blue, cooked his favourite tiffin and beguiled herself into expecting his return.

Kitcha looked away. He had always known it. Appa's dissatisfaction with everything around him – his home, his wife, his son. And with it the acrid stench of regret. Of wrong choices made. Of the meandering of the life force. Kitcha hadn't wanted to see it. If he didn't, it would go away, he thought. Like those horrific nightmares he used to have every night for a while. Amma had taught him a mantra to chant at night. 'Repeat it two times before you go to sleep and you won't have those bad dreams any more. Wish them away from the bottom of your heart!'

But Appa's sorrow hadn't gone. Instead, he had.

'I clung to him. I shouldn't have. When people stop loving each other, they shouldn't stay together. It doesn't do any good,'

Amma continued. 'I should have understood his unhappiness. I should have let him go when he first wanted to.'

'When?' Kitcha whispered.

'A year after you were born. But how could I? The child needs a father, I pleaded. I need my husband, I wanted to say but didn't. Your father wouldn't have let that hold him back. But you… I bought time with you. And I did everything I could to please him, but it only seemed to make him resent me more.'

Kitcha stood up. He didn't want to hear any more. The sordid unravelling of a marriage, the fragmenting of lives. He was fifteen, but he felt like an old man. 'You should have let him go. I wouldn't ever have known him then.'

A silence. Much later, as they prepared for bed, Amma asked him, 'Would you like to visit Kala at Minjikapuram? I have to go away for a few days. And I would go with an easy heart if I knew you were with Kala.'

Kitcha nodded. His mother had taken to visiting one temple after the other. It wasn't peace she sought, he knew. Her eyes searched temple corridors and bathing ghats. Perhaps one day she would find her husband seated under a tree, fatigued and careworn, and easily susceptible to her blandishments to go home with her. This was the prayer she carried in her heart and on her lips as she went on her pilgrimage of desperation.

It was this that Kitcha who had become Jak remembered when he looked up from his drink one evening and asked Nina who sat with a sheaf of papers, mutinous in her silence, 'Would you like a divorce, Nina?'

More and more, it seemed Nina and he had nothing to say to each other. This was a Nina he no longer recognized.

A Nina who at faculty parties and her publishing dos talked at length about Indian spices and miniatures and kathakali and the Chola bronzes, all of which she only had a fleeting knowledge of. When she was applauded for her expanse of erudition, she would say with a newly cultivated breathless laugh, 'But oh, I am an Indophile!'

The first time, Jak almost yelped in laughter. 'Nina, what's wrong with you? Indophile indeed. You are Indian!'

Soon his amusement turned into derision that he threw in her face. 'I would like to see you do this act in India. That's why you won't go back. You know they would laugh themselves silly at your Nine Yard Noose and the Grinding Stone of Desire!'

She retorted with her own observations. 'Well Kitcha, if you love India so much, why don't you go back? Look at yourself and the ridiculous lengths you go to. The leaky tap in the garden so you can hear it drip because it reminds you of the kitchen tap in the house you grew up in. The bird shit in the patio that you won't and will not let me hose away because it reminds you of the backyard in that house.'

This was a Nina quick to anger. With every day the rift widened, until they lived strangers to each other's dreams and bodies.

He wouldn't cling as his mother had. He wouldn't wait till she left like Appa had. He wouldn't make his daughters ever wonder, 'Is it our fault?' He only wanted for them what he couldn't have. Stability. In whatever form he could provide.

But as he sought consolation, Smriti too sought hers. In a faux family, to compensate for the one that Nina and he weren't able to provide.

Will it never end? Will the past never leave us alone?

Like his father, is he too guilty of parental irresponsibility? How could it be, when all his life, all he had wanted to do was not repeat Appa's mistake?

'You said you feel responsible. But why?' Jak asks, taking up the threads of his questioning.

'Smriti lied to me when she said Rishi was just a friend. I discovered that she and Rishi were seeing each other, and I went berserk. I was angry, jealous and hurt. All I could think of was how to wrest her back from him. Rishi is a good-looking dude and he'd been to these posh schools. He is sophisticated and stylish and I felt like a boy, a village boy, when I compared myself to him. But I knew Smriti and I had much more in common. Whereas Rishi and she had nothing in common. She was just infatuated with his looks and charm. He had no depth. I knew she would come back to me if only I could get her to myself for a few days.

'That was when Shivu told me about the workshop series Stree Shakti planned to conduct in Tamilnadu. Rupa, the coordinator, had asked if we could assist. We would start at Dharmapuri, move to Salem, on to Madurai, and were to cover all of Tamilnadu. There would be detours to many of the other districts, too, he said.'

Mathew felt his pulse quicken as he listened to Shivu describe what was lined up. They were to show the volunteers of the local nodal units how to put up the skit and also take it to a few villages. 'I've said yes,' Shivu said, 'I've said yes for the two of us. I know Ram, Chetana, Kripa and Maria have accepted too. It should be interesting, Mathew. But I want us to work on the script of *Dying Daughters* once more.'

Mathew nodded as he shredded a leaf to bits. He knew what he had to do.

'Smriti,' he said into the phone. He had chosen a moment when he knew she would be alone and more susceptible to persuasion. 'Think about it. You would be truly seeing India. The India that worries you. Here is your chance to do something. To talk to these women who kill their daughters in their wombs without a qualm. It is not awareness that is needed here. It is to be able to stoke up guilt, regret, remorse, the works. Shivu said you were tireless at the forum Stree Shakti organized. And even Rupa, you know how she is, cynical and aggro about everything, she said you were one of the most dedicated people she knew and if only there were more volunteers like you. They need you now. The dying daughters of India need you.'

Mathew paused. He saw himself in the mirror. He reminded himself of his uncle, the real estate broker, in whose eyes such a light gleamed as he tried to sell ugly little boxes to his non-resident Indian clients as traditional homes with modern conveniences – going back to nature in the middle of bustling Ernakulam, waking to birdsong and the romance of a time long ago. Mathew was selling Smriti a dream, appealing to what he knew would excite her. He felt dirty but he didn't care. The cause was real and she would be invaluable for what she brought to the project. Relationships were born when people shared a vision. Away from Bangalore, Smriti would see for herself what Mathew and she shared. And how flaky her relationship with Rishi was.

At first, she didn't want to. She was reluctant to leave Rishi even for a day, she said. She had changed. She had become more quiet. She had got rid of some of her piercings and got her hair fixed. Smriti so wanted to please Rishi. We could all see that. And so I told her that she was a fraud, all talk and no heart. Someone playing at being a social worker. And that she had no real interest in any living creature, except Rishi.

She didn't talk to me for a week. Then I had Shivu call her and work on her as well. Shivu seemed to know what to say to her, for she called to say she would go. She would join Shivu and me at Madurai. She would be free only then, she said.

We waited for her at Madurai. She was to have joined us on the first of March. When she didn't turn up, I was affronted at being stood up. Shivu was not so upset. He seldom is. He said she would turn up. A day later she still hadn't come and we moved on with the group.

We met Rishi's cousin a month later. He said there had been an accident. Rishi was badly hurt. But he didn't know where Smriti was. 'I guess she dumped him like she dumped the two of you,' he said. 'The bitch!'

Neither of us felt inclined to defend her. We were pissed off with her too.

The next day Rupa was at the café and she said she had read something about Smriti in the newspapers. She had gone to a small town about hundred kilometres east of Madurai. She had a freak accident there. A log lifting in the wave and slamming into her. Can you imagine? She was paralysed, Rupa said.

Then someone there wanted to know, 'But what on earth was she doing wandering around small-town Tamilnadu? These NRI chicks, they land up here and think they can solve our problems with a fistful of daddy's dollars and their self-righteousness.'

'Smriti must have gone there on one of her causes. She was so full of them,' someone said.

'Full of shit!' someone else laughed.

We said nothing but we couldn't meet each other's gaze. We didn't ever talk about it but I knew Shivu was as shaken as I was. If we hadn't asked her to come to Madurai, if I hadn't persuaded her to go with us, none of this would have happened. It wasn't as if she really wanted to go.

Shivu, who had planned to do his master's in Bangalore, stayed back in Salem. And I moved back here to Kochi.

'Think of how we felt. How we feel each day even now,' Mathew says.

Jak doesn't want to know how or what they feel. It is of no interest to him. He has no reserves of sympathy to dip into. He wrenches his eyes away. The boy holds up his crumpled face as testimony of his remorse.

Jak swallows convulsively. This banked in grief, how much is it for Smriti, the girl he has failed? And how much is it for himself? The tainting of his life that no penance, no good deeds would ever erase.

Mathew plucks at his sleeve. 'Uncle,' he said. 'How is she now?'

'The same...'

'She will get better, won't she?'

Jak stares at the boy. Should he tell him about Smriti? That would be punishment. But what were these boys guilty of? Nothing really.

'She is...' he began.

Then Mathew says, 'Have you met Rishi yet? I know Smriti and he went together to that small town by the sea. They spent a couple of days there.'

Jak knows the grinding of gears. So Rishi must have been the man with her.

Suddenly Jak feels a great weariness settle over him. He wants to walk away from it all. Go home. Go home to catatonic Smriti who has no more surprises waiting for him. Go home to Kala Chithi who was there for him, a bulwark of strength. Go home to Meera who has slipped into his life and settled there with such ease.

Go home, Kitcha. Go home, Jak tells himself. You will know respite, some peace, and perhaps even normalcy in time.

IX

Time prevails. Time that brings with it some respite, a soupcon of peace and even a modicum of normalcy.

It has been two months since that perfect September day when the axis of her world tilted forever. Meera is no longer sure of who she is. How can she be Hera when there is no longer a Zeus in her life? Some days she sites herself in another part of that mythical realm she has made her own. She is one of the golden mechanical women that Hera's son Hephateus created to help him in his smithy. They could walk around and talk and could be trusted to accomplish the most difficult of tasks. They did everything expected of them because they had no heart or soul to deter them. How the gods and goddesses must laugh to know that I, who was Hera, queen of all she purveyed, am now this – a golden mechanical woman at the beck and call of a surly, ill-tempered, ugly creature called need. But hinged to that simmering anger is something else. A certain pride at the notion that she didn't crumble or crumple; instead, she coped.

Meera remembers a night from that other life. A few weeks before Giri left.

He had come home one day with a strange expression. All evening he wore it on his face and it wouldn't go away despite the dissonance of that particular evening.

'Someone's been at my bottle. I don't like it. I don't like it,' Lily had complained in a plaintive voice, holding up the bottle. 'If someone wants a drink, they should buy it themselves.'

And Giri, who had always let Lily or Saro's patter – accusations, gossip, snide remarks – slide off his back, looked up from the magazine he was reading. He stared at her and then said in a voice that was so mild no one could fault him, yet brimming with unmistakable disdain, 'I don't drink in the middle of the week. I am not an old lush like you!'

And Saro, who couldn't bear for anyone to use that tone with her mother, had sniffed and said in her coldest voice, 'Don't you dare call my mother an old lush!'

And Giri had drawled, 'So what is it you object to? The old or the lush? Both parts being, as we all in this household know, the truth!'

Meera's hand moved to her mouth in horror. What was happening? In all these years, no matter what, there had never been an open confrontation. Meera was always the conduit for dissatisfaction, pointing out irritants to either party so a semblance of peace could be maintained. Once fractured, it would never set, she worried. Only this evening, they seemed to have bypassed her totally.

Then again, Nayantara, home for a midterm break, decided to turn vegetarian at dinner time, just as Meera was serving her celebratory kauswey. 'I can't eat this,' she said, rising from the table.

And Giri, who couldn't tolerate anyone wasting food or even balking at a dish, spooned some peanuts, chopped eggs and green chilli slivers onto his nest of noodles and chicken sauce and said, 'Well, get yourself some rice and dal from the fridge then.'

Meera looked from father to daughter. It was as if Giri wouldn't let anyone or anything get to him tonight.

As soon as they were in bed, Meera turned to him, tugging at the sleeve of his T-shirt. 'What is it, Giri? What's happened?'

'What's happened?'

'You know, first that little scene with Lily.'

'Oh that, she can't accuse me of stealing her gin.'

'And you didn't mind Nayantara turning her nose up at the kauswey.'

'Give the girl a break, Meera. She's old enough to know what she wants to eat.'

Meera knew for certain that Giri must have had a promotion at work, and a fantastic raise perhaps. Nothing else could explain this strange melding of cockiness and generosity, goodwill and unwillingness to stomach the old ladies' pernicketiness.

She leaned back into the pillows. A smile hovered on her lips. Nikhil was the same. A little triumph at school and he was Mr Heracles himself. Willing to hold up the world if it would let him.

'Meera.' Giri spoke now. 'A colleague at work took me to a

website this morning. It's amazing. You can actually recreate yourself there. I have a new name, a new persona. It's just amazing. I feel like a new man.'

Meera propped herself on an elbow. 'Is that it?'

'What do you mean, is that it?' Giri bristled.

'It's not real, Giri. It's like Nikhil playing one of his silly computer games and telling me in all seriousness – Ma, I got stopped by the police four times this morning. Get real, Giri!' Meera snapped shut the light on her side of the bed.

She cringes now, thinking about it. How could she have been so dismissive of him? So carelessly insensitive? There are moments when Meera flushes in repugnance at who she was – a smug, pompous woman who played queen of the universe with a total disregard for anything that didn't move her.

What plays in her mind now is the expression on Giri's face. Part triumph. Part excitement. Totally alive.

Second Life, Giri had called his game.

So is this her second life?

In Jak's home, Meera sits at Jak's desk. Now Meera's desk.

'Make yourself comfortable,' Jak had suggested.

There was very little in the room for her to make herself comfortable with. But as she wandered around the house and garden, collecting a cushion for her chair, a lump of quartz for a paperweight, a clutch of oleanders for a vase for the table, hanging up the stunning but unsigned seascape she had discovered behind an almirah, Meera knew she was being herself again.

She leans back in her chair and stretches. She looks at the seascape hanging on the wall and is seized with sudden pleasure at how right the room feels. To her left is a window that overlooks a corner of the garden. A riot of grass and weeds, woody shrubs, and a giant oleander whose blossoms hang heavy and deeply pink. Amidst all this wilderness is a wrought iron bench with a broken arm. 'It came with the house,' Jak explained. 'I ought to get it fixed too!'

In the pause that followed, Meera felt again Jak's helplessness. A better woman would have flung herself up from the chair saying, 'But it can be fixed, I'll find you someone.'

A better woman would have offered to find him a gardener and sort out the mess he referred to euphemistically as the garden. A better woman would have taken him, his garden and his car in hand and weeded out the helplessness. But Meera had had enough of being the better woman. No, I shall not. Not unless he asks me to. I shall not offer to be more than he wants me to be. And so she pressed down her urge to hunt for him a fixer of wrought iron benches.

It begins as a mewling. A shrill cry that becomes a long drawn shriek of terror. A wail that goes on and on. Meera rushes to the window. She thinks it came from the street.

Then she hears it again and runs to the living room, her heart thudding.

The wail becomes a howl. Meera creeps cautiously towards Smriti's room. She wants to stay where she is, but she also has to know.

Kala Chithi sits on the bed. The nurse is loading a syringe and between the two of them, locked in her inert abjectness lies Smriti. Her eyes stare at the ceiling and her fingers are curled into their habitual part fist. From her mouth emerges the howl again and Meera feels her blood chill.

She goes to stand with Kala Chithi. 'Should I call the hospital?'

Kala Chithi shakes her head. 'No, she will settle in a while.' She strokes Smriti's forehead gently. 'I don't know how she knows it. But when Kitcha is away, she is restless. That's when she starts this.'

'She sounds frightened. Could she be?' Meera begins uncurling Smriti's fist as she has seen Jak do.

A whimper. Her insides shrivel. The poor child. The poor pathetic child.

'Did it scare you?' Kala Chithi asks.

'Yes,' Meera confesses.

'This howl is all we have to cling to. If she knows that Kitcha is away, perhaps somewhere in her there is a fragment of consciousness, don't you think? Our Smriti is there in this creature. And one day she just may wake up. It has happened. I have heard of such stories. Kitcha won't admit it, but he, too, hopes for it. You must think us foolish, Meera?'

Meera is quiet. Hope. All of us thrive on it, Kala Chithi, she wants to say. Who knows what twist of fate will set right our world again?

'I have a daughter too,' she says. 'Each time I look at Smriti, I think of all that has been lost to her.'

'Lost! Stolen, I would say.' Kala Chithi's mouth is a line.

'Stolen?'

'Kitcha thinks it wasn't a freak accident. He thinks something happened to her.'

Meera doesn't speak. She knows all about clutching at straws. Grabbing at rage is easier than slithering into grief.

The phone begins to ring. 'Do call me if you need anything,' she murmurs, making her escape. How do they endure it, Kala Chithi and Jak? How do they bear it, day after day?

Six rings, and Meera holds the phone to her ear tremulously. Even now it hasn't abated. First that furtive hope. Giri. Then the fear. Lily or Saro have had a fall. Nayantara has had an accident. Nikhil is hurt. A sea of worries for Meera to rise above everyday, each time the phone rings.

Only, this time it is Jak.

'I am calling from the airport,' he says. 'The flight is late. If we take off as scheduled, I should be home by six.'

And Meera asks, not knowing what he has gone to Kochi for, 'Did it go well? The research, the meetings?'

There is silence.

'Hello, hello,' Meera calls into the phone.

'Yes,' he says. 'Yes, it went better than I hoped. I'll see you soon then, Meera.'

Meera puts down the phone. She thinks again of how much her life has changed in only two months. The smudges of uncertainty that speckled her days are erasing themselves out. She thinks of how it was before Jak found her a place to locate herself in. Of how it was before she had this – her second life. And time.

She feels a curious joy shoot through her. Joy – no, it can't be. It is relief. Sheer relief that he will soon be home.

STAGE III

The Spiral Bands of Deceit

The last painting that Salvador Dali ever did was the *Swallow's Tail Series* on catastrophes. It was the last of the series based on Rene Thom's catastrophe theory.

There are seven elementary catastrophes: the fold, the cusp, the swallow tail, the butterfly, the hyperbolic umblic, the elliptic umblic and the parabolic umblic. It's funny, this word catastrophe. A word for disaster that can also mean many other things.

The ancient Greeks considered it the climax and point of resolution in their narrative plots. Stockbrokers call a risk-linked security that shares risks with bond investors a catastrophic bond. Insurance underwriters build in a catastrophic modelling projecting the cost of losses by an act of god.

It is ironic that a natural catastrophe is referred to as an act of god. As if no one or nothing can change the course of what nature has set out to do. And it is here that theoreticians step in with their theory of catastrophe which tells us how a small variation, a tiny discrepancy that we may otherwise ignore, can drastically affect and change dynamic systems. And that is the inherent nature of a catastrophe: its capability to beguile and deceive. So you think danger lies elsewhere while the real peril lurks at arm's length.

Hidden within the cirrus canopy is a distinct pattern: bands of convective cloud spiralling into the eye wall. From these bands emerge heavy rain and squalls. But that isn't where the real danger lies. For the spiral bands are master deceivers. They make us believe this is the extent of the storm.

How utterly gullible we are when it comes to celestial forces and acts of god! The tipping point is yet to come.

Professor J. A. Krishnamurthy
The Metaphysics of Cyclones

Inside her home, there are a thousand things waiting to be dealt with. But for this moment, Meera is just another woman waiting for a friend to pick her up. She flicks the end of her light woollen shawl over her shoulder.

December. Blue skies above, with hardly a cloud. The sun shines down bright and piercing. Step out of the sun into the shade of a tree, an awning or a portico, and a chill climbs up your spine. In Bangalore, Meera thinks, it is December that wears a dual face, not January. Yet, she stands outside her gate waiting for Vinnie this deceitful December morning and feels something akin to joy limber through her.

She thinks she may have found a worthy successor to *The Corporate Wife's Guide to Entertaining*. Only this time she will not offer it to Randhir Soni on a platter. If Watermill Press wants *The Corporate Wife Abroad*, they'll bloody well have to pay for it.

No one is going to profit from her experience unless she profits first, Meera tells herself firmly. What to pack; what not to pack. What to do in those hours when your husband is locked in conference rooms. What to wear to a formal dinner. What to order in a restaurant. What to bring back home. What not to buy your household staff after a trip abroad. For years Meera has been the one Giri's colleagues' wives called for tips and suggestions. And Giri had liked it that it was Meera they turned to. It enhanced his corporate guru standing.

If anyone wants any more advice, they will have to buy it. Meera smiles.

'Coffee?' Vinnie asks as she jumps a red light with the practised ease of a habitual offender.

Meera looks at Vinnie again in admiration. How does one get to be like her? Vinnie, who runs a boutique, drives her own car, manages the dual life of wife and mistress and never ever has one varnished hair out of place. Even her chopstick stays where it should.

'So how is he to work with?' Vinnie parks the car expertly in a slot she finds on Commercial Street.

'It's still too early to tell,' Meera murmurs. 'So far so good.'

'Oh, don't be so bloody cautious for once. Tell me what you really think!' Vinnie slams her door shut.

Meera stops in her tracks. Giri had accused her of being narrow minded, Nayantara said she was stiff. Now here is Vinnie saying it too. Bloody cautious. Why is prudence always seen as wimpishness?

What shall I tell her? Meera gnaws at her lip. That the cyclone expert has had nothing for me on cyclones but instead had me open three files: Shivu, Mathew, Rishi. Titbits of information about two nineteen-year-old boys and only a blank file on Rishi. That he has me look at railway timetables and tides. That he had me google the net for freak accidents and a women's group called Stree Shakti. That he seems to have a strange purpose in his head. None of it makes sense to me.

'JAK?' Vinnie's eyebrows reach her hairline when Meera says his name. 'One of those! What's his real name? Let me guess. Jagannath? Jagdish? Jagdeep? Jagjivan?'

Meera smiles. 'Hold your breath. Jayamkondan Anantharaman Krishnamurthy reduced to J.A.K. Hence Professor Jak!'

'So what do you call him?' Vinnie laughs. 'I rather like Jayamkondan. You can call him Jay!'

'His aunt calls him Kitcha; his colleagues seem to refer to him as Professor Jak. I began with Professor Krishnamurthy but he asked me to drop the Professor. So I too call him Jak now!' Meera tells her carefully, trying to establish that the casual use of his first name is just that.

'Hmm,' Vinnie says in a quiet contemplative voice that suggests she doesn't believe it is as casual as Meera makes it out to be.

'He is a very laidback sort of a person. You'd like him, Vinnie. No airs, nothing. And he doesn't get stressed out if things don't work. The power cuts, the UPS burning out… he's easy to be around.' Meera stops abruptly. Unlike Giri. Unlike my husband, is what Vinnie must think I am implying, she thinks.

She doesn't talk about Giri any more. But she thinks of him often and though it is with a rancour that stings, she misses him a thousand times a day. It creeps up on her rather abruptly, that moment of irretrievable loss, the emptiness, a cruel hand squeezing her heart with a cold clutch and causing a whimper in her: Oh Giri.

There it is, first thing in the morning, when she feels sleep crawl out of her eyes and she snuggles deeper under the quilt, pushing herself ever so little into what used to be the receptacle of his curved hip. Feeling him nudge but lie quietly against the nest between her thighs. The warmth. The presence. The quiet content. And then the whimper: Oh Giri.

At the extra place she sets by mistake. The bottle of fish pickle only he liked. The shirt that came back from the dry-cleaners. A discarded pair of sandals. The music CDs that remain mute. His folders on the desktop. A whiff of aftershave on another man. A particular shade of blue. The hot spicy fragrance of orange peel. The curve of an emptied peanut shell. In how many ways, Oh Giri.

And then at night when she creams her face and braids her hair and slips into bed with a book, the pool of darkness on his side of the bed. The knowledge that unless she chooses to do so, the table lamp on the other side will stay forever unlit, the bulb gathering dust and time. Miss Havisham in a wedding dress never worn. Oh Giri, oh Giri, oh Giri.

Across the table, Vinnie looks at her carefully. Meera feels the import of the look. It unsettles her. 'What?'

'Nothing,' Vinnie says and begins studying the menu. Suddenly, she looks up and asks, 'How's he with you?'

'What do you mean?'

'You see it, don't you? He's a divorced man; you are separated. Does he come on strong?'

'Oh, no.' Meera smiles. 'He is very respectful. Almost avuncular. Sometimes I wish he wouldn't be so…' she adds as an afterthought.

'Are you saying you want him to hit on you?' Vinnie's eyebrows are sky high again.

Ever since that first time, Vinnie and Meera have met at least once a month. It is a friendship neither seeks to explain. If they had met elsewhere, neither would have warmed to the other. Meera would have dismissed Vinnie as predatory and cold. Vinnie would have shaken her head in incredulity at Meera: could there really be women like her, stuck in a time warp and content to be an appendage to husband and home?

Now they look at each other and gleam: it's good to be here with you.

Why is it that we veer away from men as we grow older, Meera wonders. Is it that our animal sap ceases to rise and what we seek isn't a mate but a companion? Do we find comfort in other women – their fortitude, their strength, their calm competence, their unsullied fun? Maybe that's why I need my Vinnie. This friend who picked me off the floor that first time.

Meera looks at Vinnie now. What are we doing here, she wonders. Two middle-aged women marooned in a sea of shoppers. Meera sucks on an ice cube from her drink, a tall cold coffee with chocolate topping and a swirl of cream.

'I know I shouldn't. But all day I have thought of nothing but this.' Meera smiles. Vinnie feels a tug at her heart at such an admission of want, of vulnerability. 'Have another,' she says. 'Would you like a bhatura or paav bhaaji to eat?'

Meera shakes her head. 'No, no, this is fine. One can't glut on heaven! Not good for the soul!'

Vinnie pats her hand. 'It's all right, you know. You have your needs too. We all do. Whether it is for chocolate or men. If it is Jak who makes you feel like a woman, let it be Jak.'

'You are getting this all wrong. I am talking about male attention.'

'Any male attention? You would welcome any male attention so you feel more like a woman and less like a eunuch, is that it?'

Why can't Vinnie drop the subject? She is like a dog worrying a rag. Meera doesn't want another man in her life now. Not for a long time. She doesn't even want a flirtation or an affair.

Meera shakes her head. 'No, no, you don't understand. All I am saying is, I feel hollowed out. Jak is irrelevant. He really is, Vinnie!

'But it would be nice to be seen as a woman. I get lonely

too, Vinnie. But no one would like me to admit it. Neither my children, nor my mother or grandmother. It is as if the woman in me had to die when Giri left.'

Meera sips her drink, stemming her words. What is wrong with her? All these thoughts, these words, where do they come from? She counts the dates in her head. Is her period due?

Meera toys with the cutlery on the table. She makes a V with the knife and fork. Then an N. An A and an L. With the help of the salt cellar she manages a J. But G stayes resolutely curled away. As does S. One who chose to go away. Another who was trying to sneak into her world.

'What are you keeping from me, Meera?' Vinnie demands. 'You have a secret. I can see it in your smile.'

When the phone rang a few nights ago, Meera had picked it up with a shaking hand. What new crisis lurked at the other end? Yet, somewhere in her, that glimmer of hope: Was it Giri? If so, what would he say to her?

'Hey Meera,' said the voice at the other end.

Meera paused. It wasn't Giri, but it wasn't a strange voice either.

'Hello,' she said.

'Remember me?'

That strange familiarity. A feeling that she knew the voice from somewhere.

'I know you don't!' A chuckle. A low chuckle guaranteed to send little thrills down the listening woman's spine.

It fell into place then. The actor. The Adonis of the poolside. Why was he calling her?

Meera laughed into the phone. 'Hello, Soman. Where have you surfaced from?'

'The poolside you abandoned me by.' That low chuckle again. 'But I am amazed you remember me. It has been a while. I meant to call but just couldn't summon the courage to.'

Meera held her breath

'And then I had to go away to Mumbai, Meera. I was in a TV series. I got back only a couple of days ago, and I thought I would give you a call and say hello.'

Meera exhaled. He didn't know anything about her.

'I so enjoyed our chat that day, Meera. Do you think we could meet for a coffee one of these days?'

Meera looked at her nails. 'Sure,' she said.

'Tomorrow?' he asked.

Meera knows that Vinnie is waiting for her to speak. In the end Meera does what she always does when Lily or the children ask awkward questions: *How much does Giri give you as child support?*

Do you think Daddy has a girlfriend?

Is Lily a drunk? Mummy, is Lily an alcoholic? Have you seen how much she drinks?

She changes the subject with an airy flourish of nonchalance.

A shrug and a leap into a completely irrelevant query: Has your consignment of stoles from Bhagalpur arrived? Jak wanted me to pick a couple to send to someone. A woman called Lisa. What do you think would suit a Lisa? Honey gold or moss green?

Is this really me, Meera asks herself. Did I just say that – 'What do you think would suit a Lisa?'

Half an hour later, Meera cannot hug her secret any more. She needs to confer with Vinnie. What is she to do with Soman? It niggles at her constantly, the fear that she is encouraging him.

'He must have heard that Giri and I are no longer together. That it must be a good time to call me: the woman alone who could do with some cock in her life.' Meera's hand goes to her mouth. Who is this woman who uses words like cock and fuck and not just in her head?

'Vinnie, I have to make sure that he understands I am not that sort of a woman.'

'Who is that sort of a woman?' Vinnie snaps when Meera tries to explain the confusion that rages in her. 'What woman, unless she is a nymphomaniac, or a whore, sets herself up as an available woman? We don't, Meera. Not even I. I know you think I switch lovers like I change the chopsticks in my topknot. But I am not available. You know what we are? Vulnerable!

'That's what we are. Vulnerable fools who believe that this time, no matter how often we have been proved wrong, we've found the right man. The one man who is going to enchant our lives into an extended fairy tale. The man you think you can lean into, and he'll be there for you.'

Meera shudders at the phrase 'lean into'. Nothing could explain it better. That letting down of defences. A sigh of relief. Soft, soft, softness and knowing that holding it all was a bedrock of strength. She missed that so much. To let go and know there was someone to lean into.

She thinks of the evening before. Soman had asked her to go with him to an art show.

It had involved sitting in a darkened room watching a video that was part of an installation piece. What did Meera remember of the flickering images on the screen? Not much, she thinks. All she had been conscious of was the pressure of his arm on hers. The brushing of skin; the osmosis of attraction and the constancy of that moment. Meera glanced around her. Was everyone else sitting as they were? Meera felt a flood of warmth when she saw the tiny oasis each chair was. They, only they, seemed to be leaning into each other.

'But Vinnie, won't he think I was encouraging him? I should have moved away!' Meera interrupts her.

'Listen to yourself. You are so naïve, Meera. You sat next to each other and you get so het up about that. This is a fourteen-year-old child talking, not a woman in her forties. A sexually aware woman… Meera, your daughter must know more about men than you do!'

Meera smiles then. A rueful smile of embarrassment. How could she read so much into so little? She will grow up. Become the woman that Soman thinks she is, the woman Vinnie wants her to be.

I

Who is this woman? Meera asks herself, catching sight of her reflection in the hallway mirror. Tall and straight, her face not betraying even a flicker of the sickening dread she feels. The moment she feared is finally upon her.

Nayantara just arrived from Chennai by plane. Giri paid for the flight, she says. Lily and Saro look at each other and then at Meera. But Meera nods as if it is customary for Giri to pay for an air ticket. Giri, skinflint Giri, whose cheques are accompanied with complaints of how hard it is to not ask 'why'.

She stands there rearranging the ginger lilies in a tall vase. 'How nice for you,' she says, sniping a yellowing leaf off and squashing a curious ant between her thumb and forefinger.

Nayantara has come bearing a letter from Giri. She lurks now as Meera opens the envelope, willing her fingers to not tremble and expose her.

Giri has written saying that it is almost three months since they effected their trial separation. And in that time, since they have realized that their lives aren't as enmeshed as they imagined it to be, and as they have proved that they are capable of leading happy and gratifying lives well apart, perhaps it is time to legalize the separation. So they are free to make choices and move on.

Meera feels her lips narrow into a line as she folds the paper and slides it back into its envelope. She catches the curious gleam in her daughter's eyes.

'Do you know what is in this?' Meera demands, flinging the letter down.

Nayantara stands, hesitant, unsure if she should speak the truth or feign ignorance. It is daddy's girl who shrugs.

Meera stares, appalled. 'How could you? Do you realize that your father is asking me for a divorce? Did you know that was what you were bringing to me?'

Nayantara looks away. 'Would you have preferred to receive a divorce notice by registered post? Isn't that how it is done? He was thinking of you, trying to soften the blow. Mummy, don't blame me. I am just the messenger.

'You knew this was going happen; you knew it. Don't fool yourself. You knew Daddy wasn't going to come back. It was inevitable, your divorce!'

Meera is speechless.

'I told Daddy this. I said you would hold me responsible.

That you would be angry with me. But he said that you knew, as he did, that you couldn't live together any more and be happy. He said if I brought the letter to you, it would be less upsetting. That's all I did, Mummy. Don't look at me like that.' Nayantara's eyes well up.

Meera takes her distraught daughter in her arms. 'No, I am not blaming you. How could I? Your father and I...'

'Mummy, why don't you give him what he wants? Maybe he'll come back then.' Nayantara clings to her mother, an adult child who so wants her home back with mummy and daddy together under one roof and happily ever after in a painted rainbow that rises from the house into the horizon.

Why am I so angry? For that matter, why am I so surprised? Meera asks herself as she dresses. As Nayantara said, this was inevitable. She has heard from Nayantara enough to know that Giri has begun fashioning a new life. His second life for real.

In an apartment high up in the air with a view overlooking the sea on one side and the city lights on the other. There are heart shaped silk cushions and tall candles. Vases with flowers and glass beads clinking among the stems. Neither children nor old women would ever shabby its stark chic. No one to leave rings on the table or potato wafer crumbs on the sofa. No damp stains on the wall, nor the smell of mould that is hard to banish from a bathroom with ancient plumbing. To this home Giri would bring his new trophy wife and in their newly found muscle-toned nirvana, he would start afresh.

What can I offer him, Nayantara? The only thing that may have brought him back isn't mine to give.

Meera thinks of the night some weeks before Giri went. He had watched her as she creamed her face.

'What?' she asked.

'Those veins on your thighs…' he said suddenly. 'You should get them looked at.'

'I am forty-four years old. I am not young any more, Giri. I will have veins,' she snapped back.

He shrugged then and flicked the TV remote on. 'They look terrible,' he said.

In the days after he left, Meera relived that episode again and again. Was that why? Because she was beginning to age. Those little creeping lines on the top of her thighs and the flare of grey at her temples – could they have repelled him? Or, was it something else?

At the beauty salon, Maria drapes the plastic wrap around her shoulders. 'The usual trim?' she asks Meera in the mirror.

Meera holds her gaze for a moment. 'No. Give me a new hairstyle. Short. I leave it to you.'

'Are you sure?' Maria's eyes widen.

'I am. I've had this same hairstyle for the last twenty-two years.' Ever since Giri came into my life. And I didn't want to change a thing. My hair, my home, my dreams, myself. I so wanted it to be what he wanted.

'In that case, you certainly need a new look,' Maria says, taking a swath of hair and clipping it on top of Meera's head with a yellow butterfly clip. 'It'll make you feel like a new woman.'

Out of the mouth of a salon girl, Meera thinks. It's time I became a new woman. Someone I would like to be.

As Meera walks to Jak's house, she feels the breeze at the nape of her neck. It is strange to have her neck exposed and vulnerable.

Meera sees herself in a shop window and halts in surprise. She doesn't recognize herself.

Maria had angled the mirror in different directions so she could admire herself. 'What do you think?' she asked. That she was pleased with her handwork was obvious.

'It is good,' Meera said, even though she felt a great wave of uncertainty rise. What had she done? What would the children say? What would Saro and Lily say?

Meera wanders into Smriti's room to ask about Jak. She thinks of the expression on his face when he saw her a few nights ago at the art gallery. She couldn't fathom it. Was he displeased? Should she have mentioned to him that she was going?

Kala Chithi asks, 'What happened? What made you cut your hair?'

Meera is fazed by the directness of the question. Kala Chithi seldom makes personal remarks of any sort.

Meera shrugs. 'I suddenly felt I needed a new look.'

Kala Chithi waits for her to finish.

Meera peers into her mug of coffee and says, 'Giri wants a divorce.'

Kala Chithi continues to look at her.

'I keep wondering if there was something I did, or something I didn't. What could have made Giri leave?'

'Do you think he'll come back?' Kala Chithi asks. Meera's circumstances have never been discussed, but Meera knows that Jak must have filled her in.

Meera shakes her head. 'I don't know.'

'More importantly, do you want him back?'

Meera looks up abruptly. She had never even considered it. Could she live with Giri again? Go on as if nothing had happened?

'You see, Meera, we are brought up to believe that our husband is our god. His wishes are ours, and without him we are nothing. There is a saying, *Kal analum kanavan, pull analum purushan.* Whether he is hard as a rock or as worthless as a weed, a husband is a husband. Can you make a life without your husband?'

Meera places the mug on the table. 'I don't know,' she says. 'All I keep thinking is, will he come back? I never asked myself, what if he does…' Meera's voice drops. 'What would you do?'

'I don't know, Meera. I never had to ask myself that.' Kala Chithi's eyes are steady, her voice even.

'But you left your husband!'

'What is it you want to know from me, Meera? I don't have any wisdom to offer you. My choices in life will not be yours. I had my reasons for choosing to leave my husband.'

'Was it because you thought your husband had another woman?'

'Another woman?' Kala Chithi's voice rises in surprise as does her hand. She touches her cropped head.

'Why else did you leave him?' Meera says, wanting to shatter the poise on the older woman's face.

'Why did you leave your husband?' she asks again.

Kala Chithi leans back in her chair. 'There wasn't a specific reason. Not really. Would you believe me if I told you that I could no longer share a life with him? It just wasn't possible any more. I had to leave.

'So you see, Meera, you have to decide. I can't do it for you. Do you still want to be Giri's wife?' Kala Chithi asks, rising from her chair.

Meera, looking beyond her, wonders: Do I?

II

'Have I what?' Meera asks over her shoulder.

'Have you thought about what I asked?'

Meera turns to look at her daughter carefully. 'What about, Nayantara?'

'You know, that portfolio thing... I told you. Dad's friend's wife said I should get one done. She thought she could send it to the Elite people.'

Meera frowns. 'I thought it was something you did for fun. I didn't think you wanted to make a career of modelling. Besides, what about your studies? You are at the IIT. Do you know how few kids get in there? And you want to give up that...'

Nayantara makes a face. 'What about Aishwarya Rai? She was a medical student.'

'I don't know what your father will say,' Meera tries to hedge.

'Daddy's fine. But he said you are the one who ought to be fine with it.'

Thanks, Giri. Let me be the harridan who has to say no to your daughter's silly dreams.

But hasn't it always been thus? The thrusting and entrusting of parental responsibility onto her. In those early years, Meera had protested. 'The children weren't exactly born of immaculate conception. You have to take on your share.'

And Giri, who felt justified in his aggrievement, would say without a change of expression, 'You were the one who wanted babies; I didn't. You were the one who claimed that you wouldn't be complete as a woman without a child.'

Meera, silenced by that need of hers, learnt to burden Giri

less and less with the demands of fatherhood. The children were hers to worry about, while Giri was the one to laugh and frolic with. He knew how to be the tyrant father too, but mostly he played along with their dreams and desires. Fatherhood to Giri was how he had shaped it and not what it was meant to be, Meera thinks, trying not to let her bitterness spill over.

Meera takes the sari off its hanger. 'I don't like it. The casting couch isn't a myth. You are too young to be exposed to that kind of a world.'

'Are you saying it's okay for someone to fuck me as long as I'm older?'

Meera blanches. 'Quiet!' she hisses. 'Don't talk rubbish. If you insist on behaving like a fractious three-year-old, I will have to treat you like one. You don't leave me with much choice. I would suggest that you forget all this modelling nonsense. '

Nayantara is shamefaced. 'I'm sorry. I didn't mean it like that.But Daddy's friend said…' she begins but stops when she sees Meera's face.

Nayantara watches Meera drape the sari. 'I thought you said you were not sure about going,' she says, opening and closing the lipstick tube.

'Don't. You'll snap the lipstick,' Meera says as she adjusts the pleats.

'How can you go for a party? It's just a few months since Daddy and you…' Nayantara stares at her.

'Your daddy left. He didn't die,' Meera snaps. 'Besides, he just asked me for a divorce, remember?'

Seeing Nayantara flush, Meera is contrite. 'It's not just any party. It's Vinnie's. I couldn't say no,' Meera says quietly.

She peers at herself in the floor-length mirror. 'Would you please pull down the sari at the back? It's hiked up a bit.'

Nayantara sinks to her knees obediently and tugs at the sari. 'But what will people think?'

'Nayantara, don't ever say that to me. I don't care what people think. I won't ever again.'

'I know you don't care what people think. Or would you go out with a man half your age?'

'What?' Meera yelps, turning in surprise. 'Who told you that?'

'So it is true! How can you, Mummy?'

'Nayantara, you know nothing about it.'

'So tell me…' Nayantara hugs her knees. 'You go on about the casting couch and the bad bad world waiting to pounce on me. But look at you! Do you know how it makes me feel when my friends want to know if Soman is my boyfriend? Am I to tell them that he is yours?'

'He isn't my boyfriend! He is just a friend.'

Nayantara makes a face as if she doesn't believe her mother.

'But tell me, if he was, would it be so bad?' Meera says, pretending a nonchalance she doesn't feel.

'How would you feel if I took up with a man Daddy's age?' Nayantara stands up. 'It's embarrassing, Mummy. It's gross!'

What about Daddy? Meera wants to demand. Isn't it gross that his girlfriend is only a few years older than you? Or is that fine in your vision of the world? Then she sees Nayantara's face.

'Soman isn't my boyfriend, please understand, darling. He is just someone I know. That's all there is to it. Promise!' Meera tries to cajole her daughter into accepting her explanation.

'Ok. If you say so,' Nayantara says.

Her insides quail at the forlorn expression in her daughter's eyes.

'If you don't want me to go to this party, I'll stay back,' Meera offers.

'No, it's fine,' Nayantara says. 'Do you want to borrow my stilettos?'

Meera smiles. Peace has been restored. 'If you are sure,' she says tentatively. As her share of the peace offering, she adds, 'If you want a portfolio done, I could ask Akram. He'll be able to pass it on to the right people. And I'd feel safe knowing it was him. But you can't give up your course. You need to strike a balance between the two. It's always best to have all your options open.'

And not end up like me with no plan B, Meera thinks.

'Will you be late?' Nayantara asks at the door. Nikhil and Lily are sprawled on the sofa watching a film. Saro is reading.

Meera holds her daughter to her. 'Shall I send the car back?' she asks again.

'No, no, you must go. Have a good time.' Nayantara waves her off.

Meera swallows. This role reversal is rather unsettling. 'I won't be too late,' she calls out, rolling down the car window.

Vinnie has opened the French windows so that the room and terrace merge. Here they congregate: Vinnie's friends and business associates. Vinnie's lover. Vinnie's husband. And Meera. A slightly forlorn Meera discovering what it is to be a single woman in a room full of couples.

She chews her lip thoughtfully. Has she made a mistake, she wonders, by accepting the invitation?

But Vinnie wouldn't allow her a choice. 'You have to be there,' she insisted, sweeping away any excuse that Meera could come up with. 'I'll send the car for you. That takes care of transportation. Why don't you invite your Professor? Or is there someone else you would rather? Soman? What happened between the two of you? You hardly mention him any more.'

Vinnie threw her a sidelong glance. Meera turned her head away. For a fleeting moment, she had paused at the notion of Soman.

Meera wondered how good he was as an actor. Was his interest in her an act? Or was it for real? It must be the house. Like Giri, he too must see the house as the prize. Why else would he want to be with a woman fifteen years older than him?

No, she would go alone to Vinnie's party.

'No, there isn't anyone I want to bring with me.' Meera shook her head decisively.

'That's fine then.' Vinnie smiled. 'You don't need an escort. No one makes much of these things any more. A woman by herself at a party is like a man by himself.'

Not really, Meera thinks, as she waits for someone to offer her a drink. For someone to steer her into a group and into a conversation. For someone to say hello.

Once, Giri was the one to do all of that: to fill up her glass. To introduce her to new people. To help say goodbyes. Meera feels something sag within her. Will it always be like this? Not knowing when she would be stricken by a debilitating helplessness? Wanting to scuttle into the shadows and stay resolutely there?

She still isn't used to stepping out in public by herself. In the months after Giri left, the invitations had dwindled to almost none.

She knows who she reminds herself of. The teapot lid in her odds-and-ends shelf. You don't know what to do with it. Some trace of sentiment makes you keep it instead of throwing it away, but each time you see it you wonder what you are going to do with it…

A woman alone is an awkward creature, or so it appears. A bedside table missing its companion. A lone kitchen glove. You could make do, but it really isn't seemly. Where do you seat her if it is a sit-down meal? If she has come with an escort, that's all right then. But if she is alone, you alternate between having to watch out for her and watching her so that she doesn't sink her predatory claws into your spouse. Pity is one thing. And yes, sisterhood is key. Women have to be there for women. So you have her over for a coffee morning or drinks… but for a whole evening, she is best avoided.

Meera knows the mind of a hostess. She has been one too. Choosing to forget the widow in Giri's office when she hosted a dinner to celebrate his promotion. Ignoring the unspoken plea in a newly divorced Dina's voice when they met at the beauty salon and Dina said, 'I've heard so much about your dinner parties. You must have me over the next time…'

In the end it is Vinnie's husband Kishore who rescues her. Meera suddenly has a drink in her hand, a chair to perch herself upon, a group to share her views with, and a man at her side. She wonders what she would have done if Kishore hadn't taken pity on her.

She sneaks a glance at him. The very dignified, devastatingly handsome, utterly charming and totally removed Kishore. Vinnie and he share a home and a business. For the rest, they lead separate lives.

Meera had been unable to hide the reproof in her eyes when Vinnie explained the arrangement.

'You don't approve?' Vinnie asked.

'No. I don't. You are turning marriage into a farce.' Meera was unable to keep the bitterness from her voice. 'Marriage is sacred. It is not just being joint owners of a home and a business.'

'So you would have given Giri a divorce if he had asked for it, just like that?' Vinnie's voice was dipped in steel.

'Mine is a different situation…' Meera tried to prevaricate. Would she have? What if Giri had come to her and said he wanted out? Would she have let him go?

'Ah Meera, don't kid yourself. I don't. We like what marriage means. Even if you knew Giri hated it, felt trapped, you would still have wanted your marriage… I do. Kishore does too, I think. It is the circle of security that has us enchanted. Not the house or the money, the sex or kids. Not even companionship.'

Meera was quiet. She knew what it was to be cast out of that enchanted place. She knew what it was to be alone.

She looks at Kishore again and thinks, how is it that both Vinnie and I, despite being who we are, women of the world, are still in our hearts made of the same mettle as Kala Chithi? What had she said: *Kal analum kanavan, pull analum purushan.*

In the weeks after Giri left home, Meera had wondered what she would do if she were invited to a party. Accept or refuse. Then it rankled that she wasn't invited, given the choice to make up her mind.

But here she is, holding herself erect. Saro is right, she thinks. Posture is all. You may cringe within, not knowing the degrees of civility to affect. You may not know any of the rules of your new station in life. But if your back is erect and your shoulders square, you could get away with much. Including a spider plant as a gift for the hostess.

Here in Vinnie's home, Meera feels none of the awkwardness that planted itself in her at the few parties she has been to minus Giri. There are no pauses in the conversation. No one trying to skirt around the subject of Giri and then not knowing what to talk about. Pretty much all that could be spoken in that circle was pivoted around Giri and her as Giri's wife. At Vinnie's party, Giri is entombed in a past no one has any inkling of or gives a toss about.

Someone comes to sit next to Meera. An older man. 'How do you know Vinnie?' he asks, smiling at her. 'A business associate?'

'No, a friend,' Meera says. 'I am Meera,' she adds, stretching her hand.

'Raj.' He takes her hand in his. He holds her palm for a long moment. Longer than necessary, Meera thinks, gently sliding her fingers out of his grasp.

Vinnie had warned her about him. 'Most of the men are decent chaps. Raj is a bit of a smoothie. If he hits on you, walk away. He won't be offended. He should be used to it by now. It's like he can't help himself. The one I feel sorry for is his wife.' Smooth to the point of shininess, Meera tells herself as he chats her up.

'So, are you married, Meera? Is there a husband somewhere?' he tosses at her.

'Single,' Meera says. Then, with frost in her voice, she clarifies, 'Single. And not available.'

Meera sees a nondescript woman shooting anxious looks their way. She narrows her eyes and says, 'Is that your wife? I think she's looking for you.'

Now that she has dealt with the wolf, Meera is confident enough to gambol with the lambs.

Nevertheless, it is an exhausted woman who kicks her stilettos off.

The house is sunk in sleep. Meera opens the cupboard as quietly as she can. When the handle comes off in her hand, the exhaustion in her digs in deeper. One more thing to deal with, she thinks wearily. Where does one begin with a second life?

Then from the open closet comes a whiff of sandal. A frisson of pleasure shoots through her as she takes the sachet and buries her nose in its satiny side.

The lightness of being. How stealthily it creeps up on you. One moment you think that you will buckle under the burden of all that you have to deal with. And the next moment a satin pouch of sandal dust can miraculously alleviate the unbearable weight.

It doesn't matter that this is only a fleeting sense of well-being. Now that Meera has known it again, she finds strength.

She closes her eyes and breathes in deeply of the fragrance. Again and again.

Meera wishes for something else then. That Jak could know this too. In the slump of his shoulders, she has seen the echo of defeat that gnaws at her. If only Jak could feel this lightness too. It would erase the pain in his eyes. For a while.

That is all people like Jak and I can hope for now. Temporary remission. A quick joy in a period of lull.

III

Joy needs to be worked towards. Joy needs to be sought. Joy seldom drops into our lives, we have to go looking for it. This is what troubles Kala as she tosses and turns in her bed.

She can't sleep. She lies on one side, then the other. On her back and on her belly. But no matter which position she tries, her body will not relax and slip into languor. Her thoughts keep crowding one into another.

It is the dark phase of the moon. Outside, the night is black as tar pitch and just as impenetrable. The room faces away from the road and not even traffic sounds come in this far. Kala has pulled the curtains shut and in the dark womb-like room, she curves into a little ball, drawing her knees to her chin, tucking her hands between her thighs. And yet, she can't sleep. Meera has unsettled her more than she cares to admit to herself.

She has learnt to live with her past. It seldom intrudes into the fabric of evenness that is her life. So Kala can't understand these trespassing memories that rush in and retreat like the waves.

She rises and puts on the light. She needs to talk. And in Smriti, she has found her perfect listener. Someone who hears her patiently and doesn't twist her guts with unspoken recrimination.

Kala creeps into Smriti's room. In the greenish light, she can see that Smriti's eyes are open. Is it possible to sleep with your eyes open, she wonders. You can have eyes with perfect vision and still be blind; she knows someone who has been diagnosed with hysterical blindness. So perhaps it is possible. With Smriti, who can tell? But she is certain of one thing. Smriti can hear.

'Are you awake, my dear?' Kala asks softly.

The grimacing monster stares at the wall.

Kala sighs.

I know you are listening. I know that, Smriti. I know somewhere in that brain of yours, these sounds I make are being deciphered and decoded. I know that, child.

You are wondering, aren't you, how I figured it out?

I found out the day I talked to you about making beans parpu usili.

That morning, at breakfast, Kitcha was in an unusually talkative mood. He seemed to want to talk about the past. Kala had been surprised at what seemed close to garrulousness on Kitcha's part.

'What I often dreamt about when I was in the US was your beans parpu usili,' he said suddenly.

Kala smiled. 'Yes, I had forgotten how much you liked it. I must make it for you,' she said, planning to go to the Cox Town market herself for tender young French beans with just the perfect snap to them when you broke their backs with a push of the thumb.

As Kala sat there topping and tailing the beans and paring away their stringy sides, she told Smriti how she was going to prepare it. There was no one at home that day. Smriti's nurse had called to say she would be late by an hour. I'll be there in time to bathe and feed her, Sarah had said.

Kala hadn't been pleased. She knew Kitcha wouldn't be, either. But she heard Sarah's fervent plea. Please, madam, it is really urgent. Otherwise I wouldn't ask. If you sit there in the room for a little while, every fifteen minutes or so, she will be fine. She is frightened only if you leave her alone for long periods.

Kala sucked in her breath. They hadn't known. 'You never told us this.' She heard the accusation in her own voice.

'How could I? There is no way to validate it! And with a patient in her condition, I didn't want to raise any false hopes, not even the tiniest one.'

Kala had a little chopping board. She placed it on a table and slowly began chopping the beans. 'Your father, my Kitcha, has a great fondness for beans parpu usili. It's been a long while since I made it for him. Do you think he will like it now? Memory is a strange thing, Smriti. It makes us add mythical dimensions to the ordinary. When Kitcha says, "the memory of your beans parpu usili still lingers on my tongue", it scares me. How can I compete with memory?

'See this, Smriti. The beans are all chopped. The thoran parpu is soaked and cooked. Now all I need to do is add the steamed beans to the parpu and sauté it. You know what parpu is, don't you? Dal… lentils.'

It was then Kala thought she saw a movement in Smriti's throat. Could it be that she had salivated? A wave of excitement rippled through her.

When Sarah came into the kitchen to make the pap she fed Smriti, Kala offered a bowl of beans parpu usili mixed with rice and ghee and puréed into a mess. Sarah frowned. 'What's this? The patient's intake is so little that it has to be nutritious.'

'Give this to her for once,' Kala urged. 'I think she will like it.'

Kala went with Sarah. She couldn't usually bear to watch her feed Smriti. The patience with which Sarah slid the spoon into Smriti's clamped mouth, knocking it against her teeth so she could wedge it in and allow the food to slither down.

Mush would trickle out of the corner of Smriti's mouth. Sarah would use a wet wipe. And she would continue till she had gone through the entire bowl while the heap of wet wipes crusted with Smriti's spit and food grew in a pile.

But Smriti ate more than she had ever done before and when Sarah turned to Kala with a surprised look, she hid the triumph in her eyes. 'She seems to actually like it!'

'Maybe every now and then I could give you a bowl of food to feed her,' Kala said hesitantly.

'Yes, once in two-three days. She needs the special diet to ensure she gets all the vitamins, proteins, etc.'

Kala nodded.

But she wouldn't tell Kitcha what had transpired. That somewhere in the body that held Smriti prisoner, life lurked. A life force in the movement of a muscle, in the constriction of her throat. Kitcha would dismiss it. As would Nina. But Kala had hope for Smriti.

Smriti, child, are you listening? I wasn't able to sleep so I thought I would sit at your side and talk to you. You like that, don't you?

Kitcha wanted to know what I talk to you about. I told him that I plan the menu with you. I discuss what I am going to cook.

Kitcha had smiled.

What else is there for me to talk about? I asked him, annoyed by that teasing smile.

We need to talk to her. Not just read aloud to her, I added.

He frowned then. Kala knew that he thought she was finding fault with him. Like Nina had when she discovered Kitcha reading out to her the emails Shruti sent.

'What's wrong with you, Kitcha? Do you think she comprehends anything? Snippets from the newspaper, sections from the books you read. You might as well play an audio tape for her,' Nina had said, watching Jak.

'No, don't look at me like that. You like to think I am this heartless bitch. I am not. All I want to do is take my daughter home where she can receive proper medical attention.'

And Jak had snapped, 'She will get the best medical attention, but do you have the time to be with her?'

I do. I have all the time for my daughters. My baby Shruti at fifteen is turning into an adult. But am I part of that process? She barely knows me and I, her. I know nothing of her dreams and desires, her likes and dislikes. You have made sure that Shruti has little to do with me. So you see, I am not going to give up my other child for you to put away, Jak had thought furiously, trying not to let his consternation show.

Kala could almost hear the wheels turn in Kitcha's head. She touched his elbow gently and said, 'Reading aloud makes it impersonal. When you talk, she is involved.'

How could Kala tell him what she knew? How could she allow him to hope unless Smriti give her a sign that would satisfy that forever doubting mind of his?

Kitcha turned away. 'Do you think she knows the difference? It is just the sound of a voice!'

IV

A low murmuring voice. Jak wakes up abruptly from a deep sleep, hearing the cadence of quietly spoken words. For a moment time shifts backwards and he is once again Kitcha, the boy who liked to wake up to the hum of conversation. He would lie in bed with his eyes half shut, strangely comforted by the voices. His father and mother's as they went about their morning chores, his mother keeping up a constant flow of observations while his father interjected with a short reply or a grunt. Kitcha would snuggle his face deeper into the pillow, a warmth pervading him from deep within. A sense of well-being. Even as he slept, his world continued to turn. The voices were testimony to that.

Then reality prevails and Jak sits up in alarm. Smriti. What is wrong? He slips a T-shirt on over his shorts and opens the door.

Smriti's room is cast in its greenish light. He sees Kala Chithi seated at her side. Her chin is in her palm and her face is pensive as she talks.

'I was thinking tonight of the time all of you – Kitcha, your mother, Shruti and you – came to see me in Madras,' Kala Chithi says.

Jak pauses as a memory dislodges itself.

A ten-year-old Smriti. A six-year-old Shruti. Nina still revelling in her triumph of having written a non-fiction bestseller women all over the world were lining up to buy and read. No one had expected *The Nine Yard Noose* – Nina's dissertation on the sari and its role in the condition of Indian women – to become the success it turned out to be. Neither Nina, nor the small university press. You had watched from the sidelines, amazed and amused to see Nina metamorphose from quiet academic to celebrity writer. It was Nina who had wanted to go to Madras. She was researching her next book, she said. They had stayed at the Connemara and driven around in airconditioned cars that had protected them from the heat and dust of Madras.

Then, standing outside Kala Chithi's door, you breathed in the fragrance of jasmine shikakai freshly ground coffee coriander and felt a great wave of nostalgia.

'I miss all of this!' you said.

'You would!' Nina laughed. 'Oh Kitcha, what am I to do with you?' She crinkled her nose and rubbed her face against your sleeve like an affectionate kitten.

Kala Chithi opened the door and ushered them in. Lunch was served amidst much chit-chat and catching up. Kala Chithi had cooked a Kitcha favourite, the urunda kozhambu.

Shruti had picked up an urunda and asked, 'What's this?'

Smriti bit into it and said, 'Mmm… I love it!'

And you asked, 'Better than the Swedish meatballs you like at the IKEA restaurant?'

'Yes, yes, much nicer. I love this!'

Was it then you saw a flicker of irritation cross Nina's face? She didn't seem to like the idea of her daughter preferring something that she had relegated to a distant part of her life. The 'was' section that Nina didn't like going into.

Nina said, 'Dumplings. That's all it is. Vegetarian dumplings!'

And Kala Chithi said, 'I don't cook meat. I can't bear the thought of cooking, let alone eating it!'

'You don't know what you are missing,' Nina said. 'Actually, Kala Chithi, you don't know how much you have missed out in life by choosing to remain here. You should have taken up Kitcha's invitation to join us in the States.'

Kala Chithi's voice again. 'Child, your mother said something very stupid that day. She said I didn't know what I was missing. I wanted to snap at her. There was plenty that I missed. Enough losses and absences to lament over. What does she know of my life, I thought. Yet, here she was, implying my life would have been different had I taken to eating meat or gone to America.'

Jak halts in his tracks. He doesn't want to eavesdrop but he feels compelled to stay on and listen. Kala Chithi is such an enigma. She told you only what she thought you needed to know.

At first I thought I must be the luckiest woman on earth. How could I not? He loved many things about me. He loved even my hair that I hated.

You didn't know this, did you? Once I had hair that almost reached my knees. Hair that fell like a cascade when I unpinned it. Straight as rainwater hair, with not a kink or even a wave. I could run a comb in one swift motion from the root to the tip. And every morning I would comb it through and braid it and pin it up. The weight of it made my head ache, my neck droop. The hair made me a demure girl first and then a demure woman. I was the daughter who pleased my father and later a wife who pleased my husband.

All through my school days and university too, I let my hair grow. Then I began to see how the other girls were less burdened. Only I seemed weighed down. I wanted to cut it. My father was aghast. 'Are you mad?' he demanded. 'Look at your hair. Do you know what an asset it is? Not everyone has hair like yours.'

I couldn't understand it. When everyone else stopped their daughters' education after high school, my father insisted that both my sister and I continue to study. He wanted us to be university graduates. How could such a progressive man be so regressive when it came to hair? It was my hair, after all.

It took my father almost a week to recover from the shock of what I had merely proposed. The doctor prescribed pills to tame his blood pressure, quell his anxiety and settle his nerves. The doctor who was my father's friend also advised me to not provoke my father with silly childish gestures. 'You can cut your hair off and do what you please when you are married,' he said, echoing my father. 'But why would you want to do that? It is beautiful hair, after all, Kala!'

My neck hurt that night. An ache that crept down to my shoulders and lodged there. My mother, who hadn't said much until then, found me whimpering with the pain. 'What is it, Kala?' she whispered. 'Is it the time of the month? Do you want me to give you a hot water fomentation? Will it ease the cramps?'

'It is this,' I cried, gesturing to my hair. 'The weight of it! My neck and shoulders hurt. It is worse than the menstrual cramp, Amma.'

She said nothing. I pulled at her elbow, wondering if I could rally her support. 'With the cramp I know it will go away in a day. But this… and Appa won't let me cut it!'

'No, you can't. Of course you can't. He is right.' She could be just as stubborn as he was, I realized. Or, was it that when it came to his wishes, she would be stubborn on his behalf.

'What am I to do then? Live with this pain till I die?' I snapped, angered by her inability to see my point of view.

'You don't have to tie it up every night,' she said, opening my braid and unravelling it like it was a skein of rope. She took a comb and began combing its length. 'A loosened plait is what you need so that you don't damage the hair… see,' she said, weaving it deftly. And then she began massaging my neck. 'The pain will go away, Kala. I promise you. Besides, there is much greater pain waiting for us women in our lives. How can you be cowed down by something so negligible?'

The loose plait arced around my neck and fell over my breasts and belly to my thigh. I wept then. I felt imprisoned by my hair. And she was the jailor. For my father must have confided his fears to her. 'She is impetuous. Keep an eye on her so that she doesn't do something silly like chop it off in a rage.'

When my husband and his family first came to see me, my father had my most valuable asset enhanced. It wouldn't have been seemly to leave my hair loose, not as you girls do. So my mother and my aunts combed it till it shone like silk. They braided my hair and wove jasmine into it. Thereafter, it didn't matter that my complexion was dusky or that my singing was, to put it kindly, mediocre, or that our house was shabby. My hair overwhelmed them. Even the dowry they asked for was modest. Appa needed to take a loan but it wouldn't ruin him, he said.

'See, see,' he said triumphantly. 'I was right. If I had let you cut your hair, you would still be here, waiting for a suitable boy. But this is fantastic, Bhanu,' he said, turning to my mother. 'Did you see it? I was watching them. The boy couldn't take his eyes off Kala's hair! Do you see why I insisted that she keep her hair?'

'Are you in such a hurry to send me away?' I demanded, only half in jest. I had never seen my father so animated.

'You have to go sooner than later,' my father said sternly. 'Daughters are never for keeps. They are loaned to us for a while. Besides, after what happened to Sarada, it is best to marry you off before grooms and their families start asking awkward questions.'

'But how can you blame Akka? Athimbair is the one who went away, all of us know that!' I protested. 'Amma, tell him!'

Amma wouldn't speak. She sat on the swing at my father's side, her lower lip trembling, but she wouldn't speak. I was terrified. How could I not feel as if the world was coming down upon me?

I realized then that they held Akka responsible for her husband leaving her. She just wasn't a good enough wife, one who could keep her husband at her side. She was a failed woman. My sister, who had taken to being a wife as though it was the calling of her life. 'He left her to become a sanyasi; it wasn't as if he went off with another woman. How can you hold her responsible for that?' I spluttered in my anguish. I had never been as afraid as I was then. A word of support for my sister would have given me some courage. One word of anger on her behalf and I would have known that if anything went wrong in my life, they would encompass me with their love, their strength.

But they wouldn't speak. Like Akka, I would be on my own if I didn't make my husband happy. My destiny was linked to his. I had no life to call my own. I was nothing on my own. So when I saw how much my husband loved me, I was comforted.

On our wedding night, my husband had me stand with my back to him. He looked at my loosely woven plait and hefted it in his palm. 'Doesn't your head hurt with the weight of it, Vaidehi?' he asked slowly. I had been given a new name at the marriage ceremony, as was customary. I was Vaidehi now. And expected to be as acquiescent as she had been. The ideal wife to the ideal man, Rama.

I nodded. Would he ask me to trim it to a more manageable length?

'Open it, Vaidehi. That should make it feel less heavy,' he said. Then he placed his arm on my shoulder. 'No, let me do it.'

I felt him prise open the plait, remove the flowers. He was gentle, taking care not to snag or pull. Relief filled me. He would free me of my burden, I knew. When he saw how long it was, he would do it himself, perhaps. Lay a newspaper on the floor and chop it to the length he liked best. Even an inch less would be less of it, I told myself.

I felt the hair on my back. I felt his eyes on it. I heard him say, 'Such beautiful hair. Vaidehi, promise me that you won't ever touch a hair on your head without my permission.'

The next morning I coiled every last rebellious thought with my hair and pinned the weight of it with my braid to the nape of my neck. The weight of that burden caused my neck to droop even further. The pain was ceaseless. But my husband was a happy man and so was my father.

In my husband's home in Minjikapuram by the sea, I lived the careful, well tended life of a content wife.

My husband and his family were good people. They even let me have all of Friday morning to groom my hair. My sisters-in-law helped me oil my hair. My husband filled the cauldron so I would have plenty of hot water. Every Friday morning, until I left that home, my mother-in-law would ask me if she could assist with the shikakai. Help me to work the soapnut powder into a lather. And then, while I lay on the swing, she and my husband would take turns to air the damp out of my hair with the sambrani smoke. They would sit there passing my hair over the basket in which camphor burnt, exclaiming at its length, sheen and health. I would feel my eyes grow heavy and sometimes I dozed off, weary after the rigours of the Friday wash.

On Friday nights my husband made love to me with much gusto. It was the night when my freshly washed hair fell like a shroud on my back and he played with it. When he was done, my husband was a happy man. And so, my father was a happy man.

Your father came visiting me there. He was a precious child, your father, my Kitcha. He was the son I didn't have. Only my Kitcha saw how weighed down I was. Only Kitcha seemed to understand how imprisoned I felt by my hair.

He had taken to watching the skies by then. It was a strange interest for a boy as young as he was. He had even found himself a secluded part of the beach to go to. It wasn't very far from where we lived. It was almost at our doorstep. One day, when Ambi was away on an official trip, I went with Kitcha. 'Come, come,' he urged me. 'What you see, actually sense and feel at that hour, will change you for life.'

I smiled at his intensity. At his choice of words.

I didn't tell anyone what I was planning to do. I sneaked out of bed and into the early hours of the day with Kitcha at my side.

Kitcha was right. At that hour, the light in the sky and from the sea wrapped me in a glow of – what shall I call it? Hope? Freedom? Peace? I don't know, child. I still don't have a name for that leaping of my soul. All I knew was, I wanted it forever. That feeling of being on the threshold of something momentous.

Kitcha didn't speak. He just looked at me and I knew he knew how moved I was. 'There is something else you should do,' he said.

'What?'

'Come into the water with me.'

'Kitcha, I can't swim.'

'You don't have to. We are going only a little way in.'

He took my hand and led me in. The waves licked at our feet first, then they broke against our knees and swirled around my thighs.

'Now sit,' he urged. 'Sit in the sea.'

I was wet anyway. A certain recklessness swept me into doing as he asked. Ah, what shall I say, Smriti? You probably know how it feels, the buoyancy of water. How it leeches away all the weight that shackles your dreams. For the first time, I felt weightless. On an impulse I opened my hair and let the sea seep through it. My hair rose and my neck ceased to ache. I began to laugh. Softly at first, then loudly, as I paddled and splashed around.

Kitcha smiled and joined in, splashing water into my face. And, all along, like a creature set free, my hair swirled and floated in the sea.

When the sun began to streak the skies, I knew it was time to go. I looked at my wet clothes and hair and reality set in. What was I going to do?

I looked down on myself, at my wet blouse and sari, and felt dread wash over me. Why was I afraid, I asked myself. All I had done was splash in the sea. Was that a crime? And they, Ambi's family, had never given me any reason to fear them. Besides, I had done nothing wrong. But I looked down at myself, my dripping clothes and hair, and felt fear swill through my mouth.

Have you ever known anything like that, child? The binding boundaries of those unwritten lines etched into your fibre. It is a greenish blue indelible tattoo that says what is proper and what isn't. I had been improper. I was guilty. The tattoo throbbed.

The breeze dried my clothes. As for my hair, I plaited it quickly and bundled it into a bun at the nape of my neck. When we reached home, I bathed quickly and changed my clothes. By the time everyone woke up, the morning chores were done, the coffee perking. No one suspected my impropriety. Only my hair knew.

The weight of its wetness stretched the skin of my face. My mother-in-law looked up from her breakfast and said, 'You look strained, Vaidehi. What's wrong?'

'Nothing.' I smiled, shaking my head. The very action made my neck hurt even more.

'She must be missing Ambi,' one of Ambi's aunts laughed.

I ran from the room as befitting a young wife and went to my room. I could neither stand nor sit nor lie down. My hair dragged me down to a private hell. Of your own making, my conscience rebuked me.

I pleaded a headache and stayed in my room all afternoon. In its darkened solitude, I undid my hair and let it breathe. As I combed its by now mouldy wetness, I found debris from the shore. A piece of twig, a length of seaweed, a couple of shells, and a minnow that had entangled itself in my hair and been buried alive in its coils. I shrieked as its silvery side emerged. And then I began to laugh. I was a fisherwoman and my hair was my net. What would Ambi say when I told him, I chortled. I stopped abruptly. How could I tell Ambi or anyone else what I had done?

They wouldn't approve. The tattoo throbbed again.

By the time my hair was dry, good sense prevailed. I would never again do anything so stupid, I told myself.

That night, when Kitcha asked me if I would go with him in the morning, I said no.

And yet, in the early hours of the day, when he stepped out, I was with him.

Kitcha smiled. I love that smile of your father's. It has always tugged at my heart. It is the all-knowing co-conspirator's smile. I will never tell on you even though I know all about you, it says. He smiled again and shook his head mock ruefully.

I punched his shoulder with an insouciant hand while the other was already plucking at my bound hair. I didn't understand this creature I was turning into. I didn't want to. 'Don't speak a word. Let us go.'

Kitcha and I went to the beach the next two days. Each day, while my hair fished the waters, I escaped its weight. On the bathroom ventilator sill, a collection of my hair's catch grew. It was a secret. My very own secret that lit my soul. The celestial light was your father's secret. The sea was mine. On our last day, Kitcha looked at me bundling up my hair and asked quietly, 'Don't you think there is too much of it?'

I nodded.

'Why don't you cut it a bit? Just a few inches...'

'Oh no.' I felt my eyes widen in shock. 'I couldn't. They would be most upset!'

'How would they know? No one's going to tell the difference. No one will even realize the difference, but it would be that much less for you to carry around.'

Only Kitcha had sensed the unbearable burden my hair was to me. He has that in him. An innate sensitivity that allows him to slice through all the layers of pretence, all the clouds of deceit we cover ourselves with. He sees right through to the heart. He understands most things even if he doesn't know what to do with that understanding.

Ambi was meant to come home the day after Kitcha left. If he had, I wonder now if my life would have stayed the same... who can tell? All it takes is one fleeting second for an entire lifetime to shift its axis.

Do you know the story of Abhimanyu in the Mahabharata? He was still in his mother Subhadra's womb when Arjuna his father was being taught the Chakravyuha by Krishna. Poor Subhadra. She was a warrior princess but she had no interest in war strategies. Abhimanyu listened, as did his father, as Krishna explained how to break through the seven circles of the wheel formation. And then, before he could explain to Arjuna how to exit it successfully, Subhadra fell asleep. And so Abhimanyu, on the thirteenth day of the Kurukshetra war, knew how to invade the Kaurava army but was unable to withdraw once he was in the heart of the circle.

What was he thinking of as he rode into that circle? Such foolhardiness. Such self-deception. You see, Smriti, we are all like that. Sometimes I think the Chakravyuha is a metaphor for all deceit. We let our own desires trap us into deceiving ourselves. But we do not know how to extricate ourselves without losing the life we have chosen to live.

That Friday, I woke up feeling out of sorts. I missed the dawn by the sea. And being able to shed the weight at the nape of my neck. Perhaps, when Ambi was back, I could persuade him to take me to the sea as Kitcha did.

Friday was the day of the oil bath. My mother-in-law and

sisters-in-law helped massage the warm oil into my hair. 'Why is your hair so coarse?' one of them, Rema, asked.

The seawater had coarsened it but I had no words to speak. So I smiled and said nothing. They loved that about me. That I seldom had answers.

'It must be missing Ambi Anna,' Ruku teased. 'Sometimes Akka, I think Ambi Anna loves your hair more than he loves you.'

I still didn't speak. Sometimes the very thought had occurred to me.

That afternoon the heat was unbearable. The skies were overcast. A grey settled on me too. A flat grey swath of despair.

That afternoon my hair felt even more dense and heavy. And it wouldn't dry. I looked at the ends. Rema was right. It felt like coconut fibre. Not my usual skeins of silk. I felt a great disgust for it.

What was I thinking? I do not know, but as if in a trance I took the scissors from the sewing machine table and cut a foot and a half of it.

The skies heaved. A clap of thunder.

I saw the ends of my hair settle on the floor. What have I done, I asked myself in fear. What have I done? What if my hair never grows again? What will Ambi say? What will my father say?

I felt the ends of my hair brush my hips. It swung with a new lightness. What had once lain heavy and to my knees now became a gentle creature. I felt freer. I moved my head this way and that. The hair swung with me. Such headiness. I was once again floating in the waters of the ocean.

The rains began. Heavy piercing shafts of rain that enveloped the room and caused the silence in it to swell. I looked at my hair lying on the floor. I gathered it quickly and thrust it into a cloth bag and hid it amidst my saris. When my hair was dry, I braided it and pinned it into its usual bun at the nape of my neck. No one would notice. No one would know what I had done. I smiled to myself. My secret was safe.

I realized that I was no longer Vaidehi with the downcast eyes. My neck didn't hurt any more.

Ambi arrived two days later. He sensed a difference. 'What is it, Vaidehi?' he said, peering at me. 'There is something… Is there something?' The question in his eyes unsettled me. Ambi and I still hoped that I would become pregnant soon. We had been married for two years now. No one had spoken the word yet, but I heard it in my inner ear: barren… barren. Perhaps now things would change. My eyes rose to meet his.

'You don't seem so shy of me any more. I can actually see something of your face, apart from your forehead.' I heard the teasing note in Ambi's voice and felt something like relief course through me. Ambi was my husband, not my keeper.

In our bed as I lay nestled against him, I felt his fingers caress me in an absent sort of way. My hair swathed him as he liked it to. Then his fingers paused suddenly. 'What is this?'

'What?' I asked, half asleep.

'Your hair…'

'What about my hair? I want to sleep.'

'There doesn't seem enough of it,' he said.

'I trimmed the ends,' I heard myself say. 'Just the ends. Ruku said it had split ends; it had turned coarse. She called it coconut fibre.' I was blabbering, but something about Ambi frightened me.

'Switch on the light,' he said. 'Turn around,' he ordered when the room was lit up.

He hefted a handful of hair. 'What have you done? You haven't just trimmed the ends. You have cut it. How could you?'

'It'll grow back,' I offered tentatively.

'You didn't even think of asking my permission?'

I didn't know what to say. The words formed in my head: it's my hair. Do you ask me when you cut your hair every third Sunday? Do you love me or my hair?

But I couldn't speak. I had never seen this Ambi before. This cold, aloof stranger.

'It'll grow back,' I said again. 'I am sorry. I don't know what I was thinking of.' I felt tears start in my eyes.

'You deceived me. Would you have told me if I hadn't found out? You made a fool of me. How can I trust you ever again?'

I stared at him, aghast. All this for a foot and a half of hair! 'What are you saying? It's only hair and it'll grow back.'

'Yes, it may. What if it doesn't? But that isn't the point. You flouted my authority. You betrayed my trust. You broke my heart.'

I felt the weight on my neck grow.

'Do you know how long it takes for an inch of hair to grow?' Kala Chithi asks. 'A month? Six weeks?'

Jak hears tears in her voice. Then she clears her throat.

'Kitcha taught me how to use the internet. He showed me how to find information. I know now it takes a month for a mere half inch to grow. But then I didn't know how long it would take. I was frightened.

'Each day I measured my hair. To see if it showed a

difference in length. Each day I waited frantic with fear. All the stories I had heard came home to roost. That after a certain age hair ceases to grow. That it would be weak hair and it would fall as quickly as it grew. I tried everything. Hot oil massages. Hair tonics. I made vows and offerings to all the gods I could think of and I waited. Time had no meaning. For I measured the passage of time by my hair.'

Jak chews his lip. He thinks of those first days after Smriti's accident. Of the waiting that he subsumed into a relentless stream of activity. Of the passage of time gauged by news from the hospital. Do women quantify time differently from men? Do women allow time to rule them while all around men stride through their days grinding it into the ground? While he waited, what did Nina do, he wonders now.

It took eighteen months for seven inches to grow. For the first six months Ambi chose to punish me. I had to be taught a lesson, he deemed. For six months he didn't speak to me. Six months of not even a smile. We ate together, slept together, even fornicated when Ambi had the urge, but he wasn't the Ambi I knew or loved. I was never more lonely or desolate than I was then. My father wrote me a letter. He said he couldn't believe what I had done. He said he wouldn't come to see me till I was the girl he had sent to that home. He had never been as ashamed as he was now. And I was the reason why.

I felt my heart freeze. He was disowning me. Even my father.

At first I asked my mother-in-law to intervene. 'Your son is angry with me,' I said when she commented on the silence between us. 'Won't you tell him, Amma, to forgive me? Forgive my silliness.'

But my mother-in-law didn't think it was the thoughtless act of a foolish girl. 'Silly?' she snapped. 'How could you, Vaidehi? You betrayed his trust, our trust in you. It's not the hair. I hope you understand that. But you should have consulted us before you did what you did. You should have spoken to him. That's what has made him so angry. How can I intervene now?'

I wept at her feet, seeking forgiveness for my transgression. She softened then. But only enough to say, 'Maybe he will find it in his heart to love you again when your hair grows back. He is a stubborn man, my Ambi. Once he makes up his mind, nothing can budge him. Pray to Eashwara that your hair grows back quickly.'

And so I waited. All I had to sustain me was the sea's booty that my hair had fetched me from the waters of the ocean. A handful of shells that echoed with the forlorn music of another time.

In time my hair reached the length it used to be. My head drooped. The ache in my shoulders began again. And Ambi was back to being the man he was. He had made his point and he could be magnanimous with his forgiveness and largesse.

Only I wasn't the same any more. I was like one of the shells I kept on my bathroom ledge. Hollowed out.

Seven years after we were married, we were still childless. Ambi decided that he would wed again. It would be amicable and civilized. The new wife and I would live like sisters, he said. The child he would father would have two mothers, he said. Our son would be twice blessed.

I said nothing. I knew that there was no use protesting. Ambi would do as he pleased. And he would do it so civilly, so gently, that no one would even reproach him. That was Ambi's greatest weapon: to be the most reasonable being even when he was crumbling your life and self-respect into a million pieces.

I finally had a reason to leave him. Not even my father could fault me for this. I was the wronged wife. So I left him. Before I went, I cut my hair at the nape of my neck. I gave it to Ambi. A long braid woven with jasmine and kanakambaram. 'This is all you ever wanted of me. Keep it. And let me go,' I said, walking out.

My father wept when I went home. 'What sins am I paying for?' He hit his head several times. 'I have two daughters and they are both destitute. One abandoned by her husband. The other abandons her husband. What am I to do?'

'And what is this, Vaidehi?' he demanded, his eyes settling on my shorn head.

'I am not going back. And I will never grow my hair again,' I said. 'If you force me to, I'll leave home. I will be a whore but I won't be a wife. Not Ambi's wife. And don't call me Vaidehi ever again. I am Kala, do you hear me?'

Jak swallows. The lump in his throat refuses to budge. What had he done? He hadn't meant to ruin Kala Chithi's life. All he had wanted was to see her smile again. The smile that so reminded him of his mother's, and which he seldom saw after Appa left.

He walks into the room and touches Kala Chithi's shoulder. She jumps.

'Hush, hush, I didn't mean to startle you,' he says.

'I couldn't sleep so I came to sit with her,' a flustered Kala Chithi says, not meeting his eyes.

Suddenly weary of all the pretence and deceit, Jak takes her hands in his. 'I didn't know, Kala Chithi. I didn't know any of this…'

She doesn't speak for a few moments. Then Kala Chithi reverts to being the kindly aunt he can always count on. 'How could you, Kitcha? I didn't tell anyone. Not even your mother. But you mustn't blame yourself for my life. No one is ever responsible for what happens to someone else. You have to accept that. It is the truth. Whether it is my life or Smriti's.'

Jak bows his head. Redemption on a platter. Only, he cannot accept it.

V

Accept this day as a gift. Don't clutter it up with this and that, Meera tells herself sternly.

She is all alone in her home. It is a Wednesday and Meera cannot remember when she ever had a day to herself in her old lilac house.

She looks at the envelope curiously. The return address is Watermill Press. She opens it and a cheque flutters out, and a clipping. A business magazine has excerpted a small section from her *Corporate Wife's Guide to Entertaining*. This is her share of the payment, the letter says.

Meera holds aloft the clipping.

The Corporate Wife's Guide to Entertaining
An Excerpt

1. **Invitations** – Write one. How long does it take to write an invitation? But think of the impression it will make on your guests. And do remember to send it at least two weeks in advance. Note: If you are the guest, you must RSVP.
2. **Welcome** – Be dressed and ready by the time your guests arrive. You ought to be there to greet them as they come to the door.
3. **Personal belongings** – Set aside a place for your guests to leave their personal items. Shawls, briefcases, carry bags, whatever. Find a place where they can be kept and found easily. During the monsoons, leave a bucket in the porch or entrance foyer so dripping umbrellas may be left there.
4. **Gifts** – Your heart may balk at the thought of yet another candle or wilting bouquet but learn to accept hostess gifts with a smile. It just might help to turn to your husband and exclaim: Oh, look what xyz has brought us… Note: If you are the guest, choose a small but unusual gift. And avoid desserts and flowers. The last thing a hostess needs to worry about is stretching your dessert among the guests or finding a vase for your flowers.
5. **Children** – Some guests may want to bring their children along. While you may not like it, there is very little you can do about it. The best thing to do is to ensure that you tuck the little horrors away before they get into your Swarovski crystal or scratch your antique furniture.

   If you have children, ask (read that as bribe) them to entertain the visiting kids. Or, call in for pizza and offer juice or coke in plastic glasses and send them off to watch TV in a room away from the dining area. You don't want them playing Ring o' ring o' roses or Fire in the mountain, run, run, run, around your dining table!
6. **Breaking the ice** – Before you offer guests drinks and hors de oeuvres, take care to introduce people to each other and add a sentence or two about what they do so that any embarrassment can be avoided.
7. **Buffet or sit-down** – If you are having the party catered

for, then a sit-down banquet is a great idea. It is impressive and will show you and your husband in the best possible light. Note: Check the credentials of the caterers with a few people who have used them before you hire them. Also, caterers can be expensive. In which case, unless you have adequate cutlery, crockery and household help to serve and remove the used dishes, plan a buffet meal where you can convert your dining table into a food counter.

8. **Hors de oeuvres** – If you are having caterers, brief them beforehand on the pattern of circulation and at what intervals each eat should appear. If you are doing it yourself, leave clusters of short eats at strategic places. Note: chips, peanuts, savouries are all very well for college parties. Think salads, satays, cheeses, cold cuts, etc., all of which can be either bought or prepared in advance. Note: Look for interesting bowls and platters to serve them in. You want to be seen as a hostess with an eye for the unusual. Use the nibbles time to go to the kitchen to give the rest of the meal a quick dekko.
9. **Dinner** – Allow one hour to pass before you invite the guests to the table. Make sure that the salads are crisp, and the hot dishes are piping hot and not lukewarm. Note: It may be a good idea to invest in chafing dishes.
10. **Dessert** – By carefully structuring your party, the dessert and coffee phase can be used to best advantage too. It is not just on golf courses and in boardrooms that deals are made. Make the most of that final pleasurable moment by moving the dessert and coffee back to the living room.
11. **Goodbyes** – By not delaying dinner, you can be quite sure that your guests leave on time. When they are ready to do so, go with them to the door, don't get into a long convoluted goodbye and/or make plans for future meetings. Instead, thank them again and return to the other guests. Note: If you are the guest, do not engage the host in a long conversation at the door.
12. No matter what, remember that if you don't enjoy your party, it will show. So tell yourself all will be fine, pour yourself one glass of wine (no more), and be the corporate wife you are – gracious, charming and super efficient.

MEERA GIRIDHAR

Meera's mouth twists into a grim smile. Who is this woman who dispensed such advice with the sagacity of a Sibyl? That life seemed so distant from the one she lives now.

She makes herself a pot of tea, lays out a small plate of biscuits and takes the tray with her into her favourite nook. A little tucked away veranda on the northern side of the house, camouflaged by trees. None of the others like this side of the house. It is a dark spot of disrepair. Broken ladders and bamboo poles used a long time ago to build scaffolding are stacked against the wall. Cement has hardened into boulders in sacks. Even the trees are old and dense with foliage and in one corner Meera has her compost pit. During the rains, a sweet fetid odour of rotting mulch rises from it and settles in the air.

But this December mid-morning, the sun trickles its way in through the trees, erasing the darkness and cleansing the air. Light falls on the grass and turns it an emerald green. Two kittens play hide-and-seek while their mother, the cat Meera is hoping to turn into a house cat, lolls against the ladders, peering through half closed eyes. Meera sips her tea and feels awash with content. We could be sisters, she tells the cat mother, you and I. We have our responsibilities, our burdens, but for the moment we have this: a place in the sun, a life in the shade.

The cat blinks. Meera smiles. She turns the page of the notepad in which she has begun making notes for *The Corporate Wife Abroad*. She has a gut instinct about this one, like she had with *The Corporate Wife's Guide to Entertaining*. And she isn't going to just do a proposal. She will write the full book out. There are other publishers she can write to – Penguin, HarperCollins, Hatchett, Random House, Rupa, so many of them. Surely one of them would buy it. The first thing to do is to divide the book into chapter heads. Meera sips her tea and doodles on the page.

Then, from inside the house, she hears the trilling of the phone. Meera looks at the cat. 'Should I?' she asks of her sister.

The cat pauses its slow washing of itself. You must do what you must do, while I do what I have to do, it seems to say. It rises slowly, stretches and walks away.

The phone continues to ring. And Meera, chastened by the disapproving tilt of the cat's tail, rushes indoors.

'Hey Meera, how are you?'

Meera feels her smile freeze. It is Soman at the other end of the line.

'I am fine. And you?'

'What do you expect, Meera?' he asks quietly. 'I waited for you to call me.'

Something stirs in her. She had begun avoiding his calls ever since Nayantara made known her displeasure of his presence in her mother's life. But the truth is, she misses hearing from him, being with him.

'I am sorry,' Meera says. 'I have been extremely busy.'

There is a silence. Then he says, 'What have you been doing?'

'Work, work, work, what else?' she says, careful to sound light-hearted.

'I've missed you, Meera.'

Meera doesn't speak. She doesn't know what to say.

'Can we meet?' he asks suddenly.

'I...' Meera begins, unsure how to turn him down.

'How about lunch this afternoon?' Soman interrupts. 'You have to eat, and I have to eat. Why don't we eat together?'

Meera laughs. A carefree sound of merriment.

For the day, she will cast aside all her discomfiture – Nayantara's disapproval, her own repugnance at the idea of a youthful boyfriend – and go out with him. Vinnie is right. She needs to introduce some vivacity into her life.

VI

Is vivaciousness allowed only in a young woman? Ought she to settle for sedate graciousness?

Meera searches her face in the mirror. She seldom wears make-up.

'Mine is just a water and Nivea routine,' she said airily, when Vinnie had insisted she start taking better care of her looks.

'Your mother, actually your grandmother too, are better turned out for their age,' Vinnie murmured, laying a few tubes of lipstick before her.

Meera narrowed her eyes. 'Are you serious? Lily looks what she is – an aged movie actress with her pencilled eyebrows and red lips. And as for Mummy, mutton dressed as lamb!'

'Don't be unkind, Meera. They are at least making an effort, whereas you are being priggish and self-defeating.'

Later, Meera lay in bed and wondered if that was what made Giri leave. That she had begun to look her age while he felt the need to cling to his youth. Meera bit her lip to still the trembling. Would it never cease? This drumming of doubts in her head…

Meera sits in front of the dressing table with articles of

artifice she has scrounged from the rooms of the other women in the lilac house – grandmother, mother, daughter. Where do I begin?

Foundation dots on the cheeks and forehead; the chin and the line of the jaw. Blend it in carefully, the bottle advocates. A concealer next, to camouflage the fact that she has hardly slept a full night since Giri left and that her mouth has sprung new lines at the corners. A dusting of fine powder; the calming clutch of beige dust that will not allow the ravages of uncertainty to reveal themselves. An eyeliner that turns her eyes into smoky pools of come-hither. A pencil trail that lifts her lips into insouciance. Now to disguise the nibbling, the biting, the chewing of lip when struck by a what-next. Meera unfurls a tube, deep dusky pink, and fills in the colour. Press a tissue. Take the overlay. Once. Twice. Thrice. And that final coat. Sealed with a lip gloss that Nayantara dresses her naked lips with to produce the same effect her mother has slaved over with much thought and many unguents. Youth, youth, Meera thinks. How little it meant when it bloomed on my skin. How could I have known that it would fade away so quickly.

Having turned herself into an attractive woman of an indeterminate age, Meera sets about choosing her clothes. She stares at her wardrobe, seeing its contents as if for the first time. The pastel shades and the textured whites. The greys, beiges, taupes, and the café au laits.

When did she fall into this rut of equating elegance with dull, insipid hues? Where is the effervescence of a lime green or the airiness of a sky blue or the heat of post-box red? Meera leans against the door, defeated by the thought of having to start all over again. Why bother? she asks herself. Do I need to turn into a hot babe? The siren who with a crook of her little finger will have the entire male populace at her beck and call? Do I want that for myself?

Yet Meera finds herself reaching for what might make her seem alluring. A mustard yellow top with a scooped out neckline and a slim black skirt in a clingy jersey material. Do I look like a taxi cab? she asks herself, suddenly uncertain. Or a hornet queen?

Nikhil, who has a fondness for trivia and often peppers mealtimes with his fund of useless information would call it her mating instinct, she thinks: all animals have the need to preen as part of their courtship ritual.

She looks at her bitten down fingernails and closely filed toenails. Even the southern painted turtle grows long toenails. She smells the Giorgio Beverly Hills she has atomized herself with. The rich bitch scent. The Mongolian gerbil and she have that much in common. Or is she the flamingo puffing up her feathers and strutting? Or the Madagascar hissing cockroach with its Psst... psst… I am here. And then Meera remembers what Nikhil said as an afterthought: 'Isn't it funny, Mummy, that mostly it is only the male of the species who makes the effort? The female just picks and chooses. Why does the male have to make all the effort? I am never getting married!'

Meera sits down on the bed abruptly. She has never felt so silly in her life. All this decking up, all these powders, paints, perfumes and colours. All this frantic rattling of clothes hangers to find the perfect outfit for a lunch. And for what? Meera groans and sinks into the pillow. How could she have got to this? This desperate hunger, this abject need… She is doing what she swore she would never do. Throw herself at a man. And then Meera thinks: What would Jak say if he saw her now? What would he make of her gadding about with a man half her age?

She could imagine the slow shake of his head, his lips twisted into a line and that husky voice enunciating clearly: Pathetic creature, isn't she?

It bothers her, this notion that Jak may have of her. How did it happen that what he thinks of her has become so vital, so important to how she feels about herself?

How does it matter? He is just her employer. That is the extent of their relationship.

Really? Within her head a voice that sounds very much like Vinnie asks. Is that all?

Meera knocks her forehead against the headboard of the bed gently. Knock. Knock.

What is she thinking of? It is all very well for someone like Vinnie to tell her to take a chance. Vinnie, who was unable to keep out of her voice the unspoken pain of rejection. Her lover had announced to her in bed that afternoon that he would never marry her. He had apparently coiled a strand of her hair around his finger and said, 'I am not the marrying kind, you know that, don't you?'

'But Vinnie, you can't marry him. You are married already,' Meera said quietly.

'That's not the point. He didn't think I was marriage worthy.'

'Then dump him!' Meera said. 'You don't have to put up with it.'

'I can't. I have to see it through. An affair is like anything organic. There is a birth, a blossoming and eventually, a death. It is against the nature of things to speed up the cycle or interrupt it midway. Or it will always linger in your mind, a fishbone in your throat, causing countless moments of remorse, pain. I know, Meera. I've been through it. So what I am saying is, this thing that's sprung up between you and

Soman, you have to give it a chance, allow it to be born before it can die.'

But Meera is a woman who doesn't take chances. Besides, she knows what it is about. Soman had in those first days hinted at a love affair gone wrong. The girl was much younger than he was and clung to him. He felt suffocated by her neediness, her obsessing about him, he said. Not like you, Meera, he implied. Soman is drawn to the image of who she is. The elegant home. The society hostess. The composed sophisticated woman. Sure about life and secure in her own esteem of herself. Which, Meera thinks with a pang of sorrow, has as much substance as chaff. When he discovers the truth about her circumstances and sees her for the woman she is, he'll flee. Does she really want to lay herself open to that again? The rejection, the hurt? Does she have the strength for it? Meera shrivels. She reaches for the phone to call Soman and tell him that lunch is off.

She hears the creak of the gate.

The doorbell rings. Again and again.

VII

Meera rushes to the door.

Saro and Lily are out for the day, visiting a friend Saro has known from her other life as Plantation Mem. Nikhil is at school. And even Raniamma, the maid, is away for her monthly communion with a goddess at the temple in Magadi Road. A goddess who sounded like a favourite if rather eccentric aunt with her likes, dislikes, tantrums, and a munificence only Raniamma is privy to.

Meera thinks of a woman she met at a party once. The woman cringed as a phone rang incessantly and whispered furiously, 'Why doesn't someone answer it?'

Meera had turned in surprise. The usually serene woman had a line of sweat beads on her forehead. Meera touched her elbow. 'Are you all right?'

'My brother died in an accident… someone called from the hospital. Ever since, I can't bear to hear the phone ring. It rattles me.'

I am like that woman now, Meera tells herself as she fumbles with the security catch on the door. The doorbell ringing, the phone ringing, a window slamming. I am constantly waiting. For someone to leave. For someone to return. For the backward flip of my world so precariously perched.

Through the narrow slit between door and frame Meera sees it is Soman with his doric column throat and languorous smile. On its own volition, her mouth widens into a curve of insincerity while her mind rages furiously: What is he doing here? How can he just walk in unannounced?

They were to have met at Ebony at Barton Centre. He had suggested it, in fact. And Meera had agreed without any compunction. The buffet lunch was moderately priced. And the canopied roof terrace was precisely what she hoped to steer their relationship towards – open and friendly, with none of those intimate undertones that had somehow crept into their past meetings.

'What are you doing here?' she blurts out. And then stiffens in embarrassment.

'Hello, Meera,' he says slowly.

She looks at his hands. Where is the token bunch of

flowers or box of chocolates, or even a bar of handmade soap? She clearly is way behind the times. Don't they feel the need any more to make even a token gesture, observe the niceties of flirtatious behaviour? Instead, he stands there, supremely smug in his: I bring thee myself. What more could you want?

And Vinnie, who seems to have taken permanent residence in her head, especially in her dealings with men, drawls, 'You ought to be thankful he came to see you without a carry bag of dirty laundry. Expecting you to launder and iron them into sweet smelling piles. I have had that happen to me as well!'

She takes a deep breath and says slowly, 'Hello, Soman!'

'I thought I would take a chance and come over. We could go from here to the restaurant, I thought…'

'Oh,' Meera says. And an 'oh-oh' follows in her head as he, surmising that they are alone in the room, slips his fingers through hers and murmurs, 'It is wonderful to see you again. You are looking gorgeous!'

A softness engulfs her. She feels herself sway towards him. 'Let me get the keys and we can leave right away,' she says, torn between wanting to prolong the moment and extricating herself from it. This hunger, this hunger would be her undoing.

'Why don't we stay here?' he says, dropping into a chair, his hand still clinging to hers. 'I am not particular about what we eat. Leftovers are fine too. And we could just hang out! Be together…'

Meera stands there, uncertain.

'That's settled then,' he says, lifting her fingers to his mouth. The liquid warmth of his mouth makes Meera want to offer him her lips. What is happening here?

'I'll make lunch… it won't take very long,' she says. 'There are some magazines. Or I could switch on the TV.' She thrusts a sheaf of magazines into his lap and the TV remote into his hand, hoping to hide in the kitchen till she can collect her thoughts.

Outraged, are we? Vinnie snickers. Ask him to leave then. But you don't want him to, do you?

What am I going to do now? Meera asks aloud as she tries to wrap herself in a cocoon of aromas, flavours, steam and smoke. In the mirror that hangs in the hallway passage, she sees an expression that she recognizes from her visits to the dentist. A sense of impending doom as he gathers his bits and pieces and lulls her into a state of false calm. An even, unhappy look that says, what have I let myself in for?

Meera squares her shoulders. I will just stay here and cook up a storm and he can watch. Hopefully, he will leave once we've eaten, replete and satiated.

Only, he wouldn't budge from the kitchen either. Opening the fridge and filling a glass of water with ice cubes. Stealing a finger of carrot to chew on. Suddenly wrapping his arms around her waist as she chops onions. 'Don't cry, little girl. Daddy's here!'

Little girl. Daddy. Meera blanches like the almonds sitting in a bowl of warm water. The idiot is living out some pet fantasy. Big Man. Little Woman. Sit on my knee while I dandle you. The absurdity of the scene hits her and Meera turns in his arms, takes a long, deep sniff of the cologne he has splashed himself with and murmurs, 'Will Daddy chop the onions then?'

In a few minutes Daddy dissolves into sobs. He growls, 'Why the fuck do you need so many onion rings? I'm going to smell of these things for a week now…'

Meera can't stop laughing. Suddenly, she isn't confounded any more.

I can handle him, she thinks. When in doubt, a stew. But when lightness lifts your soul, time to whip up a batch of meringues.

When Soman comes back into the kitchen with his fingers scrubbed clean of the reek of onions and his eyes bathed in cold water, he sees Meera raising little clouds of white foam in a mixing bowl. She senses him appraise her as she spoons dollops of the foam onto a baking sheet. When she bends to place the tray in the oven, he comes to stand at her side.

'Why are you all flushed?' he asks in that low, sexy voice he favours.

'Hot oven!' Meera tries flippancy, but he isn't so easily rebuffed.

'Hot oven. Not so hot Meera, is it?'

A giggle starts in her: Adonis of the Cryptograms.

'Baby, Daddy here will get you hot!'

Oh, my god, this is turning into a bad movie. Meera cringes. Yet, as she feels his hand in the small of her back gathering her close to him, her insides turn into liquid. No matter how much her brains may shriek and protest, there is no escaping the call of the flesh, the song of the nerve ends serenading her.

Meera wipes her face clean of all feeling. 'We should eat,' she says, trying to wriggle out of his arms. 'I am hungry!'

He smiles at her. 'Me too, Meera, me too!'

Vinnie in her head sniggers.

Meera wriggles harder. 'I mean, the food will get cold!'

In response Soman lowers his head and licks at her mouth. Meera gasps. She wants to push him away; she wants to nuzzle his neck. She tautens at the desperation that tugs at her.

Satisfied that she knows what he wishes of her, Soman pats her rump with a careless flick of his wrist and says, 'Go woman, go!'

And like all good cooks, Meera goes.

What do they talk about as they eat? All Meera can hear is her own hammering heart. And the sight of his rapacious appetite only makes it hammer harder. He is going to pounce on her the moment he is done. If he doesn't, she will be crushed. And if he does, what next?

The oven alarm pings. Her meringues are cooked.

'Try one,' Meera urges. Soman takes two. Meera watches the rise of wonder in his eyes. Her meringues do have that effect. Light, chewy, and utterly satisfying. But men are seldom content with the notion of forever meringues in their lives, Meera knows. She had seen such incredulity in Giri's eyes: Meera's house, Meera's meringues, Meera... Only, it hadn't lasted. For, as all pastry cooks will tell you, meringues are merely a chimera. A cloud conjured of egg white, castor sugar and a movement of the wrist. It has no substance, no aftertaste. Hence, neither the clutch of memory nor the power of enduring value.

In the end, that is what settles it. The spill of loss that makes Meera throw all her apprehensions over her shoulder. She needs this: a pinch of salt to safeguard herself from years of desolation. Meera lets Soman lead her into a room. Not the children's or hers, Saro's or Lily's, but the guest room where no ghosts live. Where the walls have absorbed the secret lives of all those who paused within them. The bare, clean room, the cool white sheets, the windows that open onto the part of the garden with a high wall. The anonymity of it will wipe clean all traces of guilt and remorse. She lets him undress her and caress her.

As he ate at her table, so he feasts on her. His mouth following an arch, a curve, the inside of her elbow, the dimples in the small of her back, the space between her toes. His lips on hers. Meera gasps. Such hunger. Where does it spring from? The softness of his lips, the smoothness of his chin… Her fingers on his back, drawing him closer and closer. Such is her need. Such is the greed of that avaricious mouth to devour. This isn't her, Meera, she tells herself. This is the false Meera. Like there once was the false Hera.

When Ixion the ingrate planned to seduce Hera, to pay Zeus back for his perfidies, Zeus created a Hera from a cloud. It was this Hera whom Ixion pleasured and sought pleasure from, while the real Hera lay untouched elsewhere.

I am the false Hera. None of this is really happening to me. It is happening to another woman, the woman he thinks I am. Meera arches her back as his hand unleashes a storm of sensations. And then on its heel, another thought: What of the real Hera? Didn't she ache for such gratification too?

The real Hera must have whimpered, crushed at being forgotten. What woman, whether she was Hera or Meera, could remain unmoved when a mouth trailed a line of wet kisses down her spine? The real Hera must have cursed the false Hera. As I curse the Meera I have become.

Cowardly Meera, seeking escape in clouds and other false gods of hope. When all she needs is this, this, this…

She feels on his back a ridge. Her fingers pause in their caress. 'What is this?' she asks, tracing the raised tube of flesh. 'What caused this?'

He flinches. 'A bad accident!'

'Is it still sensitive then?'

'Not really. But the thought of it…' He speaks against her mouth. 'I got involved in something I should have stayed out of and they, the men, held me down and one of them sliced my back. He said if I didn't leave by the following morning, it would be my face and in twenty different places…' He shudders.

'Drugs?' Meera feels her heart fall.

'No, Meera, I don't do drugs. Never did. This was something else… can we not talk about it?'

As if to silence her, his mouth descends on hers. Under his persistent lips, hers flower. The wet sulkiness of the inner lip, the darting tongue, pleasure uncoils in long spirals… has she been foolish to deny herself this?

Giri has his own life now, she understood from the children. *Daddy, Daddy, you bastard, I am through.* Meera recited Plath in her head.

A month after he left, Nayantara had started talking about Daddy's lady friend. She was with him when he took Nayantara out. Meera had ached to probe, but Nayantara was dismissive. 'Oh, youngish, Mom. Dresses nicely. Smart. Drives a Swift. Like one of those girls in Daddy's office, I think!'

Nayantara had been more enthusiastic about the apartment. 'It is on the tenth floor and he has a great view. And it's all so minimal, with clean lines. It's really chic, Mom.' Not like this shabby dump, Meera heard a reproof somewhere. 'You should see the kitchen. It's a fitted one with sliding draws and he's got new pots and pans. The cutlery…'

Nikhil flung himself on Nayantara then. 'Stop it, stop it, I don't want to know. Mummy doesn't want to hear this nonsense either,' he cried, his fingers covering her mouth.

Nayantara stopped. Shamefaced. Guilty. 'I am sorry, Mom.' She went to put her arm around Meera. 'I wasn't thinking. '

Meera feels her spiralling pleasure halt. What is she doing with this boy?

As if sensing her flagging interest, he pauses. 'What is it?' he murmurs.

'Nothing,' she says in a small voice.

His caresses are mechanical and lifeless. She aches to slap his hand away.

'Go down on me,' he urges.

'No,' she says. 'No,' she adds again, quite sternly, in a voice she reserves for her children's unreasonable demands.

He grunts against her neck. 'Hold me,' he whispers. 'There, no, not there…'

Meera feels detached from her hand as it rolls and pulls. Uncannily, it reminds her of kneading dough. Patting, squeezing, rolling, pulling. The making of pliant dough so it would rise and rise… As she lies there fondling one man whose warmth and cologne engulf her, Meera's mind walks with another.

Should I feel guilty about this, Giri? she asks him. Should I feel remorse that I lie in a bed in what was once our house, almost smothered by the weight and need of this man? But we never talked about what we meant by guilt; what made us cringe and cower. Actually, we never discussed anything significant, did we?

What is it we did with our lives? All those years of mundane details. Breakfast. Lunch. Dinner. Shopping. Spats. Vacations when we could. Hours and hours enmeshed, without our ever speaking a true word to each other. We played out our lives without ever knowing each other.

This absence of feeling I have now, is this what you felt when you left?

Do you remember the time when your father died? I wanted to go with you but you were adamant. You said your father and you were estranged. And you were going there to merely settle the loose ends, you felt no grief.

I was frightened that night. I thought, how could you sever your ties with your past so easily?

But the night you came back from your village, you couldn't sleep. I heard you toss and shift. I saw your eyes glitter. When I touched you, you turned away and pretended to sleep.

I wanted to comfort you, but mostly I felt relief. You were not as impervious as you pretended to be. Your father's death had unsettled you. Was it guilt you knew, Giri? Or did I read too much into the moment?

You left me. Why should I feel guilty? Do you know what Vinnie says? Vinnie, my new friend. She says, in the beginning, each man seems different – his skin, his odour, the texture of his hands, the shape of his fingers, even the contour of his shoulder: hard, fleshy, bony – but in that final moment when you hold him against you, there is a sameness to it. In the dark, all men are the same. That is perhaps why Vinnie feels the absence of guilt.

It is what the man means to a woman that makes him unique, irreplaceable. So what of this boy?

He means nothing to me, he is nothing but a conduit for a need.

And I don't particularly feel the need for sex. So what am I doing?

Meera's arm aches from the angle she is holding it at. She extricates her hand slowly. Soman stills. Their meringue moment of lightness has dissipated. What's left are a few crumbs of cleaning up.

'I don't know, it's never happened before,' he says against her breast, ashamed at the unwillingness of his flesh to acquiesce with his hopes for it. 'I can get really hard, really big... perhaps if you would...'

'It doesn't matter.' Meera pats his cheek and moves away, trying not to reveal her hurry to be out of his embrace.

In the shadowed room, they dress quietly and quickly. Meera looks at herself in the hallway mirror again.

He joins her reflection and Meera looks away. 'Would you like some tea?' she asks.

'No, I should be going,' he says. As they walk to the door, the bell rings. And she hears Nikhil hammer on the door. 'Open up, Mummy, open up! Where are you?'

VIII

Where are you going? What were you doing? Why are you looking away? What are you thinking?

In the days after the funeral, she feels her children's eyes dog her every step, every thought. It is unnerving, this constant scrutiny. Meera has felt near invisible all these years; an apparition who glided through the house and their lives, cooking, cleaning, sorting laundry and helping with the children's home projects. She, who in her head told herself off for being such a doormat, there and not there, doesn't enjoy the consciousness they now endow her with.

Questions. Puzzlement. Reproof. Curiosity. Fear. Meera is stung by the forked tongue of each glance. When she leaves home, it asks, where are you going? When she returns, she is greeted with, where were you? When the phone rings, it demands, what is it about? When she smiles, it queries, why are you smiling? When she lets her features settle into a mask, it nags, what are you thinking of? They, she notices, never use the word 'who'!

To accept the possibility of a who in her life would be closing the door on their father, they think. And it is this they fear.

Meera wants to gather her children in her arms and quell their fears. But how can she? For they sense the presence of a man. Nikhil has seen his mother chew on what looked like a smashed lip and murmur, 'This is my friend. He was just leaving... say hello, Nikhil.'

Nikhil had ignored the outstretched hand and rushed back to open the gates wide. That was when Meera saw the ambulance with its blue revolving siren and knew her heart drop once again.

Saro was still in the hospital, they said. Lily had needed a few stitches and her bruises had been dressed. But Saro had borne the brunt of the water tanker that had smashed into the car they were in. Saro and the driver, Saro's friend had wept.

'It was instant, the police said; she wouldn't have known any pain.' The woman touched Meera's elbow.

Meera looked around her helplessly. 'Yes, yes, I know,' she said, not knowing what she was saying and wishing the woman would go away.

She needed a few moments alone to compose herself. Her mother lay in a morgue somewhere. She had to bring her home. Then there was the funeral. She had to inform everyone... Meera slumped in a chair.

It was Nikhil who called Nayantara. It was Nikhil who insisted on speaking to his father even though he was in a presentation and couldn't be disturbed, his secretary said.

'What is it, Nikhil?' Giri didn't bother to hide his annoyance. 'What now? I told you that you can't ask me permission for anything your mother has said no to.'

'It's Grandma. Saro. She died. And Grandma Lily is still in hospital. Their taxi was hit. The driver died too!'

Giri was silent then, Nikhil told Meera later.

'Your mother. How is she?'

'Mummy is alone, Daddy. You have to come now. She needs you.'

'Son, I'll handle everything. Don't worry. Give the phone to Meera.'

From a long way away, Meera heard Giri tell her that he wouldn't be able to come that day. But he was going to ask someone from the Bangalore office to help her with the police, getting the body out, organizing the hearse and the crematorium, etc.

'Don't you want to see her?' Meera's voice trembled.

The silence again.

'You know that we were…' Giri began and then shaped his reasons differently. 'I am in the middle of a presentation, Meera. We have another round of meetings tomorrow. I'll come as soon as I am done. Don't wait for me.'

'Giri, it's my mother!'

'I'll be there as soon as I can. How is Lily?'

'She is resting. They sedated her at the hospital and sent her in an ambulance. She is in shock. Every now and then she asks for my mother. She won't stop weeping…'

But Giri had to go and Meera was left with a lifeless

phone in her hand. More than ever then, she knew that Giri had moved on. And Nikhil, seeing the slump of defeat in his mother's back, called Jak.

It was never easy, the relationship Meera and Saro shared. Saro was set in her ways and wouldn't tolerate any change. Even when their circumstances changed, Saro wanted everything to remain the way it was when her husband was alive, and it was left to Meera to find a way.

Meera had resented the demands her mother made of her. Angered, even, when her mother insisted on 'keeping up standards' as she called it. Your life may fall apart, your heart may be breaking, but by keeping a semblance of order in your routine and day, your life will be yours again, Saro said.

Her mother is dead. Their lives are askew. But as Meera lays the table for lunch, it occurs to her that she is doing precisely what Saro would have done. Keeping the fabric of their days unruffled. With a pang of remorse, Meera thinks that the only worthy thing in her life springs from what her mother had taught her. And she never thought to acknowledge that, ever.

When Meera goes looking for Lily, she finds her in her bedroom, sitting on the bed. Her face is drawn and her body is perfectly still. As if to move even a muscle would snap her.

Lily clutches the little urn tightly. 'This is my child in here,' she tells Meera. 'How can I bear it? This is my daughter, Meera.'

Meera sits next to Lily and puts her arm around her. 'I miss Mummy, Lily. I miss her so much… I wish I had told her what she meant to me.'

Lily looks away. 'I should have died. She got in on the side where I was sitting but I insisted we switch places. If I hadn't been difficult, you would have your mother here.'

Meera wishes she knew how to comfort Lily. Poor Lily. To bear the burden of guilt along with the grief. But she doesn't have the words to console her. Her own grief binds her tongue.

Nayantara lies on the bed in her room, staring at the ceiling. Meera goes to sit at her side. How would she bear it if something happened to her daughter? How does Lily? Until now, it has never occurred to her that grief can have its own weightage. What is worse? The loss of a parent or one's own child?

Meera aches to lie someplace quiet and wrap her arms around herself, to weep and grieve. Instead, she strokes Nayantara's hair. 'Darling, when do you have to go back?'

'When is Daddy coming?' Nayantara asks the ceiling.

Meera shakes her head. 'I don't know… Maybe tonight. Maybe tomorrow.'

'Do you think he will come at all?'

'I don't know.'

And Nayantara, who hasn't until then spoken a word of censure about Giri, turns away from Meera with 'What a bastard!'

Meera gasps. Don't speak like that about your father, she begins automatically and then stills herself. Nayantara is old enough to make up her mind. And yet…

'She was only his mother-in-law. And ex-mother-in-law now. So maybe he is right to stay away.'

'So you are getting divorced!' Nayantara sits up.

'His lawyer called a week ago, wanting to set up a meeting…' Meera's voice breaks. 'You knew it was going to happen.'

'And him? Are you planning to marry him?'

'Who him? There is no him in my life. You know that!'

'Nikhil said you had a man here. A young man. It was Soman, wasn't it?'

Meera sighed. 'He is a friend. Just a friend…'

'Nikhil didn't seem to think so.'

'Nikhil is too young to understand these things,' Meera says.

'Well, he's decided that you are marrying him.'

And so Meera goes in search of her son. Jak sits in one of the cane chairs in the patio, Nikhil in another. When he sees her, Nikhil gets up and walks away.

Meera drops into a chair.

'How is Lily?' Jak asks. 'You look very tired, Meera. I am worried about you…'

'I am fine. I swear I am all right. But they are not.' She speaks with a sweep of her arm to encompass her world.

'I haven't thanked you enough for all that you've done,' she begins.

'Don't be silly. I am glad I could pitch in. It was clever of Nikhil to think of calling me. And it was fortunate I was in town!'

It was Jak who knew what to do, whom to call, and he remembered to ask Meera to carry a little brass pot. For the ashes, he said quietly. They did it all together. Meera, Nikhil and Jak. And when Nayantara arrived, that strange desultory ride to the crematorium.

It was Jak who stood by her side and took the pot of ashes from the attendant.

'Yes, Nikhil did the right thing by calling you.'

Meera rubs her eyes. 'It's Nikhil who worries me most,' she says.

Jak waits for her to continue.

'It has been a really hard year for him. First, there was Giri's disappearance. Do you remember when we first met? The time you dropped us home. Giri walked out on us, the marriage, the children, all in one go that afternoon. It was Nikhil who discovered that he was missing. And now this…'

Saro and Lily were on their way to Bishop Cotton Boys, Nikhil's school, when the accident happened. They had planned to take him shopping for his birthday.

'I called home but no one picked up the phone,' Nikhil said, not meeting his mother's eye.

Meera's heart sank. Where was she then? She remembered a phone ringing far away in those first few minutes but Soman had wrapped his arms tightly around her. 'No, no, let it ring.' He had shut it out with his caresses and the frenzy of sensation he evoked had swallowed the sound.

'Grandma Saro wasn't picking up her phone either. So I thought I would wait at the school gate. Someone told me there had been an accident a little ahead where Vittal Mallya road cuts into St. Mark's road. I walked there, and Mummy…' Nikhil's face crumpled. 'It was horrible. The police were standing there near the wrecked car. They had covered Grandma and the driver with two pieces of sacking. I didn't know it was Grandma… I saw Lily then. They were carrying her into the ambulance and… I ran. For a moment, I thought it was you beneath that sacking. Then I saw the hand with the rings and knew it was Grandma. It was horrible, Mummy. I know I shouldn't have thought it, but I was glad it was her and not you.'

Meera leans forward, her head in her arms. 'I am so afraid that I am robbing him of his childhood; his father and I.

It's sad, isn't it, how children have to suffer the sins of their parents.'

Jak takes Meera's hand in his. 'Nikhil will cope. Trust me, Meera, I know. Children cope better than adults.'

IX

Children cope. How easily he had said it. That they have a greater depth of understanding than adults expect them to have. But that was what Meera wanted to hear. And so he offered her the comfort she so desperately sought: that she hadn't failed as a parent.

Jak jogs through the streets at a steady pace. The night air is cold and he has pulled a light sweater on over his T-shirt. Dogs bark from behind gates but he continues to run, trying to keep pace with his thoughts.

He feels a stab of pity for Meera. He knows what lies ahead. There is no escaping it. Those black spots in the future when certain days would come to haunt her. The vortex of fear. Nikhil may not be able to forgive you now, Meera, he had wanted to tell her. But there will come a time in his life when he will begin to understand your circumstances and with that will come acceptance and forgiveness. Until then you must seek refuge in the thought that he will cope. Nikhil will engage with life on his own terms.

No one knows this better than he does, Jak's mind and feet synchronize. Children cope but not without being marked. Children learn to understand but not without losing an element of hope. How can adults expect forgiveness of children? It is an adult emotion. It is not a child's natural instinct to make compromises on behalf of a parent. An exemplary rare child, perhaps. He wasn't one. All he knew was a black rage at what was expected of him.

Kitcha came home from college to find his mother in a strange mood. He was a B.Sc. Geography student at the Presidency College then. He studied his mother's face as if it were the sea. The ever changing sea, now so calm, now so volatile. What seismic forces had shifted, he wondered. What had brought it on this time?

From the corner of his eye, Kitcha searched the house for Kala Chithi. She had arrived a month ago, all of a sudden. 'I have left my husband and I have left our parents' home. I have nowhere else to go,' she had stated baldly.

Sarada's hand had gone to her mouth. 'What have you done, child?' she had exclaimed. 'And your hair?'

It was Kitcha who had taken the suitcase from her hand. He saw the stillness of her face and remembered her as he had seen her last on the beach, her hair loose, her eyes sparkling, her soul leaping. What had happened to her in these last few years?

'He wanted to marry another woman. A woman who could give him a child,' Kala Chithi said.

'He wanted us all to live together. The indignity! The indignity was what made me leave. And you know our parents…' She had looked away, not wanting either her sister or her nephew to see the wetness of her eyes. Kitcha and his mother had said no more. And so Kala Chithi became part of their household.

Would Kala Chithi know why Amma's eyes glittered when she talked, or why her face was lit with an unusual animation? It scared him. In the last seven years there had been two occasions when his mother had come alive from her catatonic state. Twice, when they had had news of Appa.

The first time, a relative who had met Appa at an ashram had come to them with a little pouch of dried flowers, holy ash and vermilion. Kitcha had never been more furious with his father.

'He has sent this for us, Kitcha. He has. What does it say? He hasn't forgotten us,' his mother cried in delight, oblivious to the embarrassment on the man's face. Kitcha looked away, unable to stomach the naked want in her eyes.

Later in the night, when the relative had been fed and given, the gift of a new veshti and a small sum of two hundred rupees, pressed into his hand with an 'Oh, some money for the bus fare', Amma looked up from the little pouch and asked in a voice aching with hope, 'Do you think he means to come back? Is that why he sent the kumkumam? Do you think it is his way of telling me?' She sat there caressing the vermilion dust with the tip of her finger as if it were her husband's arm. Needing to touch it to tell herself he was there and with her.

Kitcha wanted to snatch the pouch out of her hand and fling it out. What about the ash and the dried flowers, he wanted to demand. What do they tell you? That all is over. Can't you see that?

Kitcha didn't speak then. He didn't when the letter came either. It was little over a year since the relative had visited. There had been nothing until then from Appa. Amma had begun working in a small school in the neighbourhood. She had fished out her degree certificate in Mathematics which she had set aside when she married. Now the school needed a primary teacher in Maths and Amma had been fortunate to find the job, they said. So close to home; a small but steady income; regular hours and long vacations. Kitcha had been glad when she found the job. It was precisely what she needed. A diversion and a purpose. She was tiring herself by being this needy creature who rose with bare-faced hope each time someone buzzed the doorbell.

The letter was addressed to him. Amma held it in her hand as she waited for him to come home from school. Kitcha was sixteen then. 'I'm going to study the weather,' he joked to anyone who asked him his future plans. 'At least it is predictable in its unpredictability!'

Amma looked away each time he said that.

Kitcha felt a weight settle on his brow when he saw the letter. What now? 'Open it,' Amma urged. 'I didn't want to. It's for you… But it's from him. Your appa!'

Kitcha placed his books on the swing. 'Can I change my clothes first?' he asked quietly, wanting to delay the moment. Couldn't Amma see it? How could she raise her hopes so? When would she accept that he wasn't coming back?

'Kitcha…' The plea in her voice made him grab the envelope from her hand. Within was a card announcing Appa's decision to move to Rishikesh where the ashram would help him seek the unconscious better. There were shlokas and explanations, and in the final line a quiet repudiation: 'Nainam chindanthi shashtrani…' It is time to move on. As I must. You must.

It was an irrevocable parting of ways.

Amma applied for a BEd thereafter. And when it was time to pick a subject for his university degree, despite everyone telling him that he was guaranteed to be unemployed after such a useless course, Kitcha sought his clouds and seas.

Now here was Amma again with stars in her eyes. 'I have something to tell you,' she said that night.

Kitcha stared at the TV. 'Yes, Amma, I am listening,' he said, not wanting to see the anticipation in her eyes.

'I have been thinking,' Amma began. Then she reached out and switched off the TV. 'I want you to listen carefully.'

Kitcha looked up then. Kala Chithi, Kitcha saw, was pretending to read a magazine. Any minute now she would get up and leave. Kala Chithi had little time for Amma's 'one of these days he will be home' delusions. 'You have to get on with your life, Akka,' she said. 'You have to accept that Athimbair isn't coming back!'

In recent times, though, Amma no longer talked about her husband or even referred to him. She was finally learning to let go, they had decided, relieved. Appa had been a cancerous growth in Amma, gnawing away at her insides, turning a vibrant woman into a hollowed out shell, brittle and dry.

Kitcha worried that there had been some fresh communiqué from Appa.

'Your father is gone. He's never coming back. Do you accept that?' she asked, touching his shoulders gently.

'Yes, I know that,' Kitcha mumbled. 'I always knew that.'

'But my life isn't over.'

'What is it, Amma? Is it this MEd thing? Do you need to go elsewhere for it?'

Amma exhaled. 'No, it isn't this MEd thing. It is that I have met someone and we would like to get married.'

And Kitcha, who should have sprung to his mother's side, made it easy for her and said, 'Yes, Amma. You are young. You need a husband. And I… I would like a father too. A father who is here.' Kitcha, who could already read the colour of the sea, the density of the clouds, and in whom there was a natural sensitivity, ought to have found the compassion to take his mother's hand in his and absolve her of any guilt she may feel by telling her, 'You must marry again. And this time, Amma, choose a man who loves life. Not one who wants to run away from it,' had snarled, 'What's wrong with you? How can you get married again? You are still married to Appa!'

Kala Chithi hissed at the ferocity of Kitcha's tone, the venom in his words. Amma stood there, her head bent. Then she raised her eyes and searched his for a long while.

Kitcha felt shame crowd him. What had he done? But shame was erased by the violence he felt at the image of his mother with another man. He turned away, unable to stand there any more.

When he returned, he was calmer and penitent. 'I didn't mean it like that.' He fashioned contrite words to redeem himself in his own eyes rather than hers.

But she, too, could be unrelenting. 'You meant exactly what you said, Kitcha. I was a fool to think you would see it from my point of view. How can you? You are still a child.' With that his mother dismissed his attempts to take an adult stance and relegated him to what she thought he deserved – a child's place.

It took a year for her to get a divorce. And the next day she was married to her man. A quiet Physics teacher from Hyderabad. A year later, they moved to Tanzania. Kitcha heard occasionally from them and he went to visit them a few times. But something had died between Kitcha and his mother. There was no going back to how they used to be. He had failed his mother and yet, how could she blame him?

It was to Kala Chithi he unburdened his guilt and remorse. And it seemed to him that only she understood.

Some years later his mother died of cancer. By that time Kitcha had already moved to the US. He couldn't attend the funeral but as he told Kala Chithi, they had already said their goodbyes. That time when his mother left him in her care and went away with her new husband.

It was only then Kala Chithi had snapped, 'Do you have to be so unforgiving even after her death? Till the day she died, she didn't stop tormenting herself with the thought that she failed you… Let her go in peace now, Kitcha. Let her be.'

'How can you let her get away with it? How long will you make excuses for her behaviour?' Monique had demanded of you one summer evening. The two of you were working in the garden. At least, she was weeding in the backyard of the cottage she and you had been offered for the whole of two months.

Rich Monique with godparents who had a cottage in Umbria which they offered to their godchild and her lover while they were away in Argentina. Polyglot Monique who switched from English to Italian to French to Spanish, all in one sentence. Dealing with stewards, taxi drivers, marketplaces and bureaucracy with a breathtaking ease, no matter where she was. While you watched helplessly as you were subjected to what seemed like a long stream of nonsense.

Silly, frivolous Monique who could never bury her nose in a book and live vicariously through her characters. But knew every wild plant and made soup of sorrel and then went out to dinner in her Armani sheath and talked fabrics and styles to her buyers with a hauteur that overwhelmed them.

She perplexed you. A beeping dot on the radar that you puzzled over. She called you her cloud reader, her weather man, trailing kisses from the hollow in your neck to the line of your pubis. And you thought it must be the same for her: I wear the magic of the unknown.

Only now, eleven months into their relationship and three weeks into their holiday, Monique couldn't keep the vexation out of her voice when she looked up from the roses and demanded, 'This isn't the first time, right? She's done this before. Got into trouble. Didn't you know that your daughter was furious about your coming away with me? That she would do something to ensure you went back… I knew it would happen. That, or you would have had to bring her with us.'

You ran your hand through your hair, rubbed the bridge of your nose, stared moodily into your glass of white wine and said, 'I wish I had. I wish there was a way of knowing what Smriti will do next. It is ironic that I who study the clouds and the sea, I who can forecast storms and chart their path almost intuitively, I can't read Smriti, her moods and phases. She defeats me.'

Sometimes you thought that you were just paying for what you had put your mother through.

Monique didn't speak at first. When she did, she didn't hide the anger in her voice. 'You can perhaps forgive her for what she puts you through. I can't. Not when she called me a fucking cunt, and she and her friends ruined my home. I love you, Jak, but this… this is ridiculous, your quiet acceptance of her unruly behaviour. Sometimes you act as if it was inevitable!'

You flinched then.

Smriti bared fangs when she saw Monique. She saw her as an usurper. It wasn't Monique – any woman would have been subjected to the same hate. Smriti was merely replaying what you had done. 'She will like you once she gets to know you,' you said soothingly.

Monique snorted. She still hadn't forgiven Smriti or you for ruining the Christmas vacation in Venice. You had insisted on taking Smriti along. It was the safest option during the whirl of parties in the holidays, Nina and you had decided – to remove her from her environment where she could get into trouble. The two of you took turns every year, ever since the separation. Shruti was going with Nina to England. Malleable, pliant Shruti who could be trusted to amuse herself. But not Smriti, who would sneak away and do something stupid that could jeopardize her future, her life.

So Smriti had gone with them to Venice for a week of incessant torture she piled on quite easily and uncaringly. She sulked or slept in late, found fault with everything including the pigeons, dismissed the gondolas and the sights as 'bor-i-ing!' and got on Monique's nerves till you could hear them twang.

To compensate, you had plied Monique with wine and food, made love to her as often as you could and even went with her on some of her buying trips. It had been a hard time and pointless.

Smriti had her way. After you went back that summer to sort out Smriti's latest escapade, Monique and you broke up. Smriti was delighted. And the next month she announced her decision to move to India.

Jak halts mid-stride. He has not thought about it until now. This thing called forgiveness. Of how it unfurls into life. Perhaps we start learning to forgive only when our sins come back to visit us. It was only when Smriti became a sulky, fractious, recalcitrant fifteen-year-old that Jak began to understand the torment he had subjected his mother to. It was when Smriti refused to accept that he could have a life of his own that his own bristling, unyielding stance at his mother's attempt to rebuild her life seemed childish and unjustified.

He found it easier to forgive Smriti then, for the pain she was causing him. All he had to do was tell himself that it was the cycle of fate. There was no escaping it. There is some measure of comfort in this notion called karma, he thinks. There is only so much you can do, so much you can control.

Jak turns back towards home. He is tired. But it is a fatigue cushioned with calm, as if he has come to the end of a long journey. How is Meera coping, he wonders. The serenity she is usually swathed in seems to have been punctured.

'I haven't been able to sleep,' she had admitted the day before. 'I wake up with a tightness in my chest, as if I can't breathe. I don't know what to do any more.'

Perhaps tonight he will sleep well. He hopes Meera will too. It has become important to him. Her wellness.

STAGE IV

The Eye wall of Devastation

For many years now I have owned a small 8"x8" painting a Buddhist monk gave me. He was from one of the smaller monasteries in Darjeeling and I met him while I was in Cambodia in the early eighties. It is a depiction of a mandala, he said. An abstract of chaos and disorder. It was his advice that when I felt torn within, I should sit before it and look at it, and in that sacred space would emerge an order that would eventually calm me.

It is a small painting and it has travelled with me from home to home. Though it is a fantastic swirl of colour trapped within geometric forms, I have been unable to hang it up, ever. The mandala, Carl Jung said, is a representation of the unconscious self. By my constant meditation on this painting, I could perhaps achieve wholeness in my emotional life.

But the truth is, my Buddhist painting frightens me. When I look at it, what I see is the penultimate stage of a cyclone. Its most terrifying aspect.

From the heart of the storm spins an outward directed force of fury. Vicious as a herd of monsters, it raises a ring of violent storms. Sometimes twice as many. It is here that danger awaits. For the eye wall winds have no soul, know no mercy.

Professor J. A. Krishnamurthy
The Metaphysics of Cyclones

What does she feel about him, Jak often catches himself thinking. Does she think of him at all? There is no way of fathoming Meera. She gives everything and nothing away. In the months after her mother's death, Jak watched her wrestle with her demons. He watched her grapple and throw. His liking for her has become tempered with admiration. And something else. This quiet woman is a bank to shore himself upon.

Jak feels a great urge to drop a kiss on her head as he walks past to his desk.

They are in the study. They have been looking together at a paper he has to send to a journal. A paper that is already late by six weeks and has the editor frothing at his mouth while pretending to be calm and understanding. 'He must be tearing his hair out in frustration,' Jak laughs, reading the carefully worded but terse email. 'But he's so scared of pissing me off that he doesn't dare say anything outright. All this hedging merely implies: send us your fucking paper, you lazy son of a bitch.'

Meera smiles. She doesn't especially like his colourful language but Jak speaks with such a lack of malice or venom that it seems perfectly civil. 'What are you going to do?'

'I have something written down. We just need to knock it into the shape Professor Anderson expects to see it in,' Jak says, rummaging through his laptop bag.

Meera watches aghast as he pulls out a hotel pad with notes scrawled all over it.

'That's the paper?' she asks in a faint voice.

'Pretty much. Don't look so shocked. This is the crux of what I plan to present. For the rest, we'll tart it up with indices, footnotes, appendices, etc.' Jak leans back in his chair. 'That's how all academics do it. When in doubt, add a footnote. When you have to make yourself sound knowledgeable, add a few appendices. Show the workings! Show how you arrived at the magnificent conclusion. Or, even better, how you couldn't arrive at it. But show the workings, that's the trick!' Jak smiles a lazy grin. 'It's practically an art form, writing for an academic journal.'

Meera shakes her head, bemused. She is puzzled, he can see. She doesn't know if he is being funny or sarcastic. 'But you still have to arrive or not arrive at that conclusion. And this is all you have.' She holds up the three tiny sheets of paper.

'That's a good place to begin. The rest will happen. All in good time. Let the good professor stew a bit more.'

'Why don't you begin now?' Meera asks.

Jak narrows his eyes in speculation. 'You think so? Right, let's! Here, write down the title: The Metaphysics of Cyclones. What do you think?'

Meera doesn't say anything.

He knows what she is thinking. That he is mercurial. That he switches moods in a flash. How can you trust a man like that? One day he is here. And the next day he will be gone.

February. The days stretch into longer hours of light; an insidious warmth. Who says there are no seasons in India, Jak thinks as he turns up the fan regulator. Every day is a season by itself. There is no overwhelming variation to suggest a changing pattern. Instead, in a million subtle ways, the texture of each day varies from the others. How could he have missed all of this when he lived here? Increasingly, Jak finds himself looking at the world with his eyes wide open. A change prompted by Meera. He likes it that she doesn't talk at him. Not like Nina, he thinks. Instead, Meera talks to him.

'Do you know they call you Cyclone Jak? I googled you and found 39,400 entries. And almost in every entry, on the first two pages, that term was used. Cyclone Jak,' she says with a sidelong glance. 'I am not surprised!'

He cocks an eyebrow. 'Are you saying I am unpredictable?'

She smiles. 'The rest of the world does. I am not sure. I think you hide behind this unpredictable veneer. I think it is an act. What? Don't look at me like that.'

Jak's heart skips a beat. For sometime now, they have engaged in this sort of banter. Mildly flirtatious, loaded with possibilities. Who will take it forward? Will she? Or will he have to be the one? Does he want to? The wooing, the dancing, two-steps-forward, three-steps-back, the pondering, the worrying, the whole commitment thing – is he willing? Is she ready?

The nurse knocks at the door. 'Sir,' she says. 'I don't want to disturb you, but will you come?'

The lightness in the room dissipates with the ominous undertow in her voice. Jak jumps up. He sees Meera hesitate, then rise to follow him.

I

Did he follow someone in here?

He can't remember walking in. Or sitting down.

Did he stumble in blindly, drawn by its deep dark confines, the hushed silence of desolate prayer and the sight of a man interred? Could anyone else be as tormented as he is? Could anyone else bleed as he does? Where is relief? Where is escape?

Jak raises his forehead from the wooden bar of the pew. Two rows from him, across the aisle, sits an old woman with a scarf covering her hair. Her eyes are closed and her palms folded in a tight knot of supplication. Her lips move fervently. When did she come? What ails her life that makes her beseech so? And then Jak thinks: I must look the same. I am no different. We may have nothing else in common but we are both troubled souls.

The candles flicker. Jak rises from the pew and walks towards the altar. He stares at the face of Christ on the cross. Once, in some European town, he had seen a Christ in one of the smaller churches. Monique had said it was called The Christ of Redemption. 'Strange,' she had added thoughtfully. 'Michelangelo's Christ of Redemption, despite bearing the cross in his right arm, wears a triumphant expression. But I have never seen a Christ as tormented as this.'

He couldn't remember Michelangelo's Christ. But what he wouldn't ever forget was the expression on the face of this Christ hewn by some lesser known sculptor: What have I come back to, it seems to ask.

And now Jak, standing in front of Christ in the Holy Ghost church on Richards Park Road, asks of the son who died for all of mankind: What have I come back to?

He shudders.

The nurse, with the practised ease of one who did it all the time, had toppled Smriti onto her side. Then she lifted

Smriti's ankle and pointed to the skin on the lateral side. 'Do you see this?' she asked, pointing to the redness. 'Touch it!' she said.

Beneath his tentative finger, the skin felt warm and the flesh spongy.

Theresa placed the ankle back on the bed as if it were a sleeping baby. She moved briskly to her right and raised the long T-shirt Smriti was dressed in. Up and above her knees, over her thighs and buttocks. Jak heard Meera's indrawn breath.

You sensed what Meera was thinking. How can the nurse be so thoughtless and how can you, her father, not have the decency to look away? How can you stand there looking at your daughter's body? She may be the child you bathed and dried when she was a baby, but this is indecent and nauseating.

You wanted to ask her – Do you know how it makes me feel, Meera? That I, her father, have to be the one to touch her womanly parts?

There are days when the nurse is late or absent. Kala Chithi manages Smriti on her own then. But do you remember when Kala Chithi sprained her wrist? There was a day when the nurse didn't come. Could I leave my daughter unattended? I had to wash and clean my adult daughter that day. And, pathetic frozen creature though she is, she knows it's me. She never flinches at my touch. Not even when I have to separate her legs and run a wash cloth around the folds of her vagina.

The first time, Kala Chithi looked away. She was aghast, but what else was there to do? 'She is my daughter,' you said as gently as you could. 'The baby I helped bathe and feed. She is still my child!'

'It isn't right.' Kala Chithi's mouth was a line.

'What is right about any of this?' you said, dusting talcum on Smriti's back and using a powder puff to work into the folds of her armpit. Her mind may be elsewhere but her body was here.

The nurses were meant to keep her armpit and pubic hair short. But the last one had been lazy and slatternly. You were scared that you would nick her, but you did that as well. Dealt with the hair in her armpit and pubis. When it is your child, and she is suffering, none of the norms of civilized society has any meaning. What a parent may or may not do for a child is irrelevant.

You thought of when Smriti was twelve and brought her artwork for you to admire. You would frame it and hang it up. And Smriti, unable to decide if she ought to be flattered or embarrassed, would complain in a pleased voice, 'Papa, I hate this thing called unconditional love. There is nothing rational about it.'

You agreed. It was not rational. Which is why, even though she was a woman, all folds, creases, crevices and hollows, you saw your child in her, not a woman, not this wretched creature.

'Sir,' Theresa's voice rang through. 'Do you see this?'

Then Jak knew the purport of Meera's gasp of horror. For on Smriti's back was the beginning of a blister. The skin looked broken and red.

'Is that a bedsore? Is it, Sister?' Jak's voice rose.

'I told the nursing assistant what to do but these girls are careless and duty means nothing to them. She must have forgotten to move her every few hours. And it is beginning to get warm now.' Theresa's tone hovered between an accusation and an apology. And something else – the inevitability of the occurrence of bedsores.

'It's fortunate that we saw it now. It is easy to treat at this stage,' Theresa continued. 'Will you speak to the doctor, then I will consult with him.'

'Sister, is she in pain?' It was Meera who asked.

'I don't know, madam. When a patient is bedridden, bedsores can be painful. Very painful. But we don't know with this patient. We don't know how much sensation she has or can register.'

Jak can't stop looking at Jesus. It is as if their eyes are locked in a rare understanding. Our gods seldom show us this: a compassion, an empathy, and a willingness to heal bruised souls… Jak feels a pang in him. He isn't a religious man. He lost his faith when Appa left home.

'Kitcha, Kanna,' Amma tried to persuade him to go with her to Thirumulavayil, the family temple. 'Countless generations of Shivacharyas have been priests there. Our family has known the powers of Eashwara… So how can you disdain God?'

'If there is a god, would our lives be like this?' he responded.

His mother was silent then. So Kitcha went. He hated to see his mother so beaten.

He wouldn't enter the temple, though. Like the Nandi bull at Thirumulavayil who sits facing the gate rather than the sanctum, Kitcha waited in the courtyard, watching the skies, while his mother laid her woes at the foot of a god who seemed to have shut his eyes.

Later, in the bus, he had asked her, more curious than angry,

'How can you believe in god? How can you after everything that has happened to us?'

His mother looked out the window as they hurtled past the suburbs of Madras. 'Do you know the legend of the Nandi at Thirumulavayil? The king who built the temple was a great devotee of Shiva. Once when he was praying in there, enemies decided to attack him, knowing he would be alone and unarmed. That's when the Nandi came to life. It rose and sat guarding the temple while the king finished his prayers. Perhaps faith is reinstated when things happen to you. Perhaps we discover the power of divinity when there is no solace from anywhere else. I wouldn't ever wish for you to know this, Kitcha, but in one's darkest hour, God is the only glimmer of light.'

Is this his darkest hour? Jak asks the alien god whom he had dismissed as he had repudiated his own. What solace can you offer me who came crawling here seeking only a dark and empty place?

My religion taught me to accept everything that happened and will happen in my life as inevitable. That it had all been decided by someone somewhere before time or I existed. So there is peace in accepting each day, each twist of fate – Appa leaving home, Amma's marriage to another man, my divorce, my dead-to-the-world daughter, the stilling of my own life. But my education demands something else of me. It taught me to ask questions. To go beyond the surface and to probe. To know, to know, to know, for in knowledge is salvation.

Late in the afternoon, Jak goes to Smriti's room. The fan is on. The doctor had prescribed ointments and injections. 'Just to keep down the inflammation and prevent any infection,' he had said, while the nurse nodded wearily in agreement. She wasn't a difficult patient to handle but Theresa found the responsibility a great burden.

Meera watches him prise open the lid of a small bottle. 'It is a lip balm I found at a French chemist's once. It's not like Vaseline which actually dries the skin out if you don't moisten it periodically. This one keeps her lips from cracking,' he says as he applies the balm on his daughter's lips.

Jak looks up once and meets Meera's gaze. Then he drops his eyes. It scares him that she has read the raging turmoil in his mind caused by the sight of Smriti. But this creature isn't really his daughter. What lies on the bed is an ugly twisted doll, the handiwork of an evil magic. And yet, it is Smriti. He isn't offering obeisance to a memory. This is his child he is tending to.

Meera goes to stand by his side. She touches his shoulder. A gentle press of two fingers. What shall I say, it offers tentatively.

II

A gentle press with two fingers on his shoulder. She didn't know how else to comfort him. So she did the only thing she could. Offer a tentative caress.

Meera snuffles her face between the pillows. What was she thinking of?

All she knew was that when Jak rushed out of the house as if possessed, she couldn't leave even though her time to go home had come and gone… So she waited. As had Kala Chithi. Both keeping vigil and yet pretending not to.

Meera had looked at the austere-faced woman who sat purling plastic wires into a basket. 'Why now, Kala Chithi?' she asked suddenly. 'I don't understand what happened. Kitcha… he…'

Seeing him distraught had twisted something in her. A secret place in her had looped and curled, turned and knotted at his anguish.

The old woman looked up while her fingers worked the wires almost blindly. 'My mother was bedridden for several months before she died,' she said in explanation.

Meera blinked in incomprehension. Had she missed something Kala Chithi had said?

'When the bedsores appeared, I felt as if I had been clubbed. How do I explain it? You feel guilty, as if you haven't done enough.' Kala Chithi put down the half-worked basket. How could she explain to Meera the weight of guilt a bedsore can burden one with?

'You feel helpless, knowing there is nothing more you can do. You feel weary with all that is expected of you. You feel hopeless, knowing that nothing will change. You feel trapped in another person's misery while your life is put on standstill. You feel resentful, angry. You feel grief, you feel confused. There isn't enough space in one's brain to hold all this and not explode. She was my mother. Her life came before mine. So you tell yourself that this too is part of the cycle of life. That samsara consists of both joys and sorrows, of bedsores, too, perhaps.

'What made me feel marginally better was that I was there to tend to her. In the natural order of things, children care for ailing parents. But this is his daughter. No parent can be prepared for that.'

Meera swallowed. A hard lump had lodged in her throat. She thought of how it would be if it were Nayantara in place of Smriti.

Meera rose from the sofa. She knew she couldn't continue sitting there any more. It reminded her too much of waiting for Giri to come home. She was no longer that Meera. This Meera could do both, wait and keep herself occupied. She would write Nayantara an email or log into Facebook and see if she had added any updates. They could chat if Nayantara was online. Or, she might even look at the notes she had made for *The Corporate Wife Abroad*. Anything but this long wait for Kitcha to come home.

'Are you a Hindu, Meera?' Kala Chithi asked.

Meera paused. 'I am,' she said. 'Why?'

'Our epics, I have heard, tell us that the person you do the most grievous harm to in a previous birth is born to you as a child. So you pay for your sins. So you know the extent of the torment you caused. So you have a chance to make amends. When I think of Kitcha, I think it must be true.'

In the silence that crept in, Kala Chithi spoke up suddenly: 'My poor Kitcha!'

'It is a terrible burden he bears. When Nina wanted to take Smriti to America so she could get organized care, Kitcha wouldn't allow it. She would feel abandoned, he said. As if even her parents have no hope of her ever recovering… All his pain, his sorrow, what does he do with it? I have often asked myself this. Plus, he holds himself responsible in some way. My poor Kitcha. How much more will he take upon himself?'

In her head Meera formed sentences, each one meant to comfort, to heal. What emerged was a platitude. 'I wish I knew what to say. I wish I knew how to comfort him.'

Kala Chithi nodded as if comforted by even this banality.

Meera sat in front of the computer, forming sentences in her head.

Hi Nayantara, she thought she would write, what's up? And then she floundered. A tumult of thoughts, each with a little twinge. That poor child. Wouldn't it have been better if she died? Bedsores. What next?

For a moment, she wondered what Nayantara would do if she were to write to her of the searing fear that had flashed through her when she saw the broken skin on Smriti's back. The one thought that had coursed through her: 'Thank god this is someone else's daughter!' And then the panic: What happened to this child could very well happen to mine.

She remembered the summer when Nayantara was fifteen and Meera smelt smoke in her room. It must be Giri's cigarettes, she told herself. The smoke wafted in through the open window and lingered.

And then, in the toilet bowl, a cigarette end floating. No one else used the bathroom in Nayantara's room. Meera had stared at the butt and felt fear and sorrow tussle in her. Her child had grown up. Her child was no longer hers to lead through life to a safe haven that she would create for her. Her child no longer needed hand holding. But you don't know what's out there, she wanted to tell Nayantara.

In the end, what emerged from Meera's confusion was an accusation. 'I know you are smoking. How dare you?'

And Nayantara bristled, 'Have you been checking up on me? Going through my things?'

'Answer me, you are smoking, aren't you? What else are you up to? Alcohol, drugs, sex?' Meera was appalled to hear herself say the words she had thought she never would.

Accusations Saro had hurled at her when she was eighteen. But I was eighteen and Nayantara is fifteen. Still a child, she told herself.

Nayantara stalked out of the room, slamming the door shut with a loud thud.

Meera wanted to go after her. Explain to her what had triggered those ugly words. It is you I am thinking of, darling, it is your welfare.

When Meera did find the courage to bring it up with Nayantara, there was only awkwardness. 'I don't want to discuss it,' Nayantara said, brushing the tangles from her hair.

For the first time Meera saw her child had become a woman. Her flesh had curved and her mind was her own. 'Why don't you let it be? You have to let me live my life. Please. Why can't you understand?' Nayantara said quietly. 'Do you have to be like your mother?'

Meera gave up then. Nayantara would never comprehend what Meera feared. Not until she had a child of her own.

Besides, Meera couldn't forget for as long as she lived, the expression of dislike that had crept into Nayantara's eyes when Meera had continued to stand in the room. She hadn't known if she should prolong the discussion, try and reason with Nayantara. But the barely veiled resentment, the blatant dislike, had chilled her to the bone. How could her own child look at her as if she were the enemy?

Then she heard the car in the driveway. Meera stood by the computer, undecided.

Kitcha came into the room. He didn't see her at first. When he did, he stared at her and said slowly, 'You are still here.'

He went to Smriti's room. She followed him. Meera watched him open a jar of lip balm and anoint his daughter's lips. She felt a huge wave of feeling engulf her. A wave that propelled her forward to touch his shoulder in a quiet gesture of intent: 'I am here'. When he turned to her, not bothering to hide the pain in his eyes, she knew what to do. She held him. With neither coyness nor fuss, she wrapped her arms around him. He stiffened, then relaxed against her.

'It hurts... how it hurts, Meera.' Muffled words, the depth of his sorrow, all against her skin.

She wrapped her arms around him with greater fervour. To even slightly loosen her hold would break him.

'How am I to bear it, Meera? Where do I find the strength? You have a daughter of your own, Meera. How did you know what to do? How did you know where to draw the line?'

Meera shook her head. 'There is no knowing, Kitcha. We do our best for our children. We want the best for them. You can't blame yourself for what happened to Smriti.'

Meera's mouth was dry. His anguish devastated her. What must the poor man be going through? No matter how old our children grow, we do not relinquish them easily to the world. Perhaps it is only our instinct for self-preservation kicking in.

Ever since Nayantara became a young woman, Meera has known what it is to keep burning coals in her heart. A piercing, consuming heat as she waits for Nayantara to come home. Waiting by the phone for her to call, ears cocked for the doorbell to ring.

The squabbling, the heated arguments, the left hook and the right jab in places where it hurt as a once angelic child turned into a cruel monster if she didn't have her way.

Accusations, recriminations, anger – this is the coinage our grown-up children deal us:

'Why do I have to call you from Ria's home? Why do you need to talk to her mother?'

'Why can't I go for the party? All my other friends are going.'

'I was only drinking a Breezer. You should ask your grandmother to lay off the bottle if we are talking about drinking.'

'I am not fucking him, if that's what you want to know...'

And then, as if to compensate, with the minted freshness of a new coin, the return of the angel in a little deed, a thoughtful gesture, a card, a flower, a shimmery ill-fitting top, a box of napkin rings she would think twice about using, an impulsive hug. How it sparkled, that moment, the exultation that leapt within her to see her child come home to her again.

All of this was denied to Jak, perhaps forever. How did he bear it?

Many minutes later, it was he who moved away. It was he who slowly prised her fingers apart so that the embrace sundered into two bodies.

Meera did not speak. She had no words then, as she has none now. She hides her face between two pillows. What must he think of her?

Kitcha turned to her in urgent need of comfort. Anyone would have, at that moment. How could she have read more into it? He is fond of her, that much she knows. Perhaps it is her own loneliness, her own need shaping something out of nothing. She is projecting her yearning onto him.

And that way lies hurt.

III

'Are you in pain, baby?' Jak asks quietly. He sits at the bedside and looks at his daughter. Her eyes are open and staring. Smriti continues to stare. Then her jaws unclench and from the gaping hole that is her mouth, a scream emerges.

An animal howl layered with terror and pain, grief and anger, horror and disgust. An animal howl that goes on and on, snaring his soul and jerking him up from where he sits, pushing him out in blind panic.

You thought you had arrived at the stage of letting go. That tracing Smriti's days before the accident was a pointless exercise in pain. An indulgence that did more harm than good. An anxious tongue probing again and again the empty arc of a pulled out tooth. All it did was redefine the loss. The actual loss and the sense of it.

The hours with Mathew caused in you a deep weariness. The story of your daughter had unravelled to be nothing more than a teenage girl's reckless impetuosity. You abandoned all your theories of it being more than an accident. You thought Rishi, who Mathew had said would know what really happened, would only add to what you knew. That Smriti, your child, your pretty daughter, had a flair for instigating chaos. And accidents spring out of chaos.

So you decided to let it rest. You wouldn't look for Rishi. You wouldn't pursue it any more.

Then you saw him with Meera at an art event. You wondered who the boy was, at first. No, not boy. Young man. None of them, neither Shivu nor Mathew, had told him that. That the third angle to the triangle that enclosed Smriti was much older than all of them. And had the swagger of the handsome man who knows he is handsome.

Rishi Soman. Only, what was he doing with Meera?

Meera's voice had risen and struck a note of querulous fear. 'Soman. No, he's not Nayantara's friend. He is someone I know...'

You kept your expression as controlled as you could. You didn't allow even a flicker of excitement to show at the name. At the confirmation of your suspicion. You saw Meera search your face. 'Why? Why are you asking about Soman?'

You shrugged. 'I was just curious. He reminded me of someone...'

'Oh,' Meera said, the relief palpable in the relaxed set of her body. 'He is an actor. He has modelled for a few things. You've probably seen him on TV.'

'Probably!' You were cryptic in your dismissal of Rishi Soman.

You wondered what she was seeking to hide. Could they...? You paused. When it came to Meera, you found you couldn't use terms of fornication – fuck, screw, bonk... Meera wasn't that sort of a woman. Besides, he was way too young. And yet, you sensed an unease in Meera. You didn't like it. You didn't like it one bit.

It takes Jak two days to make up his mind. Two days of endlessly looking at the computer screen, trying to make sure the third boy – no, man – is Rishi Soman. Smriti's boyfriend, if what Shivu and Mathew had suggested is the truth.

Two days of sitting at Smriti's bedside and trying to see beyond the grimace that was her habitual expression. Smriti, Smriti, tell me, is he the one you were in love with? Is he the one who went with you? Was he there when it happened? Why then did he abandon you? Shall I go looking for him? Shall I demand of him the truth? Shall I, Smriti?

She lies there without moving a limb, her face contorted into a mask. She lies there looking beyond him. Seeing what? Countless versions of those last minutes? It is this replaying of what could have happened that settles it. Jak would call Rishi Soman and ask to meet him.

In the morning, Jak knows there is no point in putting it off any longer. Besides, if he doesn't do something to take his mind off what he has to deal with, his sanity will unravel. As long as he is busy, he can find respite. A semblance of normalcy, even.

The first thing to do is get Rishi Soman's number. Jak doesn't want to ask Meera, so he calls Sheela. 'What do you need his number for?' Sheela asks. 'He is a small-time actor. A charming creature, so he is on everyone's list. And he is rather pretty. Photographs well, too!'

Jak mumbles an excuse about a friend of a friend wanting to use him for something… It sounds lame to his own ears. But Sheela doesn't probe and instead, begins haranguing him for not calling her except when he needs a favour. 'When is that long promised dinner date going to happen? Or is there some hottie in your life?'

He tries calling Rishi Soman. 'I am Smriti's father,' he begins, thinking open confrontation to be the best tactic.

There is silence.

'Hello, hello,' Jak urges.

'Yes, I am here,' a low voice says.

'We need to meet,' Jak says. 'I need to talk to you.' But Rishi will not speak to him. He hedges in a most polite voice. I am busy this week, he says.

'Sure, I understand. How about next week then?' Jak offers in his most placatory voice. 'I won't take too much of your time.'

'I'll have to see. I am not sure. Let me call you…' Rishi hangs up.

Jak waits the whole week for Rishi to call. But he doesn't. And when Jak tries to reach him, he sends him a busy tone in response. Jak sinks his forehead into the palm of his hand. He is weary. How is he going to get the boy to talk to him?

'What is wrong?' Kala Chithi asks quietly.

Jak looks at her blankly. She touches his shoulder. 'Tell me, maybe I can help.'

She listens patiently to his words of frustration. Rage, even. 'Why won't he talk to me? He must know something. That's why he's avoiding me.'

'Didn't you say that you saw him with Meera?'

Jak nods.

'Then all you have to do is ask Meera to engineer a meeting,' Kala Chithi says.

'But will she?'

'Tell her. Explain to her the connection. She will then. How can she say no? She knows Smriti's condition, she'll understand why you cannot rest till you know.'

Kala Chithi pauses for a moment. Then she says in a voice soft as lace, 'Besides, don't you realize that she is fond of you…'

Jak is startled by this revelation, but he doesn't pursue it. Instead, he goes to Meera's room. He will tell her what he has discovered. And then it is up to her.

Jak waits in his car in Cockburn Road. He looks around him with interest. He didn't even know such a place could exist in the heart of the city. But here it is. A tiny bar in a row of broken down buildings and dilapidated shops curving into Bamboo Bazaar and leading on to Cantonment Station.

He looks at his watch again. Twenty past eleven. Meera should be here any moment now. He searches the entrance of Dewar's, the faded doors flung wide open, men in office clothes sitting alongside autorickshaw drivers. As he watches, a girl parks her scooter and walks in. And he knows again the thrill of discovery. Could such a place exist? And for Meera to know about it and suggest it…

Jak sees a bike come towards Dewar's. A man and a woman. The woman holds the man's waist in an almost intimate clasp. When the bike screeches to a halt, he feels the impact of the woman's breasts against his back. He grins. He has done it too, like all his friends have. That abrupt braking. The squashing of her breasts, the tightening of her grip, the smile that splashes across the face on knowing he has made it happen. The leer of knowledge – the girl wanted it as much as he did.

Jak feels a queer sense of regret. He has had those days too. A bike, a chick and endless carefree hours of youthful animation. It isn't that he longs for them any more; he doesn't. Is this what growing old means? A certain reconciliation with one's subdued spirits and not-so-youthful self?

The woman is laughing as she dismounts from the bike. She slaps the man's shoulder playfully. Jak snaps out of his reverie when he sees the woman is Meera. A Meera he doesn't recognize. He sees the casual case with which she wears the unfamiliar clothes, and her manner. Jak's mouth tightens. So this is Rishi Soman, Smriti's friend who is Meera's friend too. More than a friend.

Jak looks at the dashboard clock. Ten minutes, Meera had said. Wait for ten minutes and then call me. I'm going to ask you to join us. You wait another five minutes before you come in. I don't want him to think I set it up. And it's going to be about this key that you have tracked me into Dewar's for.

What key? Jak's eyes questioned.

'Does it matter?' Meera sighed. 'Filing cupboard key, if you need a name for it.'

'All this subterfuge…' Jak mused.

'Indeed! How do you think it makes me feel? But it is Smriti I am thinking of,' Meera said gently.

She picks up on the sixth ring. He imagines her making a moue of her lips. 'My boss. I have to answer this!' she would say, perhaps smiling apologetically. Rishi Soman would lean back in his chair and smile back at her lazily, languorously. I would if it were me, Jak thinks unhappily as he speaks the words he is expected to and hears her planned response. 'Yes, the key is with me in my bag. I am at Dewar's. Do you know the place? You do. Can you pick it up from me?'

She sits in one of the faded cane chairs facing the door. Rishi Soman is seated with his back to the entrance. Jak sees him reach over to pop a peanut into her mouth and Meera part her lips willingly enough. Jak's jaws clench. Then he sees her catch sight of him and the flash of relief on her face. Jak smiles. Rishi Soman turns his head to look at the recipient of Meera's beaming smile.

And soon Meera is saying, 'Did you have trouble finding the place?' She fumbles in her bag for the key and holding it out to Jak, she feigns confusion. 'Oh, how I forget my manners. Rishi, this is Jak. And Jak, this is Rishi Soman.'

Jak looks at the young man and with the consummate voice of the thespian queries, 'The actor?'

Rishi Soman's features relax into the wide gratuitous smile of one who aches to be recognized in public and seldom is. The little shit, Jak thinks. He really thinks that I would know him from one of those mannequins who populate the afternoon soaps on TV. What an idiot, with his wet-hair look and one size too small T-shirt and the compulsive need to show off the profile that someone must have told him is his best angle.

'Oh, do join us,' Meera says.

'Yes, do,' Rishi Soman says after a moment, not entirely pleased, but not willing to relinquish a moment with someone who actually recognized him.

Jak pulls up a chair and settles down. What now?

Meera is a practised hostess. She knows how to expand the conversation to include both Jak and Rishi Soman. So in the manner of the experienced corporate wife who knows timing is all, Meera says, 'Jak's daughter was a student at Mounts.'

'Was she?' Rishi Soman queries politely. Jak can sense his restlessness.

'I think you knew her,' he says suddenly. 'She mentioned you…'

Rishi Soman wears an abashed look but his smile is smug. He shrugs. 'College girls. Without them the actor is nothing. They are the ones who bolster our egos even if the critics pan us… For instance, would this gorgeous lady here ever ask me for a photograph and then hide it between the pages of her diary?' He throws Meera a boyish grin.

Jak thinks he would like to slap that silly, smug look away. But he can also see what it is that lured Smriti and seems to enchant even someone as sensible as Meera. She is wearing a strange expression, he sees to his consternation. The foolish smile of the besotted.

'No, she wasn't one of your anonymous fans.' Jak's voice cracks. 'I think you knew each other very well. Smriti. Smriti Krishnamurthy.'

A silence creeps into the room then. A mangy silence on the four legs of a hyena who waits for someone else to make the kill.

'You set this up,' Rishi Soman hisses. 'You planned this between the two of you. And I thought you wanted to see me, Meera,' he continues, oblivious to Jak's presence. 'I thought we had a connection. You were just using me.'

Meera flushes. Jak leans back in his chair. 'Meera did as I asked her to.'

He holds Soman's gaze steadily. 'You forced my hand when you refused to take my calls.'

'What is it you want to know? I told you I had nothing to do with it.' Rishi Soman's face contorts into a mask of misery. 'How can you hold me responsible?'

Meera reaches across and takes his hand in hers. 'Rishi, no one is holding you responsible. But don't you think the Professor has a right to know what happened? You were the only person there... Look at him. Put yourself in his place. Wouldn't you want to know?'

Jak feels Rishi's eyes settle on him.

'Tell me,' Jak says in his quietest voice.

At first, Smriti was a game. The queen of the chessboard pursued by the bishop, the rook and himself, the knight. At first, Smriti was a piece he wanted to prise away from the rest, whistling under his breath. Then one day he paused, sized her up and murmured: Checkmate?

The other two watched helplessly as he made his move. The rook toppled over and removed himself, the bishop fumed, but it was the knight who with the powers vested in him could move two paces to the front, one to the side, and stake his claim.

He had an unfair advantage, he knew. He was the older man. Older than the other two. She would see them always as boys. Playmates. But he was the one who knew how to lower his voice to a seductive timbre and toy with her already errant emotions; the one who could lean back, fold his arms, shake his head at her youthful impetuosities and say, 'You are such a child! What am I to do with you?'

The child she was flowered.

Jak's eyes narrow. This bastard, it seems, always has the unfair advantage. The older man to Smriti and the younger man to Meera. He is a professional charmer of women. Jak rubs the bridge of his nose absently, furiously.

They played house, Smriti and Rishi Soman. At first everything was a game. Days speckled with playacting and role playing. You Tarzan, me Jane. You husband, me wife. You daddy, me mummy. They cooked. They cleaned. They shopped. They made love. They made plans. They slept wrapped in each other's arms and dreams.

Everything was perfect when it was make-believe. Then Smriti didn't want it to be a game any more. In the apartment he shared with his cousin, she allowed the swelter of emotions to swirl and bank. This feeling he aroused in her, she wished him to know, it consumed her. She dressed the way he liked girls to. She ate what he ate. She switched to the music he listened to and gave up everything he professed a dislike for. She bathed using his bar of soap; she borrowed his toothbrush; she wore his shirts… She followed his every move and if he slammed a door between them, she would wait outside till he emerged.

At first, he was touched. Flattered, too, that he could raise such an excess of feeling in another person. But soon her devotion felt like clinging, her love a trap, her presence a weight on his shoulder. He didn't know if he could stand it any more. Ease up, he wanted to tell her. What is this strange intensity? We are young. We don't have to think forever. Not yet. Let's just enjoy each other.

It unnerved him to be the object of her passion.

No, it wasn't that. Passion was something else. Less consuming, less fearsome, and more to do with the call of the flesh. This was an obsessive love. And it scared him. He felt as he was being devoured alive.

At first Smriti was a coveted prize. Then she became a bloody nuisance he wished to shrug away.

The monotone pauses. Hesitant eyes. Rishi Soman clasps his fingers and asks softly, 'Do you wish me to continue the story?'

Across the room, two old men with rheumy eyes sit with half empty glasses in front of them, and a plate of crumbs. They stare at the tableaux the trio are frozen in. Meera sunk deep into her chair, fearful of what would come next. Jak bracing himself to hear the worst. And Rishi trying to school his features, his thoughts, his words.

'I thought she had unreal expectations of the life we would lead,' Rishi said. 'She was used to flinging around money. I mean, she was this typical NRI type! She drank mineral water and kept moist wipes and hand sanitizers in her bag. And I was just a middle-class boy. The truth was, I couldn't afford her.

'She wasn't really rich in that sense. Not like girls whose parents were in the Middle East. I knew her parents were academics. She had money but not enough to subsidize the two of us. And I wasn't sure when I would start making decent money.

'I hate having to say this, but I didn't think Smriti could afford us.

'I decided to go with her to Madurai. I knew she was reluctant to be parted from me for even a moment, but this was the best thing to do, I thought.

'I didn't know what I was going to do when we got there. But I knew that by the end of the trip, I would tell Smriti that it was over. I couldn't go on like this. I wasn't ready to be tied down yet. At least, not in the way Smriti wanted me to be.'

Jak's mouth tightens. Meera puts her hand on his. In that furtive gesture is a wealth of meaning: Let him speak. If he clams up, we'll never get to the truth.

His eyes seek hers in one last plea. Would you sit here and stomach silently this dismissive negation of Nayantara?

Meera shakes her head. Jak says nothing.

IV

'Nothing. It really doesn't matter.' Vinnie tries to steer the conversation in another direction.

'No, you have to explain. Why uh-oh?' Meera, already bewildered, is further confused by Vinnie's exclamation. 'You don't approve?'

'How do I explain this? I approve because you finally seem to be moving on. At one time, I thought you'd build a temple to your life with Giri and worship there for the rest of your life. Then there was the actor...'

Meera shudders. She doesn't know how to slot Rishi in her life any more.

'He was bad news, at least for you,' Vinnie continues. 'But I don't like the idea of the Professor either.'

'Why?' Meera swallows. She knows what Vinnie is going to say but she needs to hear it anyway.

'He is too needy. Look at his situation. You need someone who will be there for you. Not the other way round. You don't want him using you as a crutch and then walking away.'

'I told you. He doesn't need a crutch.' Meera's voice is flat and toneless.

'You sound hurt,' Vinnie says.

'Yes... no, I don't know.' Meera rubs the bridge of her nose. A mannerism she has picked up from Jak. She can see Nikhil shooting baskets. The thump thump of his basketball reverberates on the cement floor. 'All I can think of is, why has he suddenly become so aloof? What did I do wrong? Should I bring it up? Ask him why he is giving me the cold shoulder?'

'Meera, don't say or ask anything. You heard what the actor had to say. The Professor has to deal with it. Think of it from his point of view. He's a man with too many shadows on his soul. That's why I think he's wrong for you.' Vinnie is clear in her denouncement of Jak.

Meera doesn't speak.

All she can think of is how they parted that noon, at Dewar's.

Meera and Jak waited for Rishi Soman to leave. For a few minutes they didn't speak. Then Jak asked, 'Where are you going now?'

'Home. Where else? Why?' Meera was puzzled by his query.

At the door she waited for him to ask if he could drop her home. He seemed bereft, desolate. There are so many things that a father, a parent, ought to never know about his child. But he had listened, allowing hardly a flicker of emotion to show except when their eyes met a few times. It was this that strengthened her resolve to not shy away from him.

But he didn't make the offer. Instead, he nodded and walked to his car, leaving her to find her own way back.

Meera watched him leave with a sinking heart. This was the second time that he had moved away when she tried to bridge the distance.

He appears in her doorway the next morning, contrite and hopeful. Meera looks up from the dining table where Nikhil sits reluctantly spooning porridge into his mouth.

'Kitcha! Jak!' she exclaims, unable to decide how to address him. 'Is something wrong?' She is already pushing her chair back.

'No, no,' he stutters. 'I was just passing by…'

It is Lily who pauses her breakfast to invite him to join in. 'It's so nice to see you, Professor. We haven't seen you in a while. How are you? Have you eaten? Take your pick. There is porridge, toast and fruit. Or you can have pongal and chutney. Or would you prefer an egg?'

He lowers himself into the chair next to Meera's. 'No, just coffee will do.'

But his fingers won't still, Meera notices. He plays with a piece of toast. She ladles a small portion of pongal into a bowl. 'Try some of this,' she urges, 'Raniamma makes it well.'

'Which makes it the only thing she can cook,' Nikhil murmurs sotto voce.

Lily frowns, but doesn't speak. She is no longer the ebullient Lily she used to be.

Meera shakes her head disapprovingly. Finally Jak's face relaxes into a smile.

'It is good,' he offers.

'Don't be polite, Professor,' Nikhil continues.

'No, it really is. It's exactly what I needed,' he says, but his eyes seek Meera's again.

She is unable to hold his gaze.

'Some more coffee?' She hides behind the haus frau Meera act she can conjure up in an instant.

She hears him inhaling. Is he counting till ten? she wonders, a hysterical giggle coming on.

'Yes,' he states. 'Thank you!' Is that sarcasm in his voice? Meera gives him a sidelong glance.

Then she feels his fingers weave through hers under the table and squeeze them ever so gently. Sorry, sorry, sorry, the gentle pressure exerts. I didn't mean to pull away. I didn't mean to hurt you. I felt I couldn't drag you into the mess I am in now.

Meera's eyes widen.

She drops her head. A curve of hair hides her face. She feels him reach out and lift the strand, and tuck it behind her ear.

Meera stops breathing.

It occurs to her from the stillness that has crept into the room, so have Lily and Nikhil. And Jak too.

V

Lily wants to talk, she tells Meera. She emanates a stillness.

'You have to make the time, sneak the moment, whatever. But we need to talk. You mustn't disregard what I say until you have heard me out.'

A wind blows outside. Meera hates the wind. The constant humming fans all her fears. It tells her exactly what is wrong with the house: the roof tiles that could dislodge, the windows that creak, the door stoppers that don't pull their weight any more. And now here is Lily, her fingers plucking at a hanky, her mouth shorn of its dentures, and her face wiped clean of all artifice or expression.

'Why, Lily?' Meera says. 'What is all this ceremony in aid of? You don't need to make an appointment to talk to me… Tell me!'

But Lily will not sit. Nor will she unburden herself of the words that wait in her mouth. 'No, no, not like this. I need your full undivided attention. I need you to concentrate on what I have to say.'

Meera's brow wrinkles. Traces of the old imperial Lily. Standing straight at seventy-six without the slightest hint of a slouch in her body or tremor in her voice. That Lily had disappeared when Saro died. Almost as if her very soul drizzled away with the blood that had trickled out of Saro's mouth as they carried her into the ambulance.

'We do not know what grief is until a child dies,' Lily had said that night. 'The inconsolable sorrow of knowing nothing will ever be the same again.'

Meera huddled beside Lily, unable to grieve or console. All she knew was a numbing within.

She thinks of Kitcha, the sadness that clings to him. She has seen it come to sheath Lily, too, in the past few months. She shivers now. 'I hate this wind,' she says abruptly. 'I hate the rubbing of the branches against the roof. It makes my flesh crawl.'

Lily's mouth caves in further. 'This is what I mean,' she says, her displeasure evident. Lily will no longer make an effort. She never really had. But in the months after Giri left and in the days after Saro's death, she has become guarded. 'I need you to make the time. What I have to say is important. I don't want to talk about the wind or the trees. If they bother you so much, chop them down!'

Meera smiles suddenly. Tall trees were sacred to Zeus. And these even more so. 'How can you even think of it?' Giri had bristled when she suggested they trim their length. He liked the picture of the house framed by silver oaks, their wispy branches and lacelike leaves. Picture postcard trees that loomed and threatened to kill them in their beds, she had worried all these years. Lily is right. If they bother her so, she ought to do something about it. She will chop them down to six feet, she decides. Men and trees are the same – give them an inch and they turn unmanageable after a while. Meera Hera no longer worries about pleasing her Zeus.

Silver oaks dealt with, Meera sits in the patio hugging her thoughts. She finds that she is strangely reluctant to discuss how she feels, even with Vinnie. It is too new and too nebulous. It is also what she is yet to acknowledge to herself. That here is a man she would like to be with.

'For heaven's sake,' Vinnie would exclaim, her eyes ferreting out Meera's secret thoughts. 'Are you saying you want to marry him?'

'No, not marriage. I am not thinking that far ahead,' Meera would say.

'Then what?'

'I don't know, Vinnie. I really don't know. I just like him.'

Meera says that to herself now. Kitcha. Jak. She can't even decide how to address him in her heart. 'It's not just you,' he had told her once. 'I don't know how to address myself any more. My family calls me Kitcha, my colleagues Jak, and my daughters Papa Jak. Am I Kitcha? Am I Jak?'

'So what do you do?' She smiled.

'I take the cue from the person in front of me. Do they want me to be Kitcha? Do they want me to be Jak?'

'Who do you think I want you to be?' she asked, holding his gaze steadily.

'What do you think?' Jak, or was it Kitcha, leaned into her. She could smell the tang of his cologne and she wanted to rub her nose against the skin of his neck.

'I'll have to figure that out.' She nibbled her lip.

For, as unbound as Meera had become, one part of her was still Hera, who feared the birth of change. Hera, who waited outside Acmened's door, squatting crosslegged, her clothes twisted into knots and her fingers locked together. Let it not happen yet, let it not happen yet, Hera had willed the movement of time.

It is twilight. As the summer approaches, the days get longer and longer. Meera thinks of how on summer evenings, they would all go swimming. Giri had a corporate membership in one of the private clubs and he would send the car for them. Some days Lily and Saro would accompany them. Saro would sit at the poolside commenting on the children's lack of finesse as they swam. 'You are not a dog or a hippo to splash the water so,' she would say, pulling her legs in when Nikhil sent a tidal wave across the pool's edge.

'Why don't you show us how to swim?' Giri snapped one evening.

Saro, who would never allow herself to get into an argument with her son-in-law, cocked a finely arched eyebrow and murmured, 'Perhaps I will!'

And so Saro emerged in a bathing costume the pool attendant found her, her hair tucked into a bathing cap and as Meera watched in astonishment, clambered down the steel ladder into the waters where, with perfect aplomb and the style of a practised swimmer, she showed off her breast stroke. And the back and the butterfly. And the Australian crawl. Only, when Saro swam, the pool's surface scarcely even rippled.

The children were awestruck and so was Meera. She hadn't even known her mother could swim.

Saro never swam again. She wouldn't explain why, despite Meera asking.

Now as Meera watches Lily put on her glasses as a preamble to her important discussion, she bursts out, 'Lily, why didn't Mummy ever swim? I mean, we all saw what a stylish swimmer she was. Why wouldn't she swim?'

Lily frowns. 'I thought I said, no chit-chat!'

Meera sighs. They are sitting at the dining table, the two of them.

'It's like this.' Lily launches into an explanation for their need to sit across a table in such a manner. 'Ever since Saro died, I have been thinking about many things.'

Lily has combed her hair back and wound it into a little bun at the nape of her neck. Fine silky grey hair which she has the salon rinse with an ashy glow that makes her skin seem even more translucent. Bone china. Touch it and it would splinter. She has put on make-up and dressed herself in a heavy cream silk sari. Blue sapphires gleam in her ears and around her throat. Most importantly, Lily has put her dentures on. Her mouth stays in place and her jaw is firm in its tilt as she straightens her back and snaps, 'This is important!'

Meera rests her elbows on the table and begins playing with her rings. They did this when Saro was alive too. Invite her to a discussion where they would tell her how they hated being a burden on her and that they thought they ought to go to an old-age home.

'There are these really nice ones, you know,' Saro would say. 'Not all of them have little dingy rooms smelling of decaying bodies or stale food. I have made enquiries and you would be surprised at what is offered.'

And Meera would explode, 'What's wrong with you? This is your home. If anyone should leave, it's Giri and I!'

What if I had actually taken them up on their offer and said yes, Meera wonders. Would they have left? A stab of sorrow – this too must be part of parenthood – to feel unwanted as one grows older, to want to be needed… One day, I probably will do the same to Nayantara and Nikhil, play my version of

Do you love me? Do you really love me? Do you need me in your life?

So Meera hastens to reassure. 'Lily, I know where this is leading… no, don't even bring it up. You are not a burden. And no, I am not going to let you go into an old-age home!'

Lily sits up frowning. She works her jaws in consternation. 'Who said anything about going to an old-age home?

'Then what?' Meera's heart pounds. Is Lily ill?

Lily smiles. For a fleeting moment, Meera sees the beauty that she once was. She tucks a strand of hair behind her ear. 'My friend Zahira, you know, the actress who gave it all up some years ago and lives in Mysore now with a houseful of animals. Well, her son is a very successful television producer and he wants me to act in a new series. It's going to be dubbed into six languages.'

The excitement in Lily's voice fills Meera with dread. She has never seen Lily so animated. She is too old and too used to being the star of the show. What role would she be given?

'Lily, I don't know what to say,' Meera begins. She must dissuade Lily from this wild caper. To hang around a set all day at her age would kill her. And the children wouldn't like it. Their great-grandmother as a TV soap granny would embarrass them.

'You don't have to say anything. I am not asking you for permission. I am informing you of my decision,' Lily bristles. She can see Meera isn't pleased.

'The terms they have offered are excellent. After all, I am a national award winning actress. It will also help ease some of the burden on you.'

A dark suspicion creeps into Meera at the mention of money. 'Is that why you are doing this, Lily?'

Lily snorts. 'Yes, the money is important but I wouldn't kill myself for a two-bit role, you know that, don't you? I like the story. I like the expanse of the character I am to play. Do you know how hard I have been working to get into character? I have been managing without my dentures because I think the character requires it in the initial part of the series. Before the flashbacks, etc.'

Meera feels foolish. I am so much more of a drama queen than she is. Here I was, attributing depression and despondency to her, while she has been method acting. Meera reaches across and takes Lily's hand in hers.

The skin is papery and dry, the blue veins under the almost transparent skin criss-crossing the back of her hand. Meera squeezes the fragile hand ever so gently. More and more, she has let the irritations of her daily routine overwhelm her.

'If it makes you happy, Lily...' she says. 'I am so proud of you.'

She wonders if it is tears that bring a sheen to Lily's eyes. Lily murmurs, 'Thank you, thank you, my dear. And...' She pauses and focuses at a point in the middle distance. 'I am lost, Meera. Without Saro, my life has lost its definition. I miss her.'

'I miss my mother too,' Meera admits, realizing the vacuum that Saro's absence has created.

'There is one more thing,' Lily says abruptly. 'If there is a chance for you to make a new life, you must.'

Meera looks away.

'When your father died, I should have told Saro this. But I didn't. I was selfish in my fear that I would be alone. So I clung to your mother and let her use me as a crutch. She was too young to be a widow as I was. I should have spoken then, but I didn't. So I must tell you this.'

Blood rushes into Meera's face. 'I don't know what you are thinking but there is nothing between the Professor and me,' she says lamely.

Lily leans back. 'Not yet. But I can see he likes you and you him. It isn't about cutting your hair or acquiring a new wardrobe. That's good in the movies. A new look that turns you into a new woman. Get real, Meera. Get real before your life slips away from you.'

Meera squares her shoulders to bring more vehemence into her denial. And then she stops. Why is she denying the truth?

'By the way, there is no dark secret why Saro wouldn't swim. She hated water and I forced her to swim as a child. When she left home, she swore she would never swim except for an exigent circumstance.

'And that day at the pool, Giri was one,' Lily says, rising from her chair. 'The first thing to do is to be honest with yourself. Meera, listen to me, all of us need our dreams…'

VI

And so it happens that Meera allows herself to dream once more. Nothing elaborate or grandiose. Nothing involving new curtains or wardrobe space. She isn't hoping to build a new nest or sail into a sunset, wing to wing. At this point, she is content with the companionship that Jak gives so easily and with such largesse. Her Jak. Her Kitcha. When he ruffles her hair or leans across to cup her chin or flick a crumb from her kurta, Meera knows a sensory explosion.

Vinnie from the sidelines has done a volte-face. 'Are you ever going to make love or are you two going to moon around forever like juveniles?' she asks as Meera lists the casual caresses of the day. 'I can't believe that you get so excited by the brushing of skin. Oh Meera, Meera, what am I to do with you?'

Meera grins foolishly. All in good time, she thinks. For now she likes the woman she sees in his eyes.

For the first time in many years, she raises the spectre of a dead dream.

'Oh, Giri,' she had cried one evening early in their marriage, 'will I ever do it? I worked so hard on the research. It's all sitting there gathering dust while life slips away from me.'

'What's the point? One more literature dissertation isn't going to change the world,' Giri said, and then as if to take the sting out of the words whispered, 'The children need you. I need you. Isn't that more important?' He kissed her fingers one by one in homage to her role in their life.

Meera smiled. But the next time she brought it up during a car trip, Giri was not as cajoling. He retaliated with a joke. A cruel joke. He took to pointing out water tanks: 'Oh, there's Mummy's MPhil on the roof!' The children giggled and Meera stretched her lips into a smile and never mentioned it again.

But Jak listens carefully, his head cocked, his fingers doodling. 'I wish you had worked on it,' he says. 'You still can. Can't you?' he asks abruptly. 'Are there any books I can source for you?'

It isn't long before Meera walks in on Nayantara and Nikhil discussing her as they play a game of Scrabble. She stops in her tracks, curious as much as anxious.

Nayantara and Nikhil sense something is afoot but in the light of a father who they hear is soon going to have a baby, a moderately soppy mother is easy to deal with.

She overhears Nikhil tell Nayantara, 'He is a nice man. He doesn't put down Mom.' Like Dad used to, he doesn't say.

In recent months, both Nayantara and Nikhil have acquired a new sensitivity. Past acts of unkindness, taunts and ridicule have come to haunt them.

'He admires her and all,' Nikhil says. 'He keeps asking her what she thinks.'

'Mom! She is just a housewife. What does she know?'

'Shut up. Shut up,' Nikhil says furiously. 'She is here for us, isn't she? I admire her too.'

'Mummy's pet!'

'I would much rather be Mummy's pet than Daddy's darling, like you. Daddy didn't want us. He went away. Or, have you forgotten that?' Nikhil's voice acquires a gravity Meera has never heard before. Her breath catches in her throat.

'He had his reasons.' Nayantara rushes to defend him but Meera can see her heart isn't in it.

'I don't care what his reasons were. Did he ever ask you or me even once if we wished to go with him? He left us behind like we were old clothes or something. You should see the Professor. How he looks after Smriti. He does so much for her and he doesn't ever act as if he is sick and tired of it. Every night before he goes to bed, he sits at her bedside and tickles her under her chin saying, 'Catch up on your sleep, baby, when you wake up in the morning, I am going to make you work so hard to make up for all this lost time… Do you think Daddy would look after us like that? Daddy doesn't care about us. I don't think he ever really did,' Nikhil says, moving a tile this way and that.

Nayantara is reduced to silence. But just as Meera decides to step in, Nayantara's curiosity rears itself. 'So what do you think?'

'What do I think about what?'

'About Mummy and her Professor. Is something going on?'

'I don't know. Maybe they will marry?'

Nayantara is clearly aghast at Nikhil's line of thought. That Dad would make a new life was part of his leaving home. But Meera? Moms are meant to put aside dreams and grow old gracefully, like furniture. 'Marry?' she shrieks.

'Yeah, they seem to like each other very much. But even if they marry, at least you don't have to worry about him and Mom having a baby. They are both too old.'

Meera suffers a quiet pang. Her children are growing up. Their lives are acquiring a dimension of their own.

'What about Smriti?' Nayantara asks.

'What about her?' Nikhil is quick to defend Smriti. 'You should ask Mom to take you to the Professor's house. Then you'll see for yourself. She just lies there…'

'That's their baby then! Dad's baby will at least grow up. But this one, you and I will be changing its diapers for the rest of our lives.' Nayantara doesn't mean to be as unkind as she sounds but she is all churned up. She doesn't know what urges her to speak as she does. Hurt. Fear. Or a combination of both.

'You are being mean,' Nikhil says quietly. 'If you saw her, you would take back everything you said now. Mom takes me there now and then and the last time, she asked me to read aloud to her,' Nikhil says in the all important voice of one asked to perform a very important task.

'Did you?' Nayantara's whole being radiates jealousy.

'I did. After a while it's like reading to yourself. She doesn't even move a muscle, I think.'

Nikhil forms a word. D.E.A.D.

Nayantara looks up from the Scrabble board. 'She is that bad?'

'She is. I think I would die if something like that ever happened to you.' Nikhil's voice snags in his throat.

Nayantara doesn't say anything for a while. Then she pushes the board away and hugs Nikhil.

VII

On an evening, as Jak keeps vigil, Rishi comes to see Smriti.

Kala Chithi has gone to the doctor for her routine medical check-up. Meera has left for the day. More and more Jak finds it a wrench to see Meera throw her books, papers, pen and phone into her bag and walk out of the door. When he can, he drops her home, prolonging the moment of her going away. Sometimes he wonders if he is getting in way out of his depth. Even in those first heady days with Nina, he hadn't known such a giddiness of sensation. A luminescence. All springing from so tiny an aperture that in another time and another place, another Jak would have slapped his forehead in a gesture of protest and jeered: Oh, grow up, will you?

For the first time, he wants to rush things rather than watch and wait, as is his wont. With Meera he wants more. Not just a melding of bodies and needs; he wants all of her. 'I know you will like Meera, Smriti. She isn't like Monique or any of those other women. I know how much you resented them. Meera is different. Meera is Meera…' he tells his daughter, rubbing cream into her palms. Then he hears the doorbell ring.

Jak doesn't speak when he sees who it is. He opens the door wide and says, 'Come in. You would like to see Smriti, I presume.'

Rishi follows him into Smriti's room.

Jak hears the gasp that escapes his mouth and watches the play of emotions on Rishi's face.

Rishi doesn't speak for a long time.

'I didn't know…' His eyes seek Jak's in a plea. 'I really didn't. What can I say?' His shoulders sag as he leans against the wall.

'What did you expect?' Jak doesn't bother to hide the rage that seethes in him.

Rishi moves away from the wall and walks to the foot of the bed. He stares down at Smriti, still unable to believe that this grimacing thing, this ruin of a girl, is the Smriti he knew. The Smriti he fell madly in love with. 'They… I didn't ever think they would do this.'

'They who?' Jak straightens.

'Srinivasan and his men. I didn't think they would dare do something like this.'

'It was an accident. A freak accident,' Jak says.

Rishi's eyes harden. 'An accident they caused. What else could it be? They are evil. I know it. They did this to her.' His voice rises. 'They said they would.'

One of the constituents of all chaotic motion, Jak knows, is recurrence. That certain systems will return to a state very close to the initial one. There is no fleeing from the sensitive dependence between the original and the evolved state.

In the pit of his stomach, at the back of his skull, in that deep recess somewhere in his soul where he laid to rest the ghost of Smriti's past, he feels a flutter. The swift flapping of wings. Jak, the weatherman, knows how this by itself can cause a tornado to appear elsewhere.

The butterfly flaps its wings, again and again…

'You said you broke up at Madurai. I assumed you left her there, but it wasn't like that, was it?' Jak asks. 'What happened thereafter? How did Smriti get to Minjikapuram?'

Rishi Soman sits down. His eyes narrow as he remembers the bus ride from Madurai.

VIII

At the bus stand in Madurai, Smriti's eyes widened in glee at the blue and white chequered pattern of the buses. 'Oh look, I have never seen a bus dressed in a tablecloth,' she cried. Rishi didn't speak. He couldn't summon up much excitement. The truth was, he couldn't summon up any feelings about anything these days. He felt weighed down by what was expected of him.

'Hmm,' he said, trying to find the right bus that would take them further east to the coast where Minjikapuram waited. He had a date with freedom there.

In the bus Smriti slept with her head on his shoulder. When the bus screeched to a halt, he felt her awaken. She rubbed her cheek against his neck. He saw the man across the aisle stare at them. It made him feel uncomfortable.

'Get up, sleepyhead,' he said, squaring his shoulders and hoping this would nudge her head off.

Smriti sat up and stretched. He saw her short top rise until he could almost see the undersides of her breasts. Rishi felt again the man's eyes. Only this time they licked at Smriti's flesh. Rishi leaned forward to cut the man's vision off.

'Hey, Smriti,' Rishi said, 'put that shirt on.'

'It's so hot!' Smriti frowned.

'I know. But we are in small-town India and they don't know how to behave when they see a girl like you.'

'What's wrong with me?' Smriti demanded.

Rishi felt his mouth straighten. She was so fucking defensive. All you had to do was point one little thing out and she behaved as if he had accused her of some heinous crime.

'Nothing is wrong with you. They haven't seen girls like you. And you always said you wanted to blend with the real India. You are hardly going to do that in a tank top and no bra,' Rishi snapped and pretended not to see the hurt in her eyes. Or how his displeasure cowed her down. Any minute now her mouth would crumple, he thought.

'What's wrong?' she asked a few minutes later. 'Why has the bus stopped?'

He shrugged. 'An accident. A road block. A puncture… Could be anything,' he said. He was bored, hot and guilty. From the corner of his eye, he saw Smriti had pulled on her shirt and buttoned it all the way to the top. God, wasn't there an easy way? A painless severance? How was he going to make it happen?

'Look, everyone's getting out. Let's go too. It'll be cooler outside.' Smriti tugged at his elbow.

Outside, groups of people stood by the road. It was Smriti who asked a woman, 'What happened?'

The woman stared at her in incomprehension. Rishi

smiled, unable to help himself. Poor kid. Even when she spoke Tamil, they stared at her bemused. 'It's your accent,' he murmured.

'Yennach?' Smriti tried again.

The fug cleared in the woman's brain. She broke into an explanation of an accident further up the road at the railway gate. They would be stuck here for a while, she added.

Smriti nodded and began to walk away. 'Where are you from?' The woman held her elbow. Her pregnant daughter stood at her side and Smriti felt their eyes take in every little detail of her person. Didn't they know it was rude to stare? She shook her head, unable to decide if she was amused or irritated. But they didn't stop scrutinizing her. Nor did they stop themselves from asking her fairly intimate questions, as another group of women joined them.

One of them touched Smriti's eyebrow stud. 'Doesn't this catch in your hair?' Another woman, more censorious than curious, pinched the fabric of her shirt and asked in a whisper, 'Don't the men stare at you? They leer at us even when we are in a sari so when they see someone like you… I couldn't ever dress like you do. All those eyes stripping me naked. I would rather die!'

Another gestured to Rishi with her chin. 'And he? Doesn't he mind your dressing like this?'

'Are you newly wed? On your honeymoon?' someone asked coyly.

Smriti looked at Rishi's face. Would they see the yearning in her eyes? She shook her head. 'No, no, we are from Bangalore. He is my friend.'

The woman frowned. 'I thought you were husband and wife. You would make a nice couple! Tell your parents to marry you off to him.'

Smriti laughed in confusion. If only she could. Her eyes sought Rishi again.

He touched her arm. 'Are you going to stand here gossiping all day?'

Then Smriti spotted the hoarding for the No-Pain balm. 'Look, Rishi!' She pointed. And everyone looked as well at Rishi on the hoarding. A series of Rishi straightening from a stiff back to playing a vigorous backhand, his tennis racquet slashing the air. A dashing, dapper Rishi men envied and women sighed over.

'Do you act in the movies?' a man asked.

Rishi flushed. 'No!' he snapped.

'You should!' the man stated, oblivious to Rishi's brusqueness. 'You have that look about you! You would make a good movie star!'

The women nudged Smriti. 'He is very glamorous. You better be careful someone doesn't steal him away!'

'Have you met Rajanikanth?' A boy who had heard just the tail end of the comment latched onto the 'movie star'. He pulled at Rishi's sleeve.

Rishi shook his head and began walking away. 'What about Vijaykanth? Prabhu? Surya? Dhanush? You don't know anyone! How can you be a film star?' The boy's disappointment was a knife turning.

Rishi crossed the road to a small copse of trees.

'He is very shy!' the women told Smriti.

Smriti didn't speak. She knew he was upset by any references to his career in the movies. He had acted in a couple of films but it had stayed there. A stillborn movie career was the worst thing to happen, he told her again and again. 'At least when you are waiting for someone to discover you, you have reason to hope. But this is awful!'

She slipped her hand into his. He didn't trust himself to speak. He had to leave Bangalore. There was nothing there for him. He would have to move to Mumbai. And Smriti would have to accept that it was over.

'What is this dump?' Smriti asked, wrinkling her nose. She stood on one foot, her other foot lazily scratching the back of her calf.

Rishi paused and looked up from the register he was writing in. 'Well, this is all I can afford. There is a boutique hotel that's come up a little way up the coast. But it's too expensive for me. You can go there if you want!'

Smriti shook her head and prodded him in his ribs. 'You sound like you want to get rid of me. This is fine. It's by the sea and I can hear the waves. And it is in Minjikapuram!'

Then, once they were in the room, it didn't matter. For when the boy flung open the door and the windows of the balcony, Rishi watched Smriti's eyes glaze over. He saw her breathe in the sea. Then she was in his arms, tugging at the buttons of his shirt.

'Make love to me here, Rishi. Make love to me with the sea and the skies as our witness,' she urged, rubbing herself against him.

Rishi held her away. 'What? Here?' he asked, suddenly revolted.

'Why?' she demanded, drawing circles on his back with her nails. 'You don't want to? You never seemed to get enough of me and now you act as if you can't stand me.'

'Not now.' His voice was flat, his face expressionless. 'I am not in the mood. Button up. Let's go find something to eat. I am hungry.'

Smriti sat huddled on the bed. 'What's wrong?' she asked

abruptly. 'Why do I get the feeling that you don't want to be here? Don't you, Rishi? Don't you want to be here?'

Rishi went back into the balcony. He could see the boats in the outer seas. There was a fishing village a little further up. 'But don't go wandering there,' the man at the reception had warned. 'Especially with a woman. They are all drunks. Drunken louts when they are on land.

'There's something else,' the man had said. 'I suggest you put some money in an envelope and leave it here with me. For the police. You don't want them picking the two of you up for immoral trafficking, do you? And they will when they see you…'

Rishi felt uneasy. In retrospect, it had been foolish to come on this trip with Smriti. Severance on familiar territory would have been more easily accomplished, he realized.

He felt a curious heaviness within. He wished he could say what was on his mind. Have it over with her; get it out of his system. And then, perhaps, they could have a few decent days together. Going back to what they once were. Young, carefree, with no strings attached.

Smriti was very excited about going on the trip. 'Despite the laws and regulations, women still find a way of discovering the sex of their unborn babies. If not the women, their families. They abort the foetus if it's a girl. Soon there may come a day when there are no women left,' she said, laying out her clothes on the bed.

'What is needed is awareness. To make the women realize that the girl foetus has to be given a chance. That they can find joy in their daughters too. It's going to be hard work, thankless, too.' Smriti was flushed with excitement. 'I'll be away for two to three weeks,' she said. 'I know most of the others think that I am a bleeding heart with no real resolve. But I want to show them that I care. I really care.'

Rishi read the earnestness in her voice with relief. She just might loosen her tenacious hold on him. Shift her obsession to the unborn babies who would at least benefit from it.

'When do you have to be there?' he asked.

'The first of March is what I have said. The first batch of volunteers must be there already. You know, don't you, that I hate the thought of leaving you,' she said, taking his palm and holding it against her cheek.

Her skin felt clammy to his touch. Rishi felt a strange sadness envelop him. The surge of feelings she had aroused in him once had dwindled to this. A physical distaste and pity.

'I'll take you there,' Rishi offered. 'Let's spend a couple of days together before you go on from there. We could go to Kodai. Or how about Minjikapuram? You keep talking about how wonderful it is… we could go there. It's not too far from Madurai either.'

'Would you? Really? I would prefer to go to Minjikapuram. My father used to talk about it all the time when I was a child.' Smriti glowed. Perhaps it was the sparkle on her face that hardened his conscience further. This way it wouldn't have to be done here, where it would be difficult to hide from her desperate pleas. For he knew that Smriti would cling. This way, the women and their unborn girls would keep her occupied for a while. By which time he would have left.

Wine, she said. They would take wine to drink by the sea. 'My father's aunt used to live around there for a while. Papa spent a few days there, he said. That's when he fell in love with the skies. Until then he had watched the sea but at Minjikapuram, he learnt to watch the sky as well.'

So wine we need, she said, drawing up a list. And oranges and grapes. And pepperoni slices on a tray. They would have a moonlight picnic on the beach. The moon would be almost full then.

'Smriti, Smriti,' he said, breaking into her frenzied monologue. Giddy plans to entangle him with love and longing. Rishi kneeled at her side, thinking, how did I ever think this was love?

'Ease up, will you? We are going by bus. The food won't keep. We are going to stay in a lodge. They won't have corkscrews or wine glasses. The beach may be a long walk away… who is going to lug all those things there?'

In the end, he agreed with a resigned shrug to two cans of beer and a can of salted cashew nuts.

'Why don't you freshen up?' he said, walking back into the room. 'Let's go for that walk when you are ready. Where's the beer and nuts? I spotted a fridge in the shop outside. Let me ask them if they will chill it for us. We can go for your moonlight walk and then for dinner.'

He would tell her tonight, he told himself. He couldn't keep this going any longer.

'But I couldn't,' Rishi says. 'We went for a walk. We drank the beer and ate the nuts. I listened to Smriti talk. I was hoping for an opportune moment; a pause that I could fill. But it was as if the night air and the moon had infected her with a wildness. She ran in and out of the water, she twirled in circles. And then in one final swirl of recklessness, she leapt into the air and landed on a bit of broken glass.'

There was nothing to do but wait the night out. There was no ice, but the shop next door provided two bottles of chilled Pepsi. There was no plaster, so Rishi tore up his T-shirt and bandaged the wound.

Once they would have laughed about it. It was the kind of absurdity they found hilarious. She sat with her foot propped on his shoulder while he held a Pepsi bottle on either side of the foot to stop the bleeding. It was done in a silence punctuated by politeness. 'Does it hurt?' Rishi asked.

She shook her head.

'Would you like something to drink?'

'Later,' she replied.

This was a new Smriti. A quiet, reined in Smriti. Her meekness was like a rebuke. It made him uncomfortable. He wished he could just walk away. Close the door behind him and forget all that had to be dealt with very soon.

Rishi, who allowed himself only three cigarettes a day, lit a fourth one and went out to the balcony. He felt her eyes on him as he inhaled and blew the smoke out, and as he continued to work his way through a pack of tens.

He saw her wan face. His conscience niggled. She sat with her back to the wall, with her foot propped on the pillows. He knew she was waiting for him to go to her. Cuddle her and baby talk her as he used to in those first whirlwind days when a little cut on her thumb caused a vast reservoir of tenderness to burst forth. Now she was in pain. Her foot must be throbbing. But all he felt was a distant pity.

IX

Smriti didn't want pity. She wanted him to love her. To be as they once were. So when he suggested they see a doctor, she disdained the offer to show him how upset she was with him.

'No, I'll be fine,' she said. 'Don't fuss!'

But he wouldn't accept that. 'The cut probably needs stitches. Don't be idiotic! You need a tetanus shot and perhaps antibiotics. Look, I am already stressed out. Don't add to it by being stubborn and sulking,' he snapped.

Smriti looked at him for a long moment. 'Fine,' she said.

The nursing home was by the bus stand, the man at the reception said. He could call them an autorickshaw, he offered. Rishi looked at him in surprise. He was younger and much more friendly than the older man at the desk last night. The older man had watched Rishi help a bleeding Smriti up the steps of the lodge without a flicker of emotion. He hadn't even bothered to ask, 'What happened?'

In the dim light of the hallway, Rishi had felt a great rage surge up in him at the man's apathy.

But the young man, as if to compensate, plied them with questions while they waited for the auto to arrive. 'If I had been here, I would have asked you to stay away from the beach at night. It's not safe at all. The fishermen drink and once they are drunk, they won't stop at anything. It's fortunate that you didn't meet any of them,' he said.

'What's your name?' Rishi asked.

'Arul Raj. Why?' His eyes quickened with interest.

'I am surprised at finding someone like you here,' Rishi said.

Arul Raj shrugged. 'I've been promised a job in Singapore. The moment the appointment letter arrives, I'll be out of here. There is nothing for me here, sir. Nothing. I hate this town.'

'What are you doing here?' he asked abruptly. 'This is not a tourist town. There is nothing... so how did you end up here?'

Rishi shrugged. It was Smriti who answered, 'I am part of a theatre group that's touring Tamilnadu.'

'How long will the auto take?' Rishi demanded, suddenly impatient.

Arul Raj, irked by Rishi's imperious tone, reverted to being the polite stranger. 'Soon,' he said, opening the register.

When Rishi went to stand by the gate, Smriti as if to make amends asked, 'Is it a good nursing home?'

'It is the only one we have. My sisters had their babies there.' Arul Raj allowed himself to be drawn into a conversation again. 'There is a government hospital at the Taluk headquarters but that's ten kilometres away. So those who can afford it go to the Meenakshi Nursing Home.'

'Who's Meenakshi? The chief doctor?'

'No, the chief doctor is actually a man. Dr Srinivasan. I think Meenakshi is his daughter. In fact, he owns this lodge too. And I think just about everything in this town!'

Rishi appeared. 'How much will the auto man charge?' he asked Arul Raj.

The young man's eyes hardened. Then he saw Smriti wince as she placed her foot on the ground. 'He'll ask for fifty or sixty, seeing that you are out-of-towners. But you shouldn't pay more than thirty.' Turning to Smriti, he said in a voice softened by sympathy, 'Do ask for Vasantha Sister. She is my neighbour. Please tell her that I sent you to her. She'll help you.'

Smriti smiled. Then gritting her teeth and refusing Rishi's offer of his arm, she hobbled down the steps to the waiting autorickshaw.

'What are you doing here?' the woman asked Smriti in surprise.

Smriti looked up from the book she was reading. For a moment, she stared into the woman's eyes, unable to remember where they had met. Then it came to her, that little encounter on the roadside by the halted bus.

'I hurt my foot. I have to see the doctor. I may need to take a shot; I may even need stitches!' Smriti spoke with a little embarrassed laugh punctuating her words.

'Where is your friend?' the woman asked, her eyes darting around the crowded reception area.

'He should be here somewhere,' Smriti said. Then, wanting to steer the conversation away, she asked, 'And you? What are you doing here?'

The woman's eyes dropped. 'I've come with my daughter. She is having a scan. I was just going to the scan room when I saw you here.'

'But don't you live elsewhere? That's what you said.'

The woman didn't answer her. Instead, she said, 'I have to go. Look after yourself. Don't wet your hair for a day or two. You mustn't catch a fever.'

Smriti watched Rishi go to the enquiry counter and demand to see Vasantha Sister.

'It's her day off,' someone finally said, wanting to be rid of him.

'I can't understand this crowd,' Rishi said, dropping into an empty chair across from her.

'It's the only nursing home in the vicinity,' Smriti said.

'So many pregnant women!' Rishi said, slouching deeper into his chair.

As if to still any further need for talk, he took out his mobile phone and began playing a game on it.

Smriti watched him for a few minutes. She was thirsty. She would have liked a drink. A fruit juice, perhaps. A tall glass of orange juice with ice cubes in it. She felt a great pang of homesickness. In all these months, she had never known such a yearning for home. For cool white sheets on the bed and the familiarity of loved possessions. The fraying patch on the carpet in the living room and the creak of the bedroom window when the breeze rocked it. To smell the coffee Papa Jak brewed every morning. To swing on the glider on the porch with just a little thrust of her foot. Nina's perfume. Shruti's high-pitched squeals of excitement. So many things to miss. Her eyes filled up. The house she grew up in had been sold and what furniture Nina didn't want was given away. Where was home now? With Papa Jak? Or with Nina and Shruti? Or was it the apartment Rishi lived in? Her life quivered with fragility, with impending loss.

Smriti opened the page and pretended to read while watching Rishi. This was a man she no longer recognized. He seemed distant and cold. What was wrong?

Four stitches, two shots and a prescription of antibiotics later, a weary Smriti emerged from the casualty room. 'I'll get the medicines and find an auto to take us back. You better sit here until then. It's bloody hot outside,' Rishi said, leading her back into the reception area.

The woman from the bus sat hunched in one of the chairs. Smriti hobbled over to sit by her side.

'Is everything all right with your daughter?' she asked.

The woman looked at her blankly for a moment. Then she shook her head. 'I don't know what to say,' she whispered.

'Why?' Smriti frowned.

'The foetus is all right. But it is a girl!'

Smriti sucked in her breath. 'How can you say that? What's wrong if it is a girl?'

'She already has two daughters, she doesn't need this third one. But she is four months gone. I wish we had come earlier but this scan doctor comes only once a month. An abortion now would be dangerous. But she doesn't want one more daughter either. Her husband is already furious with her. I don't know what she's going to do.'

'How does she know it's a girl?' Smriti touched her elbow.

'The scan doctor told her.'

'But the doctor is not allowed to reveal the sex of the unborn child. It's illegal!' Smriti's voice rose.

'They do it here. Why do you think we came here? The scan doctor is not from this town. They bring him from somewhere else, and he tells us if we ask him,' the woman whispered. 'Look around you,' she added. 'All these pregnant women, they come from various parts of the district. Do you think there are no hospitals where they live? It's because of the scan doctor. And then, if you want it, they'll do the abortion here as well!'

'But it's wrong.' Smriti wanted to cry. 'How can you hold the sex of the foetus against it?'

'Tell that to the men. Tell that to the women who bore those men!' The woman's harshness startled Smriti. This wasn't the exuberant woman from the bus, her laughter loud, her merriment infectious.

'But do you believe that too?' Smriti asked quietly.

'What I believe is of no consequence. It is what my daughter wants to do. Do you know what a burden a girl child is? My daughter already has two. Her marriage is at stake here. If she delivers yet another girl child, her husband might even leave her. He has already threatened her.

'I have to go now. She is with the lady doctor. I needed a moment to myself. She will ask me what she has to do and I will have to have an answer for her.'

Smriti watched the woman walk down the corridor to the consulting rooms, her feet dragging with defeat, her head bent in thought.

It was lunch time when they got back to the lodge. They went to a little restaurant nearby, where Rishi watched Smriti pick at her food. She was in a pensive mood and made little conversation. And all Rishi could think was, she has begun to sense how I feel. That explains the awkwardness.

Another thought slithered in on its heel: had she gone off him? Rishi realized that it would be the best thing to happen, but he didn't like it.

'Don't you like it?' he demanded, irked by the way she was pushing a ball of rice from one end of the plate to the other.

'I am not hungry,' Smriti said, pushing the plate away. 'I need to rest.'

The room was warm even with the fan on. They lay side by side with their eyes shut. Rishi felt the heat close in on him. Smriti, it seemed, had fallen asleep. He gazed at the ceiling, thinking of what he was going to tell her that evening.

When he woke up, it was almost six. And Smriti was gone.

He sat up. His eyes scanned the room. Her bag was still there. Where could she have gone?

Rishi decided to look for her downstairs. Perhaps she would be at the front desk, chatting to the clerk. But it was the taciturn elderly man, and Rishi didn't dare ask him if he knew where Smriti was. He didn't look like he would volunteer any information even if he knew.

Rishi rubbed the stubble on his chin. He should shave and shower. But the thought of going back to that dingy room depressed him. He would go for a walk instead, he decided, leaving the key with the clerk.

When the white Maruti Omni slowed down on the lonely stretch of road, Rishi braced himself for what was to come. They would offer him a girl, he was sure. He was surprised to see two well-dressed men emerge from the white van. The older man in a white dhoti and a white half-sleeved shirt, and the young man in trousers and a checked shirt.

'You are new here,' the older of the men said. It was a statement rather than a query.

Rishi blinked in surprise. Who were they? And why were they appraising him in this manner?

'Why?' he asked in his most hostile voice, speaking in Tamil. 'Why do you need to know? Who are you?'

The men looked at each other. Then the older man spoke again in his low raspy voice: 'You are new here. You know nothing of our ways. I suggest you go back. We don't want to cause any trouble. But neither will we allow you to stir up any trouble for us.' He was polite, though his words were loaded with menace.

'What trouble?' Rishi stuttered. 'I don't know what you are talking about.'

The young man stepped forward. 'Your slut, she was at the nursing home this evening. Poking her nose into things that don't concern her. Go home. Go wherever you want. But get out of here.'

The older man raised his hand to halt the young man's belligerence. The gold of his watch glinted in the late evening light and Rishi saw the flash of fire on his index finger. A diamond ring. Who were these men?

The older man patted Rishi on his shoulder. An affectionate, avuncular pat. 'He understands. Don't you? They will leave!'

Rishi watched the men get into the white van and speed back the way they had come. He felt his heart hammer in his chest. His mouth was dry. He had never been as afraid as he was now. What had Smriti done?

'How could you be so stupid?' he shouted when she opened the door.

'What? For opening the door?' She raised an eyebrow.

'No, you stupid fool. For poking your nose into things that don't concern you.' Rishi found himself using the words the young man had used. 'What were you doing at the nursing home?'

'Stop shouting at me, Rishi. You don't know what's happening there,' Smriti said, walking away.

He followed her into the balcony. 'Listen to me, Smriti, you don't realize what you are doing.'

'What do you think it's all about?' she asked quietly.

'I don't know. And I don't care.' Rishi slammed his fist against the door. It swung precariously.

'I can't be like you,' Smriti said. 'I can't see and pretend that I haven't seen.'

'What are you talking about?' Rishi asked, his voice rising in disbelief.

'They have a mobile scan unit and they tell the pregnant

woman the sex of the foetus. But there's more going on. I am going to find out what's happening there. What they are doing is not just illegal, it's wrong. And somebody has to stop it!' The righteous indignation on her face filled him with dread.

'These are dangerous people. This isn't America and you are not Erin Brockovich... You can make a fuss about what's happening once you are out of here. But it isn't safe to stay on!' Rishi tugged at her elbow frantically.

'What's the point of making a report? It will be hushed up even before it is taken up. All I have now is hearsay. If I stay here a few days more, I will have the proof I need. A woman I met has promised to send me to someone who will talk to me, tell me everything.' Smriti paused. Her eyes were thoughtful when she spoke next. 'You don't have to get involved. You can leave if you want to!'

'So you left.' It is Jak who breaks the silence between them.

Rishi leans forward, his palms clasped between his thighs, his head bent low in thought. In penitence? In remorse? Jak wonders.

'I know you have already made up your mind that I am a heartless bastard. But I couldn't even bother to pretend any more. That's how removed I felt,' Rishi says with no trace of emotion on his face.

Then he falls silent.

Until Jak speaks. 'Go on Rishi, what happened then?'

It is hard for Jak to keep the bitterness from his voice. 'She gave you the opening you needed, didn't she?'

Rishi shakes his head. 'I didn't leave. Not then! I couldn't just leave like that. I knew she had got into something that was way beyond her!'

Jak sinks his head into his hands. He says aloud, 'How could she not get involved? That's how she is! She is tenacious.' Then he stiffens and corrects himself: 'Is? Was?'

He gets up abruptly and adds, 'She was never good at giving up on things – or people. And she was a great one for causes…'

X

'Causes demand martyrs. Is that what you are planning to be? A martyr? They will hurt you for sure.' Rishi Soman spoke gently at first.

The night skies were clear. A moon hung low in the horizon. The sea breeze blew, strong and laden with salt. They could hear the boom of the waves. They sat in the room, the two of them, locked in a hostile silence.

'So leave then. You don't have to risk anything. You can walk away,' Smriti tossed at him.

'No, I can't leave,' Rishi snapped at her. 'How can I? You don't know what these men are like. Smriti, they are dangerous, and I really do mean that!'

Smriti continued to play with the fringe on her blouse. Tassels swung from the hem. She said, 'You were planning to leave, weren't you? It's over. I know it. Everything about you wants to flee from me – no, don't deny it. So why don't you go?'

Rishi licked his lips. He could taste the sea on them. 'I would, if I didn't feel responsible. I brought you here. I have to take you away from here. And when I go back, I am moving to Mumbai.'

'Would you have asked me to move with you?' she asked softly.

'No.' He shook his head. 'It's over. Or it will be as soon as I take you away from here.'

Smriti sat up straight. 'You, or anybody else can't force me to leave till I have got what I want.'

'And what's that?'

'Proof, Rishi. I need proof to file my complaint. I need proof to take to the newspapers. No one is going to be able to refute the truth then. Not even your dangerous men.'

He didn't know what to say to her or how to persuade her. Neither could he leave her there, knowing that she was putting herself in danger. So he decided to stay.

They sat there in that room in the sleazy lodge, unable to bridge the silence. In the end, it was Rishi who spoke. 'Tell me,' he said.

'Why?' she asked. 'What does it mean to you?'

'Nothing,' he said. 'But at least I'll know why you are risking our lives.'

She told him of the mother and daughter on the bus. Of meeting the woman again in the nursing home. Of discovering the existence of a visiting scan doctor who sat in a room with a board outside that read 'Sex of the child will not be revealed here!' Of hints and signs for an extra fee – of an abortion arranged if the scan revealed a girl child.

'But what do you think you can do? There is nothing more complex or vicious than small-town politics. And these people know that you've been asking too many questions.' Rishi's horrified whisper slashed through the air.

'I thought I would go with her everywhere she went. At

least they wouldn't attack her if she was with me. I thought if I seemed interested enough in helping her, she would listen to what I had to suggest.

'I had friends in the media. I would rope them in. We could make a noise. That would alert the authorities. I would make those calls in front of her, so that she knew I was serious about helping her.

'By next evening, I hoped we would be on the bus that would take us to Madurai.' Rishi recounts the sequence of events as if he has relived them in his head again and again.

He trailed Smriti all morning. At the nursing home, they were turned away. 'You can't deny us entry.' Smriti tried to push past the watchman furiously.

'Yes, we can.' An elderly man had emerged from an inner room. 'For one, you are not in need of any medical help. Secondly, this is a private nursing home and finally, I decide who is permitted to enter and who isn't. Please leave.'

When he spotted Rishi, his brow furrowed further. In that same equable voice he had employed to halt Smriti in her tracks, he said, 'So you decided to do things your way. You didn't think what we said was important enough.'

'Was that your dangerous man? That mild looking schoolteacher?' Smriti turned to Rishi furiously as they walked down the alley to the main road. 'I was imagining a brawny mustachioed thug in a string vest and a lungi.'

Rishi wiped the sweat off his brow. 'The problem is, you watch too many Tamil movies. You think villains come bearing the hallmarks of villainy. That mild schoolteacher may think nothing of slitting your throat or mine. Didn't you hear the menace in his voice?' Rishi felt an icy finger run down his spine. 'Smriti, I am telling you he is dangerous, this place is dangerous!'

'Okay, I admit there is a certain hostility. But not enough to warrant our running away with our tails tucked in. Let's sit here awhile,' she said, turning into a little tea shop with benches strewn outside.

'The video cam on my phone is on. I am going to record the number of pregnant women going in. The radiologist will be here till noon and then he'll be gone. Look...'

An autorickshaw halted at the mouth of the alley. A pregnant woman and a man emerged from it. A few minutes later, two women, one pregnant, walked into the alley.

They sat there for about two hours, drinking countless cups of tea and recording the arrival of pregnant women. Twenty-two in the course of three hours.

Back in the room, Smriti played her footage for him. 'Do you see my point now? Do you think the scan is to check the well-being of the baby in the womb? All they want to know is if it's a boy or a girl. How else could he attend to so many patients in so brief a time?'

Rishi nodded. He didn't know what to say. He seldom thought too hard about anything. All he had wanted in life was a break in the movies. To be a make-believe hero. So he went to the gym and took dancing lessons. He had begun kick boxing and attended acting classes. He just wanted to be convincing as a hero. Someone who could woo the pretty girl, fight the villains, safeguard justice and uphold righteousness. But that was in the make-believe world. He left it to others more eminent than him to fight the evils of the real world.

'We should get out of here this evening,' Rishi said again.

'I have to meet a woman. Chinnathayi. Her daughter died at the nursing home after an abortion and she may still have some of the papers and reports with her. I have her address.

I'll go there after lunch. I'll probably need a couple of hours. When I get back, we can leave,' she said in reply.

'Why will she talk to you?' Rishi asked.

'She will. She lost a daughter. How can she not be angry and bitter? Once I have her on tape, we can leave. I promise!'

Rishi felt his muscles relax. He didn't like the thought of her going out alone. But it was daytime and they would be gone soon. He didn't want to spend another night in this cursed town or this dump of a lodge.

'I'll be back by six,' she said as they ate biriyani from a banana-leaf parcel. 'If you pack up, we can leave as soon as I am back.'

He nodded. 'Thank you,' he said suddenly.

She looked at him for a long while. 'Thank you,' she said in reply.

That was the last time I saw Smriti. Those were the last words I spoke to her.

They came for me early in the evening. The younger man and three other men. I opened the door thinking it was Smriti. "You are early," I said as I unlatched the door. They pushed their way in silently.

"Look, we are leaving," I said, pointing to our packed bags. "I told you we are leaving. We'll go right now."

The younger man looked at me carefully. He gestured with a careless toss of his hand.

They began beating me up. When I screamed, one of them gagged my mouth. At some point they used a knife. I was curled into a ball on the floor and with every kick and every stab of pain, I prayed I would die. I didn't think of Smriti. Not once.

This wasn't cinema, for me to fight the villains and rescue Smriti, and for good to prevail.

That was when I knew how human I was, how full of frailties. I could think only of myself and if this was how I was going to die.

They left me broken and unconscious. Arul Raj found me an hour later when the hotel boy raised an alarm.

Arul Raj took me to a hospital in a nearby town. He had me admitted. I needed some stitches on my back and my wrist was broken. There were some internal injuries too. He said I was sedated for a couple of days.

When I opened my eyes, he was sitting there. He didn't ask me what happened, and I didn't explain. He either knew or didn't want to know. 'Smriti?' I asked.

He shook his head. 'She didn't come back. I left a message for her at reception…'

I looked away. I hoped that she had escaped in time. I borrowed his cell phone and tried calling her. An electronic voice said, 'The subscriber you have dialled is out of range.' I felt less afraid then. She must be with the theatre group, I thought. She must have fled to Madurai when she saw the mess in the room. Or, maybe someone warned her to make her escape. I sought refuge in that. That was all I could do. I was in too much pain to focus. What could I do? What could I have done?

My cousin came to fetch me the next day and took me to Coonoor.

A month later, when I returned to Bangalore, I heard about Smriti and the accident she was in. I thought it best to not get involved. To visit her would mean opening up old wounds

Later, Jak sits by the bed, unable to still his frenzied thoughts that echo Rishi's words: What could I do? What could I have done? Seeking penitence in a desperate need for forgiveness for not having been there to protect his daughter.

The next morning, he waits for Meera to arrive. He will return to Minjikapuram, he has decided. A name in Rishi's story seemed familiar, now he remembers where he first heard it. Chinnathayi – the elusive sweeper at the lodge.

If she will not talk to him, she will to Meera.

STAGE V

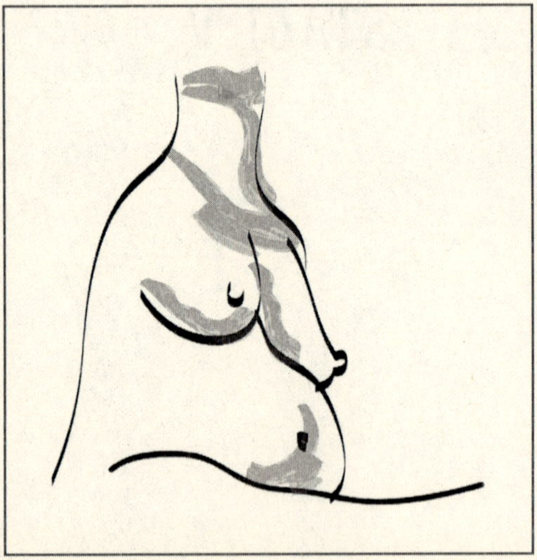

The Eye of Calm

I have often asked myself what represents a state of calm. Is it the sea that lies still as glass? Is it a clear blue sky? Is it the face of a sleeping child? Is it in the curve of a cat sitting on a window sill?

Then it comes to me. In the summer of 2006, I was in London and went to see for myself the much discussed *Alison Lapper Pregnant* at Trafalgar Square. I went prepared to be revolted, angry even. What was Marc Quinn, the sculptor, thinking of?

But in the whiteness of the Carrara marble, in the stillness of that form, in the full swell of the abdomen, I saw more than the celebration of the spirit. I saw the fall of the wind. I saw the calm that arises from the acceptance of the inevitable. A life would be born and with it all would change. But for now there was this. The quiet before the storm.

In everyday life, as in a storm, the forces that determine the nature of events are bound to spin closer as the most important moment nears. But with the increasing speed, something else is born: an outward directed force from this frenzied spinning of circumstances.

The scientific term for it is centrifugal force. The ancients called it the acceptance of the inevitable. Without it, as the science of absolute teaches us, the universe would destruct itself to nothingness.

The air spins. Faster and faster. One expects this, the eye wall, to be where the greatest fury of the storm resides. Except, the heart waits beyond the rim.

As the centrifugal force draws out the spiralling air, it causes a vacuum. 'Shunyata', or the substance of nothingness. Mathematics and Philosophy corroborate this concept of zero.

But the organic world has no room for fanciful notions. Either something is there or it is not there; everything has to become something else. For this is the law of the living world. All of nature abhors a vacuum, any vacuum. So, into that emptiness, some of the air flows from the top of the eye wall, causing it to sink.

A cloud-free aperture emerges, of sinking air and light. This is also the calmest part of the storm – its eye.

Professor J. A. Krishnamurthy
The Metaphysics of Cyclones

Meera's eyes seek his:

Do I have it in me? Do I want to be with him? For there will come a point when life and time become irreversible. Change will be born. Do I have it in me to live with that change?

Hera knew where to keep the monster she had reared. It would appear only when she summoned it. But Meera reared the multi-headed Hydra within her. Every time she wanted to do something for herself, Hydra reared. Why? it hissed. How can you? Aren't you being selfish by putting yourself first? Gradually Meera learnt to shut Hydra in its cave by submerging herself into the woman Giri wanted her to be.

But this Meera doesn't fear the hissing, many-headed Hydra. She knows how to chop its head of uncertainty off and bury it deep so it stays there.

When Jak asks her if she will go with him to the little seaside town, she doesn't hesitate.

'Yes, I will,' she says. 'But why, Kitcha?' This morning is a Kitcha sort of a morning. 'What do you mean to do there?'

He is perched on the table and she feels the pressure of his thigh against her arm. He shrugs. 'Closure,' he states, picking up her cup of tea and sipping from it.

Meera clasps her hands together. It is seldom that a woman has a second chance. Actually, it is seldom that a man does either. Perhaps this is theirs, hers and his. Theirs.

Chinnathayi flinches at the sight of the stranger framed in the doorway.

Somewhere at the back of her mind, she has always known he will seek her out one day. That first time she heard he had come to Minjikapuram, she had gone away. She heard later that he had come up against silence everywhere. That was how it would be. They had bought her silence as well. She was forced to sell it. On it hinged the lives of her granddaughters, and hers too. She didn't care about herself, but the girls would be orphaned if something happened to her. And she would have failed her daughter again.

She knew no one would talk to him. Neither was she going to give him an opportunity to find her, she had decided, as she stuffed a change of clothes for herself and the girls into a cloth bag that evening and rushed to the bus stand.

If she saw him, there was no telling what she might do. Or say.

'What do you want?' she asks baldly.

The stranger smiles. A grim smile of knowing. 'It is strange you do not ask me who I am. Does that mean you recognize me?'

Chinnathayi doesn't speak. Then she asks, even though she knows who he is, 'Well then, who are you? And what do you want?'

She moves deeper into the house. The man doesn't cross her threshold. He stays resolutely on it. 'I am Smriti's father. Do you remember Smriti?'

Chinnathayi takes a deep breath. 'How is she?' she asks quietly.

His expression doesn't change. 'It would have been better if she had died,' he says in a voice devoid of all emotion.

'Yes, it would have been better if she had died,' Chinnathayi agrees, turning away. Her face is in the shadows. 'Come in,' she adds. After all these months of dithering, her mind is made up.

She had sent Smriti away, she says. Chinnathayi sits with her back against the wall. The man and the woman are not used to sitting on the floor, she can see. Not like the girl.

Smriti had squatted on the floor easily, playing with Vana and Kanaka, her nine- and seven-year-old granddaughters. 'I told her there was nothing I could tell her,' Chinnathayi says again.

'But why did she come to you?' the woman who is with Smriti's father asks. 'What information could you have given her that she didn't have?'

'My daughter died. She was almost five months pregnant when her doctor asked that she get a scan done. The doctor said she wanted to make sure everything was all right. What is the need? I asked. Did I have a scan when I had my babies? But her husband insisted we do as the doctor asked and he said we should go to the Meenakshi Nursing Home. It was he who wanted to know the sex of the baby.

'The scan doctor said it was a girl child. Her husband walked away without speaking a word.

'On our way home, my daughter asked me if I would be her midwife. I knew what she wanted. "No," I said. "I will never be a midwife again. I swore that when you became pregnant the second time."'

Chinnathayi's voice cracks.

'She wept and pleaded. But I wouldn't listen. I thought if

I was firm, she would let it rest. Her husband arranged for the baby to be aborted. They didn't tell me. I knew when they brought my daughter's corpse home.

'I ask myself this now. If I had been her midwife, she would have wanted me to snuff that life out. I used to do it once, after all. And my daughter would be alive. Unhappy but alive.'

Chinnathayi reaches for her tobacco pouch and then pauses. 'Your daughter heard about mine… she wanted to know exactly what happened. But I sent her away. My daughter is dead, what is there to talk about, I told her.'

Jak shifts on his haunches. His leg has gone to sleep. He gazes at Meera, who looks shaken. Afraid, even. He knows remorse then. What has he done by dragging Meera into this? All he had thought of was himself – the real horror of Smriti's last hours waited in Minjikapuram and he needed a bulwark. He has been thoughtless and selfish. He finds his hand groping for Meera's.

'But it didn't end there,' he says quietly.

Chinnathayi nods. She sighs and stretches her legs out straight. The soles of her feet are cracked and there are deep furrows scoring the underside. She crinkles her toes a few times. 'No, it didn't end there.'

They came to her house a little after Smriti left. 'Where is she?' Srinivasan asked.

Chinnathayi pretended she didn't know who he was asking about. 'Who? My granddaughters? They are here… Vana, Kanaka, come here.'

Srinivasan peered at the girls. 'Don't pretend, Chinnathayi. Did the girl come here? Saravana saw her.'

Chinnathayi blanched at the name of her son-in-law. The

nursing home had bought his silence when her daughter died. He was an attender there now. He didn't see them for the butchers they were. The murderers who had killed his wife. Instead, he was their dog. Their loyal, boot-licking dog. The servile, conscienceless koodhi that he was.

'Oh, him! He is a drunk. He doesn't know his elbow from his knee.'

Srinivasan frowned. He understood her implication well enough. 'Saravana may be wrong but there were others who saw her come into this alley. They all remember her well enough. How many girls in our town will be seen wearing a jeans pant?'

'What? That girl?' Chinnathayi waved a dismissive hand. 'Why didn't you say so first? She left. About an hour ago.'

'Do you know how to contact her?'

'Why would I? I don't even know her name.'

It was Kanaka who chirped up. She had heard the flow of words between Paati and the old man who looked like a school headmaster. She could see fear in Paati. Why was Paati so worried? She knew how to help.

'Aiyah, aiyah!' she cheeped. A little bird with a big beak. 'I know!'

She felt Vana pinch her. She knew that Vana grudged her speaking out first. Vana pinched her all the time. She talked too much, both Paati and Vana said. But this time she was going to make it right for Paati. 'Aiyah! I know that Akka's name. It is Smriti and see, she gave us this paper with her number. She said you must tell Paati to talk to me and when she agrees, call me on this number. I'll come and bring with me a doll and sweets, she said.' Kanaka's words echoed in the suddenly still room.

Srinivasan leaned forward to pat Kanaka's head and remove

the slip of paper from her hand. 'Clever girl! You have saved me a great deal of trouble. Here, Selvam, give her a twenty-rupee note. Buy yourself some thenkuzhal with it. And don't eat it all at once. You'll make yourself ill. Give some to Paati and your sister, do you hear?'

Kanaka nodded her head happily.

'That akka is going away tonight, she said. She took photos of us on her phone,' she added, pleased with all the attention that was coming her way. She couldn't stop smiling.

Srinivasan stretched his hand out to Selvam.

Chinnathayi spoke into the phone the words Srinivasan asked her to: 'I thought about what you said. I will give you the papers, the scan report, everything. But you can't be seen coming here, and I can't be seen coming to the lodge. It is too dangerous. Come to the seashore. There is a vacant stretch with a casuarina grove, a little before the fishermen's colony. I will be there by six. It is better if it is twilight. No one will spot us then.'

'Thanks. Thanks. You are doing something truly noble!' she heard Smriti say into her ear.

'Don't hurt her, Aiyah!' Chinnathayi heard herself plead. 'She is a young girl. A young girl who doesn't know what she is doing. She is going away later today. Please leave her alone!'

Srinivasan smiled. 'I am not a rowdy. What do you think we'll do to her? We'll deal with her as she deserves to be dealt with. No more. Now put this conversation out of your head.'

Chinnathayi nodded slowly. There was nothing she could do.

If there was a god, he would watch out for her. But god, she knew, sometimes closed his eyes when it came to women.

Shanta had sent word for her to be there when it was time for the first baby to be born. My mother has brought many babies into this world, she must help me bring mine too. She has to be here with me, she insisted when her mother-in-law wanted to know why. Chinnathayi had said that she wouldn't go unless Shanta's mother-in-law wanted her there.

'Is it a boy?' Shanta whimpered.

'A girl! A beautiful girl,' Chinnathayi said, expertly tying the stump of the umbilical cord and swaddling the infant in a cotton cloth.

'Oh!' Shanta said, afraid to meet her mother-in-law's eyes.

'That was a fine birthing indeed!' the woman said. 'I thought you said she had a lucky hand. I thought she would bring a boy child into our home. I told you that I would call the woman who helped bring Saravana and his brothers into this world but you wanted your mother and no one else.'

Chinnathayi went about settling the mother and child without speaking. 'God decides. How can a midwife change things?' she said.

But the woman shook her head, her grim face unwilling to relent. 'We have always had boys in our family. This is the first time a girl has been born in this house.'

'Well, we also need girl children. The human race would die out otherwise. What if your mother and mine thought of us as you do now? I was so happy when my Shanta was born,' Chinnathayi said quietly.

'Perhaps. But we don't need girls in our family. Let someone else have them. As far as I am concerned, they are trouble, just trouble.'

Later Shanta would agree. Her infant sucked hard at her breast. But she had little milk. Hungry, the child wailed, its persistent wailing echoing through the house and her. 'She is right. Girls are trouble. Look at this creature. Useless waif, and it thinks nothing of demanding milk all day.'

Chinnathayi took the baby in her arms and rocked it gently. 'Don't be cruel,' she scolded her daughter. 'What does this child know? As for your mother-in-law, it is the disappointment,' she comforted Shanta. 'The next time, when you have a boy, she will be over the moon, you'll see!'

'But what if I don't have a boy?'

When Shanta's next baby was due, Chinnathayi timed herself to reach late. Let someone else be the midwife, she thought. And it was a girl again.

'What will I do, Amma?' Shanta wept.

Chinnathayi didn't know how to comfort her. It was this she thought of as she laid out her mat and curled up on it. It was three in the afternoon, but Chinnathayi felt a great fatigue wash over her. All she wanted to do was rest her head on a pillow and close her eyes for a while.

In the folds of the sari, it waited. A tiny kernel of paddy. A baby's fingernail. Glistening. Golden. Plump with grain. The ends tapering to a fine point.

Chinnathayi undid the pouch where she kept the handful of paddy. She took one and looked at it carefully. She ran her finger along its side. It was dried to a shell-like brittleness. The ends were dagger like. But she would still need to check its piercing point. There could be no errors. She pressed the flesh of her thumb down on one end of the paddy. A bead of blood.

Chinnathayi let her eyes settle on the girl's. She allowed herself this every time. It is to be your choice, she would let her eyes speak to the girl. I know what I have been told to do.

I know I will be paid for the deed and my silence. But I won't do it if you don't want me to.

The girl's eyes were shut. Chinnathayi looked at her for a long moment. The girl wasn't asleep. She knew that she was hiding behind the closed eyelids. Chinnathayi wouldn't speak. She wouldn't even sigh to register her waiting.

Then she saw the tear trickle down the corner of the girl's eye. A slow slithering tear, wet with remorse and self-hate. The salt of acquiescence. Do what you must. It is the only way.

Chinnathayi woke with a start as she always did, with wails in her head and a burning throat. Scores of throbbing lacerations. As if someone had set about slicing the inside of her throat with a razor blade. It was the same dream every night. A ghoul strangling her sleep and the few hours of peace. It didn't matter how many times she told herself that it was all in the past. The wailing child stirred her sleep. All those infants, mouths wide open, their limbs flailing. And between their parted infant thighs, the tiny slit. The silent mouth that had condemned them the moment they were born.

'What is it? What is it? Tell me…' voices would demand as they waited for the lower half of the body to emerge.

Chinnathayi's granddaughter touched her elbow. 'Paati, Paati… what is it?'

Chinnathayi stared unseeing into the girl's eyes. 'What is the time?' she asked quietly.

'Almost five,' the girl whispered, frightened by the manic gleam in her grandmother's eye.

'Take Kanaka to Rajeswari's next door. Tell them we'll be late returning. We'll fetch her when we come back,' Chinnathayi said, rolling up the mat. Her limbs ached and her head felt heavy. A chill swept through her and the insides of her eyelids felt warm and sore. She felt as if she was starting a fever.

'Where are we going, Paati?' Vana asked in the bus that took them to the other end of the town.

'Nowhere in particular,' Chinnathayi said, stuffing a wad of tobacco into her mouth. Vana looked out of the window. When Paati filled her mouth with tobacco, it meant she was in no mood to talk.

Chinnathayi rolled the wad into a ball with her tongue and let it rest against her cheek. The juice seared her mouth and stilled the countless demons that ran amok in her head. She didn't trust Srinivasan. They wouldn't let the girl go so easily. And Chinnathayi felt responsible. How could that silly Kanaka have bleated out everything? But then, she was only a child. A feckless child perhaps, but how could Chinnathayi blame her? She should have been more careful, more assiduous in her dealings with the girl and Srinivasan.

And then, suddenly, Chinnathayi was stricken by a thought. Why hadn't she thought of calling and warning Smriti? Of telling her that it was all a set-up.

'Do you remember that akka's number?' she asked Vana.

The girl nodded. 'It's in my head,' she said.

Chinnathayi looked around her desperately. An elderly man had a mobile in his pocket. 'Aiyah, I need to make an urgent call. Will you please let us use your mobile?'

Vana recited the number to him. He frowned. 'It is an outstation number.'

'I'll pay you whatever it costs,' Chinnathayi said quickly.

He punched in the keys and held it to her ear. Then he tried once again. 'It's not going through. The party at the other end is out of range. Do you have another number?'

Chinnathayi felt that peculiar grinding of stone against

stone. Of knowing that powers beyond her were reigning here.

In the twilight, the eastern sea takes on a peculiar hue. The sun, dying orb that it is, looms in another horizon. Shorn of light, the world mutes into misshapen shadows and dark spots. When the tsunami happened, the coast had been hit. An inlet further up the coast and an estuary a little down had saved the town from being destroyed. The waters had rushed to swallow the land there and Minjikapuram had escaped with not too much loss to life or property. But the coastline changed. The sand banks were eaten away and debris from the waters still littered the shore. Driftwood and rusted pieces of metal, castaways of the sea. Lording over it all, a misshapen log of wood, the stump of a dead tree from some distant land.

Chinnathayi and Vana walked quickly down the road. Would she have arrived already? Or, would some force within her have cautioned her against what lay in store?

They saw her in the distance. She stood facing the waves some distance away from the log. 'Look, Paati, Akka is there.' Vana's voice rose in excitement.

'Ssh!' Chinnathayi cautioned her. 'Be quiet. We must get to her and take her back with us before anyone else comes.'

In the end, all that Chinnathayi could do was watch. Muffling her horror by stuffing the end of her sari into her mouth and pressing Vana's face into her side so the child saw nothing, heard nothing.

The three brawny men. The swagger as they walked towards Smriti. One of them gestured with his hands. Another lit a cigarette. And the third, he stood there with his arms crossed, his head cocked at an angle. Chinnathayi had seen men take that stance. At the mutton shop as they eyed a carcass strung on a hook, the line of goats' heads on a block with their dead, unseeing eyes. Should it be chops or the brain? One thing was certain. They wouldn't leave without meat.

She stood there unable to believe what she was seeing. They were animals, these men. They tore at the girl and it seemed the more she screamed, the more excited they became. Even from where she stood she could feel the girl's fear. It was the smell of blood. And Chinnathayi knew that no matter how much the girl pleaded or sought for reprieve, they wouldn't leave her alone. She was their kill.

Chinnathayi thought she had seen it all. The depravity of the human mind in all its twisted forms. But nothing had prepared her for this, the pleasure they derived from the girl's fear. She would not forget till the moment she died, the laugh that echoed along the shore as the girl tried to flee and they rounded her in, knowing there was nothing she could do to escape them, their vile minds and bodies.

Run, run, Chinnathayi prayed. But Smriti wouldn't. She stood there wildly gesticulating. What was she saying to them? What did they tell her? The wind ate away the words.

The third man, the mutton shop man, he was the one who moved suddenly and pushed her down. They loomed over her as Smriti tried to get back onto her feet.

Don't, please don't. Chinnathayi's mouth widened but there was no sound. Fear stifled every shred of decency she had. If she gave herself away, there was no saying what they would do to her and the girls.

So Chinnathayi was a mute witness to the ease with which they held Smriti down and slapped her. The casual stripping of her clothes. The scream of terror that turned into a catena of howls as they, one by one, quickly and methodically, entered her.

As if that wasn't enough, one of them turned her on her back with his foot. The others laughed aloud. A murder of crows in the twilight sky.

As the others watched and urged, he entered her there as well. The girl tried to shake him off, sought to pull away, finding the strength to crawl on her hands and feet through the sand. Panting. Heaving. Sobbing. Seeking to escape. The booming treacherous sea waited, but anything was better than what these predatory beasts could do to her.

And then the monster king of the rubbish – the giant twisted log that lay on its side – rose with the wave and came to slam against her head.

'What will you do now?' Meera asks.

They are sitting in the balcony of their room. A sea-facing room in a boutique hotel, complete with little touches for the discerning traveller.

Jak sips his drink. The ice in the glass clinks. 'I don't know,' he says.

It was dusk when they returned from Chinnathayi's home. Neither Jak nor Meera had been able to speak. He had held her hand all through the car ride. It was Meera who urged him to sit in the balcony and called room service for drinks and dinner. It was Meera who poured him his drink and pressed it into his hand.

'What is it that I can do?' His voice breaks.

This could have been my Nayantara, she thinks. If it had been my child, how would I have endured it? All this, and the knowledge that she is trapped in a frozen world of odious beasts and winged demons. That her last conscious thought must have been a plea.

'Why do we love our children so much?' In the darkness his voice cuts through her.

She shakes her head and whispers, 'I wish I knew. I wish I could tell you, Kitcha, that there is another way to love our children rather than this. Sometimes I wonder if that was why in earlier times people had more children. As self-preservation. When you have to spread yourself among so many, you are less overwhelmed.' Meera subsides into silence as she sees his shoulders heave.

His pain fills her with anguish. It is not the sorrow from witnessing the pain of a suffering soul. It is Kitcha. The extent of his grief. How could this man have come to mean so much to her in so short a time?

'Kitcha, Kitcha...' she says. Her fingers reach for his.

'I have never felt so alone. So bereft. So defeated,' he cries against her cheek.

She shuts her eyes tight. But into them swims an image of Smriti with her mouth open in an animal howl. What if it was Nayantara... 'No, no,' she says, as much to herself as to him. 'You can't think like that. You have to be brave. You have to be strong.'

'When Smriti was a baby and wouldn't sleep, I would take her out of the baby cot and walk her. I held her to my chest and rocked her each night. As long as I held her close, I thought she was safe. She would come to no harm. How did I forget that? How did I let her go?'

Meera tries to not think of the expression she glimpsed in Nayantara's eyes each time she held her back from an impetuous move. The animosity, the dislike. In the end, she would buckle and let her have her way just so that she would smile at her.

'Kitcha, there is no getting it right. All we can hope for is that we do right by our children, and someday they will understand. And that eventually it will all work out...'

'There is not even that with Smriti. There is nothing to look forward to.' His voice is flat, his eyes shut.

With great care and gentleness, Meera cups his face in her palms. Slowly she leans forward and presses her lips to his eyes.

She feels his eyeballs move beneath her lips. She thinks again of what he must be seeing. The broken child. His lost daughter. The break with eternity. For isn't that what they are to us? Children, our children. A line that takes us beyond tomorrow.

Meera shrugs away the sadness that threatens to swamp her. Her lips move, searching the contours of his face. Gently, ever so gently…

He feels something squeeze his very being. Such tenderness. Such sweetness. When had he last known such solace? She rains kisses on him. The gentle afternoon rain, washing away the past. He feels cleansed, alive, and as life stirs beneath the gentle but persistent pressure of rain on earth, within him a movement, an awakening, a tentative shaping of possibilities.

He gathers her to him with a fierceness that he hopes will say all that he has no words for. She can read him. That much he is certain of. One day, perhaps, he will find the words. But for now all he has is what he murmurs against the curve of her neck: Meera, oh Meera, my Meera…

Other people baffled Meera. They always had. Giri had teased her in the early days of their marriage, 'Honestly, doesn't anyone else exist for you but your family?'

She had shaken her head earnestly. No, no, no one else did, but you do now.

Only later, much later, he had narrowed his eyes and said scornfully, with a furtive admiration, 'Other people don't exist for you, do they?'

By which time Meera had some knowledge of other people's lives. How they lived. What they ate. Who they slept with. And with the confidence of someone who had pieced together a difficult jigsaw, she tossed back a disdainful 'I don't know what you mean. I know everything about everyone you and I know, including everyone you work with. So who doesn't exist for me?'

But Meera knew that she still didn't comprehend people.

She thought she had fathomed Jak. This man who paints seascapes of utter stillness or violent storms, of a musical leaning that veers from old Tamil songs to Barry White, Cat Stevens and Leonard Cohen; of the extra large sizes he wears because confinement of any sort stifles him. She knows that his mind races into territories she will never be able to understand. That he hides his intensity, so he appears a big bland man of indeterminate likes and dislikes, hard to pinpoint, hard to capture. Loving him will be frustrating and even self-defeating, she fears. And yet, as his 'Oh Meera, Meera' washes over her, it unsettles her.

It excites her. It makes her turn to him with a voracious hunger she hasn't known before.

'Oh, Jak!' she whispers. 'Or should I call you Kitcha… I don't even know what name to use.'

'It doesn't matter, as long as you know it's me.' His fingers move as if to memorize all of her by touch alone. 'How I need you… oh Meera, my Meera.'

Meera leans into him.

Later, she will remember precisely how it was. The swelling of consciousness, the knowing of her body. The languor. Meera searches the clock face and then the pearly tinged skies outside the window. Is it night or day? When has she last seen this hour carve itself out of time? This riddled-with-sleep-and-multiple-dreams, dig-deep-into-the-pillow hour. Meera brushes the hair off her cheek and lies on her back.

Then she hears a sound from the bathroom. Meera clenches

up. How is she to arrange herself at this moment? Who is she to be? Like the indefinite hour, Meera's mind hovers. Between sleep and wakefulness, arousal and embarrassment, guilt and a curious lightness of being.

Her eyes glitter in the dark.

All these years she chose to bury herself as Hera, the perfect wife. When Zeus sought her body, she responded. She was his for the taking, never asking herself if she could know desire. Silly Hera, who thought it was men who delighted in the sexual act and all a woman had to do was acquiesce. When Teiresias, who had known sexual pleasure both as woman and man disagreed, she was enraged. How could it be that if pleasure were marked on a scale of one to ten, women derived nine and men knew only one!

For that blasphemy she had blinded him. But this is a Meera who has removed the scales from her eyes, her desires.

What will Vinnie say when she finds out? A smile settles on her face. Vinnie wouldn't exactly approve. No, she won't dwell on what Vinnie might say. Instead, she will think of what Vinnie would have done in her place. Would she lie as she did? Afraid and dreading the moment he appeared from the bathroom. Or, would she reach out for the bedside lamp and switch it on? Sit up in bed propped against the pillows with the sheets draped casually over her breasts and thighs. The cat who has fed on cream but isn't averse to more. Would she fluff out her hair and call out languorously, 'Where are you?'

Would she be able to muster up such courage? Meera's toes nudge the bundled heap of her nightie. She sits up and tugs it over her head in one swift movement. Should she pretend to be asleep when he comes in? Should she? Should she not? Should she? Should she not? Daisy petals drop to the floor till there is only one. She licks the dryness from her lips and waits. Meera once again.

Just after Appa went away, Kitcha had accompanied a few relatives to Rameswaram. Early in the morning, he had been woken up by Kala Chithi.

'Can't it wait?' he had whimpered in sleep.

And Kala Chithi had whispered, 'Look at the sky, Kitcha, it will be dawn soon. We have to be at the temple before the sun appears. That is the rule!'

Kitcha had looked at the night with its grey underbelly and wondered how anything could be more fascinating. And about a god who shied away from the sun.

Thereafter, Kitcha had set the alarm for three and much to the consternation of his aunts, he woke at that hour, every day, the whole week they were there, to study the celestial light. 'Show him a few constellations,' an uncle advised. 'What is the boy doing reading the vacant skies?'

But Kitcha wanted none of it. 'No, no.' He shook his head and looked away resolutely.

The rest of them grimaced. Reproof lit their thoughts. Just like his father. Obstinate as a mule. Everything had to be his way!

Only Kala Chithi understood. 'Let him be!' she said in her soft voice that cloaked steel. 'Maybe he has a point. Once you know what there is to know, where is the magic?'

And so Kitcha saw all he wanted of the three o' clock sky. Of a light that drew nothing from the sun. Of the sea echoed in the skies. Of a world that was the same up and down, when in between was chaos in his thirteen-year-old world.

Kitcha in the bathroom – only he is Jak now – searches the skies from the ventilator slats. The mother-of-pearl sheen. It fills him with rapture as it did then. An endless vista of possibilities. He wonders if this is the moment of truth Appa talked about.

Then he hears tiny muffled sounds in the room beyond. His hand pauses on the tap.

Jak stands framed in the doorway. She is feigning sleep. He sees it in the way she holds her body, aware of his every breath. He goes to sit by her side. He sees with amusement that she has pulled her nightie on. He gropes on the bed and finds his boxer shorts. He pulls them on and then reaches out and touches the tip of her nose. 'You can open your eyes now,' he murmurs softly. 'I am decent. Decent enough.' He laughs.

Her eyes open abruptly. He sees the flush of embarassment. He feels again that swoop of tenderness. 'Oh, Meera, Meera,' he says softly.

Jak leans over her and ever so gently lays his cheek against hers. He nuzzles his face into the side of her neck. 'Come,' he whispers. 'Come and look at the skies with me.'

He pulls her up from the bed and leads her to the window. He takes her hand in his. She lets it lie there for a few minutes and then slowly, she weaves her fingers through his. Outside, the skies heave and the clouds shift.

She hears his whisper, half in hope, half in marvellous wonderment. 'I have to finish what Smriti set out to do. How can I not, Meera? Remember that Cohen line? About ringing the bells that still can be rung…'

Meera doesn't speak. Last night was waiting to happen. He responded to her embrace and she matched his manic hunger with hers, entwining limbs and desires. But Meera was struck by the very nature of their slaking of need: two desperate people clinging to each other. Is that all we will ever have? Will it ever become something else? A more enduring bond. A more sustaining love.

Now, as Jak seeks her as his anchor to root him in what could be a long and frustrating quest, Meera knows yet another qualm.

All of her aches to rush forward and give herself to him. To make his battles hers. To mesh their lives and hopes. To fashion something out of nothing.

But she knows that if she does this, the Meera she has become will wither and die forever. She will be there for him, Meera decides. But to keep herself alive, she will need to dredge all the selfishness that lies deep within her. That alone will ensure that Jak does not swallow her up, as once Giri did.

'Yes, you must,' she says.

In the way he holds his body, she knows he waits for a pledge of her troth.

But Meera cannot speak it. Not yet. She cannot give him the reassurance he wants from her. Not yet. Meera thinks of her favourite fruit: the pomegranate. Of how she savours it best when she eats it seed by seed rather than as a handful thrown into her mouth. She will take a cue from that. Of how resurrection is to be fashioned one day at a time.

So Meera does what she can. She rests her head against his arm. This is all she has to offer for now.

Perhaps one day there will be more.

And a thereafter.

Thereafter...

The man shifts in his sleep. He has been restless all night. A series of images chase themselves in his mind. A montage of thoughts that he doesn't like to dwell upon. He knows where they spring from. Like his little toe and the coccyx, the vestigial organ called conscience announces its presence in these unfamiliar beds across three districts.

In the early days, he ran the probe on the bellies of the women with an easy hand. It was a prestigious hospital. The diagnostic centre attracted many patients. After a while, he ceased to even look at the faces of the women. It was routine work. And it was best not to get involved. Only if there was an abnormality did he look up from the monitor and speak.

Sometimes, a hesitant voice would query, 'What is it?'

And he would snap a question back: 'Why?'

Then he learnt to temper it with a careless flick of his hand. 'It's too early to tell.' Those days the Hippocrates Oath was still freshly etched in the palms of his hands: for the good of my patients according to my ability and my judgment and never do harm to anyone.

Until the day the director of the diagnostic centre summoned him to his room. 'You know why they come here,' he said. 'If you do not give them what they want, they will go elsewhere, and I can't have that.'

'But sir, it isn't ethical,' he protested. Nor will I give a woman a pessary to procure abortion, Hippocrates murmured in his ear.

The director gazed at him with a strange look. 'Which

world are you living in, sir? It is their choice, not your decision, you know. And if you don't meet targets, you won't leave us with much choice either.'

Choices. It came down to that. The patient's. The hospital's. To keep or to kill. To stay or leave.

He succumbed, as the director knew he would. He learnt to answer the 'What is it?' He stopped being a fool.

He lies on his back, staring into the darkness. I should be used to it by now, he tells himself. It isn't as if I am actually committing a crime. I am not playing god. I am merely fulfilling my professional obligations.

Soothed by the thought, the man feels his eyes close again. Soon it will be time to wake, bathe and dress. It is going to be a long day.

A man needs his rest.

Elsewhere, in a room cast with a green light, a thought sails through many months of nothingness, through a morass of deadened cells, and remembers:

Her blue denim shirt. Papa Jak's shirt. The mother-of-pearl buttons that gleamed in the dark. Papa Jak's here. No, no, it's only his shirt. Papa Jak, where are you?

Look, Papa Jak, I am here. Where you were once. You would never tell me enough about your days here. Maybe you didn't want me to come here.

The sea, Papa Jak. The sea. I can smell it. It is a violent sea. The waves crash. Boom. Boom. Boom.

I wanted to do something real. I wanted to stop what they were doing. See, Mom, I wanted to say, I didn't squander my future when I chose to come back home…

Remember the time the cat got my budgerigar? Birdie lay

on her back. The cat raised its mouth, entrails dripping. I screamed, Get away! The cat stared at me and snarled.

They came for me in that purple hour before night. All three of them. In their eyes, I saw what lurked in the cat's.

I am on my back. I scream. Get away! I try to push them away. I scream. Papa. Papa Jak.

Catatonia quells. Within a frozen abyss, a tiny vein splinters. A nerve cell is born. A toe wiggles. *Smriti. I am Smriti...*

There is a crack, a crack in everything, that's how the light gets in. And then all the grace, all the joy will be hers.
All of life heeding her bidding.
One perfect day.

A Note on Hera

Hera, usually taken to be a Greek word for 'lady', could also mean Herwa (Protectress).

She is the daughter of Cronus and Rhea. Her childhood was spent in Arcadia, where the Seasons were her nurses. Hera's twin brother Zeus banished their father Cronus and wooed her. However, she disdained him until he disguised himself as a bedraggled cuckoo. Hera's pity was stirred and she gathered the cuckoo to her tenderly, warming it in her bosom. Thereupon Zeus took on his true shape and ravished her. Hera was so shamed that she had no alternative but to marry him.

Zeus and Hera's marriage was tumultous. Humiliated and hurt by his constant infidelities, she often resorted to ruthless intrigue to get her own back. Their constant squabbling would end with him flogging or even hurling a thunderbolt at her. Strangely, Zeus would confide his secrets to her, and even at times accept her advice. But he never fully trusted her.

Hera had several children but she bore Python parthenogenetically, to spite Zeus. Another of her sons was Hephaestus, the Smith-god.

The winds were originally the property of Hera, and the male gods had no power over them. Her symbol is the pomegranate and it represents death and the promise of resurrection.

— adapted from *The Greek Myths*
by Robert Graves

Bibliography

The Greek Myths [Complete Edition], Robert Graves, Penguin Books Ltd, 1992.

Special Series: The Art of Hospitality, Part V, Dinner Party Etiquette, Tamera Bastiaans, www.homecooking.about.com

Acknowledgements

As always, this book wouldn't be what it is, were it not for V.K. Karthika – anchor, bulwark, rudder and then that final gust of wind that steered the book through its course.

Jayant Kodkani for once again being my first reader and celestial navigator.

Camilla Ferrier, Geraldine Cooke and the team at The Marsh Agency for their sustained support.

Mini Kuruvilla for making a veritable difference to the mechanics of producing a literary work.

Sudha Pillai who made available to me material on cyclones.

Sumentha and Franklin Bell, Francesca Diano, Leela Kalyanraman, Gita Krishnankutty, Chetan Krishnaswamy, Achuthan Kudallur, Carmen Lavin, Dimpy and Suresh Menon, S. Prasannarajan, Sunita Shankar, Rajini and Sunil, Jayapriya Vasudevan, Vishwas and Patrick Wilson – friends who made everything and every day so much easier to deal with in countless ways.

My parents, Soumini and Bhaskaran, for being there for me. Always.

Unni, Maitreya and Sugar – the triumvirate without whom life and literature would have neither meaning nor relevance for me.